SCOURGE
TRISKELLION
BOOK ONE

By Rodney W. McWilliams

If you enjoy this work of fiction, please post a review or rating on Amazon, Goodreads, or whichever service you use. Independent publishing depends heavily on ratings, reviews, and word of mouth advertising to be successful.

Second Edition

For Beth, my wife, the love of my life, and my strongest supporter

PREFACE

Long ago, the world was a very different place. What we know and what we believe to be true may prove to be no more accurate than the myths and legends from our past. The truth does exist, unable to be completely shrouded from view. The Age of Kalanak, concealed from all but the select few with the eyes to see it, ended the world's true roots, and gave birth to a future doomed from the beginning.

ChAPTER ONE

Ellen walked home from the diner the usual way, but something didn't feel usual about it. She couldn't put her finger on what it was – maybe it was something in the air or in the way the light reflected off of the snow in a myriad of never before seen colors. The neighborhood was her home for almost twenty years and she never once felt uneasy; but as she walked, shadowy phantoms began playing at the edge of her vision so she quickened her pace. She sensed she was being followed, but each time she made a cursory glance behind her the street was devoid of any other life. The outdated mercury vapor street lamps provided a meager golden glow which made the shadows darker and even more threatening.

My mind is playing tricks on me.

She could sense darkly shrouded figures all around her leaving behind only surreal wisps that would vanish when she turned to look at them. She knew something with ill intent was close.

What was that?....Ghosts? Ridiculous...oh God!

She broke into a run as the hair on the back of her neck stood on end, warning her of immediate danger. Sparks of adrenaline and fear spiked down her spine. She was barely able to keep from falling on the wet, salt-thawed concrete. Fear utterly consumed her mind, supplanting all thoughts of fight with flight.

Home! I've just got to make it home!

Home—safety—was only three blocks away.

Ellen's stomach blasted directly into her throat, churning with an unsettling cadence, and making breathing become more difficult. As her need for oxygen increased, her skin shifted from shades of bright pink to almost red. She could feel something bearing down on her while she tried to stifle her ever increasing nausea.

No, no, no, NO!

She was two blocks from home, trying to close the distance faster, but unable to do so. She cut behind a parked pickup, leapt over the furrow of snow left behind by the plows, and followed an angle across the shiny blacktop of the street.

A cry for help hung in her throat, unable to escape her lungs as they burned all the air she could supply, not allowing any to be wasted.

She knew her strict exercise regimen, geared to keep her diabetes in check, was the only thing granting her a scant lead over her pursuer.

She chanced a look over her shoulder, terrified of the hand she knew was about to grab her, drag her down, and rip her to pieces. The sidewalk behind her remained empty, but it did nothing to belay her fear. She kept at a dead sprint.

Please let me get home! God, I'm almost there.

Tears welled in her eyes, blurring her vision, ready to gush forth in a tidal wave. Lines creased her face and across her forehead as she grimaced with stress and fatigue that aged her with each stride. The front porch steps were only a block away.

Ellen's body physically hurt under the strain, unable to keep up the pace. She tried to conjure more speed from her aching legs, but her body, already beyond its physical limits, refused. Voices, barely at a whisper, filled her ears, pouring even more fear into her in an unbridled rush.

Dear God!

The words were unintelligible, in a language she could not comprehend, but the intent of evil was as clear as day. The tears ran from her eyes even heavier, like a swell of water breaching the top of a dam. Twenty feet separated her from her front door.

Keep going. Don't give up. DON'T GIVE UP!

As quickly as it took hold, the fear vanished without a trace. Ellen felt completely calm and secure, albeit exhausted, almost as if the last few minutes never happened. She stopped running and looked around as she tried to catch her breath, leaning forward with her hands on her knees for support. As she heaved with exertion, she could see her breath fog in the cold air. Everything was just as it should be. She wanted to laugh at herself, but she couldn't shake the feeling that what happened was more than wild imagination.

What had me so spooked?

She turned to walk up the steps, blotting the tears from her cheeks and eyes with the sleeve of her coat. Her breathing worked back towards normal to remedy her used up and hollow inside condition.

A man dressed in black with his face hidden in silhouette stood on the second step. Ellen's fear returned a hundred-fold the second her eyes realized the shadowed visage. His hands were around her throat before her vision could focus, trapping the scream in her lungs.

NOOOOO!

Desperately trying to break free, she lashed out, striking him in any way she could. Oh God, I was running right into this, not away from it! His lips moved, speaking in the same dialect as the voices that plagued her during her flight of fright. She felt her throat collapse, sealing off her airway, under the mammoth pressure of his grip.

Please, not like this!

Bright spots of light shone around the edges of her vision, bolting her forward through an expanse of stars. She stopped flailing, finally succumbing to the firestorm burning in her chest that stole her air. Her sight faded to black as a sharp pain shot through her neck, followed by a sensation of numbness. The utter lack of feeling spread down her body like warm molasses, fading into the blackness of eternal sleep.

chapter two

The wind, laced with ice and other small debris, swept through the filthy alleyway, scattering new pieces of trash into the already present refuse. Metal garbage can lids rattled in time with the clicking of sleet on the frozen macadam. The orchestra of nature backed the voice of the wailing gusts of wind carrying the snow that bit Thomas Gianelli's face and stung his eyes. He moved quickly through the rubbish, gripping a bottle wrapped in a brown paper sack with one hand and trying to protect his face from the elements with the other. He could only ward off the cold with movement and sips of the shrouded strawberry wine in his grasp.

The sight of home overjoyed him, even though it was nothing more than an amalgamation of old refrigerator boxes he found behind the neighborhood's appliance repair shop. Borrowed duct tape worked to seal off the seams and hold on a few layers of plastic wrap that partially weatherized the corrugated abode. Pieces of other boxes, also attached with duct tape, helped make the structure somewhat sturdy.

Winter's icy tendrils firmly grasped the city of New York. The season was especially harsh, only expected to worsen, as new low temperatures and obscene snowfall amounts replaced long-standing records almost daily. Most inhabitants could cope with the bitter cold, but the less fortunate percentage of the population was devastated. Old Man Winter's death toll on the city's homeless was breaking long-established records.

Thomas Gianelli was one of the lucky ones since his prime piece of backstreet real estate, sheltered in a covered section of the alley, harbored him from all but the most violent gusts of wind and deep drifts of snow.

The little patch of paradise was one-of-a-kind due to a blueprint error. The architect that designed the building to be office space made a typo that was not discovered until the first phases of erecting the building were complete, making it too costly to correct. The result was a back wall fifteen feet shallower than the buildings that already stood on each side. The owner settled with the architect for the addition of a large roof style cover that spanned the distance from the building to the alleyway. In the beginning, it proved to turn a small profit as reserved parking for surrounding tenants until it became too difficult to manage. The area was slowly filled with junk. The chain link barrier placed along the alley's border fell into disrepair, allowing access to anyone willing to go through. The current owner, unwilling to spend the money necessary to effect repairs, epitomized the term "cheapskate" in regards to the building that he rented out as apartments, offering no resistance to anyone squatting there.

Gianelli did not like to think of himself as a squatter, even though he knew it was the proper term. He made an effort in the beginning to contact the owner and reach some agreement for his use of the space, willing to offer his labor as barter. The owner never responded or tried to have him removed, so the situation had some level of acceptance by both parties.

Thomas' middle-aged body still produced enough internal heat to keep him from freezing to death as long as he stayed inside out of the wind, and kept wrapped in his sleeping bag. He earned one hot meal a day by volunteering at the local shelter at least three days a week, but he rarely took the meal for himself. He usually extended the hospitality to someone that he knew needed it more. Most of the street people he befriended were several years older, and many would have succumbed to the elements if not for his generosity.

Listening to the torrents of frigid air flow through the winter night, he settled into his old olive-green U.S. Army sleeping bag, pulling a tattered quilt up over it to enjoy the bottom half of his bottle. Staying drunk most of the time helped him make it through the joke he called his life, if it could even be considered living. The booze gave him the edge against the cold and bewildered his demons to the point he could forget his worries. He only sobered up to work at the shelter or to go without if he couldn't scrape together a couple of bucks for another bottle of courage.

The wind tore at the sides of the boxes, mercilessly trying to shred the cardboard and devour the man inside. It howled as it passed, furious it couldn't attack Thomas directly. Weird, haunted sounds lingered in the frost-laced gusts. At first, he thought nothing of it—the wind's voice could take many forms—but the most recent variation held qualities beyond Mother Nature's talents.

That sounds like a voice.

The next volley was a scream that penetrated to the core of his soul like shards of frozen metal ripping through skin, muscle, and bone, forcing him to take notice. He tried to ignore the unsettling timbre, but his conscience was victorious. He concealed his bottle of wine and stepped out into the relentless wind. The cold cut through his layers of clothing, stealing his breath. Snow stung his exposed face. The voice of the wind sounded somewhat satisfied.

Why am I doing this? I turned away from this.

The scream came from somewhere deeper in the alley, easier to identify without the added distortions from echoes, cardboard, and random piles of junk. He turned and moved in search of the tormented soul. The disturbing scene he found about fifty yards farther down the back street would remain with him for the rest of his life.

A young woman, in her mid-twenties from the look of her, sat in a murky puddle of dark slime. Her knees were drawn up to her chin and her arms wrapped tightly around her legs, forming a little ball. Her straight black hair draped down, concealing her face and her knees. A brown grocery sack full of food rested beside her, falling apart from the moisture drawn into the paper. Her muscles were taut enough to snap, visibly rippling with tension. Driven into a state of hysteria by what lay at her feet, she rocked slightly, screaming herself hoarse.

The body of a man—obviously dead—lay in a crumpled and broken heap in the center of the alley. His head was turned at a precarious angle, and quite close to being unattached, confirming that his neck was broken. The corpse reminded Thomas of a marionette with freshly cut strings, forever still on a morbid stage. The young lady kept her face buried in her legs; the horror of the image burnt into her mind's eye forever, refusing to accept the hard fact of what happened to the mangled corpse.

Thomas stood frozen, staring in disbelief as if denial would make it all go away. He even closed his eyes and shook his head, trying to shake off any effects of his drink, praying the alcohol was impairing his vision. Opening his eyes revealed the brutal scene unchanged.

He approached the woman, prepared to offer whatever he could, when he finally saw what truly pushed the poor woman to the edge of mental collapse.

Lord in Heaven!

The corpse had a huge, jagged-edged cavity marring the torso. Organs that were situated by birth were completely missing. Gravity coaxed blackish-red ooze slowly out of the opening, increasing the size of the

14

coppery, rotten-smelling pool, drifting thickly to the spot where the woman sat. The man's face was not spared of the mutilation either.

Thomas forced himself to control his bodily urges. He felt his last meal, and part of the one before that, tickle the back of his throat. The fervent female at his side needed help, which he couldn't provide if he lost both his composure and the contents of his stomach. He realized she was injured when he spoke and reached out to touch her.

"Are you all right?"

It looked as though the killer, intending to turn on her next, lashed out at her while performing the grisly act. The initial stroke was obviously not fatal, but her neck was still bleeding, soaking her forest green turtleneck with blood. It looked bad, but worse than it truly was. Clotting blood slowed the flow from the wound, but she still needed medical attention. He draped his camouflage jacket over her shoulders and ran the distance out of the alley to call for help.

Knowing he would be under immediate suspicion, he didn't look forward to talking to the police, especially with his elevated blood alcohol level. He thought he would probably be hauled off to jail as a prime suspect until the police muddled through the evidence, if they would even bother checking his story. Instinct told him to make an anonymous call and vanish, but he yielded to his conscience a second time. The reticent young woman needed help and didn't need to be alone, not to mention that the killing took place too close to her home. He dialed 9-1-1 from a payphone on the corner and explained the recent events to the efficient dispatcher. He returned to the frightening scene to await the arrival of the police and offer what consolation he could to the distraught young woman.

She had not moved from the spot where he first discovered her, and she was still rocking back and forth slightly. She was no longer screaming, but entrenched in a different stage of severe shock, mumbling something in her native tongue almost inaudibly. Thomas didn't know the language, so the meaning of her words was lost to him, but he felt certain she was speaking a Slavonic dialect, most likely Russian.

Gianelli involved himself at the scene of the attack at roughly seven o' clock, but it was almost seven forty-five when the police and the paramedics arrived. The time was commendable considering the weather and the bustling traffic which kept the city's roadways at a virtual standstill.

The two EMTs went to work, slowly coaxing the woman into the back of the ambulance so they could treat her injuries while the police started their standard procedures.

Officer Dupree, a very tall, stocky African-American man, roped off the section of the alley where the attack took place with black on yellow plastic tape, attaching it to downspouts and whatever else was handy. His partner, Officer Hernandez, finished up the initial call to the precinct. He could see the body of a man lying in the alley, facing away from the squad car; and without having to look any further requested a unit from homicide and the coroner. The dispatcher confirmed the call and stated that the requested parties would be in route shortly. He got out and pulled a small steno pad from the inside pocket of his standard issue parka.

Emilio Hernandez was a rather short, toothpick-skinny Hispanic man with black hair, brown eyes, and a light complexion. He appeared to be in his late twenties, due more to his air of confidence and practiced posture than any physical traits. His defined cheekbones, manicured moustache, and virtually unblemished skin tailored his face into a very distinguished look. However, he didn't appear like the type of person who would commit his life to serving and protecting others. In fact, he looked like the person who would lead a rogue gang of militants with an iron fist, all the while convincing them everything was their idea.

Malcolm Dupree, on the other hand, looked as though he was perfectly suited for a life in law enforcement. His face was long with sharp, chiseled features. His eyes seemed to interrogate everything they looked upon with an all-penetrating gaze that took the subject of interest apart layer by layer until only truth remained. His countenance emanated a sense of trust, modesty, and confidence; he wore the uniform well. The unlikely pair worked together with the fluidity found only in well-tuned and oiled machines.

Thomas' tension abated slightly, allowing him to fully realize the soreness developing in his muscles and the dull ache filling his head in the void left by the wine. He desperately wanted the last of the bottle hidden in his refrigerator box to give him strength as the stress tested the measure of his resolve.

"Sir!" called Officer Hernandez, requesting Thomas' presence as he moved away from the car and finished jotting down a quick note. "We need to ask you a few questions about what happened here tonight.

Would you like to sit down in the car and get out of this wind? I have some hot coffee with me; you look like you could use a warm-up."

"Sweet Mary, Mother of Jesus!" blurted Malcolm, catching everyone's attention. He put his hand over his mouth and stifled what he would later define as a cough. He shook his head from side to side as he moved around the body, finally getting a close look at the victim in the last moments of his life.

"Are you okay?" yelled Emilio over the wind, obviously taken aback by Malcolm's reaction. "You don't startle easy big guy. Is it that bad?"

"Bad doesn't begin to cover it compadre. I've been a beat cop for over fifteen years and did a tour during Desert Storm and I've never seen anything like this." Some of the color drained from his face as he continued his inspection. "It looks like this guy's heart was cut out! And I don't mean with a blade, I mean ripped out. There's a huge hole here!"

Emilio's face flushed slightly as his mind painted a picture for him. "Looks like the detectives will be busy on this one. Let's get that body covered. I don't want anyone else besides homicide and the coroner seeing it. The last thing we need is someone with the press showing up and starting a panic."

"No problem Amigo, I've seen enough already." Malcolm stood up, releasing a held breath in a plume of visible vapor as he went to the trunk of their car to retrieve a blanket they carried for emergencies. He shook his head again, wrestling with his own denial and disbelief.

Emilio turned his attention back to Gianelli.

"Sir, can I get your name, address, and phone number?"

This was followed by the other usual questions. Thomas wasn't surprised when he was asked how much he'd had to drink, but he was caught off guard when he was asked how he got blood on his pants.

Blood, what blood? When did I get blood on my pants?

Questions ran through his mind as he looked down to see the stain, trying to find an explanation and recall the events of the last hour or so. He hadn't noticed the blood before the officer called his attention to it.

Emilio saw the blood as soon as he laid eyes on Gianelli, but he didn't say anything at first. He interrogated suspects with a unique style that made the questionee feel comfortable, establishing himself as someone to be trusted. He always started with the basic, simple queries that calmed the subject and coaxed them into dropping some of their defenses. By the time he reached the incriminating questions, most people would state things they hadn't intended to say. His appearance seemed to work against his actions, swaying people to answer truthfully even if they had doubts.

The wind continued to buffet everything in the alley, voicing its opinion on the matter and creating a wind chill that would unsettle the hardest Eskimo. An unending supply of trash rode the currents of air down the alley's length, dancing with the ice pellets and snow.

Emilio got out of the car when he finished with his questions, instructing Thomas to stay put and went to talk with Malcolm in front of the hood. He squinted as the frigid wind hit him, having to readjust to the colder air. They pieced together the gathered facts in the form of a preliminary report they would surrender to Homicide upon their arrival. After that, they would be able to call it a night. They knew they would meet soon after at their favorite pub for the traditional this-was-a-damned-rough-shift longneck or two of their preferred stout ale.

The paramedics cleaned up the woman's neck, packed it with Bactroban, and stitched it up with measured care before covering the area with more antibiotic salve and a sterile bandage. Triage was limited, but luckily the wound was not as bad as the amount of blood suggested. They were much more concerned with the nature of the wound. The laceration was not a cut, as they first suspected, but akin to a bite. Grooves, similar in shape to the teeth of a crosscut wood saw, fell together like puzzle pieces when the gash was closed; her jugular was missed by mere millimeters. The threat and fear of any blood borne diseases made them cautious as they were aware some criminals intentionally bit their victims to spread disease. It was also good practice to avoid taking chances.

They advised Marina Makovoz, as the green card in her purse identified her, that she still needed to go to the hospital. She needed a blood test to confirm she wasn't infected with any nasty organisms at the very least, as well as a prescription for an additional antibiotic to keep the wound free of infection until it completely healed.

Ms. Makovoz refused, turning her head from side to side hard enough to aggravate the fresh wound. She seemed unaware of the pain as the stiches strained, allowing a small amount of blood to leak through the bandage. Her body shook uncontrollably as she mumbled in incoherent spurts.

In a flash of movement, she burst through the back doors of the ambulance and bolted down the alley at full speed. Disadvantaged by surprise, the EMTs had no chance of detaining her,. They jumped up in unison towards the back door that was only wide enough for one person, forcing a fumbled exit out of the vehicle and giving her an even wider head start.

Marina screamed as she ran away, catching the attention of everyone in the alley. The word "necheseiveds" trailed in the frigid air behind her as she ran towards the avenue, increasing the distance between herself and the ambulance.

The police officers laid chase right behind the paramedics as they realized what was happening. Only a few feet separated the public servants from each other, but the closest of them was still over thirty feet behind Marina, and she was gaining ground. Fueled by adrenaline and fear, she exited the alley and turned north a good three seconds ahead of her pursuers.

Malcolm and Emilio stopped by the EMTs on the curb at the alley's opening. They looked north, then both ways, dumbfounded. Marina had disappeared without a trace. The question of how ran through the minds of all four men. She had not been far enough ahead of them to be able to hide before they regained a line of sight.

Malcolm was visibly irritated, but he didn't focus his frustration at anyone directly. His mumbling inaudible to the others, he reprimanded himself for not being more cautious and standing guard at the back of the ambulance,.

"She was sitting stark still and just bolted," offered the first paramedic. "We weren't expecting it at all."

"Yeah," continued the other EMT, "it was like she was completely paralyzed with fear. We see it pretty frequently with this type of situation. The victim is suffering from such severe shock that the

19

brain just shuts the person down until it can right itself. Her adrenaline was very high, and her heart was just racing. She was oblivious to the pain she was inflicting on herself, not to mention all the other hurt she's got to have. The brain has to do something to keep the body from damaging itself. She wouldn't move, and she hardly spoke once we got her in the ambulance. She would only mumble off and on."

"Did she ever say anything coherent?" asked Emilio curiously.

"Not anything I could make out, and in some other language. It sounded Slavic, but I'm not great with accents. The only thing I could make out was the same thing she yelled as she ran away – it sounded like she said 'knee ches e vee eds' or something very close to it. What does that mean?"

"You got me," replied Emilio. "I'm only down with Spanish and English."

"She also left this," offered the other EMT, holding up her green card. "We were checking her purse for ID, prescriptions, or medic alerts when she took off. This was the only identification we found. The rest of it is just normal stuff like lip balm and tissue."

"That'll help," said Hernandez as he scanned the face of the card. "We can call immigration in the morning and get Ms. Makovoz's address."

The four public servants walked back into the alley, wrapping themselves tighter in their coats to ward off the cold. The paramedics locked down their equipment and left while Malcolm and Emilio waited in their car for the unit from Homicide to arrive.

"Do you really not know what that word means partner?" asked Malcolm, sounding the word out in his head.

Emilio was actually fluent in four or five languages. His family moved to different spots on the globe due to his father's job in the military, which immersed him in different cultures while growing up. He took a lot of courses in college to refine his understanding of the languages he'd picked up along the way. His partner was privy to his ability, but he didn't make a point of sharing it with very many people. It was amazing what some people would say before they realized he could understand them.

"I have no idea. I don't think I've ever heard it before. I'm not even sure what language it is, although I think the EMT was close when he guessed Slavic. Whatever she saw really scared her. Do you have any ideas on that?"

Malcolm thought for a second, scratching his head. "No, but I don't think she was referring to the John Doe out there," nodding his head in the direction of the body. "I think she may have seen the perp."

"I think it might be Russian," offered Gianelli from the back seat, forgotten in his silence.

Malcolm turned his attention to Thomas.

"What makes you think that?"

"It just sounded Russian. I probably heard it on TV or something. She sure seemed to be afraid to look around though, almost like she thought something was still out there and she would see it again."

"Did you see anyone else out there?" Malcolm asked with a lift in his voice, encouraged that someone else had the same thought.

"No," said Thomas, "well, not exactly."

"What do you mean by not exactly?"

"I thought I saw the shadow of someone moving away down the alley at first, but I'm not sure." Thomas fidgeted in place, clearly uncomfortable under the added scrutiny. "All I could make out was a darker place in the air. It seemed to be shaped like a person, but I think my eyes were playing tricks on me."

Malcolm got out of the car and zipped up his coat. "Emilio, I'm going to go check this out. Stay here with Mr. Gianelli until I get back. I'll signal you if I get in trouble. If I remember right, this alley stops in a dead end a few hundred yards down. If there is another person back there, he won't be able to get out without coming through us."

"I don't like this. Be careful Malcolm." Emilio's voice took on the tone of a person far wiser than his years. "I don't want a double homicide on my hands here. Whoever we're looking for is one sick individual."

"You know me – I'm always careful. I'll be back in a few," he consoled with a wink and a quick pointing of his finger. He closed the car door and walked deeper into the alley, looking for any other clues or unaccounted-for homicidal maniacs. He was out of sight of the squad car quickly, concealed by the unrelenting snowfall.

The backstreet was one of the stranger ones in the neighborhood because the outlying streets tapered down at angles to a point. The buildings, constructed along those intersecting angles, caused two alleys to merge into one that reduced in width until it terminated in a dead end. The crime scene was in the bottom bar of the virtual "Y" the building arrangement created. Several cutouts and depressions stood on both sides, leading to the back doors of shops who offered their wares on the street side. Malcolm walked cautiously with his sidearm readied in case someone hid in those recessed depths. He felt the familiar twitch start in his left eyelid.

Here you go Mal.

His mind drifted back to some of his unit's operations during the war, where he picked up the nickname. He held the rank of Captain and led a small group of Special Forces soldiers tasked with entering enemy strongholds and eliminating any resistance. It was mostly going through a bunch of deserted caves, but the occasional occupied bunker found its way onto the agenda. They had more missions than they could count, and completed several without a single injury. The work was a necessary evil, but it never made them feel better or justified for doing it.

One of his men jokingly called him "Burro Mal de Capitan" after one of the missions. It was intended as a compliment due to Malcolm's track record, but he asked his man, not understanding the language, "what the hell that meant?" in a tone indicating he didn't care for a joke, if that's what it was. The response was "uh, Captain Bad Ass...Sir." It was the hardest Malcolm had laughed since setting foot on foreign soil. Mal was the only part that stuck, but the whole unit always used it as a term of endearment. He took responsibility for the lives of the men under his command, as expected, but it went beyond his job duties. He truly cared for those soldiers, and they knew it. They were also willing to do anything in return for that care and respect.

His memory settled on the mission when their "unscathed" record fell.

It was a bunker bust in the dead of winter in those godforsaken mountains. Intel indicated it was just another cave, probably empty. What they found were fortifications built far stronger than apparent

22

necessity. Standard Operating Procedure was the same, dictating a room to room search, clearing them one by one.

One of the last rooms was checked, found clear, and Malcolm advanced to the next position per protocol. The bullet passed through his right shoulder. The shooter knew the weak spots of the body armor. Luckily, the shot missed the bone. The ammo was high caliber, exerting enough blunt force to knock him backwards, off balance. He felt the heat of the second bullet pass his left eyelid as he spun and fell to the floor. Two of his men died before they killed the sniper, and the bunker was otherwise abandoned.

Without conscious thought, Malcolm checked and double-checked every spot large enough to conceal a man in the alley.

Headlights reflecting in the rearview mirror alerted Emilio of Homicide's arrival. He got out and walked over to their car with Gianelli in tow, showing his badge as he briefly introduced himself and Thomas. He uttered a quick verbal summary of what they included in their preliminary report and informed the detectives, who identified themselves as Joe Anderson and Angela Benson, that his partner was deeper in the alley looking for a possible suspect. He surrendered Gianelli and the report to the detectives and headed into the alley at a jog, unsnapping the leather strap that confined his sidearm in his hip holster.

The detectives asked Thomas Gianelli to get into the back seat of the car and wait while they went to check out the crime scene. He didn't have a choice since the rear doors could not be opened from the inside and the opening in the Plexiglas shield separating the front and rear seating was far too small for a man to fit through.

The driver was a man in his early fifties, dressed sloppily, with two to three day's growth of black and silver stubble on his cheeks, chin, and neck. He left the car idling and the heater running as a courtesy. His salt and pepper hair was severely mussed and being disturbed even more by the howling gusts of wind. The places beneath his dark brown eyes were a deep, uneven ashen gray with hints of black, indicating a severe lack of sleep. His suit, looking as if he slept in it, was wrinkled and equally disheveled.

In sharp contrast, his partner was an attractive brunette in her late twenties wearing a neatly pressed, conservative pantsuit. Her jet-black hair was hung just below her shoulder, with the sides tucked behind her ears, keeping it from getting in front of her deep blue eyes, until the wind hit her, throwing it into disarray. Her badge hung from a lanyard around her neck, glinting silvery sparks as she stood in the beams of the headlights. She conveyed a strong sense of preparedness that acted as a highlight to her alert persona. She kept herself in excellent physical condition, based on the cut of her clothing, and carried herself in a way that suggested a sense of purpose, very much unlike that of her partner's.

Hernandez and Dupree returned ten minutes later. They looked perplexed at coming up empty handed. They combed through every nook and cranny in the alley and came back without a suspect or anything else of use to add to the investigation. The detectives pulled heavy coats from the trunk to wear as they started their sweep.

"Evening Detectives," started Malcolm. "I'm Dupree and this is my partner Emilio Hernandez. We didn't find anything back there. I guess our witness just saw a phantom."

"Thank you, Gents," returned Joe. "We'll take it from here."

The uniformed police officers nodded in acknowledgement and returned to their car. Emilio drove away from the crime scene as the homicide team got to work. Malcolm updated the dispatcher and indicated they were going off shift.

"Time for O'Grady's, Amigo?"

"Si," returned Emilio, playfully butchering a Spanish accent. "I tink ve should close it down, Man!"

"Now you're talking partner," returned Malcolm, laughing away some of his demons.

O'Grady's Pub wasn't one of the local hot spots for New York's Finest, which was one of the reasons Emilio and Malcolm frequented it. It was a reasonably quiet bar with decent food, cold beer, and an atmosphere that encouraged relaxation. They discovered it in their second year as partners after responding to a domestic disturbance call in the apartments above the pub.

"Will it be your usual boys?" asked Tabatha.

She was a working mom with one little girl, holding down two jobs. She did a fine job waiting tables, and earned the tips to prove it. She always worked nights, so she waited on them most of the time. Ironically, she was also the only thing truly Irish about the pub. Her deep red hair framed her good looks and highlighted her emerald-green eyes. Her normal voice carried only a hint of Irish, but she exaggerated the accent and retained every ounce of the trademark fiery personality when she worked. On two occasions that they knew of, she dealt with overly infatuated, hands-on, drunk patrons with a wicked right cross before the bouncer or the manager even realized her honor was besmirched.

"Yeah, that'll work for me, Tab. What about you Malcolm?"

"Let me have a shot of bourbon and a chaser of dark stout."

"It'll be right up, boyos."

Tabatha hustled away to check on another table, leaving the partners alone.

"Are you sure you're okay Malcolm? You've been on edge since we left that last call tonight. You don't usually start with a shot of anything."

"It feels like something bad is coming our way," he answered, not willing to bring up his war stories. "Be glad you didn't get as up close and personal like I did with the victim."

"Blood and guts don't usually affect you like this, and we've seen some bad things in our time on the streets since you became civilian. I imagine you saw worse in the Marines."

"It's not the body that bothers me. It's the pure carnage of it that's so unsettling. I mean, what kind of person can do that to another human being?"

Tabatha dropped off their drinks and gave Malcolm an odd look as he set the empty shot glass back on her tray before she had time to serve Emilio his beer. She recovered quickly and without comment, but she was aware that something was troubling him. She was known to offer an ear to listen to customers that she deemed deserving. Malcolm and Emilio both fit into that category for her, but she knew them well enough to know it wasn't a good time to offer comment or consolation.

"I understand where you're coming from. Whoever did this is just…for lack of a better word, evil."

"I think that's exactly the right word. That wasn't a mugging, or a dispute that went south. I think the killer did it just for the sake of doing it."

They sat in silence for a long time, slowly nursing their beers.

Emilio used the quiet to recall a louder time in his life.

His parents died when he was only ten years old in a freak airline crash. The wreckage gave evidence to a mid-air collision, but no other jets were in the area at the time. This left him in the care of his seventeen-year-old brother, Juan. Emilio idolized his older brother, and that grew stronger once it was just the two of them.

Juan was able to provide for them both very well. Emilio never questioned how he did it. He thought it was Juan that wanted him to dress the way he did, especially the dark blue bandana that he wore, tied around his left upper arm. He wanted desperately to wear his on his right arm, just like Juan.

His life was loudest when he found out what he would have to do to shift the position of that banner. At the age of sixteen, that rite of passage cost one human life, enough to prove he was worthy to become a member of the Bandas. Juan led the gang, and Emilio suddenly realized that "Jefe" was more than a nickname.

It was a price Emilio could not, and would not pay. Hurt, with his morals betrayed, he felt lost for several months, not sure what to do or where to go, but always knowing he had to stay away from Juan. He was able to stay with school friends for short periods of time, between bouts at the school of hard knocks. He tried to eliminate some of the mannerisms he picked up from Juan, but they were hard to put to rest. He would find himself walking with that confidant swagger when he let his guard down, that he now understood was met with negative connotations to those watching.

He was to the point of mentally tearing himself apart when a door opened, just like his late father always told them it would. He could clearly hear his dad telling them "boys, life will be very hard sometimes, but always remember that if God closes a door, he will also open another one for you."

The door was opened by a police officer that took a bullet, fired by a gunman sporting dark blue on his left arm, saving the life of an elderly store owner. He read the story in the *Times* a few days after it happened.

Officer Gerard McCreedy died before he reached the hospital, in route to a life-saving surgical procedure to remove the bullets. He was off duty, shopping for the week's provisions for his family of four, when the gang member came around to collect his "fee" for protecting the store from rival gangs. He fired one shot as he fell to the floor of the small grocery. McCreedy's bullet found it's mark and left Emilio without a brother.

The story described the funeral for the fallen police officer. Every officer that could attended to show their honor and respect for their fallen comrade. The widow, holding her daughter and son, broke down completely when she was presented a United States flag as the twenty-one-gun salute, accompanied a bagpipe version of Taps, echoed in the background.

Emilio walked through the door God opened, and it was the entrance to the police academy. The badge represented every trait that he wanted to embody. It offered him a way to fight, and hopefully right some of, Juan's wrongs.

"Is that all that's bothering you, Malcolm?" asked Emilio when he slipped back to reality from his memories. "You know you can tell me if you need to talk." Emilio was acting like a big brother, even though Malcolm was over a decade older. His devotion to family was very strong, and he considered Malcolm family, even though he wasn't blood.

"Am I a book that's that easy to read?"

"I watch what's going on around me. You'd be amazed at all the things you pick up just by paying attention. Are you having trouble with Beverly again?"

"Guilty as charged. She's been on me for a few weeks now about getting off the streets and taking a desk job. She's worried that I'll take a bullet in the line of duty and leave her without a husband and the kids without a father. I'm just not ready to give it up yet. Our oldest, Mark, told us a few days ago that he wants to join the force. She told me to talk some sense into him, so I told him to get his degree first."

27

"I don't imagine that went over very well."

"I've slept on the couch the last couple of nights. She'll come around like she always does, but it's got me thinking all the same."

"She's just worried about you. Sylvia feels the same way, but we agreed in the beginning that I could do this as long as I wanted. She knows what it means to me. I hope you aren't telling me you're thinking about retirement."

"No, I'm not, not yet anyway. I've still got a few years to work before I can retire the way I want to. How are things with you and Sylvia?" asked Malcolm, shifting the attention away from his problems. Trusting Emilio was not an issue for Malcolm – it was just uncomfortable for him to talk about his problems. He knew Emilio saw him as an older, surrogate brother, even though it dredged up memories of things forever lost.

"It's about the same. We've talked and talked about the wedding, but she can't decide on a date. She wants everything to be perfect. I told her we don't have to have perfect, but she won't settle for less. The baby's due in four months and I'd really like to be married first."

"Do you know if it's a boy or a girl?"

"I'd like to find out, but she doesn't want to know and it's not worth getting her ire up over it. She's in that stage right now that scares the crap out of me anyway."

"You, scared? How does she do that?"

"Oh, it's the 'we're doing this my way or I'll kill you in your sleep' trimester."

They started chuckling as Tabatha swung by the table to pick up the empty bottles and ask if they needed another round. Reaching a laugh finally broke some of their tension, so they told the Irish Miss they were done drinking for the night and ready for their ritual nightcap of dark roasted coffee. They didn't depend on alcohol to shield them from the wounds of the job, but it could sure dull the blade on particularly sharp days.

Joe and Angela finished up and waited in the car until the Coroner arrived to take possession of the body. They were relieved that the murder took place deep in an alley so they didn't have to deal with the occasional passerby or the guaranteed rubberneck that would alert the media.

"How cold do you think it'll get tonight?" asked Angela, looking for a new subject.

"They're predicting eleven degrees," answered Joe, "but I think it'll get a little colder. I've seen a few little glints of starlight through the clouds, so this storm may be breaking up. It'll get even colder before that new storm system hits in the morning. They're expecting another eight to ten inches of snow."

"I never thought I'd ever experience cold like this. Winters in Texas could get cold, but never relentless like this."

"You get used to it after a few years. I'd rather deal with this than the hot, dry summer heat."

"Now that's what I'd like to have. I'd love to be stretched out on the beach working on my tan."

"Angela, you don't strike me as the tanning type."

"And what is that supposed to mean?" she asked jokingly.

"You just don't seem like the kind of woman that would be worried about having a good tan. You only expect that kind of thing from a ditzy blonde, you know."

"Then I guess I should take that as a compliment?"

Joe didn't answer, but his expression gave him away. Angela's lips shifted into a small grin.

"When can I go home?" interjected Thomas gruffly from the back seat.

"It won't be much longer, Mr. Gianelli. After the meat wagon gets here, we'll take you to the Precinct to get a formal statement, then a uniformed unit will give you a ride back," said Joe, using the rearview mirror to reflect a stern look to the back seat.

"Is that really necessary?" He fidgeted a little under Joe's stare, still wanting to climb back into his bottle and reach the peak of his numbed world.

29

"I'm afraid it is. I apologize for the trouble, but you'll only have to bear it for a little while longer."

They sat in awkward silence for another five minutes until the van with "Coroner" stenciled on the side and rear doors pulled into the alley. Joe tapped the horn and waved in lieu of getting out of the car as they backed away from the scene.

The flakes of snow steadily grew smaller as less and less sleet came down with the mix. The relief would prove to be short lived, but any relief was more welcome than none at all.

ChApteR three

Webster Avenue was unnaturally quiet. The swollen gray clouds trapped the city's light, illuminating everything with an eerie mockery of daylight. Even with the occasional clear spot through the nimbus, the sky looked as though it could explode at any moment, plummeting New York into an Arctic Pompeii.

Julie Romanowski gladly stepped out of the cab at the building addressed 2420 at 1:50 AM. The driver completely unnerved her during the trip, pressing forward faster than the road conditions dictated, weaving in and out of traffic like a pro skier. She was relieved when they stopped in front of the brownstone, still alive and in one piece.

She shuddered when the heat from the cab gave way to the elements outside as she paid the meter and tipped the cabby. She jogged up the stairs, hastened by the cold nipping at her skin, wincing with the harder bites. She was glad to finally be home after the near hour-long commute from work, made longer and more frightening by the bad weather and dangerous driving.

Julie worked at a nightclub called The Black Knight, a renowned hot spot for New York's elite, where many of the rich and eccentric went to play. They enjoyed living in a world of fantasy behind those doors and every night was a costume party. Everything about the club carried a medieval theme. The staff wore uniforms resembling medieval garb, as did many of the patrons.

The furniture looked as if it came straight from Camelot. The hand carved chairs were a bit much for a bar, but the clientele didn't tend to abuse them. The interior walls supported gray stone veneer and most of the accoutrements were black wrought iron, finishing out the theme. The few food items offered were finger foods that were modernized versions of 13th century cuisine, even though the only similarity was the names listed on the menu. The bar drinks had special names too, like the Lancelot and the Steel Gauntlet.

On several occasions each night, the staff performed for the crowd, taking them farther away from their lives of worry and responsibility. They staged a duel that night, and Julie played the damsel-in-distress to two knights fighting for her favor. The highlight was the mock sword fight, complete with fake blood and a riveting death scene at the end that earned a standing ovation from about a third of the customers.

Julie wanted to get out of her costume, one of three she actually owned. Costumes were provided by the club. It was her fanciest "duchess" gown that she picked especially for the staged duel. She stripped it off, threw it over the footboard of her bed, and sat down on the edge of the mattress. Her legs and feet ached from the performance, which made taking her shoes and hose off a near biblical experience. The heavy stage makeup was losing its freshness, making her face feel oily. Even so, the night didn't seem as bad as usual since it was her acting encore.

She leaned down to massage her calves, hoping to work out some of the soreness. She then rolled her bare toes back and forth over the carpet. She still thought the little trick was weird because she heard it in a movie as a remedy for jet lag, but it actually worked. She followed that with a few deep breaths that she held before letting them out slowly, which forced the tension to just roll out of her shoulders.

She took a long, hot shower to feel human again before slipping into flannel pajamas and a thick terry cloth robe. The heater was set low to save electricity, forcing her and her roommate to dress in layers during the winter months. She entered the kitchen to find the lights off, indicating she was still home alone.

Julie's excitement about work renewed as she relaxed, thinking about the promotion she was given when she got to work. She was moving up from a waitress to bartender, which meant better pay and better hours, not to mention that she wouldn't have to perform any longer. She would also be making "bar tips"—the bread and butter at the Black Knight. She couldn't wait to share her news with Ellen.

chapτεʀ fouʀ

The warehouse was dark and musty. The air inside carried a strong scent of salt brought in from the surf of the Atlantic, while layers of dust and mildew covered all of the boxes and equipment stored in the building. The facility once belonged to an import-export company that had bankrupted eleven months prior. The court locked up the warehouse and all of its contents pending appraisal and sale, designating that the proceeds be used to pay off the company's debts. The crates held a cornucopia of products since the company dabbled in virtually every market. Some boxes indicated they contained electronics from Japan, others had clothing sourced from China, while others stored preserved foodstuffs from various regions of South America. It was a seven-hundred-thousand square foot treasure trove set apart from the rest of the world, but hidden in plain sight.

Unfortunately, the court overlooked locking up the skylights, leaving them unsecured and allowing unhindered access to anyone aware of the oversight, like the two vagabonds standing at the building's center.

An old, rusted camping lantern provided light for the two intruders. They stood in a clearing among the rows and rows of crates and equipment. The lantern's feeble light couldn't ward off all of the darkness of the cavernous building, yielding to complete pitch darkness at a ten-foot radius.

"Freddy, what are we doing here?" asked Todd insecurely, wincing as his echo returned to him in a voice he did not recognize. He trembled under his clothes and shifted his gaze quickly, trying to keep an eye on everything at once, like a rabbit hiding from a pack of coyotes. "This place gives me the creeps. Let's get the hell outta here!"

"What's the matter, Todd, you gettin' scared?" teased Freddy with a mocking tone. He raised his hands to frame his face, mouthed the word "Boo," and gave his best shocked look. It smoothed the small wrinkles around his eyes and showed how many front teeth he lacked.

"What are you trying to say?"

Todd mustered all the courage he could and pushed his chest out in an attempt to stay the shakes that visibly rattled his hands. Deep seeded fear was a new experience for him, and one he wasn't well equipped to deal with a run of down-and-out bad luck. A few poor decisions stripped the self-esteem of a once confident man into the fearful vagrant that took his place.

"I'm saying you need to get a handle on it. We're the only ones that even know about this place, so there ain't no reason to turn yellow."

"Okay, okay, it's not that bad," he returned with a rattling sigh, still looking around nervously. "I'm just worried about being in here. What are we doing in here anyway?"

"This is that big score I told you about a few weeks ago!" exclaimed Freddy triumphantly, spreading his arms wide to represent the extent of the new-found wealth. "Look at all this stuff in here."

"And what do you think we're gonna be able to do with it? Don't tell me this is another one of your schemes."

"No! No, Todd, you ain't seein' the whole picture here. This place used to ship all kinds of stuff. There's plenty of stuff that we can sell, pawn off, or just use to get by."

"And what if we get caught?" asked Todd, working some of the possible outcomes through his mind. He knew he wasn't always the brightest crayon in the box, but he didn't think this venture was going to be the cakewalk Freddy predicted.

"What'll they do to us, even if we do get caught? We're a couple a bums; besides, I rigged the doors. If anyone comes in, it'll make one hell of a racket, and we'll have enough time to get out."

"And what will they do if they find anything missing?"

"God Todd, you ask too many questions! They won't be able to do anything. They won't know who took the stuff and they probably don't even know what all's in here. Nobody's gonna miss a few things."

A loud, metallic clatter echoed in the darkness from the west end of the building. Both men snapped their heads in the direction of the sound, fear and uneasiness on both their faces.

"I thought you said no one else knew about this place?" asked Todd nervously.

"No one does that I know of, and it bothers me that the sound came from that way."

"Why?"

"There aren't any doors or windows over there." Freddy's expression took on a hardened edge, like a 49er getting ready to deal with someone on his stake. "Someone else must have come in here like we did and I'll be damned if I'm gonna share this gold mine!" He grabbed the heavy crowbar he used to break seals on the crates and ran off into the darkness towards the origin of the sound.

"Freddy! No! Wait!" called Todd, as loud as he dared, but his friend was already gone. The new nervousness turned on itself, tarnishing his fear with the dread of isolation. He backed into a corner created by the stacks of wooden crates and pallet-stored items. The light from the small lantern flickered and shook in his trembling hands as he resigned himself to sit and wait. Freddy's footfalls passed out of earshot, and he could hear nothing besides his rapidly increasing heartbeat and fear-lined breathing.

Freddy's eyes adjusted to the darkness, but it was still very difficult to see. He moved more slowly, careful not to get ahead of his limited range of vision as he realized how limited it really was. He had covered almost four hundred yards when he heard something a short distance behind him. He spun around wielding the crowbar like a two-handed sword, prepared to strike whatever was lurking in the darkness. He stealthily moved back towards the clearing where he left Todd, seeking out the source of the new noise and wondering if he had actually heard anything at all. The mind liked to play those kinds of tricks. Another clatter resolved any doubts. He increased his pace, hoping to trap the uninvited guest between himself and his partner in crime.

Freddy ran and tripped on something, forcing a fall to the cold, hard concrete floor. The crowbar escaped his grip and rattled off into the darkness, thudding against one of the crates as sliding off on a new vector. He sat up quickly, trying to find his weapon and to see what he stumbled over. A quick glance and cursory feel around didn't discover the crowbar, but it did reveal the broken remains of the still warm camping lantern just beyond his feet. He was back in the clearing where he started without realizing he had backtracked over that much ground.

Todd was gone.

It looked as though he had gotten scared and dropped the lantern, probably kicking it as he ran away. Freddy guessed those were the sounds he heard, followed by Todd scampering through the skylight. He leaned back against the nearest crate, took a deep breath, and laughed. He would give Todd a real hard time for turning yellow and running. The sound he heard before he left Todd alone had slipped his memory.

Freddy stood up and headed back towards the center of the warehouse. He had a box of emergency flares and some cans of tuna he'd taken from some of the crates stored there, so he was going to eat, get some rest, and wait to find Todd in the morning. He decided to hold off on looking for the crowbar until daybreak so he wouldn't waste any of the flares.

He brushed his hands on the seat of his pants as he walked, attempting to clean off the thick layer of dust that clung to him from his tumble across the floor. He sneezed into his sleeve as some of the old silt tickled his sinuses. He discovered the sleeve was wet. The moisture had not soaked through the material; thus, he couldn't feel it on his skin. The liquid had a strange, almost slimy texture and smelled strongly of copper. Freddy froze in midstride, gasping in a breath, when he realized what it was. His sleeve was covered with cold, coagulating blood.

"TODD, WHERE ARE YOU? Is this some kind of joke? Real funny, you jerk! Ha ha, I'm just laughing my ass off now! Come out here! This stupid game's over!"

The sensation of suddenly being very alone in a very bad place swept through him like a wildfire. He looked in every direction, trying to make sense of what was happening. Unexpectedly, he felt something sharp pierce the back of his neck, slashing through flesh and bone. It only hurt for a second before the pain gave way to a sense of light pressure. He grabbed the nape of his neck to assess the nature and extent of the wound. Blood flowed quickly through his fingers and down the small of his back. Weakness gradually increased with the beating of his heart, pumping blood out of the gash. He collapsed on the cold floor and tried to call for help, but he was unable to form the sounds. Dizziness rushed in, coupled with disorientation, as the shadows at the edge of his vision grew darker and the temperature in the warehouse dropped.

What's happening?

Freddy drew all the strength he could and crawled towards the skylight. Each advance came harder and slower than the last, and the wetness on the floor made it more difficult to keep his hands under him.

I can get out and get help. I'll just rest here a second and catch my breath.

The air felt overly chilled. Strange sensations tingled along his spine, riddling his skin with goose bumps and spiking as odd pains throughout his body. Running on will power alone, Freddy propped himself up against another stack of crates. Sweat purged from his pores while cramps twisted and attacked his stomach. In just a few short moments, Death was there to claim him.

The sound of the garbage truck startled Julie awake. The clock on the wall in the kitchen read 3:12 AM. Disappointed that she dozed off and missed her roommate's arrival, she went to her room, crawled into bed, and quickly fell back to sleep. Her news would have to wait until morning.

ChAptER FIVE

The cathedral of St. Christopher's loomed high in the night sky, a Gothic shadow against the winter clouds, ashen with the captured light of the city at night. It stood for one-hundred seventy-four years, making it one of the older churches in the city. It was not as striking as Renwick's masterpiece of architecture that was erected at Fifth Avenue and 51st Street in 1853, but every bit as unique.

The quarried stone walls narrowed to tall spires that cornered the steeply pitched, copper-gilded rooflines. Multiple arches graced the walls at street level and permitted access to the covered walkway that stretched along three sides. Bright stained-glass windows balanced with darkly stained, massive oak doors and accents gave the holy place a feel more reminiscent of Jim Shore's creations.

The interior was warm and inviting, made even more so by the inclement weather outside. Small clusters of ivory-colored candles burned in the narthex, creating a comforting and serene ambiance. The gentle scent of vanilla and lavender hung in the air, providing an aromatherapy-induced calm.

A large, hand carved red oak arch supported by wooden columns opened into the nave. Many more candles were peppered throughout, almost completely filling the holy space with a soft, pure light. Rafters in the same wood and design as the entrance arch supported the vaulted ceiling rising high above the floor of the nave. The vicinity around the outside edges of the pews, beyond the altar, and along the face of the confessionals was shrouded in deep shadow. The confessionals were rarely used at this time of morning and generally left unattended until daylight hours.

The priest was already awake and about, finding that age brought a tendency to begin and end the day early. The first hour or two of his typical daily schedule gave him time to clear his mind of any problems before he turned attention to his flock.

Father Samuels heard the door of one of the confessionals pull open and click closed. The action made little noise, but it came to his ears easily with thirty-eight years' of experience doing the Lord's work in the venerable church. The priest waited a few moments before entering the side of the confessional designated for him. He discovered, a few years into the priesthood, that most people allowed themselves to open up a bit more if they had a few moments to relax and compose their thoughts.

Once Samuels entered, he began. "Welcome to St. Christopher's, a house in the rite of our Holy Lord." His voice was as warm and inviting as the church, and he commanded a reassuring and gentle tone that extended the overall sensation of calm to those needing counsel. "How may I be of service?"

"Forgive me Father, for I have sinned."

The parishioners voice, obviously male, was very deep with a slight scratchiness that made him sound aged. The tone was weary, but every word was spoken clearly.

"I killed someone and I will have to kill again."

Father Samuels, utterly dumbfounded, stared at the wooden lattice separating him from the shriving stool in the other half of the free-standing booth. He was taken aback, never having anyone confess this mortal sin to him. The ease with which the penitent revealed the unforgivable act, and the commitment to repeat it, bothered him even more. His breath came in shortened gasps and he felt dizzy, confined to an emotional roller coaster. Penitents just don't confess to the worst of all sins unless it's followed by a step up to the gallow's noose.

To further his predicament, the priest was bound to a vow of confidence; he could not and would not reveal anything for any reason that he was told during a confession. He acted only as the ears of God to allow His followers forgiveness from their venial sins, and as the voice of God to those who needed His comfort. He was not permitted to pass judgment or render his personal opinions–he could only convey God's teachings. The confession put immense pressure on his shoulders and his oath of confidentiality.

Was it God's intent to allow someone to confess to murder and walk away unpunished?

The irony unnerved Father Samuels. He lost his composure, unbeknownst to the confessor, and felt the need to reassert his position, which caused him real physical pain. He knew his duty to God and to the Church. He knew, as he was ordained, he would not reveal the man's dark secret to anyone, regardless of the sin's severity. The brutal realization of the fragility of life forced him to question his own morality along with his vows.

"Father, are you still there?"

"Yes, of course," answered Samuels, clearing his throat and trying desperately to recover from his dumbstruck state. "I'm sorry for losing my bearings for the last few moments. You do realize that murder, the taking of another's life, is the worst of all sins?"

"Yes, I do, and I am sorry for putting you in this position. I cannot explain my actions or my intentions, nor am I here to justify what I've done. I merely needed to confess to cleanse the burden from my soul."

Murder being downplayed to burden was beyond the father's threshold of tolerance.

"You can't simply wash your hands of this sin from the eyes of God!" barked the Roman Catholic, audibly irritated. "What you have done will be with you from now on, even into the afterlife. I pray that your very soul has not been lost for all eternity!"

"I know this is overwhelming, and I believe I would feel the same way in your position. I don't expect you to understand or approve of what I'm doing, but you must believe me when I tell you that my intentions are pure."

Samuels was left utterly speechless.

The sinner paused a moment, collecting his thoughts, unsure if he should continue or if he had already said too much for this first meeting. It had taken him several weeks to find Samuels, and several more to decide if he was reliable. He fervently hoped that his time and effort would not prove to be a waste.

"I have an appointment to keep with an old friend, so I must go, but I will return each time I've completed one of my tasks. I must show my respect for the dead regardless of the reasons for which I have taken their lives. I pray that their souls will have a safe journey into the next life."

The sound of the door opening and closing again indicated the man left the confessional. He slipped away unnoticed, just as he entered. This anonymity allowed him to follow his path without resistance, his freedom of paramount importance to see his tasks through to completion.

Father Samuels waited much longer than normal to leave the receiving side of the confessional; his mind too entangled in the recent event to function properly. He could feel his accelerated heart beat through the pulse in his hands and along his temples. He sat in silence, hoping for divine intervention to offer a solution to his problem. On exiting, he excused himself from the primary chapel to be alone in his chambers. The killer left the church, headed for what he called home. It was a relatively short trip and someone awaited his arrival.

"You are late."

"I had to make a quick stop."

"You should have told me. You are making my job more difficult when you don't let me know what you are doing."

"I apologize. I needed to speak to Samuels."

"Ah, I see. I take it you are not injured?"

"No, but I have to take care of a loose end that cannot wait."

"You don't have much time. Are you sure that's wise?"

"I have no choice. I'll be back in time." He stepped back into the night and disappeared into the darkness.

The killer's partner worked through the nightly ritual of checking and double-checking all of the building's doors and windows, making sure they were securely locked or barred shut. The place was once known as St. Francis, but the cathedral had remained empty for months after the church received enough donations to build a new place of worship. Church officials postponed the decision of what to do with the old building, so it sat–waiting.

The two discovered the cathedral very soon after their arrival to the city, knowing it would serve them well. The bell tower was ideal since all but one of the bells themselves had already been relocated. The one that remained sported a small crack near the bottom and was set back in one of the corners. All the doors and windows at street level were nailed or barred shut, leaving the only point of entry through the bell tower, which served as an excellent location for defense. He climbed the ladder from the topmost floor of the church to the trap door in the floor of the airy bell room, positioning himself in a dark corner to await his partner's return and the break of day.

Samuels' chamber was quite large, but the room was put to good use. The space felt very cozy, which was the reason he chose it. He believed the church, and his representation of it, should exude peace and comfort. He didn't condone breaks from the established conduct of his religion, but hard-earned wisdom showed him that it was far easier to guide a congregation at ease.

A mammoth, solid walnut desk, with a neatly organized desktop, stood at the room's center, facing the door. The surface was uncluttered, and all of his administrative paperwork rested neatly in a wooden box sitting on one corner. An old-style banker's lamp provided a warm circle of light below the hunter-green tinted glass shade, which illuminated a leather writing pad on the desk's center. The high back chair, made of the same leather sat ready for use behind the desk. The furnishings were expensive, but not extravagant in nature. Visitors saw lasting quality, not flourishes of wealth.

The walls were lined with bookshelves containing various religious texts and other reference materials he had collected during his extensive pilgrimages of the world. Samuels, now sixty-eight years young, settled down at St. Christopher's after his forty-eighth birthday, with a very broad base of knowledge on the world's different religions and belief systems. Understanding the pretense of other religions and denominations helped him to better understand his own, while providing well-rounded counsel.

He took a bottle of drinking water from the small refrigerator in his office and noticed his hand shaking slightly as he unscrewed the cap. He sat the bottle on the desk and clasped his hands together to still the movement as he prayed for strength and guidance. He had confronted many hard decisions throughout his life, more difficult ones since his induction to the priesthood, yet he found himself at a complete loss for what to do. He wished his mentor was still alive. Stephen always knew the right thing to do. During times of peril, Stephen would always turn to the written Word to clear his thoughts.

Samuels found that reading scripture eased his mind as well. Picking up his worn copy of the Good Book, he went through several verses, searching for the calm that accompanied the presence of divinity. Later he even pulled a few tomes from his shelves for variety, but after an hour, his hands still shook the pages as he turned them.

ChAPTER SIX

Angela tossed and turned restlessly all night. The fifth sleepless night helped the deprivation show. She looked at the clock to check the time. "Five twelve in the morning. This is insane. The only thing I should see this early in the morning is the backside of my eyelids." She rolled to her back and stared at the ceiling, thinking about what she wanted to do. She finally decided to just get up, tired and unwilling to fight with herself any longer to fall asleep.

A short stroll put her in her kitchen, where she fixed herself a cup of Earl Grey and listened to the news on a local radio station. The newscaster's voice had an annoying quality, like he spoke through his nose, as he gave all the bad news that happened overnight. Angela paid very little attention to his monologue. The weathercast called for more snow and even colder temperatures, no surprise in the dead of winter. She shut off the radio and walked to her desk, clutching her favorite coffee mug full of hot black tea. A military style block font stated "I Hate Mornings" on both sides above a line that appeared to be written in black marker that stated "and morning people, all six of you."

She woke her laptop and started the media player for background noise as she checked her e-mail. She deleted the usual spam, offers of large sums of money from the Central Bank of Nigeria, the sale to beat all sales with the same discounts as last week from an online retailer, and discount pharmacy ads for pills to help men with erectile dysfunction.

"You'll never see my shade or the sound of my feet while there's a moon over Bourbon Street" flowed melodically from her speakers as she sent a quick message to her mother. They shared a secret e-mail address that her father didn't know about so they could keep in touch. Angela and her father hadn't spoken a word to each other since she moved away from home.

Home was Hale Center, Texas. It was a typical small West Texas town, home to good people, over-priced groceries, and one flashing four way stop sign at the town's hub. She left at the age of seventeen after graduating high school a year early. She wanted more than the small town could offer and set her sights on the University of Michigan.

They offered a very good forensics program where she earned her law enforcement degree simultaneously. A good scholarship from a near perfect SAT score and a few grants got her through school. After graduation, she left for New York, hoping to start a career as a detective.

Her father didn't approve of the move or her choice of higher learning institution, and he especially hated his daughter's intention of becoming a policewoman. He felt that police work was a field dominated by men because it was meant for men. The reality shows he watched religiously only furthered his ill-informed beliefs. New York was a vile place full of sinners, rapists, and terrorists that would do nothing but grind his daughter through the wheels and spit her out when she was just like the rest, leaving her with no option but to return home, broken and defeated. He absolutely refused to accept Angela's decision and virtually disowned her.

What would his pastor think?

It was one of her many trivial worries. At this point he was beyond changing, and it made little difference since what was done was done.

Her mom, Susan, understood that Angela was the inquisitive type, more interested in the how and the why, always open to new ideas, and supported her daughter even when it caused tension with her husband. It was the same during her childhood, and she was determined to put Angela first and encourage her to better herself, especially in terms of education. "Susan, make sure you get a good education. It's the one thing that you'll always have with you and it can never be taken away," were her mother's words that she shared with her daughter early on.

Angela was very bright and showed a desire to learn at a young age. She showed a special interest in animals, especially horses, that also irked her father. She could still hear the first thing he said when she expressed her desire to have a horse, "Those things do nothing but eat, crap, sleep, and cost money. Where's the sense in that?"

Even so, Susan spent many hours watching Angela ride, helping with training, or explaining the importance of health and exercise, quenching her daughter's thirst for knowledge.

By the age of twelve, Angela completely trained a then three-year-old mare from the ground up. She couldn't be happier than coming in for dinner covered with hay, smelling like a barnyard, and satisfied with ending on a good note.

43

Susan never missed a single riding competition or horse show, or the chance to offer her shoulder when some boy broke Angela's heart. She was forced to keep her continued relationship with her daughter a secret to prevent problems with her husband Marlin. She didn't like to do things behind his back, but she refused to push her daughter away and pretend she didn't exist. She loved Marlin dearly, even with his unreasonable problems. They both came from the old school where husbands and wives understood the meaning of "for better or for worse."

The ringing of the phone startled Angela.

Who would call at this hour?

She answered on the fourth ring.

"Hello."

"Hi, Angie," said her mother.

"What are you doing up at this hour, Mom? Am I going to have to get the Sharpie again and update my mug to 7?"

They enjoyed the laugh they shared. Susan bought Angela the favored mug for her 9th birthday, surprised that she had such an emotional attachment to it.

"I should ask you the same thing. For me, rites of passage I guess. It seems like I wake up about four in the morning every day now with a craving for something made out of whole grains with a lot of fiber."

Angela laughed again, filled with warmth. Her mother could always make her laugh and feel better.

"Why are you up so early, Angie? You, to use cleaner words than you would, absolutely detest mornings."

"Amen, Mom. It's the case I'm on. I'm having some trouble sleeping. I wish I could tell you about it, but you know the rules, and I wouldn't want you losing sleep on my account."

"I know you can't. Do you ever wish you'd stuck with Geography as a major? Rocks don't usually kill people unless they're pushed from high places."

"Mom, that's not funny!" she exclaimed, trying to prevent her escaping giggles.

"So why are you laughing?"

44

"Okay, it's a little funny. I just feel like I need to help people. I want something more upbeat that plate tectonics."

"You've been that way your whole life, Ang. You probably don't even remember taking up for the smaller kids on the playground when you were little. What, four or five?"

"I'm pretty sure the memories I have are from what you've told me. I think I would remember if I really was the Wonder Woman you tell me I was."

"It's the honest truth young lady! The next time you come home, we'll pull your outfit down from the attic – magic lasso and all!"

She paused for a few seconds, unsure if she wanted to ask the question that came to mind at the mention of home.

"So, how's Dad?" she asked, choking on the words. She loved and missed her father, even though they hadn't been civil towards each other for years.

"Just like always, Angie. He's in pretty good health and he stays busy with the church and the guys at the Lodge. I've never told you, but I'm really sorry about the way the cards fell between you two. He just seemed to change when you got old enough to start making up your own mind about things. He was so supportive when you were younger. I'd like to think that he wants to set things right, but I just don't know anymore."

"I tried so hard to make things work Mom, I really did. It was bad enough when he decided to sign me up for the softball team without even asking, but I couldn't take anymore when he forbade me from taking that forensics class. I told him I wasn't trying to hurt him or be disrespectful, but I had to live my own life."

"I know and I tried to get him to see that Angie, but it was like talking to a different person. I tried to get him to understand a couple of months after you moved out, thinking he would have cooled down about it all by then, but he wouldn't have any part of it. I don't bring it up much anymore, we just argue when I do."

"I know, Mom. I'm glad you tried, but I guess we can't have everything. I know I could be the bigger person and take the first step to apologize, but that goes against everything that I am. I wasn't in the wrong to make my own choice. I know you understand where I'm coming from with this."

45

"It'll work out one way or the other. I don't imagine this is going to help you sleep any better, so it's time to change the subject. How's Ellie?"

"She's doing fine, Mom. I don't get to ride her much up here, but I go to the boarding stable three or four times a week to see her. She gets brushed and loved on, and more treats than she really needs."

"That's my girl!"

"I learned from the best! I just wish I had enough time to take her out for a full day's ride. The people up here don't seem to see a problem with their horses being stabled all day."

"It's not their fault! They're Yankees!"

Angela's laughter eased the rest of her tension away.

"Thanks Mom."

"Well, you better get back to bed if you're planning to catch any bad guys today. Try to get some sleep, and don't let all the demons you had to leave here bother you. I'm going to finish my oatmeal before it gets cold."

"Okay, I'll put them to rest. I love you, Mom."

"I love you, too. You know, no matter how big you get, you'll always be my little girl, and I'll never be more than a phone call away."

"Talk to you soon."

Angela grinned as the warmth of good feelings swept into her heart, mimicking the flow of her bergamot flavored tea.

"Bye Angie."

Angela hung up the phone, feeling better if only temporarily. Talking with her mother always made her feel better, but it didn't last. The stress, and occasional homesickness, crept back into her just like always. She hated being so far away from her mom, but she wouldn't allow herself to back slide. She'd come too far to give up.

Her thoughts shifted back to her father, bringing a tear to the corner of her eye. She knew the relationship was too far gone to be reconciled. She wiped the sadness away, took a deep breath, and refused to once again let her father have any degree of control over her or her emotions.

The echoes of sleep returned, so she took her empty mug to the kitchen sink, went back to her queen-sized feather bed, and climbed under the covers. She hoped to get at least an hour or so of rest before her alarm officially announced the ridiculously heinous hour she had to start her day.

The New York City Police Department, one of the largest law enforcement organizations in the United States, scrambled to perform its sworn duty of serving and protecting the Big Apple. The sprawling population provided the "men in blue" with a multitude of crimes to solve, disputes that required intervention, and endless traffic violations that help fund the city's coffer. However, even the pride that supported the gold shield wasn't always enough. The Gateway City's Finest worked severely understaffed with increasing caseloads daily. Moral, on a good day, was fair to poor for most of them.

Duty Sergeant Miles O' Toole, one of the exceptions to the rule, arrived at headquarters at a quarter before six in the morning. By his agenda, he was late, even though payroll would complain about him coming in over an hour early. The city's streets, covered with a new layer of snow, made commuting slower than normal, and the unchangeable fact did nothing to alter his outlook.

I should have left earlier. I knew more snow was coming.

His face carried the shade of irritation as he approached his desk. He needed to go through the departmental logs to prepare for the morning's briefings. The logs were updated constantly throughout the day, making note of important events like new APBs, hot sheet crimes, recent arrests, and the like. He summarized the daily information into a more usable report that he issued every morning during shift change.

The widowed son of an Irish immigrant, Miles served on the force the 37 years since his eighteenth birthday. He worked the streets for all but the last four, forced to go behind a desk due to unrelenting near-sightedness and age-slowed reflexes. He could no longer pass the field evaluation, but he took the test every year, even though he knew he was unlikely to pass. He absolutely loved working the streets, wanting nothing more than to be back on them again. He settled for Duty Sergeant because it was the closest to the streets as he could be without actually working them and because he could remain an active member of the force.

O' Toole finished his third cup of coffee when one of the case files brought on déjà vu. He knew he hadn't read it before, because it was entered into the logs the previous night, but it seemed very familiar. He chose to investigate his hunch, spurred on by the uneasy feeling in the pit of his stomach.

The case he read again concerned a murder on the previous evening. The victim, slain in a very grotesque manner, was the tone that rang familiar to Sergeant O' Toole. He scanned back through the logs, expanding his search to include all the precincts, and found three other homicides with similarities, specifically mutilation as a common thread. He was one of the few Duty Sergeants that went through the logs for every Precinct, not just his own. It was easy for similar details to be overlooked until something became a crisis if the focus was on a single Precinct.

All four of the victims had no identification, no witnesses, and all the bodies were ravaged extensively. The absence of the victim's heart in two of the cases was even more disturbing. No evidence existed as to why the organs were removed or where they ended up. He jotted down the numbers of the four cases and returned to his desk where he sent a quick e-mail to the morgue asking the coroner to have the three prior autopsy reports reviewed. With luck, the most recent body would still be in custody so they could forego having to exhume one grave. The newest cadaver was scheduled for autopsy that morning according to the agenda the Coroner's office posted electronically, so a quarter of the work would be easy. He shifted his focus back to assembling the packet of information to distribute that morning. The gut feeling still nagged at him, telling him that something much worse than the weather was about to take the city by storm. He finished up and made his way to the briefing room.

Miles was known for two things across the entire department, his integrity and his hunches. The first was infallible and the second had never proved wrong.

O' Toole stood behind a tabletop podium as the first shift's officers filed in. Most carried cups of coffee, quick breakfasts, notebooks, or a combination of all three. The last officer sat down as O' Toole began roll call. "Officers, can I have your attention please!" he said, slightly louder than the dull roar of the room. "Let's get started this morning. Officer Stewart?"

"Here," came from the middle of the room.

Miles ran through the rest of the roll, noting who was present and who wasn't.

"Okay, it looks like we're missing four today."

The group broke its silence with mostly silent mumbled complaints and groans.

"I know it makes it a lot tougher out there, but it is what it is. This shortage is hard on all of us and it's not going to get any better belly aching about it. You wouldn't appreciate knowing that you were out for a day and all your fellow officers were acting like this about it. Those officers know what it's like to cover someone else's beat as well as their own, so I don't want to hear anymore of it."

The room fell silent out of respect, even though not all agreed. Miles was one of the most respected men on the force. His integrity never wavered, and surviving three gunshot wounds and five near fatal knife attacks in the line of duty didn't hurt either. He was a highly decorated officer that didn't let it go to his head. If anyone asked, he was just doing his duty and didn't deserve anything more than the next cop in line.

He flipped through his notes to find his place. "Welcome back, Davis. How are the toddler and the Misses?"

"Just fine, sir, thank you for asking."

Miles stood in silence for a moment, as if he was waiting for something. "Well, aren't you gonna at least tell us his name?" prompted Miles in a cheery tone.

"Jeffrey Adam Davis. He was born day before yesterday at five-twenty in the morning. He's five pounds, 15 ounces, has the required number and fingers and toes, and is very healthy."

The group gave a short round of applause accompanied by cheers, whistles, and at-a-boys.

"Okay, listen up people. I want the patrols stepped up in Davis' neighborhood. He's coming back early from his leave and I don't want anything bothering Mrs. Davis or little Jeffrey."

The directive was unnecessary. The police made special efforts to look out for their own, just like family, and all of the shifts would make extra rounds by other officer's homes just to make sure everything was in order.

"Now, let's get down to the nitty-gritty. We have a new APB, issued today, for Rocky Malone. Most of you have seen this loser, and I think a few of you have had the pleasure of bringing him in. He's been on parole for three weeks, and our sources tell us that he's already running a car-jacking racket this time. We have surveillance footage that ID's Rocky in some of the recent thefts." O'Toole paused for a few seconds to take a sip of his coffee and recheck his notes.

"The next big thing is the Cicero Drug Ring. A team from narcotics managed to catch one of the Ciceros in a sting, and it seems he was happy to tell us what we needed to know after a little persuasion. Check with your Supervisors; they'll be assigning several four-man teams to pick up some of the other members of the Cicero organization."

"Which Cicero did they bust?" asked Temple.

"It was Alberto. Rico is still at large, but he's the dumber of the two. We're hoping to catch him in some sort of bust using Alberto as bait. It will be too late for Rico to do anything by the time he realizes his brother sold him out for lesser charges."

"The last new item on the books today is something I ran across this morning. I can't confirm this hunch yet, but it appears we may have a serial killer on the loose."

The officers focused on the Duty Sergeant simultaneously and all the side-line conversations stopped. Most of the work was the same, day in and day out, but serials were serious business. They made up a whole new breed of criminal, doing what they did because of some sick, twisted perversion. Perps like that were real threats to a cop, not to mention the fear and paranoia that spread like wildfire behind them.

"I ran across a few similarities between three homicides in the last few months and one that happened yesterday, but we have very little useful information on any of these crimes. I want you all to be careful and watchful out there. I've put together an information packet I'd like you all to go through before you hit the streets. We don't have enough time to cover everything here in the briefing, but I've got a feeling that this is going to get much worse.

"In summary, we have a real twisted individual out there. It looks like he, or she, has a taste for the extreme in the form of mutilation. The case notes from all four files are included, but a solid connection has not been established. I have no idea what's driving this psycho, so watch your backs."

O'Toole left the podium and walked to the door. A stack of packets awaited him. "Dismissed. Please get a copy of the homicide information from me as you leave."

The officers left the room, quietly in single file, collecting the documents as they passed. Miles patted Davis on the shoulder when he went by, giving silent thanks for his commitment to his duty. As the last officer left the room, O'Toole gathered his papers and returned to his office to send a copy of his information to Homicide.

Captain Bishop sat at his desk signing paperwork when his computer notified him with an annoying beep of a new e-mail. He was not the most computer literate member of the force, actually much closer to the illiterate end of the spectrum than he let on, so the notification alarm remained. The one time he tried to alter the settings to prevent it, he managed to delete his e-mail account and lose all of his e-mail. The techs in IT told him not to worry, ID-Ten-T errors were common. They didn't share the moniker was actually labeled "ID10T" and kept the joke within the department.

He turned to face his desktop PC after he signed the last paper in the current stack. The message was from Duty Sergeant Miles O'Toole, flagged as priority. It briefly said something about clues for a homicide case and a file was attached to the e-mail. Bishop managed the double-click after three tries and inspected the file. The concise message it contained prompted him to take immediate action.

He called for the detectives assigned to the previous night's John Doe murder to compare the older cases to the new one. He was amazed the evidence hadn't been linked any earlier. He figured mutilation would stick out like a pink gorilla suit in a tuxedo shop, but it was hard to maintain good communication between the Precincts with the shortage. A single case could be lost in the shuffle as the constant flow of increasingly violent crimes had a desensitizing effect, making it all a part of the daily grind.

Joe was up early, like most days of late, finishing his first pot of coffee before his alarm went off. He had the ability to sleep, but he lacked the desire because his dreams pulled him back to times in his life that were better left in the past.

He made a couple of rounds through the house, checking all the rooms, windows, and doors as he went. Of the three bedrooms, he slept on a cot in the one that doubled as an office. He still couldn't bring himself to break the sanctity of the other two rooms.

He settled back into his desk chair with the first cup from the new pot of coffee and flipped though his notes. After he picked up his partner, they had a meeting with the Captain first thing, and that was not a good way to start the day. To top it off, he would have to forego his normal practice time at the firing range, which didn't improve his mood.

He looked forward to the practice time. Not because he needed it, he was an excellent marksman, but it was a good way to vent frustration and stress. He learned how to manage turmoil and deal with it in a healthy manner. Some would say that his method was too violent to be truly healthy, but those critics weren't police officers. Paper targets were safe targets, and the entire process reinforced the rules and structure required to properly handle firearms. His adherence to that structure was very healing for him.

He made the decision to not refill his current SSRI prescription four months earlier, and he promised himself that he would never rely on that crutch again. It was a weakness, and he was seeing the tremor side effects, which interfered with his ability at the shooting range.

He glanced at the digital face of his alarm and realized it had been beeping through almost ten minutes of his reverie. He turned it off and went through his routine to get ready for work. Five minutes later he armed the house's security system, locked up, and walked across the darkness of the front yard to the car.

It would take about forty-five minutes to get to Angela's from Jersey. Her apartment was on the way to the Precinct, and it saved her from having to deal with the sea of angry motorists, surging this way and that through traffic. He liked making the drive. He used the quiet of the morning to prepare himself for the day's offerings from the criminal fraternity.

He honked when he pulled to the curb in front of her apartment. The light over her doorstep was on, so he knew she would be out in a minute or two. They devised the signal a couple of weeks after they started carpooling to work. If the light was off, Joe didn't even bother to stop. It was rare for the light to be off and he resisted the urge to question her about the times she found her own way to the Precinct.

Angela heard Joe honk outside. She finished her last sip of tea, cut the lights, and headed out. She actually didn't mind getting up a little earlier to ride with Joe. She wasn't used to driving in New York and she was leery of what might happen to her car if she did drive it. She considered herself an intelligent, logical person, but driving through the sprawl completely unnerved her. She had a hard time dealing with lane changes that kept the corners of everyone's bumper clean or the absolute conviction required to be behind the wheel. Joe had several years of experience navigating the turbulent waters and he didn't mind driving in it. She hastened down the steps when the morning's chill hit her. She hopped into the front passenger seat and immediately started rubbing her hands together to get the cold ache out of her bones.

"Morning Benson, we've got a meeting with the Captain as soon as we get to the Precinct. It has to do with last night's John Doe."

"I know," she returned, sounding discouraged. "I checked my voice mail about thirty minutes ago. It sounds bad."

She opened her bag and adjusted something inside before she turned to face her partner. They were still getting to know each other, but she felt comfortable enough with him to tell him when something troubled her.

"I really don't like dealing with that man. He always talks down to me and he doesn't listen to anything I say. To top it all off, the only place he can't stare at is my face. He's a chauvinistic jerk that thinks I'm only on the force to look at! The only things he hasn't done is change the dress code so I have to wear one of those stupid 'sexy cop' outfits when I'm on duty!"

53

Joe didn't expect the personal revelation, but it made him feel good that she confided in him. Trust was the make-or-break component to every good partnership.

"Lucky for the rest of us he can't change the dress code. I'd look pretty bad in one of those getups."

Angela turned to face him with an angry look, but she almost immediately started laughing. Joe had a knack for finding a way to make her not feel so uptight or angry about just about anything that bothered her, which still surprised her. Until she starting working with Joe, her mother was the only one she knew that possessed that particular talent.

"He's just an old-fashioned cop, Angela. He doesn't think that women should be allowed to work out in the field. It's not that he thinks you're incapable of doing the job, he just doesn't feel that you, meaning women in general, should. He sees the role of protector as a requirement if you're male."

Angela thought of her father again, but from an angered perspective. She didn't show any of that anger outwardly as Joe was just the messenger in the scenario, and he was just telling it like it was.

"As for the other problem, you're an attractive young lady, you should be flattered."

Joe pretended to look at something outside of the car on the driver's side so she couldn't see his smirk.

"Flattered? OH-NO-YOU-DIDN'T! I cannot believe you just said flattered!" Angela was flabbergasted and unsure how to take her partner's comment.

Is he serious? Did I make a mistake telling him?

Joe couldn't contain his laughter. He just partnered up with Angela a few months earlier, but he already knew how to get her riled up too, and more importantly, when. Angela cooled off when she realized he was just rattling her cage, and she felt better, too.

"You just need to lighten up a smidge. I think you're making a little more of this than is really there. I've never noticed Bishop doing that. Besides, I won't let anything bad happen to you."

"I know. Let's just get there and get it finished."

Angela spoke flatly, unable to put her feelings into words. She could not and would not adjust to what her Captain deemed his "leadership style." The situation frustrated her, but it was worse that she let Bishop get to her. She wouldn't let her father have control of her emotions, but she was allowing a virtual stranger to do that very thing. On the other hand, it was reassuring to know that Joe supported her and had her back. It had been a few years since she had someone she could see and touch to do that for her.

"Yes, ma'am! Next stop is the Precinct House."

Joe gave her a loose salute and then reached over and gave her a reassuring squeeze on the shoulder. He could tell this was really bothering her and he made a mental note to pay more attention to Bishop's "style."

He pulled into the garage for the police station ten minutes before eight. It would take them a few minutes to get up to the third floor and gather their notes before they went to meet the Captain, but they would be there at 8:00 on the dot.

A knock sounded from Captain Bishop's door.

"Come in."

Joe and Angela walked in and sat down.

"What do you have for us, Captain?" asked Joe.

"I received a memo from the Duty Sergeant this morning about some possible connections to your current case," said the Captain, looking towards Joe's partner.

Bishop did tend to stare at Angela. Joe hadn't really noticed it before. He joked about it earlier, but it was on the assumption that it was her imagination. His whole take on the situation changed.

"I want you to attend Dr. Palmer's autopsy personally. It's scheduled in a few hours. I wouldn't normally assign something like this to you, but Miles made the connections. His reputation for instinct precedes him, as you already know. I want you to report back to me after you're finished at the morgue. Do you have any questions?"

"No, sir," answered Joe.

"No," said Angela, taking no time getting out of the office.

The detectives hastily returned to their desks.

"Don't get too bent out of shape, he's harmless," offered Joe insecurely, reading his partner's body language. She was trying to hide the fact she was affected by the Captain's behavior.

"Harmless or not," she said quietly, looking down at her desk, "I just don't like him or his attitude towards me. Now we get to go to the morgue which is my SECOND favorite thing to do first thing in the morning." Angela started for the elevator, obviously deflated by the recent events. Joe followed at a comfortable distance, making a few decisions as he walked.

"What's the FIRST thing?" he asked, trying to lighten her mood.

"Don't ask."

chapter seven

Dr. Allen Palmer, the chief medical examiner for the city of New York, arrived at the morgue midmorning. He was late due to unexpected delays at the airport associated with new federal regulations related to the transportation of human remains, which was his personal responsibility when bodies required shipment back home for burial.

The autopsy was supposed to begin some twenty minutes earlier. The work order was labeled urgent, so the doctor moved very rapidly, trying to make up for lost time. The autopsy would take almost an hour, and then he had to go back across town to attend a social luncheon to raise funds for children's diseases. He knew he would be late, but he wasn't the keynote speaker. It would not cause a problem unless he was absent altogether.

As he approached his office, located in the basement of the hospital, he found two people awaiting his return. "I'm sorry I'm running a little late. Airport regulations are tighter since 9/11, and the four-car pile-up on the interstate didn't help either. I'll probably see some of those drivers again tomorrow." The doctor allowed a small grin to form on his lips, which faded when he realized the detectives did not appear amused. "Sorry, I guess you have to work down here to appreciate morgue humor. You have to throw an occasional joke at a job like this if you intend to survive it."

"No sweat, Doc," said Joe. "I know you guys don't get out much. I think I'd take as long as possible to come back, and don't worry about the joke; I found it...refreshing." Joe turned to Angela. "I don't think you've had the pleasure of meeting my new partner. Dr. Palmer, this is Detective Angela Benson. Angela, this is Dr. Allen Palmer, the senior medical examiner for the city."

"It's nice to meet you," said Angela, slightly restrained, as she extended her hand.

"Likewise," returned the Coroner, shaking it. "I'm sure we'll be seeing a lot more of each other in the future. Our lines of work do tend to cross."

The Coroner opened the door to his office, letting the detectives enter first. His office was very spartan, due primarily to the battleship gray concrete floor and all-metal office furniture. The city didn't allow anything besides stainless steel in the basement, especially in the morgue. Metal furnishings were easier to clean and sanitize, and they would survive in the event of flooding.

"Please, have a seat." He indicated the chairs facing his desk. "I'll have to get some of the paperwork together before we can proceed. Would either of you care for a cup of coffee or a soda?"

"No, thank you," responded Angela, "we ate breakfast on the way over."

A slight look of irritation crossed Joe's face, but it vanished just as quickly. He never turned down free food, but he didn't want to embarrass his partner or himself.

"Very well, I'll be right back. I've got to gather a few things as well, and make sure my assistant is here."

Dr. Palmer left his office to perform his errands. Angela rubbed her arms through her jacket.

"Why does it have to be so cold everywhere down here?"

"So the dead bodies won't stink."

"Really? You're the only person I know that would say something like that out loud."

"Thanks, I try."

Angela let a small laugh escape, even though she tried not to encourage him. Her partner's sense of humor took some getting used to, but he had a way of making people laugh. She found herself warming up to the way he behaved and carried himself because she sensed a soft heart in her brackish bull of a partner. The Coroner returned.

"Everything is set and ready. I must ask you to put on some basic coverings, regulations again, I'm afraid. You'll find the PPE in the cabinet behind you." Dr. Palmer pointed to the cabinet on the wall facing his desk. Angela and Joe both looked perplexed and slightly put out. "It's for your own safety. We've had a few cases where the deceased was still infectious, even after death. Trust me, you don't want anything that can still work in a dead body." They both knew the routine, even though they didn't like it.

Dr. Palmer stepped into his large closet to change into light blue medical scrubs, returning to wash his hands with antimicrobial soap.

Joe and Angela did as instructed and the Medical Examiner led them to examination room four.

The room looked very much like a hospital's operating room without all of the equipment to monitor vital statistics. A shiny examination table sat at the room's center that was built differently, with a large bank of lights hanging just above it. It had a small trough that ran around it, with a square drain built into the foot end as well, to capture liquids.

A smaller table, independent of the exam table, stood against its side. Another man, dressed like Dr. Palmer, stood next to the side table, organizing the multitude of instruments on the green cloth that covered the table's surface. He finished his straightening and left when the detectives entered with Palmer.

Palmer began. "Please stand at the head of the table. Dr. Murphy will be back in a minute; he went to get the body out of cold storage. You'll be able to see what we're doing without being in the way there. Are you sure you're up for this, Ms. Benson? This isn't a good place for anyone with a weak stomach." He noticed the slight hesitation on her face when she first looked at the examination table.

"She'll be alright, Doc. She's seen a lot worse than this out on the streets."

Angela nodded in agreement, but still looked uneasy. Her last autopsy was at the academy, and it wasn't one of her fonder memories. She tried to avoid the entire morgue whenever she could. She could handle witnessing death, either naturally or from violence, but cadavers bothered her. She felt her phobia was ridiculous, but she couldn't change the way her stomach churned back and forth and the way her throat knotted up. She would not be surprised if the corpse sat up in the middle of the procedure and started attacking everyone in sight, mumbling something about brains. It was something about the clammy, pale skin, and the way the bodies looked mostly dead, but not completely dead to her.

"Ah, come on partner. Don't tell me you're going to get sick on me," mocked Joe. He'd seen it before with first timers. In a few minutes she'd be down the hall in the ladies' room regurgitating her breakfast.

"I'll be okay!" she snapped back with a little heat in her voice. She didn't like to show weakness.

"Yes, ma'am," he answered, satisfied that he ruffled her feathers again. He had to break her in if they were going to become true partners. They had to work like a team, which meant establishing a kind of mental link with one another. It was more than knowing what the other would do, but what the other would think and feel. The link was vital. Without it, one of them could end up getting killed.

Dr. Murphy returned with the body. It rested on a gurney, covered with a white sheet that crested and fell, revealing an outline that didn't look quite right. He parked the rolling table next to the exam table and they transferred the body. Murphy rolled the gurney out of the way and stood fast, awaiting instruction.

"Let's begin," said Palmer, starting his digital recorder. "For the record, it is January 29th. I, Dr. Allen Palmer, am about to perform an autopsy on one John Doe, case number 1137-636. Dr. John Murphy is assisting. Detectives Angela Benson and Joe Anderson are attending as representatives from the Homicide Division of the Police Department at the request of Captain Ronald Bishop, and they'll double as witnesses. The purpose of this examination is to determine, or try to determine, the exact cause and time of death of John Doe. I'll begin with an overall summary of the condition of the body before the physical procedure."

Dr. Palmer pulled the sheet off of the body. The victim's clothing was long since removed, no longer required by the owner. The corpse's skin was pasty white and rubbery. The eyes were open wide and solid black as if the soul was stolen away just before death.

Oh God!

Angela caught her breath as she first looked at it, understanding why the form looked wrong when it was still shrouded. She forced herself to keep her focus and not shy away from the body. She knew she would never master her fear if she couldn't face it.

"At first sight, the areas of the body not marred by the visible damage from the attack appear to be well muscled and toned, supporting a good physical condition prior to death. The victim was a Caucasian male, in his middle to late twenties I surmise, as no proof of age has been presented as of this time. His approximate weight was 225 pounds. I do not see any distinguishing marks or means of identification besides the unique damage to the torso." The Coroner moved down the table to stand next to the cadaver's chest and turned his attention to the head.

"The deceased suffered severe facial trauma in the form of multiple lacerations. The lacerations themselves number in the teens, and they all appear to be similar in origin. I don't see any evidence of concussion or other blunt force trauma." Palmer reached out his hand and requested a probe. Dr. Murphy produced an instrument that resembled a small screwdriver, but the metal came to a simple, rounded point on the end opposite the plastic handle. Palmer used the probe to move the tissue around inside a few of the lacerations, and he pushed the metal point into a few of them as deep as it would go.

Angela felt her stomach tighten. She held a mental picture of the corpse grabbing Dr. Palmer's hand and stabbing him to death with the metal probe, angry to have his final rest disturbed, and grouchy because it was craved cerebellum. She felt afraid and silly at the same time, guessing she watched too many horror movies when she was a kid. She could rationalize what was happening, but she couldn't shake the slight chill tickling her spine.

Palmer requested a pair of forceps. The tissue made a tearing sound as he pulled the flesh aside to look at the internal composition of the lacerations. He looked for a minute or two before he stood back, still holding the probe.

"It appears the deceased was struck in the face multiple times with a serrated blade of some kind. The lacerations can be divided into separate sets, and each set contains cuts that are almost parallel. The series of attacks came from slightly different vantages, and each identifiable set of wounds follows the same angle of incidence and similar depth of tissue damage. It is also evident that the weapon was thrust from below twice and once from higher overhead. Using a clock as a reference, these three attacks came from seven o'clock, six o'clock, and two o'clock, respectively. The two o'clock strike looks like it occurred as the victim fell." He rechecked the damage at the bottom of the victim's face, still using the probe and the forceps. He requested another probe with increments marked on the metal.

"The first of the laceration sets starts just under the jaw, cutting the mandible and leaving grooves in the bone. The depth is about a quarter of an inch at the point of incidence, and it decreases to one thirty-second at the point of exit. The second cut runs deeper than the first and actually severed the bone. The weapon was thrust with a great amount of force, as it takes roughly five hundred pounds of force per square inch to break human bone. The blade itself must be exceptionally strong to remain intact, and sharp, under such high-pressure use, which just seems very rare."

Angela's stomach was settling as her curiosity took the foreground, enthralled by the doctor's words.

This is amazing, in a weird sort of way, but still amazing.

She imagined the murder in her mind, recreating the events based on the information she heard. She recalled her forensics training to run calculations in her mind.

"It appears the last of these unique strikes occurred as the victim fell. This strike came from a much higher angle. It's impossible to determine if the attacker was very tall or if the victim was already on his knees or lower, but I would assume the latter scenario. These lacerations also indicate that the blade is somewhat long, more akin to a sword than a knife.

"Of the other two unique attacks, the one closest to the nose and mouth, which I'll define as site number one, actually breached the integrity of the skull. The breach is approximately one inch in length." The Coroner paused again to ascertain his findings.

"I do not, however, conclude the injuries to the facial area were the cause of death. The trauma was very severe, but not enough to kill someone of this size and fitness. I'll move to the damage on the torso next."

Dr. Palmer switched sides with Dr. Murphy. The wound in the victim's chest was centered on a slight angle, pointing out more towards the deceased's left side.

Angela took a quick glance at Joe. He hadn't offered any comments, which wasn't typical for him. She noticed that he looked unusually pale, and he seemed to be trying to look at other things in the room.

The Coroner started prodding and pulling at the tissue around the cavity in the victim's chest. Dr. Murphy assisted him with the exam, as he needed to check all the damage in detail. The moving of the tissue on the protruding ribs sounded like meat ripping away from the bone, much like that of a pack of wolves devouring a fresh kill.

Joe couldn't handle the sight any longer. He excused himself and made a beeline for the nearest men's room.

How about that?

Angela was proud of herself for not letting the nausea take control; she expected she would have been the one needing a bathroom.

The two doctors poked and prodded at the damaged site for several minutes in silence, occasionally exchanging understood glances. They discussed their findings at length, too quietly for the detectives to hear, coming to an agreement before Dr. Palmer spoke loud enough for recording. The law allowed medical examiners to conference in private when assisting one another. They could both voice their professional opinions separately if they disagreed, or one examiner could give the results if they reached the same conclusion.

"Dr. Murphy and I agree that the damage to the torso is very similar in angle and force of attack. We can't identify a distinct set of lacerations, but the blade paths descend in patterns similar to a slowly closing circle, much like the mark left in a piece of wood when a screw is started. It appears that the serrated blade of the weapon was thrust in and out of the victim's chest in a saw-like motion at least three dozen times. The projected paths almost touch at the deepest part of the chest cavity, almost to the spine. We have never seen this kind of damage before."

Stabbed to death with a Goth traffic cone is definitely a new one on me, thought Angela.

Palmer handed his tools to Murphy.

"Obviously, the damage to the torso is the cause of death. Unfortunately for the victim, he was probably still alive when this attack began, only stunned and in shock from the facial trauma. Death would have been sudden, as the aorta and other major arteries were severed immediately based on what we can discern from the attack. John Doe here may not have felt that part as the amount of adrenaline and endorphins running through his system would have rendered him completely numb. This is mere speculation, but it appears the intent was to literally remove the victim's heart, as it is the only organ entirely absent."

Why would someone want to remove someone else's heart? That's even off the chain for most psychos.

Palmer looked up at Angela to see her reaction. She did not appear confused, just inquisitive and repulsed.

Dr. Murphy walked to a small refrigerator on the wall behind him. He took out two vials, and then he picked up a receipt book on the counter next to it which he handed to Dr. Palmer. The senior Medical Examiner flipped to the page referenced with the same numbers printed on the adhesive labels that were placed on the vials when the samples were checked in.

"The lab technicians are required to take fluid samples from the bodies at the time the victim is pronounced dead," explained Dr. Palmer. "I will run a couple of quick tests that will allow us to determine an approximate time of death. The tests will take a few minutes, so you can take a short break if you'd like, Detective Benson."

Angela left room number four, looking for her partner with questions running through her mind.

What could provoke that kind of attack? What happened to his heart?

She found him coming out of the restroom. His face was flushed, and the rims of his eyes were lined with the remnants of tears.

"Are you okay?"

"Yeah, I'm fine. Those donuts must've been bad." Joe tried to hang on to the few fragments of dignity he had left. "What did you find out?"

"So far, he's looked at the wounds themselves. He said it looks as if the killer attacked with a specialized weapon of some sort with a serrated blade. They're perplexed, and even more curious as to why the heart is missing. They are testing bodily fluids right now to determine the time of death."

"I'll wait out here for you. I'm going to go find a soda machine. I think a drink will help settle my stomach." Joe rubbed his hand over his rounded stomach gently, as if it would help calm the tsunami battering his bowels.

"Okay, I'll be back out shortly," said Angela as she turned to go back to room four. The walk to her destination was short.

"We have the results," started Palmer as Angela entered the room and approached the exam table. "We can test the rate of cellular breakdown in the fluids and compare them to a time chart. The results indicate that this man died approximately ninety-six hours ago."

"What the hell? Excuse me, sorry, but could you say that again?" Angela's jaw dropped slightly, weighted down with confusion.

"I said this man died approximately ninety-six hours ago." Palmer appeared slightly offended.

"Are you absolutely certain, Dr. Palmer?" she asked, giving a sheepish grin and trying to not appear disrespectful.

"Absolutely certain," he stated firmly, on the front end of becoming defensive. "The margin of error is four hours, give or take. The cells decay at a set rate from the time of death. We can also measure the percentage of coagulation in the blood stream. Under a microscope, the amount of deterioration to the cells is visible, which allows us to formulate a time of death. You seem overly surprised by this. This is your case, isn't it?"

I think I deserved that.

"Yes, and therein lies the problem. This man was killed last night at about seven o'clock. My partner and I were called out just after it happened. I don't see how this can be possible," said Angela, astounded. "Our evidence indicates he was killed about 15 hours ago – that's an 80-hour discrepancy."

Now Dr. Palmer looked somewhat astounded.

"That is very strange indeed. I'll send this off for a second analysis. It's unlikely, but possible, that the equipment here is not calibrated properly. I'll let you know when and if I have a better answer." Dr. Palmer was doing a horrible job of concealing the fact he was totally confused. Dr. Murphy's expression mirrored that of Palmer's.

"Thank you. Could you also send a copy of the autopsy to Homicide for me when you've finished the report?" asked Angela. "We've got other leads to run down today."

"Yes, I will. I should have it finished tomorrow morning or early afternoon."

"Thank you, Doctor. It was a pleasure meeting you."

"Likewise, Detective," added Palmer. Dr. Murphy nodded in agreement without saying a word. He was deeper in thought concerning the mystery that lay before them.

Angela stepped into the hall to find her partner waiting. Most of the color had returned to his face, but he still looked squeamish. She moved slowly, partly for his benefit, and partly to keep her mind clear while she tried to fit the pieces of the medical mosaic together into some kind of pattern that fit.

"How's your stomach?"

"It's not bothering me as much as it did a little while ago."

Joe's tone and demeanor held a simple, honest nature that he didn't always share with her. That unspoken trust was very important to her. He was dropping his tough guy persona more often around her.

They stepped into the elevator to ride back up into the normal world.

chapter eight

Joe pulled the unmarked police car out of the hospital's parking garage, grimacing in the brightness awaiting them. The sun was still veiled behind thick layers of swollen clouds, but the contrast was enough to make them squint after their subterranean adventure. They were bound for the Precinct to report to Captain Bishop as ordered. The promised storm system moved into the area as they drove, slowly darkening the sky.

The late morning traffic thickened as drones of yuppies escaped to early lunch appointments. The sidewalk traffic was lighter by contrast. The economic recession slowed the burn of cash in pockets, even though most storefronts displayed deep discounts.

The drive took three times as long due to the congestion on the streets and two fender benders. By the end of the commute, most of Joe's ability to cope with the other drivers had faded, replaced with the beginnings of road rage. The frustration was visible on his face and he mumbled obscenities under his breath. Angela tried, with difficulty, to think about other things. Joe was a safe driver, but he couldn't account for the gaggle of idiots driving around him.

"What lead do you want to follow after we meet with Bishop?" asked Joe flatly, keeping his composure and temper in check for his partner.

"I think we should go over to INS and try to get a lead on our only witness. I think we'll waste time talking to Gianelli again this soon. I don't think he's got any more information that will be able to help."

The ache in the knuckles of her right hand finally registered with her brain, prompting her to notice her death grip on the door handle. The back of her hand was bright pink with stark white knuckles. She let go and tried to hide her hand between her leg and the car door, but she could tell Joe had already seen.

"I agree. Let's get this visit over with and get down to business. By the way, you should loosen up a little. You keep doing that and your fingers are going to fall off."

Angela blushed as she rubbed the feeling back into her hand. She wasn't pleased that Joe noticed her nervousness, but he didn't chastise her the way she expected either. The ache crept into her palm as they exited the garage.

The second meeting with Captain Bishop went better than Angela hoped as she managed to stay at her desk while Joe talked to the Captain. Joe filled him in on the autopsy's preliminary findings and informed him that the final results would be ready the next day, hopefully by morning. Joe promised their report by the close of business the next day. He then told him they had several other leads to follow up on that afternoon. Bishop seemed satisfied with the work and dismissed Joe from his office.

Angela had a small grin on her face when Joe returned, trying to not look smug. "How did it go partner?" she asked, trying to keep the line between her lips straight.

"He said you need to clean out your desk; he fired you. I tried to explain why you weren't there, but he wouldn't accept any excuses. He said he wouldn't tolerate anyone, especially a woman, disobeying direct orders. I even tried telling him how much of a pain it would be to get another new partner, but he wouldn't listen to that either. I told him he was a chicken shit for not coming in here and doing it himself."

Angela's jaw fell open. She was totally speechless, not believing what she just heard.

"How can that man do this to me? I didn't disobey any orders or do anything to deserve walking papers. Especially a woman, MY ASS!" Her face flushed red with anger as the veins on her forehead swelled visibly, primed to rupture. Some of the Texas accent she tried to suppress slipped through. With a cowboy hat and a pair of clippers, she would have looked ready to castrate a few bulls. Her eyes shifted wildly as she tried to comprehend her situation, finally gaining focus as her anger peaked. She got up and started walking straight for the Captain's office.

Joe caught her by the arm, unable to contain his laughter any longer. "I really had you going for a while there. I don't think I've ever seen you this mad."

She was unable to speak, but the look she shot him could have melted all the polar ice caps at once, which only made him laugh harder.

"You…are…a…Jerk."

He tried to give his best "who me?" look in between guffaws, but tears were welling up in his eyes.

She picked up a stapler and readied to throw it. Joe raised his arm to block.

"Made you flinch!" She went back to her chair. "I should have known you were full of it when you said you called Bishop a chicken shit. You wouldn't have been that complimentary of him."

The office conducting daily business for Immigration and Naturalization Services was totally swamped when they arrived, the opposite of what they were, for some reason, expecting.

The space was very large, presenting as if it was an active time capsule, obviously constructed several decades earlier and maintained, but never updated. The floor was tiled with vinyl squares common to 1960s era public school cafeterias, hued is avocado tones with yellow flecks. A few small pieces of unmatched furniture, covered in long outdated and no longer popular fabric, was littered around the edges of the room, mixed with fake fiscus trees and other greenery, creating make-shift waiting areas.

Some of the office machines visible through the glass partition that separated customer from employee were built when quality was still a concern, not yet replaced with newer technology. The expanse beyond the front of the line was ensconced in cubicles just short enough to see each worker's head and the top of their computer screens.

Fluorescent lighting nestled at even intervals throughout the suspended ceiling provided harsh and uneven illumination as about twenty percent of the bulbs were either burnt out, or flickering in the final throes of death and throwing odd shadows in spaces around the people waiting.

Each line was roped off and labeled for whatever purpose it served. Two lines were used expressly for the replacement of permanent visas, one line accepted only new visa applicants, and another was reserved for immigrants filling the requirements to become citizens of the United States. The other three lines appeared to be used for inter-office routing, as they were identified by form names and numbers.

Each clerk had a line of at least thirty people of varying ethnic backgrounds, grumbling and fidgeting as they waited for assistance, careful to avoid eye contact with one another while they looked around as though trying to find the easiest escape route. The lines trudged forward mere inches between long delays, making the group look more like a herd of cattle moving through the shoot, sans mooing. As each one reached a window, the unpleasant attitudes that brewed during the wait were focused on the clerks, who listened without enthusiasm. To make things worse, which wouldn't seem to be within the realm of possibility, the over-crowded proximity was too hot to be comfortable, contributing some unpleasant smells that wafted through the throng.

Joe and Angela couldn't seem to work their way towards the front desks, so they rounded the perimeter of the lobby area to reach a door labeled "employees only" that led to the back office. The door was locked, so Joe rapped on the door soundly, but not hard enough to draw attention from the people in the lines.

A couple of minutes drudged by without a response.

The clerks worked a few more of the herd out of the lines.

Angela told Joe that the ceiling over the lobby had 256 tiles and only about a dozen didn't have water stains.

Joe's face was red with impatience and frustration; he knocked again. The glass separating the closest clerk from her line of customers rattled from the vibration. Many of the cubicle heads turned their attention, as did many of the people waiting. An employee could be seen scurrying through the field of cubicles in the general direction of the door, which opened roughly ten seconds later.

The ID badge that the short, skinny man with glasses wore identified him as Seth Thomas. He was quite frail, unable to weigh more than one hundred pounds fully clothed and soaking wet, with a pocket protector full of pens and a short-sleeved shirt buttoned all the way to neck, even though he wore no tie.

"What can I do for you?" demanded Seth, trying to sound as authoritative as possible.

"You can get me the information I need," returned Joe. "We are investigating a homicide/missing person's case, and we don't have the time to deal with these, or all the red tape." Joe indicated the lines behind him by pointing over his shoulder with his thumb.

Angela watched as the room full of people continued to take notice of Joe's conversation with Seth because he was talking loud enough to share his comments with most of the audience.

"Have you even taken the time to get the proper forms?" said Seth, in the most rude and annoyed voice he could muster between the high, nasally tones jumping into his oratory. He pushed his glasses back up his nose, furthering the damage to his image.

"Look, Seth, I'm just trying to get to the bottom of this case before I have any more corpses on my hands. I have questions that need to be answered and wasting my time dealing with the bureaucracy isn't helping!"

"You have no choice, sir! That's the way it works here. I can't...."

Joe grabbed Seth just below his shoulders and Seth felt the floor move away from his feet. An overly tight belt combined with his skinny frame pulled his clothing up more than the rest of his body, completing the nerdy look with off color socks now exposed due to the temporary highwater effect. Angela was taken by surprise and completely unsure if she should intervene. Joe was overstepping his authority.

"You should really reconsider doing what I've asked. I could haul you off to the Precinct for obstruction of justice for hindering a police investigation. I've got friends in booking. They could keep you there over a week before you even got your phone call, just to impress upon you the joy of waiting." Joe could feel Seth trembling.

Angela noticed a mixture of emotion work through the crowd in a wave. Some looked nervous, as she was, but others looked defensive, and some outright angry. Those troubled her. A wrong move could set off a reaction, she envisioned a stampede, that would not bode well for them. She lightly touched her partner on the side, careful with her angle of approach so the smallest number of people could see it. Joe did not indicate he felt it, but he set Seth down gently and straightened the wrinkle in his shirt where he gripped him.

"I'll see what I can do for you, sir," responded Seth, only meekness in his voice. "It'll just take a few minutes." He immediately backed into the office area, holding the door open for until Joe assumed the weight of the door.

Moos of approval came from the herd, and a few applauded. "Hey, do you think you can help me out when you're finished?" called someone from the other side of the room. "I've been here for over three hours!"

Joe let the door close behind them, slowly separating them from the lobby as the pneumatic closer did its job.

The restricted area was a much larger chasm of cubicles than they realized with the now unhindered view, skinned with sheer, dark blue-grey carpet with wear lines that showed the highest traffic areas. A few spots were showing frayed threads, but nothing was completely worn to the foundation below. A cacophony of voices, ringing telephones, shuffling feet, and the light hum of office equipment swirled into their ears, adding a low background noise to the ambiance.

"Please follow me."

Seth led the detectives through the maze of workstation cubicles and meeting areas, into a cross thatch of hallways, to an office near the back of the building. As they passed, they saw a mixture of old and new equipment in the too small to ever be comfortable duty stations. The close proximity led to an odd mixture of scents, like rose-scented coffee served with garlic-glazed donuts, that finished with antibacterial spray.

"Please wait here. My supervisor will be with you shortly."

Seth quickly vanished, taking his leave through the labyrinth of corralled city workers. The office Joe and Angela sat in front of had the name Wendell Harris on the glass that made up the top half of the door, with the word "Supervisor" centered underneath in smaller letters.

It was relatively quiet, but they could still hear some of the noises echoing from the office area. Angela leaned over to whisper in Joe's ear. "It reminds me of the ant farm I had as a kid. They didn't really do anything, but they were sure busy doing it."

Joe allowed himself a small laugh.

"You know you may get us in all kinds of trouble for this don't you?" she expressed, slightly above a whisper but maintaining privacy.

"Yep; wouldn't have it any other way."

She rolled her eyes as Seth returned, approaching them with an older man wearing a very outdated suit. His hair was almost completely gone from the top of his head which he tried to hide with a comb-over of his remaining white locks. His wire-rimmed glasses rested on the end of his nose, the lenses, coke-bottle thick, making the trifocal lines easily visible.

"Good morning, Detectives. Seth tells me you have a problem that I may be able to remedy." His gaze rested on Joe, mostly pleasant with just a hint of disapproval.

"Yes sir," said Angela, standing and cutting Joe off before he spoke, extending her hand in greeting. She guessed that a little more tact and finesse would expedite the case at hand, not to mention preventing Mr. Harris from calling in a complaint. "My name is Detective Angela Benson. This is my partner, Detective Joe Anderson. Is there somewhere we can talk privately?"

"Of course, young lady, please, step into my office." Wendell Harris motioned towards the door, opening it for Angela. He stepped in after her, intentionally cutting Joe off and letting the door start to swing shut.

Harris' office provided sharp contrast as it was very modern. It was larger, but still not large enough for the contents, with a new modular desk supporting a brand new PC, telephone, and basic desk accessories. The three chairs, one behind the desk and two facing it, were obviously new as well, still bearing tags. The two bookshelves rounding the walls were newer than most of what they had seen, and his carpet showed no signs of wear or stains.

"What can I do for you?' asked Harris, once everyone was seated, taking pleasure in the frustrated look on Joe's face.

"We are working on a homicide/missing person's case," started Benson. "The only witness to the crime, unfortunately, is the person that's missing. The killer is still at large, so you can see how important it is for us to find this witness for questioning. She should be able to give us some of the answers we need, and she should be able to describe the killer. All we have to go on is the green card that the paramedics recovered at the crime scene. We're here on the hope that you can give us a home address, or some other means to make contact."

"Well, that shouldn't be any trouble at all," stated Harris. "If I could take a look at that card, I can query the system's database for the home address. We aren't supposed to do this without the proper forms and warrants, or written consent from the cardholder, but I can make an exception," he added, shifting his gaze towards Joe, "since she could be in danger."

Angela handed him the card.

"I'll be right back. My computer isn't networked to the new mainframe yet, so I'll have to use one of the other terminals in the office. Excuse me for a moment."

Harris left the room to gather the requested information, softly closing the door behind him.

"Sorry for cutting you off, Joe. I just thought we might get farther using a little less brawn."

"Don't worry about it. We're starting to act and react to one another as partners. I was counting on you to play 'good cop' to my carousing. It's cliché, but it almost always works. Besides, this guy is more worried about being passive aggressive with me than hindering you. I don't think we'll get any of those complaints."

"Thanks, Joe."

Angela felt her lips curl slightly, enough for a little of her smile to show. She liked the way the nod of approval felt and she savored it for a moment as being a rookie was hard enough. He was very difficult to read most of the time, so she was glad to hear confirmation that they were getting along as well as she felt they were.

Mr. Harris returned, holding a two-page printout. "I believe this is what you need. The address was updated a few months ago, so it should be current. I'm sorry we don't have a phone number on file, but it appears that she didn't have a phone the last time we updated her file." He gave the INS card and printed information to Angela, purposely ignoring Joe.

"Thank you, Mr. Harris. We really appreciate all of your help."

"You're quite welcome, young lady. If you need anything else, please don't hesitate to contact me. Here's one of my cards," he retrieved from the holder on the desk, "and that's a direct line to this office. I would hate for you to have to muddle through the automated system on the main number."

Angela gently guided Joe out of the office to work back through the hallways and field of workstations. Joe never spoke a word, but he did have a sneer on his face that insured no interference from anyone else.

She wasn't sure if it was from interacting with Mr. Harris or preparation for the possibility of reencountering Seth, but he dropped the demeanor when they exited the building.

"I really enjoyed that," he said as they reached the parking lot. "I know I shouldn't rile people up like that, but it is so much fun."

"You're right," she said.

"Really?" he muttered, shocked. "I never took you for someone that likes to mess with people like that?"

"I'm not. I'm agreeing that you really shouldn't do that."

Angela managed to control her expression as she watched Joe deflate. A pathetic look graced his face, like a child getting caught with a hand in the cookie jar. She let it ride for a minute or so until he was wearing a full-fledged pout and she could no longer keep from laughing, turning his frown into a classic I-will-so-get-you-back-for-punking-me look.

"I do, however, get a kick out of watching you do it," she added as she got into the car.

Joe still looked a little surprised. It was the first time she really got one up on her partner.

Joe pulled out of the parking lot, turning left. The address for Ms. Makovoz was in the borough of Queens. About halfway to the address, Angela turned to Joe with a perplexed look on her face as a thought came to her.

"Is it just me or is this going to be a long way from the crime scene?"

"Yeah, but in a place like New York, you never know. Stranger things have happened."

"I realize that, but from what we know, she was on foot. We didn't find a driver's license, or car keys, and that's a long way to go for groceries. I can't see anyone going out in this cold without a coat either. It seems like she only planned to be out for a few minutes."

"We have to assume she was," answered Joe. "We just don't know the reasons why she would be there like that. She may not own a coat and had no choice but to face the weather, or she may not be playing with a full deck. Anything's possible in the Big Apple."

"I'll call the cab companies. They should have a list of their pickups for last night. Maybe that's the explanation."

"Good idea, Angela."

They arrived at the address. The apartment building it identified appeared to be in good shape for its apparent age. No broken windows or peeling paint, which was more the norm in the neighborhood. The inside was immeasurably worse.

The paint on the interior walls was faded, cracked, or gone, exposing raw sheetrock, and it was different colors in sections. The majority of the light bulbs in the hallway were broken or missing, shrouding it in eerie darkness. The light from the outside offered no respite as the bulk of its rays was cut off when the door shut behind them.

In several places, the sheetrock on the ceiling and walls exposed the wall studs through crumbled out holes resulting from age, severe neglect, and outright abuse. About a third of the holes were obviously caused by violent tendencies of some of the tenants. Chunks of sheetrock scattered the floor, some so long that only a layer of gypsum powder remained, ground into the carpet pile as though a bag of flour exploded. Most of the carpeting that did survive sported stains of various origins, only some of which were identifiable. The smell emanating from floor and walls reinforced the adage that ignorance is bliss.

Only a few of the doors still had numbers, some gone so long that the ghosts of the digits that once hung on them had already faded from view. Splintered gashes marked some of the others, while one or two had gaps big enough to see through if they had not been covered from the inside by the renter.

The yellowed paper sign duct taped on the elevator door with out of order scrawled on it in black marker obviously meant apartment 607 was now a six-story climb. Angela took point as they ascended the stairs. She was in much better physical shape than her partner and her lighter weight made it safer for her to go first, considering the condition of the stairs. The aged wood squeaked in protest as they settled onto the mostly barren treads. Whatever once covered the steps, whether it was carpet or stain with clear coat, was long gone. The wood was worn, raw wood in the center from repeated foot falls, and dingy with unidentifiable grime around the edges. Many of the steps had deep gouges, some filled with filth and some still bare, likely caused from tenants moving heavy items up and down. The handrails were mostly intact, but they decided not touching them was the lesser of two evils.

Joe lumbered behind, never getting closer than an entire flight. He was taken by surprise when he heard Angela yelp from above. He couldn't see her or what happened, but he double-timed up the flight to reach her. He found her as he turned onto the fourth floor landing.

She was sprawled out on all fours halfway up the flight to the fifth floor. One of the risers broke on her ascent, flipping the back of the tread to a forty-five-degree angle, which then cracked in two underneath her, causing her to fall forward. The plunge fed her leg to the hungry wooden splinters and a row of rusty carpet tacks in the abused and broken oak. Her ankle twisted when the wood gave, and the force of her fall pushed her foot through the corresponding riser and back to the next lower step, adding bruises and cuts to all but her calf. Her pants leg shredded as it passed through the sharps, making the damage easy to see. One of the lacerations, caused by an exposed brad nail that originally bound the tread to the riser, qualified as a gash and bled freely.

"Are you okay? That looks pretty bad. Do you think you'll be able to walk?" asked her partner, concern on his face.

"I'm not sure. It really hurts…throbbing and burning. Some of those…splinters feel like…they went pretty deep. It's…already starting to swell." Her expression twisted with pain, laced slightly with fear.

"I'm not sure how we are going to get you out of here. I don't think I can carry you all the way down."

"Why isn't this damn building condemned? I'm surprised this dump hasn't fallen in on itself!" she forced through gritted teeth. Her pride was bruised as badly as her leg, allowing frustration to seep to the surface. She guessed that she would never hear the end of it once she was cleared by the doctor she would be seeing in the very near future. She expected the fatherly "you-need-to-be-more-careful" speech even sooner.

"You never know, the building inspector may not come out here very often. They can get sidetracked pretty easy, especially if it means staying out of the bad parts of town. They can't fine the owners if they can't find them, and if they do, there's no guarantee they'll have the money to pay for upgrades."

The blood from Angela's smaller scratches and cuts started clotting. The gash wasn't bleeding as heavily, probably due to the increased swelling. She ripped one of the wider shreds of fabric from her pant leg to bind over it to maintain pressure as it would likely start bleeding heavily when she tried to put weight on it. Shock was replacing some of the pain, making it at least bearable, but increasing her concern, which only pumped up the stress.

Joe helped her to stand, and she now had to use the hand rail for support as she tested her balance. She started to ascend, slowly and hopping, unable to put any weight on her leg at all, and taking the chance that the other stairs might fail as well. She stuck to the sides of the stairs where there was likely more structural support.

"Don't you think you should start working your way back down instead of up?" asked Joe, completely shocked.

"Probably, but...I can't back my partner if I'm not with him. We don't know what we're going to find up there."

"You're a pretty tough cookie," he said, patting her on the back and supported her from the other side as she finished the climb, careful to stay on step behind her so they never stepped on the same tread at the same time.

When they finally reached the sixth floor hallway, it ran both directions from the centrally located stairs. They chose left, and Joe scouted ahead, searching for the door marked 607. The first apartment he passed that actually had a number on the door was labeled 615. He realized he was going the wrong way when he reached 623. He turned and went back to get his partner.

"Who numbers a building...from the right to the left?' she mumbled under her breath, still having difficulty curbing her frustration as they started in the right direction. She relied heavily on the wall to keep herself standing as the hallway wasn't quite wide enough for Joe to stand beside her for support. The hall was littered with obstacles like bags of trash, broken furniture, and even a derelict dog house.

"Why don't you just wait here, close to the stairs? I can check this out and you can see all the way to the end of the hall from right there. If someone is in there and gets the jump on me, you can stop them out here. You need to save what you've got left for the trip back down."

"I'll be okay...but thanks for the offer. It doesn't hurt as much as it did." She lied. The sparks of pain were shooting up her entire leg like a cattle prod was held against it, arcing electric shocks. The muscles in her lower back were tingling with the onset of a spasm from trying to compensate for the injury.

Joe moved ahead, drawing his revolver as he closed the last few steps to 607, finding the door halfway open. The interior was pitch black beyond the threshold. His first concern was that the killer somehow got there first to finish the job. He turned and silently signed his intentions to Angela.

She was just a few feet behind him, leaning against the wall for balance, with her nine-millimeter already drawn. She had an angled line of site through the open door. She assumed a makeshift shooter's stance and nodded, saying nothing.

He pushed it fully open with his free hand – his sidearm readied in his right.

Dr. Palmer had to attend a luncheon, so he charged Dr. Murphy with preparing the samples to be sent to the lab for testing. They decided to have the backup lab provider check the samples since they couldn't verify if their equipment was working properly and they didn't have the time to wait for the calibration of their instruments.

All the samples had to be properly labeled and identified with the donor's information. The associated paperwork had to be filled out completely, without any mistakes, signed, countersigned, and then attached to the outside of the transport box to give the requests to the lab for the tests that needed to be performed. That paperwork was required in triplicate, and the lab could refuse to do the work if all three copies didn't come through clearly. All three slips were also color coded so a copy couldn't even be substituted in a pinch.

Murphy also had to clean up before he left. Once everything was finished, he walked the samples to the courier's station himself. It was required that all specimens in homicide cases were hand delivered by one of the attending medical examiners to insure proper handling and delivery, the consequence of some previous serious mistake before his time.

The samples were signed in and tagged after the paperwork was inspected and approved. One half of the tag stayed with the sample, and the other half went to the examiner as a receipt, with everything logged by the courier. The only person allowed to obtain the test results was the person that delivered the specimens, and that person had to present their half of the receipt.

The courier explained during the exchange that the procedural overkill was cumbersome, but generally viewed as a necessary evil. A few security breaches and instances of mishandled evidence resulted in the dismissal of charges in a couple of judicial proceedings. One high profile case was all it took to have the procedures modified to the point that it was virtually impossible to make a mistake that could go that far.

Once the paperwork was handled, Dr. Murphy grabbed a quick lunch at the hospital's cafeteria. He was due at the university to give a lecture on his craft to a group of medical students, followed by four more autopsies before he could call it a day.

Joe breached the threshold scanning left and right for any and all possible threats, using instinct and muscle memory since he couldn't see anything. He felt for the light switch with his free hand, and immediately realized the room was barren when illuminated. He motioned Angela to keep her position outside the primary door while he swept the other rooms. He checked the small apartment quickly, holstering his weapon by the time he returned to the hall.

"It's empty, except for a few wire hangers in the bedroom closet. It doesn't look like anyone's lived here for a while. Harris said the information was updated recently, but this obviously doesn't fit. We can try the office downstairs to see if Marina was the last tenant, but I doubt if they'll have a forwarding address if she did live here. We'll have to go back to INS and try again. I guess you were right on the way over."

Angela holstered her weapon and leaned her back against the wall, eaten up with pain and frustration. They were empty-handed and all she got from the whole deal was a twisted ankle, an unavoidable limp, pain like a SOB, and a rat's nest of soon-to-be scars.

"I hope this was just a computer glitch," she said with a deep breath, trying to release some of the stress. "I don't want to waste time searching the city on wild goose chases. After the INS, I think we should go back over the crime scene. We may see something in the daylight that we missed."

Joe shook his head in disagreement. "We'll handle that after you get some medical attention."

"I can see the doctor later. We're losing daylight."

"Partner, I understand what's going on here. You're new and trying to prove your worth. I was a rookie once, too, so I know how it is, but we need to get something straightened out right now," rejected Joe, not looking angry, but visibly being firm.

Oh no, here it comes.

"My partner comes first, and I don't care how hot of a lead might be lost. You've got all the makings of a great detective and you're already well on your way. You didn't have to prove yourself to start with, so there's really no need to prove yourself now. I saw your profile before I ever accepted you for assignment as my new partner and I knew that you were the best one for the job before I ever met you. Now, let's get you down to the car, sans the bravado, and take care of that leg. I should have never let you come all the way up here in the first place."

She stood in shock for a few seconds, unsure of what to do or say. The words he spoke were the last words she expected to hear anytime soon, but what she needed to hear most. She almost succumbed to the emotions coursing through her, but she avoided breaking down when she was able to respond.

"I don't think it will do the situation justice, but…thank you. That…really means a lot to me."

Joe just nodded and started helping her down the stairs, moving no faster than she could handle. He was obviously frustrated with their results, but it didn't put a rough edge on their conversation as they descended. He knew the address could have been bad from the beginning, but he couldn't shake the feeling that Wendell Harris misled them intentionally. Maybe Mr. Harris is just passive aggressive. He knew he crossed the line with Seth, and it seemed odd that he wasn't threatened with a complaint about his conduct.

About halfway down, Joe moved to descend backwards in front of Angela to insure she couldn't fall down the stairs. She was moving a little easier, probably due to her leg going numb, which wasn't a good sign, and made no better by the increasing amount of blood staining her makeshift bandage. He wanted to be ready if anything gave out on her. She tried to cover it up, but she couldn't hide the ever-increasing stress lines on her face. They both learned about trauma on the way to becoming detectives, and they tried not to worry about worse case scenarios.

He knew that she was already being too hard on herself for getting hurt, even though it wasn't her fault and could have happened to anyone. He saw a lot of himself in her. He understood what she was going through and he didn't want to do anything that would add any grief.

chApCER NINE

Pratt's opened at 11:00 like every other morning for the last seven years. Rick inherited the family business when his father died, and he followed his father's wishes to keep the diner open as it had been for the last forty-two years. It was more than a mere place to eat; it was an icon in the neighborhood. The customer base was deep and loyal, and it usually doubled as a good, clean hangout or a meeting place for the neighborhood kids. The food was very good, and the cheesecake, made with his mother's recipe, was about the best available in town. A few restaurant critics even advised him to focus on the cheesecake and start selling it through a website and by mail, if he wanted to get rich. Although the idea held appeal, his goal was to uphold the high standards the diner was founded on, pay homage to his father's legacy, and keep Pratt's unique in a rapidly evolving cookie cutter world.

Rick inherited his family's cooking sense and he developed a recipe for one of the best Rueben sandwiches on the East Coast. He added a little of this and a little of that to the rye bread he baked fresh daily, and his homemade thousand island dressing had once been declared the "eighth wonder of the world" by one of the cheesecake critics.

By 11:15, customers occupied a little over half of the tables. An exceptionally good deli wasn't easy to find, and it was remarkably rare to be in a restaurant that wasn't exclusively a deli. The combination, along with the ambiance, kept the joint jumping.

It was a warm and inviting place that felt more like a favorite relative's house than a business. The walls were covered with autographed pictures of all the famous people that had eaten there, mixed with vintage memorabilia and framed restaurant reviews that ranked the diner in the upper echelon. Although the Mother Road never reached New York, the keen eye would notice that the mostly covered walls displayed a huge map of the historic highway. It graced all four walls and was strikingly accurate from California to Chicago, but it offered an addition, labeled "under construction," that stretched from the windy city to Pratt's. Rick Sr. loved the allure of 66, so he added the fictional "NY Expansion" when the diner was built, going so far as making up a few stories to support that is was really a part of the original plan. The most popular one involved Al Capone being behind it all, trying to get his bootlegging operations moving west and east.

Rick asked Ellen to come in early today when her shift ended the previous evening. A construction crew was renovating a tenement building up the street and they adopted Pratt's as their "place" while they were working. Most of the crew came in everyday for lunch, and some patrons either had to order "to go" or stand to eat. The normal crew couldn't keep up with the extra customers. Joyce, the regular day waitress, worked very well under pressure, but she still had her limits. Rick's watch showed almost 12:15 and still no sign of Ellen. She was an outstanding employee that rarely missed work and was as dependable as they come, making her absence all the more unusual.

He picked up the phone to make a call, and the phone rang three times before it was answered.

"Hello."

"Julie, it's Rick. May I speak to Ellen?"

"Sure, give me just a sec to get her."

Julie set the handset down on the small phone table and crossed the hall to Ellen's room. She knocked twice, waited, and then opened the door. Ellen was not in her room.

"Rick, she's not here right now. Can I take a message?"

"I asked Ellen to come in early today for the lunch rush. She's about forty-five minutes late. Please have her call me."

Julie heard concern in Rick's voice, not the tone of an irate boss. She could relate. She roomed with Ellen for over four years, and in that time, she had never known her to call in sick or go in late.

"I'll do it," she said and hung up the phone.

Julie looked around to see if Ellen left her a message or some kind of note before leaving that morning. She found nothing, so she decided to check Ellen's room again. That was when she realized that Ellen's bed had not been slept in. The cleaned sheets were still folded by the pillows, as she didn't have the time the previous morning to put on the fresh linen.

That was very strange and very unlike Ellen, which made Julie start worrying. She looked for any indication that Ellen had come home. No other dishes were dirty and the refrigerator and cupboards were just as she remembered from the previous day. Ellen's blue uniform that she wore on laundry days was nowhere to be found.

84

She took a deep breath and decided to check back with the diner, even though only a few minutes had passed.

There was a first time for everything. Maybe Ellen was just running late. It could happen. She thought, trying to convince herself.

"Pratt's Diner, this is Rick."

"Rick, it's Julie. Has Ellen made it to work yet?"

"No, not yet."

"When was the last time you saw her?"

"Last night. I finished the books for the day and Ellen said she would lock up after she finished mopping the dining room. Why do you ask?" asked Rick, his tone increasingly concerned.

"I don't think she ever made it home last night. You know Ellen isn't like this at all. I'm afraid something may have happened to her."

"Is there anywhere else she could have gone?"

"No, I don't think so. She always comes straight home after work. I don't have any idea where she could be. What should we do?" returned Julie.

"Have you considered calling the police and reporting her as missing? I feel uneasy about this, too."

"Yes, but I didn't want to overreact. I hate to say this, but I've got a very bad feeling."

"Please let me know what happens, or if you hear from her."

"I will. Please do the same."

Julie hung up and grabbed the phone book. She started to dial 9-1-1, but wasn't sure what she would say when the dispatcher answered. She felt like this was an emergency, but that didn't mean the NYPD would share the sentiment. She looked up the non-emergency number for the closest Precinct.

"New York City Police Department 42nd Precinct, how can I assist you?"

"I think something has happened to my roommate. Can you help me?"

"Please elaborate on what has happened?" asked the dispatcher, maintaining a calm demeanor.

"She never made it home last night, and I cannot find her."

"One moment, please."

The phone clicked and fell silent. Julie thought the officer hung up on her when an instrumental version of "Suspicious Minds" filled the void. The second chorus ended as the extension transferred and rang.

"Missing Persons Division, this is Officer Smith. How can I help you?"

"I think something happened to my roommate! Can you help me?"

"We need to start with a few things first, okay? What is your name, miss?"

"Julie Romanowski."

"What is your address and phone number?"

"It's 2420 Webster Avenue, apartment C, like cat. The number is 572-0945."

"What is your roommate's name?"

"Ellen Clark."

"When was the last time she was seen, and where?" he asked with a mundane manner to his voice.

"It was the night before last about midnight, just before she got off work at Pratt's."

"You mean the home of Rick's Reuben?" His tone changed, gaining a little warmth.

"Yes, that's the one."

"Your address is what, maybe a mile or two from the diner?"

"Yes, that's correct."

"Do you have the exact address for the diner, ma'am?"

"Yes, just a minute." Julie flipped through the address book they kept by the phone. "It's 4103 Webster Avenue. The number there is 572-3625.

"About what time did she leave the diner?"

"I guess about one or two in the morning. Rick said she left the diner after close, and I don't think she ever made it home."

"Could she have gone to a friend's house for the night, or maybe a boyfriend's place?"

She sensed Smith's perception of the situation.

"No, she doesn't really know too many people here, and she keeps to herself a lot. She doesn't have a boyfriend, and before you ask, all of her family lives in Minnesota."

"Can you tell me anything else about your friend's disappearance?" His voice grew a little warmer, almost like he was leading her with his questions.

"I don't really know, but she was the last person to leave the diner. Rick said he left before she did. She closes at the diner every night and walks home. It's not very far. Something must have happened to her on the way here."

"How well do you know Mr. Pratt?"

The question caught her off guard and seemed irrelevant to her.

"Ellen has worked for him for several years. They're friends. Why?"

"All possibilities need to be considered. That's all I need for right now. Call me back the day after tomorrow and we'll get the case started. Please let me know if your roommate shows up before then, or if you get additional information."

"The day after tomorrow, are you SERIOUS? Why aren't you going to do anything right now?" Julie couldn't believe what she was hearing. Only God knew what happened to Ellen, and the police apparently weren't very concerned.

"Ma'am, please try to calm down; it's our regulations," started Smith. His voice sounded troubled as he continued. "I can't declare a person officially missing right away unless something very concrete, like foul play with solid evidence, is suspected. You said yourself that you 'think something happened' and you 'guess about one or two in the morning.' That's not solid. A high percentage of people believed to be missing return within the first twenty-four hours. We don't have the manpower to utilize that many searches, just to find the 'missing' sleeping off a hangover at a local hotel."

"But, but you…don't know Ellen, " mumbled Julie as she started to cry.

"I understand the way you feel, I really do. I wish I could do more right now."

She didn't want to accept the answer, but she felt a genuine air of sympathy in his voice.

"We have an enormous caseload, so we have to be sure of what we're dealing with before we devote the resources. We have to keep the possibility open that your friend could have just gone away for the day, or gone out of town on a last-minute emergency and just hasn't called yet."

"You…you just don't…know…Ellen. That's not like her at all. I know something bad happened."

"I truly hope you are wrong, Ms. Romanowski. I need to give you a case number. It's 235-H-5733. I'll be in touch. Please call me if you hear from her."

The phone clicked and the line went dead. Julie dropped the handset into the cradle, sat down at the kitchen table, and pulled her limbs into a ball. Tears soaked the knees of her light gray sweat pants. Her friend was gone, no one would help for another forty-eight hours, and she knew in her core that something terrible had already happened.

chapter ten

Joe and Angela went to the New York Hospital Queens emergency room. They couldn't tell if her cuts were still bleeding, although her makeshift bandage was entirely soaked. The burning was mostly gone, replaced with a throbbing that felt like she took a hammer blow to her leg with every heartbeat. The lack of movement from the car ride, combined with the swelling, resulted in a stiffness that no longer allowed walking as an option. She held onto Joe for balance and support, afraid she would not be able to get up again if she sat back down in the car. Luckily, an orderly arrived with a wheelchair.

The waiting room was full of people in various states of discomfort and disrepair, which seemed fairly typical. The orderly rolled Angela to the end of a row of chairs while Joe gave Angela's information to the attendant on duty. She thanked him as he hurried away to help the next person coming for treatment, lowering her head and closing her eyes to try and focus on something other than the pain.

Low groans, grunts, sneezing, and muffled sobs set the ambiance. Bursts of cold air rushed into the room each time the automatic sliding doors opened. She looked up and around after a few minutes as her own pain lessened with the lack of movement. She needed to move her leg, knowing the decrease in pain was not a very good sign, but still thankful for the respite.

She noticed one young woman sitting as much by herself as she could, which put her very close to the main entrance, and in one of the spots hammered the hardest by winter when the doors opened. The twenty-something brunette looked like the typical college student in her blue jeans and Columbia t-shirt, but very underdressed for the weather.

Joe was barely seated next to Angela when a nurse came from the back to wheel her to an exam room. The wait was short since there was no one present with more critical injuries, and her status as a police officer moved her to the top of the waiting list. They went straight into a service area. The nurse lifted Angela to a standing position and helped her onto the bed.

"There we go. My name is Dale, and I'll be your nurse today. If you can just lay back and relax, we'll get you fixed up."

He was a big man with a gentle face and a calm voice. Angela felt immediately at ease. Joe must have felt the same way as he offered no protest.

"I've got to take your vitals. Would you slip that coat off for me so I can get your blood pressure? I'm sorry about your leg and your clothes. I've got to get this shoe off and cut what's left of this pant leg away so the doc can get in there," he explained as he pulled the privacy curtain closed.

"Don't worry about it. They're trashed anyway."

She offered what smile she could as he washed his hands and gloved up to start prepping her leg. She gasped as he lifted her foot to remove her shoe. The slight twisting motion sent jolts of sharp pain pulsing through the numbness that had settled over the injury. She had Joe's forearm in a death grip before she realized it.

"Sorry, miss. I've almost got it. We'll get you something for the pain in just a minute. The doc will write the order once he's taken an initial look at you."

She nodded her understanding, unable to speak as she ground her teeth in response to the agony. She was afraid she would cry out if she opened her mouth. Joe gave her shoulder a light squeeze of reassurance with his free hand, using the other to make sure she didn't jerk around too much.

Dale donned a fresh pair of gloves, removed the temporary bandage, and cleaned the cuts as gently as possible. He lightly wrapped gauze padding over the wounds, and formed a small gauze pad that he slipped under her calf, to catch any renewed bleeding until the initial examination occurred.

"This will just keep everything protected until the doctor can take a look and provide treatment. Can I get you anything?"

Angela shook her head no.

"Dale, are you clear?" came from outside the privacy screen.

"Yes, sir."

The screen parted just enough to allow the doctor to look inside the exam area.

"Hello Detective Benson, I'll be with you in just a moment. Are there any breaks, Dale?"

"No sir, there don't appear to be any, just a lot of tissue lacerations. One is pretty deep, there's significant bruising, and the ankle seems to be badly sprained."

"Okay, very good. Let me see what I can do about some pain management." He closed the screen and walked away.

A moment later a second nurse breached the cloth wall carrying three loaded syringes. She surrendered one to Dale and left.

"If I can see your right arm, we'll get this started."

She volunteered her arm for the shot, barely noticing the stick. Dale was putting the spent syringe in the sharps container as she felt the first effects. The medicine burned like ice as it crept up her arm, but it quickly changed into soothing warmth as it moved through her shoulder. The pain in her ankle ebbed almost immediately, and she quietly sighed with relief. She let herself lean back into the pillows when a less desirable sensation shocked her system.

Oh no. Please don't. Not in front of Joe!

"Joe, I'm going to be sick!"

She tried to get up, but there was no time. She managed to get her head over the side of the bed in time. A gush of sick splattered to the floor. She felt the color slip from her face even though her embarrassment fought to keep it there. She leaned back against the pillow as a second wave of nausea hit her. Joe already had a trash can in hand, ready to catch the second volley. He was rock solid, even though only mere sounds turned him green in the morgue. He didn't offer a rebuke or even break a smile.

Dale returned with a second syringe and quickly administered it.

"I'm sorry, Miss. It'll be okay. That happens to about half the people that get that pain med. The doctors wait to see if there's a reaction before they write the order for Phenergan. It'll stop that nausea pretty quickly."

He spoke to Joe as much or more than Angela due to the look of concern on his face. He barely had the curtain closed before Angela needed the trash can again. Gratefully, the Phenergan worked as quickly as the Demerol, settling her stomach before a third volley.

Joe set the trashcan down and washed his hands at the small sink in the room. He returned with a small plastic cup of water.

"Swish that around. It might get some of that nasty taste out of your mouth."

"Thanks, Joe."

"Don't mention it." He then handed her some paper towels to wipe her face.

The doctor on duty again stopped just outside the curtain to request entrance.

"Come in."

"Hello, Detectives, I'm Dr. Carroll. I apologize for the nausea from the Demerol. I like to prescribe it because it's very effective for pain, and we can manage the side effects efficiently. From what I see in your chart, I need to send you to radiology for a couple of quick x-rays just to make sure we have no fractures and we'll go from there."

Joe was asked to wait while another orderly relieved Dale and took Angela for x-rays. He caught about fifteen minutes of a cooking show on the wall mounted television before his partner was wheeled back, bed and all.

"How are you holding up?" he asked when they were alone again.

"I've been better, but I've also been a lot worse."

"Are you still in a lot of pain?"

"No, not really; the pressure from the swelling is uncomfortable, but it doesn't really feel like pain anymore."

Dr. Carroll returned with Dale in tow.

"I just checked your films and you don't have any fractures either. Let me get prepped and we'll get you patched up."

He cleaned out the lacerations, leaving nine blood-soaked splinters in various sizes on the triage tray when he was finished. He packed the wounds with antibiotic ointment, closing the large gash with six sutures and the others with Steri-strips. He finished with a thin application of lidocaine cream. The slight tinge of pain and the burning caused by the procedure melted away as the lidocaine soaked into the aggravated tissue. He wrapped a light bandage around her entire calf.

A lightweight air splint over the wrap of gauze was necessary for the ankle. The total of the damage was a moderate ankle sprain that would stop hurting in a few days with proper medication and rest, and several lacerations that would heal completely in 10 days if not aggravated. He prescribed oral medications for pain, swelling, and the unavoidable infection that would follow without antibiotics. He also provided two small tubes of ointment and lidocaine cream for dressing changes. He elevated her leg and added a cold compress while they waited for the business side of the visit to be completed.

"Well, I guess you won't be jogging for a few days," said Joe when they were alone.

"Ya think?" popped out of her mouth with a sarcastic flourish. She immediately lowered her head and looked down at the bed. "I'm sorry, Joe. I'm stressing out a little, but that's no excuse. That was out of line. It means a lot to me that you stayed in here with me; you didn't have to."

Joe reached for her shoulder and gave another fatherly squeeze.

"It could have happened to anyone. Don't lose sleep over it. I doubt this was the first time, and surely it won't be the last. Can we call it even on the upset stomachs today?"

Angela smiled at his jest, knowing it was in fun.

"Yes, I think we're more than even, just don't call me Shirley," she said, putting her hand over his as she quoted the line from one of her favorite comedies.

"How long have we been in here?" she asked, unable to see the clock in the exam room.

"Close to an hour. Why?"

"Something's been nagging me since we got here. Do you remember that young brunette that was sitting in the waiting room when we got here?"

"I don't remember seeing her, but I was at the front counter most of that time. What's bugging you?"

"It didn't register with me until now. She was sitting over by the automatic doors and she wasn't wearing a coat."

"What's so strange about that? Maybe she wasn't cold."

"She just sat there in a kind of daze, but the strange thing is that she didn't flinch any time the door opened. I know that wind was extremely cold and it hit her full force over and over, tossing her hair around like crazy, and she didn't move."

"Maybe she was just in shock. We don't know why she came here."

"That occurred to me, but she was holding the side of her neck. Thinking about it now, it seemed she was mumbling to herself, too. It's just a little too much like our missing witness."

The same thought had already occurred to Joe and he took off for the waiting room. The girl matching Angela's description was not there, but she could be in one of the treatment rooms. He approached the check-in desk and inquired about the girl.

"No, she never checked in," said the clerk. "I saw her come in. She sat right there and didn't move for a long time. It's almost like she was afraid to come inside. I was going to go over and ask her if she needed help after it quieted down a bit since she didn't seem to be in any immediate jeopardy. I didn't see her leave, but she wasn't there when I was going to go check on her."

"How long ago was that?"

"It couldn't have been more than a couple of minutes. She was sitting there when I answered the last phone call. When I hung up, she was gone and you were standing there."

"Thanks!"

Joe rushed out the front door. The parking lot was well lit, and the snow helped brighten the view to near daylight. The girl was nowhere to be seen. The abundance of vehicle and foot traffic around the entrance didn't let him see what direction she went.

Damn.

He went back to Angela's treatment room.

"She's gone, and I only missed her by a minute or two at most."

The detectives returned to the alley by mid-afternoon the next day, much to Joe's chagrin. Angela was supposed to be off her feet with her foot elevated, but she insisted on going with him. Under normal circumstances, the department would have forced the issue, giving her no choice but a couple of days of administrative duty at best, pencil pushing to recover. Since they were so short-handed and working such an important case, Captain Bishop put Angela in Joe's charge with clear guidelines about what she could and couldn't do in the field.

The scene was a macabre Christmas present wrapped in snow and ice. Yellow crime tape ribbon coiled around the scene, trimmed with a white chalk line under a small cover that was set up to keep the snow from covering that spot on the ground where the body was found.

Joe combed the scene a second time, while Angela leaned against the hood with the help of a crutch, looking for anything they might have missed without the benefit of daylight. She didn't notice anything, but she didn't expect to while forced to stay in one place.

The throbbing was back in her ankle, grumbling about like a frustrated child after the Demerol metabolized out of her system. The pain pills she had worked fairly well, but not with the same effectiveness as the injection.

The puking would almost be worth it.

It was hard for her to concentrate. The pain would lessen long enough for her to get focus, only to hit her again with another throbbing wave. She gave up trying to reassess their notes and just waited for Joe to finish. She caught herself drifting back to the nightmares that plagued her restless sleep.

Upon waking that morning, she tried to convinced herself the pain medicine was the source, but now she wasn't so sure. She couldn't remember the visions the unpleasant dreams put in her mind, but they left her feeling disoriented, somber, and scared. She wouldn't dare mention it to her partner due to the weakness she showed at the hospital.

It wasn't long before Joe was ready to give up as well. He started moving, actually throwing, the trashcans at the edge of the crime scene. He wasn't truly looking for anything as much as venting his frustration. A shiny flicker of gold caught his attention during the tirade.

The glint came from a gold bracelet that was lodged between the trashcan and the building it rested against. The face was stamped with the insignia of physicians and the words "Medic Alert" in red. The back of the bracelet offered an engraving that read "Kelly Richardson" with a phone number centered beneath it. It identified Kelly as an insulin dependent diabetic with a severe allergy to penicillin. The clasp was connected, but one of the links was broken open, as if stretched farther than the metal's strength could prevent.

"Angela, take a look at this," said Joe as he walked to the car and handed it to her. "I wonder what it's doing here."

"I don't know, but it sure is clean. It doesn't look like it's been out here for very long. Not to mention it's an unusual find at the scene of a murder, especially since it doesn't belong to Marina."

"I agree. What do you suggest we do now?"

"Why don't we see if Gianelli is around since we're already here? Maybe he knows Miss Richardson. I'm guessing the phone number is a direct line to her doctor's office or an emergency service that can direct us to her doctor. One of the two might point us in the right direction."

"That sounds good to me."

They got back into the car and Joe backed toward the entrance of the alley where Gianelli said he lived. The alley offered several unusually shaped cutouts and depressions on both sides, some exposed and some covered. Many contained a large number of metal trashcans, ringed thickly with soot, which the street people used to burn anything that might provide warmth. The largest of these offshoots fit the description Gianelli provided. A little looking led Joe to the refrigerator box condo he called home, but Thomas wasn't in.

"This just keeps getting better," said Joe. "I feel like we are just spinning our wheels here. All of our 'leads' are leading nowhere."

Joe paced angrily around the space of the offshoot, not sure what he should do with the new frustration building up.

"Why don't we go get something to eat and collect our thoughts," offered Angela. "It seems like we are missing something, but we aren't in the right frame of mind to figure it out. We need a break, and I need to take some more pain medicine. My ankle is killing me."

He sighed to let off steam.

"Okay, I know just the place." The pair left the crime scene headed for a local joint Joe frequented.

The cafe was built in an old train dining car, coupled with the original kitchen car, and parked on a short run of track in front of an old depot. A second short section of track supported two box cars that were used for storage.

The appliances were updated to make the kitchen modern, and the junction between the cars was enclosed and finished to allow weather-free, unobstructed access back and forth. The mahogany trim and royal blue upholstery was still in amazing condition for its age, as was most of the Persian designed interior.

It was built by the Pullman Palace Car Company and originally served on B&O's flagship train, known as the Royal Blue that ran from Washington, D.C. to New York in the late 1800s. The proprietor ran across it at an auction for the estate of a one-time executive for the Baltimore & Ohio line who purchased it after it was decommissioned in 1958. He couldn't believe his luck, as the sister car, named the Waldorf, was never sold and went directly to the B&O Rail Museum.

A bold neon sign mounted along the front edges of the old-style train depot's roof read Flip's Astoria in an art deco font. The depot had the name Mertzon painted under the gable. Angela was impressed with the restored exterior of the train and the relocated station that rested beside the four train cars. Two short stretches of track ran side by side with two cars on each track. It looked like the rails, train, and depot had been there all along and the rest of the city grew in around it. They walked a ramp onto the platform and could step directly into the dining car. Joe grabbed a couple of menus and led them to a table near the kitchen.

"Afternoon Joe," said a man with thick gray hair and deep green eyes. Angela guessed he was in his early fifties, but it was hard to tell since he had apparently aged well. His body was still defined with toned muscle. He reminded her of the actor that played Wade Garrett in the movie Roadhouse.

"Hi Flip. I thought it was high time to introduce my new partner to the place. This is Detective Angela Benson. Angela, this is Flip Tuttle, retired police Captain, expert fly fisherman, washed up cowboy, mean short order cook, and all-around pain in the ass."

"Hello, it's nice to meet you Mr. Tuttle," said Angela, grinning.

"Well, I can see we're going to have a problem," said Flip, looking at Joe disapprovingly. "I guess you haven't had the talk with her yet."

97

Angela's face flushed. She looked at Joe, unaware of her offense. Joe just shook his head knowingly as Flip sat down beside him.

"We can't have any of this 'Mister' business," he said cheerfully with a Texas drawl and a smile. "Flip will do fine. If you call me 'Mister' again, I'll have to poison your dinner and tell the man upstairs you died. You limped a bit coming inside. How'd you get that hitch in your get-along Missy?"

"It's a long story, Mi...Flip. What part of Texas are you from? I hail from the Lone Star State as well," she added, letting some of her accent return.

"Now you've done it," offered Joe.

"I'm a might glad you asked. You can't cover up your accent completely, young lady. I can tell you're not from these parts, so I'll oblige, regardless of the toil it has on this Damn Yankee."

Joe laughed and Flip's smile widened.

"Are you two putting me on?"

Flip answered. "No, but Joe's giving a subtle hint that he doesn't want to hear the story again."

Angela looked at her partner and scolded him with a heavier accented "shame on you."

"I was born in Texas in a little place called Mertzon that you've probably never heard of before now, or when you read it painted on the gable out front. My dad worked for the railroad after he got out of the Army, but it didn't pay that well. He wanted better for me and my mom, so he saved up and paid our way here. He was supposed to come for us, but mom got a letter from the railroad saying he was killed making some track repairs. She found work after the railroad benefits ran out, holding down three jobs to get me through school and into college.

I lost her a few months after graduation. She was mugged walking home from her third shift job. I joined the force to try and make sure that didn't happen to anyone else's mother, or anyone for that matter. Joe pretty well simplified the rest. Growing up around the trains in those early years is what inspired this place. But that's enough about me."

"That's no lie," mumbled Joe from behind his menu.

Flip swatted the back where it read "Daily Specials," making it lightly hit Joe in the face.

"Now, you both look hungry. What'll you have today? It's on me."

Angela released the breath she didn't realize she held, not sure if eating was such a good idea after all.

Joe smiled like he knew what was happening the whole time and motioned for her to make her request. "If he ever poisons anyone's food, it'll be mine, I can assure you. My saving grace is that he knows I'll bad mouth his cooking in the afterlife and he just doesn't want to hear it for eternity."

Flip laughed heartily as he took their orders then headed off for the kitchen car. Angela fell in step with the joke and felt as if she'd known Flip her whole life. His personality was so endearing that she knew if Joe did talk trash about his cooking, no one would believe him.

Flip turned just before he entered the kitchen. "Oh, I almost forgot, it was nice getting to meet you, Miss Angela. Let me know what you think of the fare. I haven't had an unsatisfied customer yet. It seems the ones that survived enjoyed their meal."

"We can't have any of this 'Miss' business either," she shot back at him.

"Joe, I really like her." Flip went through the swinging doors. His jovial laugh could be heard from the kitchen.

"How long have you known him?"

"It's been almost twenty years. My old partner Tom was partnered with Flip until he promoted to Captain. I replaced Flip as Tom's new partner. After Flip retired from the force, he took everything he had and bought these old train cars to open the diner. Tom and I used to come here at least twice a week. After Tom retired, I stopped coming as much, but I still try to make it in once or twice a month."

"He's a very friendly man. It's obvious why people like him."

"He's a great guy, and he was an outstanding police officer. He's one of the most decorated officers in the history of the NYPD, and he didn't stab any backs to get there. His reputation precedes him, as it should. He's known for his exemplary integrity and honesty. I learned everything I know about police work from Tom, and he learned it all from Flip. I'll be satisfied if I end up half the cop that he was."

Flip returned to the table carrying a large tray piled with food. Angela had a grilled chicken sandwich with a side salad and Joe had his usual. The "usual" was a triple meat cheeseburger, two orders of fries, an order of onion rings, a slice of cheesecake smothered in cherries, and a large chocolate shake with a mega-sized soda to wash it all down. Angela had no trouble seeing why Joe was such a large man. She liked Joe as a partner and a person, but she quickly discovered that she could go without watching him eat. Joe ate very quickly and sloppily, talked with his mouth full, and didn't concern himself with the grease that ran down from the corners of his mouth.

Angela ate slowly and neatly, taking small bites, waiting to see what her stomach would decide to do next. The food tasted fantastic, and about halfway through her meal, the icky feeling washed away like smoke on the breeze. Likewise, the slight offense she took to Joe's mannerisms yielded as well as she saw the truth for what it was. Joe was just being himself, which for her was like a somewhat obnoxious but lovable older brother. He didn't care what anyone thought about him, especially if they only looked at what was on the outside.

Flip came back to the table as Angela finished.

"What did you think?"

Angela's face flushed a little and she reached for her throat, starting to twitch with an oncoming seizure. A wave of anguished pain washed over her face, dulling the sparkle on her eye. Flip's eyes almost popped out of their sockets as he reached out to do what he could to help her. As soon he reacted, she couldn't hold the rouse and started laughing behind her hands that she was using to cover her face. Joe's guffaws filled the café.

"Okay, you got me. I guess we're even now."

Angela was laughing so hard, she had to use her napkin to catch the tears in her eyes.

"Okay, that's really just not that funny, but I still like you anyway."

Joe laughed himself into a spasm of coughs. Angela was afraid his over-sized lunch might see daylight again.

"I can see why Joe likes you so much, and it really was very good," she added, letting him off the hook as she finished dabbing her eyes. "I'll make Joe bring me here more often."

"Good! There's nothing like good food and good company. Can I get you anything else?"

"No, thank you. I'm stuffed."

Joe managed to stop laughing, but he hadn't finished eating, so Flip didn't direct any conversation towards him. He knew Joe long enough to know to leave him alone when he ate. After he finished, he neatly stacked his plates, pushed them to the outside end of the booth, and used his napkin to wipe his face, and the condensation off of his glass, and the mess from the tabletop. He started laughing again as he put the napkin on top of the stack of plates. He was full of little contradictions.

"I feel better," said Joe. "I hate working on an empty stomach, and that look on Flip's face was priceless; never a camera around when you need one."

Angela curtsied from her seat.

"Why don't you try the number on that bracelet?"

"I guess it is about time to get back to work." She realized she left her cell phone in the car when she discovered her pocket was empty. "Do you have your cell?"

"I don't even own a cell phone, partner. Why don't you use the payphone in the back? You've been sitting for a while. The doctor told you not to let it get too stiff or it would really hurt."

"Thanks for reminding me. I'll be right back."

Angela was warmed again with Joe's concern. She didn't realize he was paying such close attention when the doctor gave her instructions, and he apparently intended to make sure she acted in accordance with them.

She walked to the phone that was nestled in a small privacy alcove at the back of the diner, limping a little. The profound wobble she just knew was in her gait was barely noticed by the other patrons. The medications she took with lunch were handling the pain well enough to mask any outward signs. After she reached the phone, she deposited the required change and dialed. The call was answered after two rings.

"Good afternoon, Dr. Arkits' office. How may I help you?"

"Hello, my name is Angela Benson. I'm a detective with the New York Police Department, and I need some assistance. I've got a few questions involving an active investigation."

"Yes, ma'am, you'll need to speak to Dr. Arkits directly. I don't know what he'll be able to tell you considering HIPAA."

"That'll be fine," returned Angela, suspicious that the receptionist felt obligated to offer such a disclaimer. The phone hummed quietly for a few seconds while the call transferred.

"Hello, Dr. Arkits here."

"Hello Doctor, my name is Detective Angela Benson with the NYPD. I have a few questions about one of your patients."

"I'd be happy to help. What can I do for you?"

"My partner and I found a medic alert bracelet that belongs to one of your patients at a crime scene last night. The phone number I just called to reach you is engraved on the back."

"What's the patient's name?"

"Kelly Richardson. What can you tell me about her?"

"Let me check my records. It will only take a second. Ah, here it is. I finished working with Ms. Richardson about three months ago."

"Can you give me any contact information for her? Do you have any pictures of her?"

"Under normal circumstances, no, but since this situation implies she could be in real danger, I'll bend the rules, off the record of course. I remember now. She was diagnosed with insulin dependent diabetes last summer. I had a hard time getting her blood sugar stabilized because her body tried to reject the insulin. I had to try several different types before we found one compatible with her system and determined the proper dosages. We had to fit her with a continuous blood sugar monitor that would automatically administer the insulin as needed. Once we got her blood sugar to stay in the control range, it was far easier and safer for her to keep it there. The monitor is also designed with a help call feature."

"What does that do?"

"In the event her sugar becomes too low, from something like a malfunction, the device basically makes a cellular call to a help center. It transmits her current blood sugar level, the rate the level is changing, and her location in the event an ambulance needs to be dispatched."

"So, you're saying the monitor is equipped with GPS?"

"Oh yes, it's very cutting-edge medicine. She qualified for the pilot program."

"Can you find her now?

"Unfortunately, no, it doesn't work that way. The unit runs on battery power, so the GPS transmitter doesn't activate unless there's a problem. It's a one-way connection. The makers would never have gotten FDA approval if the device could be used to track patients without their knowledge."

"Have you heard from her recently?"

"No, I haven't. She was in once for a device calibration, but that was back about six weeks ago and my PA handled it. I see a note flagged on her records. It says that Ms. Richardson called four days ago requesting a prescription for a new medic alert bracelet. She realized her bracelet was gone when she got home one night from work. She had a backup to use, but she wanted to replace her primary one that had the updated information."

"Well, that seems to answer the question. Can you tell me where I might find Ms. Richardson?"

"I'm sorry, but I can't bend the rules quite that far. I need written consent from the patient to release contact information. Her medical information is already cleared, at her request, because of the nature of her insulin device and her medic alert status. Since she called about the missing bracelet, it seems that she likely isn't in danger."

"I understand. Thank you for your time Dr. Arkits."

"You're welcome, Detective. Let me know if I can be of further service."

Angela walked back to her seat with a puzzled, dissatisfied look.

Joe asked Angela as he nursed his milkshake and as she slid into the opposite side of the booth, "Do I want to know what you found out?"

"Probably not, it'll only make you mad again."

"That covers the disappointment I see on your face, but what about that perplexed look?"

"I just have this gut feeling about Dr. Arkits, and I don't like that way it feels. I can't quite put my finger on it, but something isn't right."

"How is that?"

"It's almost like he answered my questions from a script."

After Joe finished, he and Angela headed towards the INS office from Flip's, doing what they could with their leads. The radio crackled as Joe changed lanes to make a turn.

"Homicide, Unit 23, come in please."

Joe picked up the handset. "This is H23, go ahead."

"Report to Seventh and Grand for a 10-73. Sanitation is already on site. No one else is available."

"Ten-four, we're on our way."

Joe made a U-turn at the first place he had the chance. The intersection of Seventh and Grand was about thirty minutes away, give or take with the road conditions and traffic.

A uniformed police unit was on site when Joe and Angela arrived, as Sanitation requested assistance from both. All of the preliminary work was completed and the crime scene was already cordoned off. One of the uniformed officers approached the Detective's car as they arrived. Joe rolled down the driver's side window to address him. The bristling wind carried snow into the car.

"Afternoon, Anderson and Benson, Homicide."

"Detectives," he replied, nodding his head to both. "My partner is talking to the Sanitation Officer and the employee that found the body this morning. I've got the preliminary report."

"Good, let me get parked and we'll get started."

Joe pulled into a small lot, adjacent to an idle trash truck nestled in between several tall tenement buildings. The garbage truck was next to three trash dumpsters, set in a row, at the back edge of the space.

The truck, dumpsters, and a good portion of the parking lot rested within the yellow crime tape perimeter.

Joe got out and approached the crime scene to start his inspection. He could tell the area was relatively undisturbed. The snow surrounding the truck and the trash bins only showed two sets of footprints that were already getting shallower from the falling snow. The tire tracks behind the wheels of the NYWM truck were the only set in the area. The rest of the snow was still virgin. The truck had a fresh layer on its top, but it wasn't enough to conceal any disruption if it had occurred.

The officer greeted Joe and Angela, surrendering the report to her at Joe's indication. She returned to the passenger seat of the car to look it over, feeling more pain with the onset of the colder air. The wind picked up, giving the swirling currents a sharper blade. Snow fell in thicker sheets.

The report stated the sanitation worker, Mr. Eli Lebowski, arrived at roughly 10:30 that morning to empty the containers as part of his normal route. He'd gotten out of the truck because several bags of trash were stacked around the containers instead of in it. It was unusual for this set of bins since they were rarely ever full. Some of the bags even appeared to be thrown from a short distance, which caused them to burst and allowed the contents to scatter along the ground. Most of the loose debris was already gone, either blown away by the wind or buried out of sight by the snow. He assumed the mess was the result of laziness, but he noticed an unusually strong and pungent odor when he approached the dumpsters.

When he checked the middle container, the stench from within made him nauseous, and the sight of the corpse inside caused him to vomit violently. He called Sanitation when he regained enough composure to make the call and waited in his truck until the Sanitation Officer arrived at approximately 11:40. Sanitation called for a regular unit to assist. The uniformed team made a visual inspection of the body and set up the restricted area when they arrived after which the Sanitation Officer was free to question Eli. All three officers conferred to establish the preliminary report that would fall to Homicide for them to conduct a more detailed investigation.

Angela got back out of the car and walked over to question the driver herself when she finished reading the preliminary. She wrapped her trench coat around her body tightly in hopes it would keep the wind from slicing through her. It did a fair job protecting her body, but the attack on her ankles was brutal. The frigid air aggravated her injury, making her limp even more profoundly.

"Mr. Lebowski, this is Detective Benson," stated the officer that supplied the report. "She needs to ask you a few questions about this morning before we can let you get back to work."

The other three officers finished up their duties meaning they could leave when the detectives gave them clearance.

"Mr. Lebowski," started Angela, "I can tell you're pretty shaken up by this, so I'll try to keep it as brief as possible. The information the other officers gave me said you found the body this morning. Can you tell me about what time it was?"

"It was a little after 10:30."

"Are you sure of the time?"

"Yes, I was listening to a talk radio show that's on every morning at 10:30. The intro music was starting as I pulled into the lot."

"Did you know the victim, or recognize him from the neighborhood?"

"No, I don't know who he was. I ain't never seen a dead person before," answered Eli.

He lost the little color that had returned to his cheeks as he thought about the corpse again, replaced by the greenish hue reserved for seasick landlubbers rafting through a hurricane.

"It's okay. It's very natural to feel that way. I see this all the time and I still get queasy sometimes. I can imagine how hard it is for you right now."

He merely nodded in agreement, afraid that vomit would erupt from his body if he provided an answer by opening his mouth.

Joe conducted the site investigation while Angela questioned the worker from the Sanitation Department. His search was fruitless, and the only thing certain at that point was the body was dumped in the trash container after death. The trash bins were emptied once a week; now they were less than half full with several other bags sitting around the containers. The body was probably discovered within twenty-four hours, but no one wanted to come forward, too afraid to report it. It was a common problem in many neighborhoods, especially ones like this. He guessed the body was dumped three or four days earlier, maybe five, but that was a stretch.

The lack of blood on and around the body supported Joe's theory. If the victim had been killed there, the contents of the bin would be coated with blood to evidence a struggle. The amount of blood and lymph caked around the wound was far too little for the type of injury as well.

He got the digital camera from the car and started taking pictures of the entire scene. The other officer's camera wasn't working, or they would have already handled the photographs. He took as many as he could and then he went to the car to wait for Angela. He scrolled through the images on the camera's view screen to see if anything just jumped out at him that he overlooked. The camera's eye didn't miss anything.

Angela instructed Mr. Lebowski to return to Sanitation as she finished. She would call if she needed anything else, and she cleared the other officers to leave the scene as well. She hobbled back to the car, trying to keep most of her weight off of her now-throbbing ankle.

"What did you find out?" asked Joe, as Angela closed her door.

She took a deep breath and leaned forward to check her injuries before answering. She ran her hands lightly over her ankle and lower leg without applying pressure, trying to warm the joint and soothe the pulses of pain.

"Well, Mr. Lebowski has worked for Sanitation for almost three years. He has never seen a dead body, which actually surprises me in his line of work in this town. He generally keeps to himself and he lives alone. He doesn't know or recognize the victim, and he is very scared and confused. He doesn't want to be in any trouble, and he just wants to get back to work."

"Can I take a stab at this one? No pun intended."

"Shoot."

"No leads?"

"Good guess, but MO seems to be the same as the John Doe from last night. I'm starting to think O'Toole may have something with his serial killer theory."

"That sounds possible to me, but last night's victim was a lot worse for wear. Serial killers usually duplicate the crimes in every possible detail."

"That's true, but we don't know enough about our killer yet. If these cases are connected, the killer works fast. We better get to the bottom of it quick."

"I hope the Coroner gets here soon. We're wasting time we should be using to find Marina. I want to get back to INS today and I hope for Mr. Harris' sake he didn't give us a bad address on purpose."

"I seriously doubt it, even though you probably deserved it."

Joe looked at Angela, incredulously.

"I'm just kidding. Besides, what would he have to gain from it? You've already taken at least ten years off of Seth's life."

Angela tried to keep from laughing at the priceless expression on Joe's face. Even though it was wrong, Seth's reaction was pretty memorable, looking like he was going to wet himself, cry, or both when Joe picked him up.

The snow kept coming in thick, white flakes. The spot where the trash truck sat was already covered by a thin layer in the relentless snowfall. One of the city's Coroners finally arrived after another half an hour. Joe was visibly irritated because he and Angela were burning up time they needed. He went to the Coroner's car alone, telling Angela to hold tight as there was no reason for her to get back out into the cold and aggravate her ankle again.

"Looks like you guys are pretty busy," said Joe as he reached the van.

"Yeah, it's been a really busy month so far. Old Man Winter is devastating the homeless population, and we have to perform autopsies on every one of them, even though we know that they each froze to death. We've probably all get a month's worth of overtime trying to catch up."

"Here's a copy of what we have so far. You can forward a copy of your autopsy report to the e-mail address at the bottom of the page when you're finished," instructed Joe as he passed the paperwork.

"No problem. I've got to get started here. I've got an assistant coming to help me with the body, but I need to get the initial procedures out of the way first. That'll also let us get out of this weather a lot faster."

The Coroner began his work as Joe walked back to the car. The snowfall thickened to a virtual white-out. Less than twenty feet separated the public servants, but they could not see each other.

Joe got behind the wheel and started the car. He turned the heater up full blast and routed the warm arm to the floor vents with the dashboard controls. Angela was still lightly massaging her ankle.

"Is it time for another round of pain meds?"

"No, it's okay. The wind is just brutal at these temperatures. It's settling down."

"We can stop somewhere and grab you a little something to eat if you need to take more, just say the word. The doc said the medicine goes down easier with food."

"Thanks, Joe."

"You're welcome, Partner."

They swung by the Precinct on the way. They wanted to get some of their paperwork finished and filed, and Angela wanted to see if the Coroner's office got the lab results from the autopsy they attended earlier that morning.

chapter eleven

Julie pulled herself together enough to shower and change clothes. She tried to eat but couldn't force herself. She choked down two bites devoid of flavor and pushed the plate away. She barely touched her pot of coffee.

After a couple of hours of anxiety-riddled waiting, Julie decided she needed to do something, anything, if she felt it could help Ellen. She wanted to start by walking to the diner so she could retrace Ellen's normal route back home. Julie was convinced, although she wasn't sure why, that Ellen made it part of the way home. She wrapped up in heavy clothes and a coat and stepped out into the cold. The brisk air stole her breath, making her stand still to allow her body to adjust. The frozen air hurt her lungs for the first several breaths, feeling like she swallowed several angry fire ants. Once she was able, she started the trek up Webster to Pratt's.

The walk wasn't very far, but it seemed to take a lifetime. Julie filled her mind with possibilities about Ellen's whereabouts, all of which had happy endings. When she reached the corner of Webster and 51st, she considered going inside to talk the Rick. She knew she would only loose her focus and break down, so she turned around and started, with resolve, back towards the apartment. She knew the route well because she made the trip with Ellen several times. On many occasions if she got away from the Black Knight early, she would go to the diner and wait for Ellen to get off work, like she did the last time she saw her.

Julie walked very slowly, scanning the sidewalk and the surrounding area for any clues. She paid close attention in front of Al's TV Repair where the sidewalk was cracked and uneven. It was an easy place to fall on the ice. Ellen always chose that over crossing the blacktop of Webster at that point. The street has a low spot that caught the runoff that froze solid in the winter. Ellen's view was that it was better to just fall on your butt than fall on your butt and get hit by a car.

The snowfall covered the sidewalk damage, and memory guided her over the safest parts. The street and gutter along the curb held a filthy conglomerate of frozen slush laced with oil, dirt, and debris.

Julie found herself back at the front porch to her apartment, her search yielding nothing. She didn't know what she expected to find, but she was hopeful that she would find something, anything. Her determination to find her friend was strong, so she decided to start again, convinced that she wasn't paying enough attention to detail.

The ice buried under the snow was very slick. She lost her footing and fell when she turned to walk back, hitting the concrete hard and knocking the air from her lungs. The palm of her left hand started to ache and throb immediately from trying to break her fall. The snow stung her face and eyes from her forehead connecting with the rock-hard sidewalk, and the pain from the blow immediately turned into an intense headache. She knew she didn't have a concussion, but that was just dumb luck. For all intents and purposes, she knew she should have been knocked unconscious for at least a few minutes.

She started pulling in her limbs to get up when something glinted in the corner of her eye. A parked car at the curb had no snow underneath it, meaning it had been parked there for a while. A small metal object reflected the beams from the headlights of the passing cars, calling for her attention.

Julie crawled to the curb on her hands and knees to investigate. The cold seeping into her hand numbed the pain from the fall to the point that it stopped hurting. Her clothes soaked up the cold water that melted under her body heat when she touched the ground. She could just reach the object under the car by lying flat on her stomach. The icy water attacked her skin as it soaked into her clothes, reaching her now unprotected body.

The shiny object was a small metal keychain holding a single key. The keychain's face bore a coat of arms on a green background with the words "The Black Knight" etched just below. Julie gave Ellen a keychain, just like this one, a few months earlier. She scrutinized the area under the car, hoping to find something else. The cold water soaking into her clothes became too painful and her head throbbed violently. She got back on all fours to get back up and started brushing the snow on the sidewalk into the street. Aside from the snow and ice, the sidewalk was also clean.

The delicate crystals riding on the wind bit into her skin ferociously. She knew each sting would make her skin glow a bright pink and her knuckles turn white. She finally walked to her front door when she mustered the strength, praying she wasn't holding Ellen's key. She put the key into the lock, telling herself it was coincidence.

The Black Knight was a popular club. Several people could have keychains.

111

She burst into tears when the lock's tumblers yielded and unlocked the door. Whatever happened to Ellen happened right here, not ten feet from the front door. A wave of guilt flowed over her, carrying a riptide of nausea right behind. She never heard a thing and was just inside when it happened.

Julie ran to the phone, barely able to dial the number as she trembled. She hoped that the key might be enough to get the police to do something. The phone rang four times before it was answered.

"New York Police Department 42nd Precinct, how can I help you?"

"I-need-to-speak-to-Officer-Smith-in-Missing-Persons-right-away!" she sputtered so rapidly that she sounded incoherent,

"Ma'am, can you please repeat that a little slower. I can't understand you."

"I need to speak to Officer Smith in Missing Persons. Please hurry!"

"Let me transfer you, one moment."

The phone made a familiar buzz following by a misleading silence, making Julie think the call had disconnected this time.

"Missing persons, this is Smith."

"Officer Smith, you've got to do something! I found Ellen's key! I know something has happened. Can you start looking for her now?"

"Whoa, slow down ma'am. You're talking faster than I can keep up. Try to slow down and let's start over. What can I do for you? Do you already have a case number?"

"This is Julie Romanoski, and yes, I have a case number. We spoke this morning about the disappearance of my roommate."

"I remember. What was the case number I gave you? It'll save us some time."

Julie looked for the notepad that usually rested by the phone.

"The case number is 235-JH5-732."

"Okay, give me a second to pull the information up. Here it is. What can I do for you Julie?"

"I found Ellen's house key under a car parked out front."

"Are you sure it's hers?"

"Yes, it's on a keychain I gave her a few months ago. I tried it on the lock on the front door to be certain."

Tears ran down Julie's cheeks. She was finding it difficult to speak as sadness swelled her throat. "Please help me," she sobbed.

"Okay, this is what I can do. Due to the discovery of the key, I can upgrade the case because we have reasonable suspicion of a crime. I'll have to send a unit out to ask you some questions and get a formal statement, and they'll also check out the diner, since that was the most likely the last time she was seen.

"Thank you."

Julie tried to lighten the tone of her voice to show appreciation, although the pleasantry did nothing for her sadness. She hung up the phone, went to the living room, and sat on the couch, ignoring how cold and wet she was.

Her thoughts swam in confusion and disbelief. She did not want to accept the fact that something happened to Ellen, even though she still held the discovered key. She was convinced that things like this only happened to other people. She stared at the key, thinking she could somehow undo what was happening by simply wishing it away. She refused to let hope slip from her heart, even though her mind told her it was hopeless.

A pair of uniformed officers sat at stools mounted along the polished mahogany lunch counter. The man working behind it paused long enough to fill the coffee cups they turned right side up and nodded in their direction.

"I'll be right with you, Officers."

He recradled the pot on the burner of the Bunn coffee maker and walked away, carrying a plate of food.

"I'm a little short-handed this morning. Sorry about the wait."

Officer Dupree set his radio and keys on the counter next to his coffee. His partner laid out a five by seven notebook and a pen. They drank their coffee while they waited for the waiter to return.

"What can I get for you today? We've got our nearly famous Rueben, and there's a pretty good matzah ball soup simmering back there, too, unless you want breakfast. We serve that all day, too."

"We're not actually here to eat, sir, but thank you anyway. I've heard a lot of good things about the food here though," replied Emilio. "We just want to warm up a little and have a few words with Mr. Rick Pratt."

"Well then, those coffees are on the house, and I'm the man you came to see. How can I help you?"

"We need to ask you some questions about Ellen Clark."

After she cleaned up and got into dry clothes, Julie found herself flipping the pages of the photo album she and Ellen started a few weeks after they started sharing the apartment, thinking about how they became friends. In the beginning, she answered an ad in the paper that Ellen ran, looking for a roommate.

Ellen was so particular that Julie was convinced she'd be rejected as a candidate without even getting to see the place. Ellen was a divorcee from an abusive marriage, finally able to get her feet back under her. She was very protective of her apartment and lifestyle, determined to maintain her independence after making the move from a single rented room. It took her almost a year to decide to look for a roommate. She didn't want to continue living alone, but she also didn't want to deal with any kind of new relationship while still nurturing a few deep, emotional scars.

When she called about the ad, Julie was new to New York, fresh off the bus from Kansas and filled with dreams of making it big on Broadway and being the next famous starlet. She loved theatre and decided New York was the best place to get started, even though the city scared her to death. She was in complete awe at the mere size of it, and surely looked like a lost tourist, gawking at all the things most inhabitants saw daily.

She expected to be turned away, yet Ellen offered her the room. Julie wasn't sure why at the time, but they hit it off from the start. Over the first few months they became great friends and relished in always having someone to talk to, confide in, and spend time getting the most out of New York. Ellen eventually told her that she saw a lot of herself in her young friend and she just couldn't bring herself to refuse letting the room. It was obvious that Julie was terrified, but Ellen sensed strong values of commitment and responsibility under the mask of fear the Midwestern girl wore.

Julie found herself staring at a picture of Ellen and herself at Coney Island. They paid an old man five dollars to take their picture in front of the roller coaster they just rode. He had a hard time figuring out how to operate the camera, so they ended up with about six pictures of the sky, the ground, or the man's thumb. The picture she focused on was the only one the man took that was decent. It was at an odd angle, but it got her and Ellen with the sign for the roller coaster and one of the cars climbing the first big rise.

A few pages closer to the front she found the photo that Ellen took of her in front of the Black Knight a few days after she was hired. Julie wore one of the costumes she donned at work and acted goofy, swooning over one of the suits of armor standing by the front door as if it were her damsel-rescuing savior. She kissed most of her lipstick onto the metal shell and the red kiss marks were visible in the photo.

Julie heard her tears drumming on the plastic cover protecting the pictures. She gave the keychain that now sat on the coffee table to Ellen just after her armor besmirching incident. Ellen had transferred her house key onto it right away so she'd see the gift every day and handled it as though it were a solid gold ingot.

"Has something happened to her?" asked Rick, obviously concerned and hopeful. He set the coffee pot back down and gave the police his undivided attention.

"That's what we came to talk to you about, Mr. Pratt. It seems you were the last person to see Ellen Clark."

"I guess I was, and I assume this means you haven't found her." Rick's demeanor changed from anxious to melancholy. His face visibly dropped, and his eyes swelled to the point that it looked like he might cry. "What can I answer for you?"

"How long have you known Ellen Clark, and what can you tell us about her?" asked Emilio.

"I've known her for about four years. She came here looking for a job to get away from her husband. Her marriage, if you could call it that, was falling apart. He was an alcoholic and very verbally, mentally, and physically abusive. She started working for me as a second job and packed away every dime. She even had me keep her pay for the first several weeks to make sure he didn't find out what she was doing. One night he came home after tying off one too many with a shade of lipstick on his face that Ellen never wore. He almost broke her arm when she asked him about the other woman. When he passed out, she grabbed everything she could manage and left.

"She asked for a few days off, which wasn't her style, and then asked about taking a full-time position and maybe getting some double shifts. I had the opening, so I gave it to her. I tried not to pry, but I recognized the address she gave me when she told me she moved. It was for a local shelter that I used to deliver food to with my father when I was a kid. I felt very bad for her, so I talked to my wife about renting her our extra room. My wife was a little reluctant at first, but she warmed up to the idea when I told her I suspected she was fleeing an abusive husband. My wife grew up with a stepfather like that, so she knew what Ellen was going through. They made an instant connection and got along very well.

"When the first month's rent was due, my wife wouldn't accept the money. Ellen worked hard for me at the diner and she worked just as hard at the house, helping with the chores and even watching our kids. She was more like family, you know, my kids even call her Aunt Ellen. Ellen's real family lives in the backwoods of Wisconsin somewhere. All she told us was that they had a big falling out when she was seventeen. She left home and never looked back, even though she came to New York with nothing more than a dream and about $14.

"She moved out a few years ago because she wanted her own place again, and she found one back here in the old neighborhood. Her ex-husband's mistress apparently had a husband with a bad temper, and Ellen's ex picked the wrong time to take a swing at him. He threw one solid punch, but the whiskey threw off his aim and he wound up face down in the street instead of flooring his opponent. The bus driver never even saw him. With her ex permanently out of the picture, she knew she could return safely. She still comes to have dinner with us at least once a week."

116

"Can you give us a rundown of what happened the last time you saw her?"

"Sure. It was a pretty typical night. We were busy until about ten o'clock with people coming in for a late dinner. After that, it whittled down to the regulars. We stay open until one in the morning every night and we usually get the same group of locals from around 11:00 until midnight, usually two or three times a week. They all happened to come in that night. They're never any trouble, but they tend to stay until closing time and it makes us get out late because we can't really start cleaning until they leave. I always stay late on Mondays to reconcile the books and take inventory for the week, so Ellen entertained them until one so I could finish. She offered to lock up for me since she had to finish mopping. I agreed and went home."

"So you left her here alone?"

"Yes, that's exactly what I did, and regardless of my protests, it wouldn't have ended up any other way. Ellen had her talk with me about it a long time ago. She said she was not going to live in fear any longer and she couldn't very well do that with me looking over her shoulder all the time. The first few times we had that argument, I left the diner, but I only drove around the block. I parked down the street until she left and followed her at a distance to make sure she got home okay. On the fourth night she told me she'd close up, and she joked that she would slash my tires if I followed her again instead of going home. I had no idea she knew."

"She sounds pretty independent."

"That will prove to be one of the understatements of the year."

"Do you how Ellen went home that night?"

"I'm sure she walked like always. She told me on several occasions that this neighborhood is her home, and with her ex gone, she felt the neighborhood was safe, even at night. Until now, she's never had a problem getting home."

"What happened after you left the diner?"

"I made sure everything was locked since Ellen was here alone and I drove home. I took a quick shower and went to bed. I get up at six in the morning to get the kids up and ready for school. My wife has to be at work at eight, so I try to help her out as much as I can since I don't have to be here until about ten."

"So Ellen was here by herself?"

"Yes."

"What time did you leave?"

"I left about a quarter after one."

"Was everything the way it should have been when you got here this morning?"

"Yes. The doors were locked and the alarm was armed."

"Which company services your alarm?"

"It's Long Island Security. Why do you ask?"

"We should be able to determine an exact time of departure for Ms. Clark. Security services are required to keep logs on their alarm systems. The log will show when the alarm was set last night, and they can tell us if it took an unusually long time for Ellen to leave. Does Ellen have her own code?"

"Yes. Ellen, Joyce, and I all have our own codes."

"Who's Joyce," asked Malcolm, giving Emilio a short break to finish writing down a few notes.

"She's the day waitress. She comes in at nine to set up the tables for the day."

"Do you know their codes?"

"No. The codes are set up over the phone through an automated system. The technicians at the security company don't even know the codes."

"Does Ellen always work the late shift?"

"Yes, I put Ellen on evenings and moved Joyce to the day shift a few months ago. Their shifts overlap in the afternoon when we're slow so some of the heavier cleaning can be handled by all of the employees."

"Did Joyce have any problem with the shift change?" asked Emilio, ready to take the lead again.

"No, not at all. She was relieved actually. Her husband promoted at his job and moved off of the graveyard shift. They almost never saw each other because one of them was at work while the other was at home. The change helped them both. Ellen wanted to work nights because she wanted to take a few classes at the local community college during the day."

"Do any of the other employees dislike Ellen?"

"Not at all – they all like her. The only other employee I have is Luciano, my cook. He gets along with everyone. I don't think I've ever seen him without a smile on his face. He respects Ellen very much because she's been helping him learn English since he started working here. He came from Guatemala a couple of years ago and he's trying to become a US citizen. He sees Ellen like a big sister. I haven't said anything about this to them yet, but I think they know something isn't right."

"When did you realize something was wrong?"

"It was this morning when I tried to reach her at home. I asked Ellen to come in early for the lunch rush today. She was supposed to be here at 11:00, but she never showed up. It's very unlike Ellen to be late, and she's never missed a day of work since she started working full time for me."

"How long have you known Ms. Clark?"

"I've known her for almost four years, like I told you a little while ago." Rick's tone was a little rougher, some of the polish worn out by the repetitive questioning, but it was the only sign that he was getting frustrated. He knew the police were just doing their job, even though that meant asking the same question in different ways.

Emilio took the last sip of his coffee to wet his throat and give his hand a short break from writing.

He's telling the truth.

"Who are the regulars you mentioned?" asked Malcolm.

"We had the whole group, like I said. John Bergowitz works the graveyard stocking shift for a local grocery store. He goes in at one and he usually stops in to eat on his way to work. Elliott Hill is a veteran in his eighties. He meets his friend Russell Miller here three nights a week for coffee, dessert, and conversation. They served together in the Pacific during World War II and they've both outlived their wives. Jennifer Tomlin is a college student. She comes in the most of the whole group. She does her homework and studies because her roommates like to stay up late and party. She sure can drink a lot of coffee. I don't see how she doesn't just vibrate all the time. Joe

Craven is the last one. He drives a cab for Checker and he gets his lunch break around midnight to one. He comes in about as often as the vets, unless he gets a big fare. They all pretty much know each other now and they sometimes even sit together. Elliott and Russell can keep them all entertained with their war stories, and Joe usually has a 'worst-fare-ever' story to share with them."

"Did any of these people stay until close?"

"No, they didn't. Elliott and Russell usually close us down, but I overheard Russell say he had a doctor's appointment early the next morning and something about getting old. They were the last to leave, about 12:40."

"Can you think of anything else that might help us find Ms. Clark?"

"No. I can't even see how what I've told you will help. I just pray that she's okay. I have no idea what I'm going to tell my wife and kids, or Joyce and Luciano for that matter, if she's not."

"Thank you for your time, Mr. Pratt. We'll be in touch," said Emilio as he stood up. "Please make sure you're available until we give you the okay; we may need to talk to you again."

"Am I a suspect?" asked Rick, making no attempt to conceal his shock.

"We have to make sure everything checks out, Mr. Pratt. Everyone is a suspect until the evidence we collect indicates otherwise. Please don't take it personally. It's routine procedure."

Malcolm picked up his radio and keys and followed Emilio out of the diner. They walked across the snow-covered parking lot to their squad car.

"Do you think he had anything to do with Ms. Clark's disappearance?" asked Malcolm.

"No, my instinct tells me he's on the up-and-up. Besides, he gave us too many ways to check his story and he wouldn't offer so much information if he had something to hide. I'll still run a check on him, but that's because it's procedure. I don't have an issue trusting him. I'll call Long Island Security when we get back to the Precinct if you'll start running backgrounds and records on the regulars."

"I'll check with the local hospitals, too. She could have been admitted as a Jane Doe if she was hurt."

"That's a good idea. I hope this doesn't turn out like so many of the others. According to Smith in missing persons, Ms. Clark's roommate found her house key just outside of their apartment. It appears that she almost made it home when this mystery began. I hate the sound of it, but I think we're dealing with foul play."

"I hope this isn't connected to the string of homicides they told us about in the morning briefing."

"I agree. Let's run down and talk to Ms. Romanowski. Her address is 2420 Webster, apartment C. I'd like to take a look at things there. If Ms. Clark made it that far, we may find something."

Malcolm pulled out of the diner's parking lot headed for Julie's and Ellen's apartment. The slush on the pavement allowed the tires little traction, forcing slow driving. It gave Emilio a chance to survey the surroundings.

chapcerčwelve

Joe parked the car in the INS parking lot for the second time. Infuriated couldn't accurately describe his mood, but it came close to the mark. He hated wasting time and energy, especially when someone's life hung in the balance. Angela forced him to promise he would stay calm as they entered the lobby.

The clock on the wall read four forty-five, indicating the office would close for the day in fifteen minutes. Joe and Angela cut directly through the lines of people, which were just as long as before, to the door leading to the back offices. They were certain they recognized some of the people waiting from their first visit as they parted the crowd. Angela lifted her hand to knock when it moved away from her fist. Joe was already pushing it open and hustling Angela through the doorway. She had to double-time to get in front of him in spite of her ankle. She was glad she left her crutch in the car.

"Remember, you promised to stay cool! Let me handle this – you'll attract more flies with honey, remember?"

"Okay, but you've only got fifteen minutes before I come in guns blazing."

"It's a deal."

She turned and headed for Wendell Harris' office. Joe felt a pang of guilt as he watched her walk away since her limp was markedly worse after rushing to gain ground on him.

Angela knocked on the office door, entering when allowed. Joe took his post in the hallway. Seth turned the corner, headed for somewhere, and almost killed himself stopping, turning, and going back the way he came in an effort to avoid Joe.

"Mr. Harris, we had a little trouble with the address you gave us. The apartment was vacant, and it looked like it's been that way for a while."

"That's odd. Let me check that file again. I've still got the reference number here on my desk. I'll cross reference it with the old system this time. Please, have a seat."

Angela slowly worked around the chair and sat down, using her arms to handle the bulk of her weight as she sat.

"Are you okay?"

"Yes. It's just a sprain. Thank you for asking."

"This won't take long. Can I get you a soda or some coffee?"

"No, thank you. We just ate."

He punched in the info the terminal requested.

"The address I gave you should be correct, but let me dig a little deeper."

He tapped a few buttons and clicked the mouse several times.

"There are some active notes here. The account on the new system didn't have any notes attached. My staff are generally very good about updating our information."

He clicked a few more times and called up a note the system flagged.

"This may be the problem. It looks like this file had an error when it tried to transfer into the new database. For some reason, the file updates didn't append. The base file was all that transferred. This update is from four months ago, and it says that Marina was going to move at the beginning of September. The forwarding address is here. Let me write it down for you. I'll have to contact our IT department to get this bug fixed. I wonder how many more files were affected this way by the upgrade?" he questioned as he handed over the new note.

"Thank you, Mr. Harris. I'm sorry to bother you again."

"Not a problem at all, my dear. Let me know if I can be of further service."

Angela limped out of the supervisor's office as the clock struck five.

"Okay, it's my turn," said Joe as he stood up, almost bumping into his partner.

"Joe, I got it!" she said, putting her hands on his chest to block the way, putting the note in his field of view. "I'll explain on the way."

She grabbed his arm and steered him in the direction of the lobby. They cut through the dwindling crowd and returned to the car, determined to get to the new address before they called it quits for the day.

"It looks like Marina wasn't very far from home after all, less than half a mile actually."

"That makes more sense," said Joe, as he worked the car into traffic. "Why didn't we get this address the first time?"

"The computer system and software were recently upgraded and all the files had to be transferred from one system to the next. Mr. Harris checked the new system this morning, but he didn't cross reference their case file with the old system until just now. The files were supposedly transferred from the old system to the new one, but only the base files copied over. All of the updates on Marina's file were still active in the old system. It seemed to surprise him, and he was concerned about how many other files suffered the same problem. I think he genuinely felt he gave us good info the first time."

"I'm hoping this isn't another dead end," said Joe flatly. "This case feels very strange and I just want to get it solved and closed, if there's a snowball's chance of that. It's as if something dropped out of the sky, killed John Doe and attacked Marina, then flew off into the ether without ever having to touch the ground. The only thing we have is the medic alert bracelet, and that doesn't seem to have anything to do with this case."

"Yeah, I'd call it creepy. The uniforms at the scene checked out the rest of the alley and found nothing. There's no other way out of that alley. We've got to find Marina; she's the only one who can tell us what happened."

"The only one except for the killer," Joe added.

Night fell on the metropolis as the detectives headed for the new address. The streets and sidewalks were bustling with people going about their normal lives in spite of the weather. Eateries were busy, cabs were flagged, and the snow continued to fall in a meager attempt to hide the blemishes. The thick cumulus trapped the glow of headlights, sodium vapor light poles, and neon shining up from the city, making an eternal dusk graced by delicate flakes of snow that swirled and danced as it traveled to the cold ground.

ChAPTER ThIRTEEN

Fred Jamison, Commissioner for the NYPD, settled into his oversized leather recliner and switched on the television. The chair was old, but the cushy seat was extremely comfortable, letting his muscles relax for the first time all day. He didn't bother to change out of his work clothes into something more relaxing, but he loosened his tie and unbuttoned the collar and cuffs of his shirt. Reaching for the cold bottle of Budweiser sitting on the end table, he clicked the remote to change the TV to Channel 17. He muted the game show that ran just before the seven o'clock news.

A man of forty-six years, he lived alone since the divorce. He was thirty-seven then. The one-bedroom apartment he called home for the last nine years was crude but functional. The furnishings were mediocre in quality and very spartan, much like a college student's first apartment. He was always at work, collecting overtime and going in on his days off, so he had little need for anything more.

Work consumed his life, which was one of the main reasons behind the divorce. He ran his hand over his buzz-cut hair and checked the time on the watch he was given by his Commanding Officer when he retired from the Navy. He turned up the volume as the newscast began, wanting to watch an interview he'd given a reporter for WJNY that morning.

The station was covering a charity program he developed. As Commissioner, he wasn't only responsible for keeping the department and its officers in line, but for handling the upper echelon of its public relations as well. His program was called "An Hour for the Children" and over seventy percent of the officers were already signed on. The enrollees would spend time each week with a child assigned to them. All of the children were from broken homes, and the goal was to provide mother and father figures for them. The officers would be paid for their time, but the wages would be directed into a central fund. The fund would be allowed to grow and earn interest until a workable amount was in the account; then, payments would be dispersed from the account to various local charities for children. Jamison felt the program was a good one, designed to help the kids and get some good PR for the department.

"Good evening. Welcome to the WJNY Channel 17 Evening News. The top story for today is unsettling, so all of you in the Big Apple better brace yourselves," said anchorwoman Denise Rigsby.

She was a very attractive natural blonde holding the post of star anchor. However, it had nothing to do with her skills as a reporter or her degree in mass communications. It was all about her miniskirts that rode too high, the plunging necklines of her tops, and her sympathetic shock style of speaking. She didn't leave much to the imagination with her looks or her storylines, but she generated good ratings, especially in the male demographics.

"It appears that some type of serial killer is running loose in our city and the police are refusing to comment."

Son of a...

"We learned of this heinous criminal when one of our reporters discovered this information."

She held up a packet of papers for dramatic effect. The Commissioner recognized it as one of the handouts Miles gave the force that morning.

"This file contains information about several other killings from the last few months. It describes the crimes in great detail and highlights what is believed to be the common thread between them, the murder weapon. We have an artist's rendering of it."

The image of the anchorwoman was replaced with a sketch. It looked like the red-headed bastard child from the mating of a meat hook and a pitchfork. A grip-sized handle housed a large metal shaft with bladed hooks attached to the opposite end at varying angles. The artist even made the hooks appear used, to increase the shock-and-awe.

Just when I thought it couldn't get worse.

Denise's voice transmitted as the sketch was displayed. "The killer has been dubbed as the 'Hook Man' because of the weapon he uses to mutilate his victims."

The drawing of the weapon reduced to a small box on the screen so the reporter could be seen with it simultaneously.

"Be careful out there, citizens of New York. I'm afraid we're in for a long, cold winter, and we don't know what the police are going to do about it. We'll be back after these messages."

126

The commissioner realized his lower jaw was sitting in his lap as a commercial ran for a local organic grocery store named the Garlic House. The newscast took him by complete surprise. Not only was the charity story bumped off, the reporter dropped a bomb on the police department, and almost half of the report was news to the Commissioner. He felt his blood pressure rise with his anger, making his face feel hot. Someone had some explaining to do. The whole thing turned into a media circus in a matter of minutes.

Sections of the city lost phone service as the number of calls grew exponentially until the switchboards overloaded and shut down. The calls that did get through to the police precincts ranged from scared single women to furious patriarchs, all of them wondering what the police intended to do about the "Hook Man". The frenzy of panic and fear sparked a wildfire that quickly engulfed the city.

Another gust front swept across the city as the next winter storm system arrived. All the people of New York could do was ride it out.

Jamison turned off the TV and swallowed the bottom half of his beer. He got up and went to the kitchen to start on the rest of his six-pack and start looking for the circus-inventing SOB when the phone rang. He walked to the refrigerator first and opened his next beer, already knowing who it was. He didn't really feel like talking to him just yet; he wanted to have answers before he was asked the questions. He chugged the longneck and opened the third bottle, picking up the phone after the sixteenth ring.

"Commissioner Jamison!" bellowed from the receiver. He quickly pulled the phone away from his ear, and even holding the receiver almost two feet away, the Mayor's voice was still very clear and loud. The Mayor's words were jumbled slightly at times; he was so mad he mixed some of his words together and didn't finish all of his sentences.

Jamison finished the third beer during the tirade, having enough time to start the fourth. He caught himself trying to smile, as some of the mayor's obscenities were exceptionally creative. The idea of the Mayor blowing up like this was comical since he was always known for his level-headedness. The Commissioner put the phone back to his ear after he heard, "What in the hell do you intend to do about this?" trail off into a silence.

"I'm sorry, Mayor Simmons. I don't know where the station got the information, but I'll find out. Internal Affairs will assist me since we apparently have a leak. I also have no idea where this 'Hook Man' business started, but I'll find that out too. About half of the story I never heard before now – I don't know if they made it up or what."

Another outburst, albeit shorter, came across the line.

"No, sir, I don't know why they didn't run the charity story. I know it was supposed to be the top story and I fully realize what this has done to the Department's reputation."

Jamison continued to drink as he finished listening to the Mayor.

"No, sir, it won't happen again. I'll get right on it."

Jamison started another beer as he sat back down in his easy chair. A rapid buzzing started in the kitchen, coming from the handset dangling from the wall mounted phone. He left it off of the hook after the Mayor finished his belittling and abusive monologue. The sound was a little irritating, but he knew it would timeout and stop soon. The alcohol wasn't hitting him hard enough to ease his anger. He just took the worst ass chewing of his professional life and he wanted to know who made it all possible.

chapter fourteen

"What's up Lefty?" asked Joel.

"I'm just trying to keep warm. It's really cold this year and the snow just won't let up."

Joel and Lefty shared the warmth emanating from a trash fire burning in a rusty fifty-five-gallon barrel. They were street people, living off of the wasteful habits of the city, barely able to stay clothed and fed. Thomas Gianelli stopped by their alley on the way home from the shelter with some extra food.

"Hey fellas, I've got some extras tonight I thought you might be interested in," he said as he gave the two men the sack full of food. "Where's the rest of your crew?"

"Who knows? It seems like a lot of the regulars don't come around no more. I'm surprised we ain't seen hide nor hair of Todd and Freddy, they's always here to get a free bite to eat," answered Lefty.

Lefty was a veteran, nicknamed such because he lost his right hand and forearm in Vietnam. He couldn't find a job that he was suited for because of the missing limb, and his disability checks from the government weren't enough to make ends meet. He couldn't remember how long he'd been on the streets. His graying hair was long in the back, just like his unkempt beard and moustache in the front. The small amount of face you could see was smudged and dirty. Even a reeking dumpster would choose to stand at a distance to avoid his body odor.

Joel was a down on his luck dock-worker, born and bred in New York. He took to a life in the streets after the company he worked for went belly up, leaving a few hundred workers without jobs. The company was the Thornquist Corporation, and his service was just under ten years. Unfortunately, it didn't mean anything to anyone else.

The few jobs that were available were always filled with younger, less experienced help. Joel expected as much; you didn't need a Ph.D. to work the docks and the younger guys could work longer hours and would settle for lower pay. Joel tried to stay as presentable as possible without easy access to things like hot water and soap. He kept his hair slicked back in a blackjack style ponytail that hid the frizz and some of the dirt. Some of the tattoos that covered his arms peeked through the holes in the shabby coat that he never seemed to take off.

"I seem to remember Todd saying Freddy was really excited about something, like he made a big score, but he didn't really know what is was about. Freddy wouldn't tell him anything else. I guess it's a big secret," said Joel.

The three men stood in silence for a few long moments, watching the flames jump around and enjoying the temporary respite from the cold. Lefty and Joel divided the food and stuffed most of it into pockets and other hiding places in their clothing. They each ate a little after the rest was stashed, only being seen with a little at a time was much more conducive to being left in peace by the other homeless.

Thomas left to go check on the two absent alley men. It was right on his way home and only a couple of blocks away. Todd and Freddy lived in the alley between 47th and 48th. He couldn't find them and no one had seen them for a day or two, so everyone assumed they really landed something good. It was an odd phenomenon that ran through the homeless populations. Thomas expected a group forced to live at rock bottom wouldn't have such an optimistic view, but the perspective may change when you have no farther to fall. In spite of the bright outlook, Thomas wasn't convinced about their situation and he wondered what really happened to them. The other people living in this unseen, impoverished world didn't live there by choice.

The backstreet was more affectionately known as Beggar's Alley. It was true to its namesake and it kept its secrets. Thomas wasn't sure why he was taking such a strong interest in the two homeless men, but he felt he was duty bound to make sure they were okay. It was not unusual for street people to come and go for several different reasons. They had a certain kinship, but it wasn't considered bad taste if someone broke free and never looked back.

The events from the nights before worked him over more than he realized, even though he kept telling himself it was probably nothing. Some street folk would get lucky and reenter society, while others were just docking into the port at the bottom of the world, struggling to learn how to survive. The fact that the two men seemingly disappeared without a trace was the strange part. A stroke of good luck was usually shared with the others, even if it was just for rubbing it in. This loose brotherhood existed with all of New York's street people. They all tried to look out for each other because they knew no one else would.

Thomas went to Todd's "house" first. Todd lived behind an old café on the north end of the alley in a little lean-to he fashioned himself underneath an old patio style cover used to keep rain and snow out of the trashcans. He didn't find anything helpful. Todd had a couple of old quilts and a tattered pillow, and an old, metal, military issue ammo box hanging in a dark corner near the ceiling. The box contained five votive candles, a box of matches, two small bottles of cheap wine, and some loose change. He put the box back just as he found it because it probably contained all that Todd currently owned in life other than the clothes on his back.

Freddy's place was a little farther north, on the opposite side of the alley. His living conditions were very similar to Thomas'. Freddy's place was also fashioned out of old refrigerator boxes. A dirty fragment of an old blanket served as a door, and the floor was covered with an army issue sleeping bag, probably from the local surplus store. It was strange to find it wasn't somehow concealed, being worth more than gold in this world during the winter.

He found a flashlight stuffed under the sleeping bag in one corner, and he noticed a couple of pictures attached to the ceiling. One was a snap shot of a young man in a uniform, an Army private looking very proud and virile. It was obvious that the man in the picture was Freddy. The other picture captured an attractive young lady sitting on a park bench waving to the person taking the picture. He guessed the woman was an old flame or an ex-wife.

As Thomas turned to leave, he noticed several cuts in the side of the box that butted up against the back of the building. He ran his hand over them, curious to their purpose. The side gave a little more than he expected under the light pressure. The cuts extended to the ground, forming a flap-door in the side of the box. The corrugated portal opened to reveal a broken out window leading into the basement of the building. All the shards were removed, leaving clean and easy access through the opening. Thomas grabbed the flashlight to look inside.

The flashlight didn't help much, but it was enough for Thomas to climb through the window safely. A couple of large crates pushed up against the wall under the window doubled as makeshift stairs. The room was about fifteen by twenty feet, with a large double door in the wall opposite the window. It was very dark, so Thomas moved cautiously as he looked around the room.

Something tickled his ear as he walked towards the door, making him flinch. It was the pull string hanging from the light fixture mounted in the ceiling. He was surprised when a pull on the string turned the light on. It was very weak, but enough to allow him to stop using the flashlight.

He thought he was in the basement of the old Piermont Theater, which had been condemned for years and meant no electrical service would run to the building. Thomas was not very familiar with the street side of the alley, and he realized that he could be in a different building. It looked like Freddy had a pretty good setup, which made it all the more unusual that he wasn't around.

The room he stood in was apparently used as a storage closet. Six rows of metal shelves, holding boxes of various sizes, stood in the space to the left of the door. The other end of the room was empty, but the floor was lined off with yellow and black markings, designating areas for large crate storage. Curved black markings, left by either a small forklift or crate dolly, linked this space to the door itself. The floor itself was completely devoid of dirt and trash, leading him to think that he might be in someone's active business. Thomas stood still and listened for several moments, hearing nothing.

With his curiosity piqued, he tried the door. It led to a dark hallway that ran both directions, so he switched the flashlight back on. He could see the end of the hall looking to the right, but the other end was beyond the flashlight's reach. He noticed right away that the hallway was extremely dusty except for a clean track through the center. The pattern looked to be caused by foot traffic, and as if someone walked down the hall recently. Thomas followed the path that led to the left, realizing the hall was wider than a normal hallway.

The hallway ran almost two hundred feet before turning to the right. It looked as if the hall ran all the way to the front of the building. The left wall of the hall was solid, but the right side offered four evenly spaced doors, two person-sized and two doubles like the smaller storage room. He walked to the second door, still following the path in the dust. He heard a low humming coming through it as he reached out to open it.

He stood, motionless and quiet for a moment, trying to identify the sound. The humming was rhythmic, unaccompanied by any other sounds, and it was much louder when he opened the door. An air compressor on the other side of the room was running. He guessed the tank must have a leak and it was maintaining pressure.

The room was very large and he discovered all four doors led to the same room. It was a garage with a door large enough for a vehicle to enter in the wall to his left, and it was full of various automotive tools and equipment. The path on the floor led to a long workbench along the back wall of the garage, supporting a peg board storage system on the wall above it. Some of the tools were gone, and he guessed that Freddy was slowly taking them to pawn off.

It looked as though Freddy had not gone anywhere else in the building, but Thomas made out a single faded set of footprints going away from the workbench in a different direction. They ended at another door that sat alone in the wall opposite from where he entered. Thomas followed the path and ended up in what was the front office. The rooms in this area were carpeted and paneled, obviously made suitable for conducting business. The office windows faced the street, but they were all boarded up. All of the office equipment and furniture remained in place, just like everything in the garage except for the missing tools. The chair behind the oversized desk was pulled out with the dust disturbed from someone sitting in it recently. Thomas sat down after he wiped the rest of dust off of the seat and inspected the desktop before him. It was covered with wildly strewn pieces of paper. Thomas couldn't imagine what Freddy hoped to find.

Officers Hernandez and Dupree left their police car at the curb and approached the door labeled 2420. A panel of buttons, labeled with the apartment's letters, were built into the wall to the right of the door. Through the glass, they could see the foyer that took up the center of the building. It was all stairs and landings that allowed access to all the apartment entry doors inside. Malcolm pressed "C," and after a few seconds a small voice came through the metal grille at the bottom of the panel.

"Yes?"

"Ms. Romanowski?"

"Yes," answered Julie.

"My name is Malcolm Dupree, and I'm here with my partner Emilio Hernandez from the NYPD. Officer Smith from missing persons sent us out to check on your roommate."

"Yes, just a minute."

A buzzing emanated from the metal panel and the lock disengaged, allowing the officers to enter the foyer. They climbed a half of a flight of stairs to the first landing. The apartment labeled "C" was to the left and the door opened with a soft creak as Emilio reached up to knock.

"Come in, please."

It was obvious that she had been crying. Her eyes were red and swollen, as was her nose from the repeated use of facial tissue. The distress on her face was nothing short of heartbreaking.

"Please, have a seat," she offered as she led them into the small living room. "Can I get you anything?" she asked, trying to be a good hostess in spite of the circumstances.

"No, thank you," said Malcolm, as the three sat in in the small living area.

"We wanted to touch base with you about the case," started Emilio. "We just spoke to Mr. Pratt about your roommate, but we need more information. We can narrow down the time of her disappearance with your help. We know she left the diner and about the time she did, but we don't know when she got here. What time did you get home that night?"

"It was just before two o'clock. I came in and tried to stay up until she got home. I fell asleep here at the kitchen table, knowing she'd wake me up when she came in."

"That narrows it down to about a one-hour window. We still don't know exactly what happened, but we're working on it," said Emilio.

Julie nodded her head in understanding. She didn't have the strength to actually speak.

"We are concerned about your safety as well. We don't want whatever happened to your roommate to happen to you. Take my card; it's got several numbers you can call if something happens. It will get you in touch with me and it'll be faster than 9-1-1."

Again, Julie only nodded.

"Is there anything else we can do to help you, Ms. Romanowski?" offered Malcolm.

Julie eked out a soft "no" and looked down at her feet.

They took their leave, letting themselves out and reminding her to lock the door behind them. They could see the tears welling up that she didn't want to release until they were gone.

ChApteR fiFteen

The pager clipped to the driver's hip beeped and displayed his office number on the crystal quartz screen. John Murphy was bound for home after thirteen hours of solid work, but apparently that wasn't enough by someone's standards. He desperately wanted to go home, eat, shower, and get some sleep. He looked longingly at the bag of Chinese takeout sitting in the passenger seat as he u-turned his car, knowing it would be cold before he got the chance to eat it. He moved his Corvette into the fast lane, accelerating as much as he could without losing control of the sports car, but unable to pull away from his frustration. He ate one of his egg rolls so he could have something before it got cold.

He was an excellent physician, and the city had to offer him several perks to give up his private practice. Bonuses aside, his long-standing friendship with Dr. Palmer was the real reason he took the job. Palmer was planning to retire and he wanted the responsibility for the Department to fall to someone he could trust, someone incorruptible.

Murphy worked as the assistant medical examiner, answering to Palmer while being groomed to take over the top job when the time came. He was paid well above average, and the job brought a certain amount of recognition. The long hours and the current life-on-call status were the undesirable aspects of the job, but they didn't outweigh the pros.

He pulled into the hospital's parking garage after he gained entry with his security card. He parked in his reserved space that was wider than normal and very close to the elevator. The luxury was afforded to all of the senior staff. At this hour, the garage was empty except for Dr. Palmer's Mercedes.

Why are you still here Allen?

Murphy boarded the elevator for the three-story ride up to sub-basement level one, holding his Kung Pao Chicken, hot and sour soup, and remaining egg rolls. The morgue, exam rooms, and coroner's offices consumed the entire floor. The city employed fifteen staff coroners, led by Drs. Palmer and Murphy, bringing the total to seventeen. He entered the main exam room in the morgue to find Dr. Palmer writing notes in his journal next to the two microscopes they used. Allen looked up when he heard the door open.

136

"Evening John, I'm glad you were able to come back so soon. Sorry for calling you back, and ruining your dinner, but I really want you to take a look at something for me." The look on Allen's face was not its normal seasoned and status quo demeanor. It was closer akin to fear. He had known Allen for many years; few things surprised him and he rarely showed any emotion close to concern.

"No problem. What's up?"

"I want to get your professional opinion. Take a look at the slide in the microscope on the left, and then take a look at the one in the other one."

Murphy approached the scope, curious, and asked, "What am I looking for?"

"Just look at the cells and tell me what you see."

He nodded and followed the instruction.

"It's a blood sample, obviously," he said as he looked up briefly at his senior. "I'm seeing a high amount of white blood cells, which tells me the donor suffered from some type of disease or infection, and all of the cells seem to be in the first stages of deterioration. It suggests the disease ravaged the donor's body, or this sample was taken shortly after death."

John looked up and faced at the senior examiner again.

"Allen, am I missing something? This is pretty much textbook stuff here."

"No, you're not. Take a look at the other one."

"This sample also has an abundance of white blood cells, but these cells are much more deteriorated. It just looks like old blood or a contaminated sample." He looked up again, puzzled. "I'm not following you here, Allen. What's this about?"

Dr. Palmer walked to an overhead projector and flipped the power switch, throwing the images of the two blood samples onto a large silver screen hanging against the wall.

"There was something about the autopsy on the John Doe this morning kept bothering me, but I couldn't put my finger on it. The discrepancy between our findings and the information Homicide provided just seemed too far off. I came back about an hour ago and started investigating from the beginning to make sure I didn't miss anything."

Allen pointed at the screen. "The connection between these two samples is that they are from the same donor, taken on the same day. The question of the day is how could these two samples come from the same corpse, namely John Doe, only hours apart?"

"That's not possible," remarked Murphy, guessing his face looked much like Allen's did when he arrived. "Those samples are days, if not weeks, apart in age – not hours. We both know that cells break down at a fixed rate after death, excluding unfavorable conditions in which the body is stored. That corpse has been here, maintained per protocol. This morning we determined the time of death to be no more than ninety-six hours prior to the autopsy. What am I saying? You were here when we did it. Homicide put the time of death approximately twelve hours before the autopsy. Are you positive the samples weren't mishandled?"

"That was my primary concern, which is why I took another sample just over an hour ago. The only indication it might be blood at all was the fact it still had a tinge from the hemoglobin. That's when I paged you. The slides were prepared less than twelve hours apart, and they are from the same donor."

"What is going on here? Did he have some type of rare disease that accelerates decomposition?"

"I don't think that's it. I've never heard of a disease that's capable of this. I've been searching the AMA database, and others, for a match, or even something close, but it's coming up empty. I also skimmed through some recent online medical journals and research publications, but I can't find anything there either."

"I think we should take another look at the body. We could be losing valuable information about this mystery as we speak if this is really happening."

John's mind was already buzzing with unanswered questions. His second wind took him by storm, leaving thoughts of Asian cuisine and fence jumping sheep in its wake.

"That was my thought, and another reason why I paged you. I'll start prepping the instruments and get my digital tape recorder if you'll go get the body."

"Will you grab me a smock while you're back there?" asked John.

"Yep." Murphy left the exam room, bound for cold storage, and Palmer went for his half of the job.

John was leaning against the empty exam table when Allen reentered the room.

"Where's our patient?" asked Palmer quizzically.

John said nothing as he walked towards the door, motioning Allen to follow.

"You have to see this for yourself."

Dr. Palmer followed the assistant medical examiner to the large cold storage room. Two of the walls were lined with drawers, looking like a bank of small, heavy-duty stainless-steel freezers. Each drawer slid out on high capacity rollers made to support the heaviest of corpses at full extension. The topmost drawers were chest high, allowing for three compartments vertically from the floor.

Murphy opened John Doe's assigned compartment and pulled out the drawer. The body rested on the metal surface of the drawer covered with a white gossamer sheet that rested in all the wrong ways. A rush of cold air escaped the drawer, expressing a putrid, rotten smell. Dr. Palmer could tell that something wasn't right, but his jaw dropped when John drew back the sheet.

"What could have done this?"

John Doe was nothing more than a blackened skeleton. The tissue was completely decomposed into a fine black powder, and the eye sockets revealed the empty skull. The shiny surface of the drawer peeked through the small piles of dust through the rib cage and the back of the skull.

"What happened to the body? And what happened here?" queried Palmer as he put on a pair of latex gloves, his attention turned the hole in the back of the skull.

"I don't know. That wasn't there this morning."

"Has anyone been down here? If this is a joke, it's not funny!" said Palmer in a loud voice, looking around the room, expecting half of the staff to appear out of the walls, laughing.

"I don't think this is a joke, Allen; it's just too much for a prank. I want to take a look at that hole."

139

John turned the skull to one side to take a look. Some of the vertebrae flaked away and fell to the tabletop from the stress, even though he was being very gentle. He ran his latex covered fingertip lightly over, around, and inside the area to examine the surface, letting his sense of touch draw a mental picture of the damage. The thicker bone withstood the friction of examination.

"This is a gunshot wound. From the size and shape of the hole, and the damage to the bone in the surrounding area, I would guess he was shot at close range with something powerful, like a .44. Let me borrow your pen."

Dr. Palmer surrendered his pen, which John used to project angles.

"The angle of entry suggests the shot was fired from a lower position, like the shooter was shorter than John Doe. The bullet path exits the skull through the left eye. I can feel tiny fragments of bone inside the skull. How can this be possible? We didn't see any tissue damage or scars when we did the autopsy, not to mention the fatality of this kind of injury. Even if he survived, by some miracle of God, he would have been a half-blind invalid in a vegetative state!"

"Let's run some more tests on what we do have. We've got to find some answers, and they're all in these bones," stated Palmer.

"We should also double-check the other cases the police mentioned in the memo issued earlier. We can cross-reference all the records to see if anything jumps out at us," added Murphy.

The two examiners worked long into the night, running every test that came to mind.

chapter sixteen

A knock sounded off of the thick wooden door, solidly three times, echoing through the silence.

"Yes."

The man, known only as Viktor, pushed the door open and entered the darkened chamber. A lone candle flickered on a table near the door, providing little light and leaving the back half of the room in total pitch darkness. Viktor seemed unaffected by the acrid fumes hanging in the air, musty motes masking decay and sickness.

"Why have you disturbed my sleep, Viktor?"

"I beg your forgiveness, Master, but I come with a message from Arkits. I felt you would not want to wait to hear it."

"Really, and what did he have to say?"

"He was very adamant in his demand that you be more cautious. He said the local authorities approached him about one of the arrangements. He threatened to stop offering his services if it happens again."

The master laughed slightly.

"Why do you find this humorous, Master? This mortal is challenging you."

"Viktor, your concern is trivial. Arkits has no idea what our deal is, and he is obviously too naive to realize that he's not in a position to make demands. He is nothing more than a convenience, expendable and easily replaced."

"Shall we pay him a visit to remind him of the terms?"

"No, I will handle it personally. I don't want him to think I won't handle my own matters. He needs to be reminded who is in charge."

Viktor softly closed the heavy door behind him as he left. It placed him back in the main boarding area of an abandoned subway station. The city closed and bricked it off from the rest of the network after they finished adding newer tunnels. It provided a perfect location for a small group to hide without discovery.

Viktor was the clan's second in command, earning that status in the scant two years he followed his Master. His skills made him the perfect candidate. Oddly, he couldn't remember anything before his service began, but the lack of memories didn't bother him. The others would be out until early morning, but Viktor would venture out for a couple of hours in the dead of the night, only what was necessary.

The clock in the terminal struck two in the morning, serving as an alarm for Viktor. He entered the night looking to slake his thirst. The bars just closed, giving him exactly what he wanted.

Trokar sat in his chamber, memorizing the text before him after Victor's departure. He ran the incantations through his mind over and over, making sure he understood all of the subtle nuances. He knew the passages from the three books he possessed from cover to cover, but one wrong inflection of voice could cause violent side effects instead of the desired result. He wasn't concentrating as hard as necessary because the problem with Arkits, as well as the unknown status of the missing book for which he sought, nipped at the edge of his mind.

His lifelong search for the book led him to New York almost a year earlier. He left England after he made arrangements with Sayer to transport the book, and it should have been waiting for him when he arrived, considering the slowness required of his trip across the Atlantic. Sayer could not be reached, and Trokar never got the final destination from him. He was forced to have his clan search all of the local ports to try and find it.

Chapter Seventeen

Candice ran down the path, unable to find her voice. She was bound for home from her study group at the junior college she attended, deciding to cut through Central Park to save time even though she knew better. Now, she felt like she was running for her life. She had already shed her backpack and purse in her flight and forgotten about them.

A man dressed in black blocked her path as she reached the center of the park. The sight of the man didn't startle or scare her. She just stood there, staring, while her mind started tripping like a five-alarm fire. She was directly in front of him, looking, as if in a trance. She didn't know why she just stood there instead of fleeing.

Fear set in when he reached out and grabbed the front of her shirt, ripping small holes in the fabric and almost pulling her to the ground. His nails brushed her skin ever so lightly, leaving a razor burn sensation in their wake. She realized she could move.

She bolted towards the trees just off of the path hoping to find cover. The brush and brambles cut her face and caught on her clothing as she ran away from her assailant. Sturdier branches and brambles ripped more holes in her top. One caught on her bra, twisting her body until the thorn broke and the branch left a shallow gash across her side. He was right on her heels every time she glanced back.

"That's right, little girl, I want you to run," Mekune spoke in a whisper just loud enough for her to hear.

She felt more burns slash down her back and the back of her thighs. The slices didn't feel deep, but they were enough to draw blood and burn intensely. The skirt, leggings, and undergarments she wore were riddled with tiny slashes and holes; the contact was almost enough to push her forward to the ground.

She tried to find a way out of the thicket as she ran, hoping she would have a better chance to gain distance in the open. A firm blow to the center of her back hurtled her forward, crashing her through a row of bushes and into a small clearing and roughly landing face first on the frozen ground. The snow stung her skin as she slid through it, offering no padding for the fall. The cold numbed the cuts, but she couldn't catch the breath the impact knocked from her lungs. She regained her footing as quickly as she could, but her legs refused to run. She stood, tears running down her face, as short breaths of air entered her lungs.

Mekune emerged from the trees, walking within arm's length. He did not speak, but he grinned as he looked her over with a sinister expression. He was completely clean and orderly, which puzzled Candice in spite of her predicament. His clothing was still intact as well, even though he held chase along the same prickly path. His skin was very pale, appearing almost pure white in contrast to his clothes.

"Quite the feisty one, aren't you? We're playing by my rules, my sweet. It must be absolutely terrifying to know you must escape to survive, but you just can't and you don't know why."

He circled around her slowly, letting the backside of a nail make contact here and there, sending chills up her spine.

"How does it feel to know that you are no more than a piece of meat that will be used and discarded?"

The realization of utter helplessness washed over her with the force of a tidal wave as a snow laced gust of wind pushed through the clearing. The cold air pushed through the holes in her clothing, attacking her skin directly where it wasn't numb, causing the cuts to throb.

"My, my, what do we have here?" said another voice from behind.

She didn't think anyone else was around, but she knew this addition wasn't to her benefit. She was surprised she could actually turn her head to look, seeing a second man, also dressed in black, approaching her.

"You've found a nice one, Mekune," said Damok. "I think we should have a little fun with this one."

Another surge of tears cascaded down her cheeks.

Damok snapped his fingers and three more men emerged from the edge of the clearing. She was on display for the five men that circled her, closing the radius in a coyote-like fashion.

Damok put his hands, that were colder than the snow, on her body, not skipping anything. Each of them went in turn, feeling her where they chose and adding new scratches where it suited them.

Mekune took over and grabbed her right arm, closing his mouth over her now exposed shoulder and puncturing her tender flesh. He backed away, his lips brushed with fresh blood.

144

Candice felt a hot rush from the two holes and realized she could move. She lurched for the edge of the clearing, but another cold hand caught her by the throat and threw her to the ground. She kicked and struck out as she felt ten hands on her body, groping and pressing, but she was no match for even one of them. She closed her eyes as each one descended on her, methodically destroying her weakening resistance. She felt several sharp, intense pains, at points all over her body. She was unable to look, unable to understand, unable to move.

All at once, the weight on her was gone and she opened her eyes. She found herself alone, broken and flat on her back in the clearing and losing feeling from exposure to the cold. What was left of her clothes and her exposed skin was tinted red with her own blood and the snow around her was slowly turning crimson. She tried to sit up, but she was too weak to move. The word "why" formed in her mind as she blacked out.

New snow fell, sticking to the cooling wet of her skin as her body lost temperature. It quickly covered her body, the blood-soaked snow, and all the evidence of the attack.

Mekune left Central Park through one of the gates along the north side. The pink backpack and purse strung over his shoulder contrasted sharply against his black attire. None of the city's early risers would pay any notice. Stranger things happened.

chapter eighteen

The day started poorly for Angela. Her night was again plagued by graphic nightmares that slipped from her consciousness when she tried to focus on them. She woke in a cold sweat, rigid with tension, her mind filled with fantasies about the scene in the alley and the body in the dumpster to visions she couldn't decipher. She guessed she was just overly nervous and concerned about the killer. She got out of bed, wrapped in her robe, and walked slowly to her desk. The pain in her ankle shifted between dull aches and sharper pains, but she knew had to move it to keep it from becoming any harder to use.

Disturbing scenes of computerized fish in a digital aquarium, she woke her computer and sent a quick e-mail to her mother. The phone didn't ring in response this time, but it was earlier than she usually rose each day, and the simple action of doing it helped ease her mind.

She went to the kitchen and opened the small cabinet above the refrigerator. She chose the bottle of Stranahan's single malt and poured a shot. She rarely drank and her lack of appreciation for it was obvious. The tepid liquor stole her breath and burned as it went down her throat, but it took the edge off her nerves. She returned to bed and finally drifted into peaceful sleep around four in the morning for a scant three hours.

Duty Sergeant O'Toole called roll, just like every morning. Only two officers were absent, partly due to the fact that it was a good day and partly due to the panic taking its toll on the city. The media got everyone's attention with their "Hook Man" story and the phones at all the Precincts wouldn't stop ringing.

"Okay you Gurriers, let's get started. I'm sure everyone knows about the media circus from last night's newscast, which means our jobs are about to get much harder. We got a lot of complaints and everyone is effin' and blindin' from the Mayor on down. We have to do everything by the numbers out there."

He paused for a sip of coffee and to check his notes.

"We don't know very much about what's going on. The Coroner's office is working diligently to get answers and we should know a lot more at that time. I'm cutting the briefing short today so you can all get out there. I want hourly check-ins from everyone until we get to the bottom of this. No excuses. We'll transmit the key elements from the Coroner's report to your on-boards when we have them. You're dismissed."

The group of men and women filed out, somber and miserable.

She slept through her alarm, waking up over an hour late, exhausted and sporting a massive headache. She got ready for work as fast as she could with the pains inside her head and ankle. The swelling was almost gone, but a little remained that sleep created, filled with an area-wide ache. She didn't have time for her morning coffee or the will to iron her pant suit. Needless to say, Angela Benson was irritated. She called a cab for the ride to the precinct, unsure if she trusted her ankle enough to drive.

She tipped the cabbie as she finished the last chocolate donut of her makeshift breakfast and saw Joe waiting in their squad car.

"Sorry I'm late."

"Don't worry about it. I figured as much with that ankle of yours. That's why I didn't come by this morning; you're in line for using a sick day. Things like that always hurt more the second and third day. By the way, we're having a meeting with some of the higher ups at ten because they want to go over concerns and the Coroner's findings in private, but we've got some time. Let me buy you something real for breakfast."

The detectives left the garage, heading towards a restaurant that promised a good morning meal. Angela eased out the breath she was holding, trying to keep her sigh of relief inaudible. She expected a reprimand for being late, not a free meal.

"Looks like you had a rough night. You really look like hell."

"Why thank you, Joe. You really know how to make a girl feel special, and I'm suddenly feeling so much better. I was beginning to think you didn't love me anymore."

"No need to doubt me partner. I'm not trying to be mean and I'm not talking about your bumps and bruises. You look like you've been through a mental ringer. I thought you might want to talk about it."

Angela felt her cheeks flush. Joe caught her off guard again, especially with his concern. The hint of affection in his voice when he said 'partner' was becoming more and more evident.

"Thanks, Joe. I just…. I didn't sleep very well. I keep having the same nightmare over and over, ever since we took this case. It's…well…really creeping me out."

"How so?"

She turned in the seat to face him.

"I can't quite put my finger on it. It's very vivid, but I can't focus on the details. I always wake up feeling like I'm missing something important, something I'm supposed to see. The only sure thing is a feeling of wrongness. Does that make sense?"

"Yeah, I've had those before. My shrink said that your brain uses your dreams as a way to work out problems that you weren't able to solve during the day. What you dream is a type of metaphorical representation of something real in your life, and your brain keeps running through all the possibilities, looking for a solution."

"Really?"

"As I live and breathe."

"No, I mean you have a shrink?"

"Sure. Doesn't everybody?"

Marina woke up feeling rested and exhausted at the same time. She was in her apartment, but it didn't feel right. She was at a loss, confused and disoriented, lying on her couch, fully clothed, and not knowing how she got there. The muscles on one side of her neck were sore, probably from sleeping at such an extreme, odd angle. She stood up, looking towards her wall clock in an attempt to gain her bearings. Her entire body ached as she moved and stretched, but she couldn't imagine why.

The mystery lunged to terrifying depths when she realized her blouse was caked with dried blood. The fabric stiffly held its shape, pressing against her body in an odd fashion. In a state of panic, she pulled off her clothes to see where she was bleeding. A thin red tinge, in the pattern of the top's fabric, covered her skin from the neck, down over her chest to her waste. A few lines of it ran down her right leg to just above the knee as well. She ran to the bathroom to continue her self-inspection in the mirror. She looked over her entire body, but she could not find any sign of a cut or a wound, just bloody residue.

If the blood isn't mine, whose is it?

Her stomach twisted into knots and her knees weakened. She collapsed to the floor, sitting in a crumpled heap on the cold tile, trying to ward off waves of nausea and dizziness.

A reserve of inner strength filled her and she jumped up and into the shower, turning the water on as hot as she could stand. She bathed vigorously four times trying to cleanse her body, each with a new washcloth. She looked at herself in the mirror after she dried off. Her tan skin radiated a bright pink from the near-scalding water, looking like she was sun burnt over most of her body. She double-checked her head and neck, looking for any type of cut or abrasion, anything to explain the blood. Her search yielded nothing and she realized from her reflection that she was crying.

She swam in the blackness of total loss and confusion with no recollection of the last several hours. The only clue she did have was the bloodied clothes on her living room floor. She got a pair of rubber gloves and threw the clothes into the laundry hamper. It never occurred to her to throw the clothing away. The severe state of shock she slipped into induced denial and called for familiar routines. Out of sight and out of mind was all her psyche could handle.

She found herself sitting at her kitchen table drinking coffee. She didn't remember making it, or even the trip to the kitchen from the bathroom. Her hands trembled at sporadic intervals, sloshing hot coffee over the sides of the cup and onto her hands. She felt the brew scald her skin, but she couldn't let go. The pain was tangible, giving her something to focus on and use as a bridge to her sanity. Vertigo battled relentlessly to take control of her soul, but she kept it at bay and regained enough composure to realize what she needed to do.

Joe and Angela entered the conference room just before ten o'clock. Everyone was present except the senior medical examiner, but he had called ahead, advising the group he would be there no more than fifteen minutes late.

As they waited, Joe's thoughts drifted to the old days when he was a beat cop out on the streets with his old partner. At the time, Bishop was a rookie, and the Commissioner served as the duty sergeant. Joe worked up to Detective and stayed there, just like Tom, wanting to stay in the action. He was eleven years younger than Tom and the senior officer mentored him. He learned everything from Tom, and it was all Old School.

On a dreary winter night in the distant past, Joe and Tom were responding to a request for backup from a pair of uniformed officers. They pulled over a car that was swerving erratically along a rural stretch of the freeway. At first, it appeared to be a standard DWI traffic stop. The driver pulled to the shoulder, stopped, and rolled down his window. Senior Officer Jason Mattox, approached the driver's side to make the standard requests while his partner, Eddie Wakowski, took a position at the rear passenger side of the car.

Mattox never even saw the gun in the dark. Eddie saw the blood explode from the exit wound in Jason's back as the sound of the gunshot reached his ears. The driver threw the car into drive to flee when Wakowski opened fire on the car. Of the four shots fired, one was found in the trunk, one ruptured the front passenger side tire, one shattered the rear window, and the last found the driver's right arm. The blown tire and the wound was enough to cause the driver to lose control. He slid off of the road and ran headlong into a tree.

Eddie was able to call for help and get his partner off of the blood-soaked pavement by the time the detectives arrived. Luckily, they were already in the area and the first on the scene. Wakowski yelled for them to get the drunk driver as he tended to his fallen partner.

Tom and Joe approached the car slowly, guns drawn. There was no movement in the crashed sports car, but the passenger door was open. They quickly found tracks in the snow that lead into the trees, dotted with drops of blood. The path led them to the driver. He was leaning against a tree, blood running over his right hand and the gun he held in it, dripping off of the barrel to the snow-covered ground. When he saw the detectives approach, he used the strength he had left to pull the gun into firing position.

Joe fired first and his aim was true, but neither of them saw the girl hiding behind the tree. She tried to shield her boyfriend and took the bullet in the chest. Tom's shot hit the driver in the head, killing him just before he pulled the trigger and shot Joe.

The driver was a meth addict named Leonard Hudgens. The blood toxicology from his autopsy confirmed a significant level of his drug of choice in his system at the time of his death.

His girlfriend's name was Carla Angela Swanson. She was a nineteen-year-old sophomore in college and generally a good kid. She made good grades, her parents were very proud of her, and she was on her way to becoming a veterinarian. She got mixed up in Lenny's world, convinced that she loved him and that she could get him off the drugs.

Lenny and Carla had gone out for dinner and a drive that night, but she didn't know he took two hits when he went to the restroom. They were on the freeway when the rush hit him, leading to the tragic string of events.

Joe and Tom were investigated per procedure and found to be free of wrong doing or error, but Joe didn't see it that way. He was unable to forgive himself for Carla's death, even though her own family could.

He requested a few weeks of desk duty and was on the verge of resigning from the force. Tom soon realized that his partner was not just going to bounce back like always, so he went to the only person he thought could help. That was the first time Joe ate at Flip's Astoria. Tom retired from service seven years later, making way for Angela to become Joe's new partner and the roles reversed; the student became the teacher.

"What's wrong Joe?" Angela whispered, pulling him from his reverie and trying to read his expression. He was looking at her much like the way a father looks at his little girl on her wedding day. He didn't realize he was doing it until Angela broke his concentration.

"Oh, it's nothing. You've just got some toast crumbs on your cheek. They're stuck in that little dab of jelly."

"Oh my God, I do!" she mouthed, digging in her small purse for a pocket mirror and Kleenex when she heard Joe snickering. Angela made a quick check and shot him a rude glance, acting like she was angry. She was learning to expect his sense of humor, and she enjoyed it, although it would come hell or high water before she'd ever tell him. She chose not to pursue the feeling she had that something was bothering him.

It was almost noon when the meeting ended. Joe and Angela headed for the new address they obtained from INS, both convinced that Marina was the key to finding the killer.

chapter nineteen

Michelle, the receptionist, answered the phone. The sky-blue letters WJNY were emblazoned on the front face of the desk where she sat.

"Good morning. WJNY, Channel 17, how may I direct your call?"

"I'd like to speak to the station manager."

"He's in a meeting at the moment. I'd be happy to take a message for you."

The caller's tone changed from pleasant to livid in the space of one breath.

"This is Police Commissioner Jamison. You need to get the station manager out of his damn meeting and onto the damn phone right now! I've already got half a mind to shut your worthless station down for as long as I deem necessary, which is rapidly approaching forever!"

Michelle was taken back, unsure how to handle the call, so she put Jamison on hold and buzzed Mr. Adams during the meeting. Jamison listened to the stale hold music, getting madder with every lame note.

The intercom in the meeting room beeped, calling attention to it. Jack Adams ignored the interruption and continued without pause.

"Gentleman and ladies, our ratings are climbing off of the charts! Praise the 'Hook Man'! Everyone is tuned in for miles and that's exactly what we need. The public just loves flashy journalism and it's putting City Hall in a bad light at the same time. This is a journalist's wet dream! I want you all to hit this hard and keep the exclusives coming."

The intercom beeped again. Jack still acted as though he didn't notice.

"I want you to get in touch with the national networks and get this story on every TV in America. The advertisers will be begging us to air their spots and we'll have it made!"

The buzzer sounded a third time. With irritation, Jack walked to it and pressed the button to offer his response.

"This had better be good."

"Mr. Adams, I'm sorry to bother you..."

"Then why did you?"

"I've...um...got the...Police Commissioner on hold. He said it's urgent that he speaks to you."

"That's nice, Michelle, but I don't really care who it is. Take a message, like I told you when I said I didn't want to be disturbed and I'll call him back when I get around to it!"

"He's very adamant, sir. He mentioned taking us off of the air."

Jack threw a maniacal glance at the intercom.

"That pompous ass doesn't have the authority or the right! Put that blowhard through right now, right to the intercom. I'll deal with him. Where does he get off thinking he can waltz in here and pull the plug – he's got another thing coming!"

"Yes sir."

The intercom speaker fell silent as the call transferred. The low beep alerted the room that the call was live and the caller could now hear what was being said.

"Jack Adams, Station Manager," he introduced, using a tone of voice that was disgustingly sweet and sincere.

"Mr. Adams, this is Police Commissioner Fred Jamison. In light of the newscast your station chose to run last night during the seven o'clock hour, you are hereby ordered to cease and desist your 'Hook Man' broadcasts."

Jack looked very smug and confident, making a face to indicate that he thought Jamison was a complete idiot and utterly unable to match wits with him.

"I'm quite sure you think you are in a position to order me to do that, but you are not. Our First Amendment rights allow us to tell the public. You cannot infringe our freedom of speech."

The other meeting attendees cast nervous glances at each other, unsure of what they should do, if anything other than stay silent.

"If that's the way you feel about it, I can take care of this very quickly. The story you ran contained more fabrication than truth, but I can handle both. The latter is confidential evidence in a pending homicide case and the release of that information is hindering an official investigation, which is against the law. The rest of the story, the part someone in your office made up and threw the city into a panic, which is inciting a riot and also illegal. After the story aired, the phone lines

154

were so tied up with calls the city's switchboard overloaded and shut down. 9-1-1 service was lost for over two hours. Not only is this direct interference with official police business, it puts you directly responsible for any damages that occurred during that time frame. If someone died of a heart attack because they couldn't make a 9-1-1 call, that death will be added to the other charges I already have against you."

"Charges, what charges? You can't charge me with..."

This time Jamison did the cutting off.

"I can and have. I have a warrant for your arrest. The judge was gracious enough to allow me the freedom to handle this warrant any way I see fit. Considering your opening comments, where should I send my officers to pick you up, unless you'd like to discuss your options?"

Jack's face flushed to the point it looked like all the blood in his body was trapped behind his face. No one had the right to speak to him that way, especially in front of the rabble that worked for him. He would not allow this disruption of his authority to go on.

"Commissioner, I'm transferring this call to my office so we can straighten this out."

Adams transferred the call.

"You all get back to work. I'll be making the rounds after I handle this jerk off!"

He excused himself from the meeting and made a beeline for his office. The meeting room was silent when he slammed the door. They waited long enough for him to reach his office before the outbursts of laughter began. Some of the people laughed so hard they cried, while others made flamboyant mockery of the man that just left. They all hated Jack Adams for the pompous ass he was and anything negative happening at his expense was welcome.

"Commissioner," started Jack as he picked up the phone in his office, "what do you expect me to do?"

"I thought you might see it that way. You need to run a retraction during the next newscast, and I don't mean during the end credits when no one is watching. I expect you to run it at the top of the show. The parts of the story that were made up need to be corrected and you need to inform the public that they can call the non-emergency number to get all of the information that is cleared for release. We have the right to withhold certain types of information when it's in the best interest of the public's safety. You seem to have such a working knowledge of the law, surely you are aware of that."

Jack listened, fuming. He couldn't stand losing, and he truly despised anyone getting the better of him, and the hint of sarcasm in Jamison's voice was just icing on the cake. Jamison put himself on the top of Jack's list labeled "revenge." He was, at least, relieved that he was alone this time. All journalists knew that the police had the right to withhold information, but most chose to ignore it since the consequences were never enforced.

"Yes, I can see how this made your life more difficult. I will speak to the crew about the matter. We'll have that retraction on the air at seven o'clock."

"Perfect. I hope we don't have to discuss this matter further."

The Commissioner hung up before Jack had a chance to respond. Jack always got the last word and being thwarted again tied his insides into tight little knots. The veins on his forehead looked as though they would rupture, split open his forehead, and finally allow the vile little creature inside to get out and show itself to the world. His mind started working on a way to even up with the Commissioner and get around his threats.

Jamison called the Mayor's office and left a message. He wasn't ready to talk to him directly, but he wanted to let him know that the problem they discussed was resolved.

The door to Jack Adams' office slammed shut hard enough to knock a picture off the wall, shattering the glass when it hit the floor. The entire office took notice as Jack stormed back through the work area, bound for the elevator. The path in front of him cleared like Moses parting the Red Sea. Workers either stepped aside inconspicuously or scattered like mice. The buzz of curiosity took flight after the elevator doors shut, taking the tyrant to another floor.

Adams walked into Denise Rigsby's office without as much as a knock. She had her back to the door, which was a good thing since she was topless. She was changing clothes to get ready for the lunchtime newscast when he burst in, but she didn't get upset when she saw who it was. He wasn't seeing anything new.

The fact that Jack was married didn't stop him from sleeping with her. His wife was too wrapped up in her own social events to notice what was happening, if she would even care if she did know. They rarely saw one another and had little to say when they did. He was convinced that she was sleeping with someone else, but he didn't care either. They maintained the status quo to avoid a messy divorce that would undoubtedly go public. He didn't have any particular interest in her or any desire to have a meaningful relationship. He was only in his marriage for the physical gratification.

Denise didn't care about him either, but his happiness kept her at the star anchor post and continued sexual favors would keep it that way. She let him do what he wanted to do to her and it drove him wild. He not only got off on the experience itself, but the illusion of power he held over her invigorated him.

"I like it when you're forceful and domineering," she said coyly as she dropped her top and unbuttoned her skirt, revealing her entire body to him. "Do you want me to just bend over the desk? I like it when you're rough."

"I'm just ecstatic about that," he answered with a sarcastic tone. "This is business."

Denise put her clothes back on, irritated. She would find a way to make him regret that remark later.

"What's up, Jack? You better make this quick, I've got the midday report starting in a few minutes."

"You go on when I say you go on! This is about the 'Hook Man' story. The police Commissioner just called and threatened to pull the plug if we don't play by his rules."

"I imagine that just burns you up, doesn't it?" added Denise with a pointing hand gesture.

He grabbed her wrist and twisted it roughly.

"I'm not playing games with you! You will run a retraction about last night's newscast, but you'll do it in a way that won't hurt our ratings! Is that understood?"

"You're hurting me."

"Is that understood?"

He squeezed tight enough to make his own hand ache.

"Yes," whimpered Denise, pulling away as soon as he loosened his grip.

"That's what happens when you cross me. Don't think I can't find another piece of ass to sit in the anchor chair."

Denise's gaze could have burnt a hole through a mountain. She was furious at Jack for hurting her, and she was even madder at herself for losing some of her control. She didn't have a trump card to get it back, not yet. He was virtually untouchable and acted like a heartless dictator to prove it. The other employees agreed when the "tator" was left off that moniker.

Denise sat for a few moments, plotting her next move and massaging her wrist and forearm. The purple ring forming there darkened with each heartbeat until it was an angry, ugly bruise. She looked for another top that had long enough sleeves so she wouldn't have to offer any explanations.

chapter twenty

The apartment building Joe stopped in front of looked much worse than the first one. The tenement was run down and old, but it seemed to be holding together. Joe credited the craftsmen from the old days. They didn't build anything shoddy back then. It wasn't a fault of theirs that it wasn't being maintained.

"I hope this one is better than the last one," mused Joe.

"I'm not getting my hopes up. I just hope I don't manage to tear up my good ankle this time."

Angela wasn't very happy about the expected interior or the stairs to climb. Some of the swelling had already returned to her ankle and the apartment they sought was on the seventh floor.

The inside of the building was in surprisingly good shape, obviously taken care of with earnest. The stairs, the focus of Angela's attention, looked very solid. The carpet pile was slightly worn down, but it didn't show any holes or excessive damage. Joe stayed behind Angela as they ascended the flights. He wasn't concerned about the stairs giving way, but he didn't hold the same confidence in Angela's ankle.

They reached the seventh floor without incident. A sign at the top of the landing directed them to the right down the hall.

Joe knocked firmly on the door marked 723. It sounded as though the frame might splinter away taking some of the wall with it. The door remained closed. Joe knocked again, as hard as the first time. They couldn't hear any sounds from within the apartment. Due to Marina's importance to the case, and the potential harm that could come to her without police assistance, they had no choice but to expect the worst and act accordingly.

Joe unholstered his service revolver and announced he was a police officer. He kicked the door open, entering cautiously, and Angela followed according to SOP. She wasn't sure the force was necessary, but all she could do was back her partner, regardless of her take on the situation. They went room by room, meeting in the kitchen, where they holstered their weapons.

"Was that really necessary?" asked Angela, trying to keep her weight on her good leg.

"We don't know what we might find in here. I realize that I should have let you know what I was going to do, but I didn't want to take any chances with a killer on the loose. I'm just glad we haven't found another dead body."

"Okay, I just wasn't ready for that."

"Don't worry about it. It'll come in time, partner. Tom and I could anticipate each other's moves. I'm not used to having you as a partner yet; no offense, but it will get better."

"None taken. I wonder if Marina made it back here last night."

"I don't know. I'll start in the living room."

The apartment felt right. It was sparsely furnished but cozy, and everything appeared to be in order even though they had never seen it before. Joe worked his way back into the kitchen while Angela checked the bedroom. It was very clean, organized, and offered no clues. Joe checked for things like an address book, or a notepad by the phone, or a bulletin board on the refrigerator; he found nothing.

Angela found herself in a hospital clean bathroom. The medicine cabinet was empty except for a bottle of aspirin and a box of bandages. She noticed an odd smell as she got closer to the bathtub. A foul coppery smell lingered in the air, just noticeable over the basket of potpourri on a shelf by the window.

Drip.

Angela thought she heard a noise, but she wasn't certain.

Drip.

The second occurrence confirmed it, and it was coming from inside the bathtub. The shower curtain was pulled shut, not allowing her to see inside.

Drip.

The smell got stronger. Angela tensely reached for the curtain, ready to pull it aside.

Angela found the bathtub empty and clean. Another drop of water fell from the showerhead and quickly disappeared down the drain. Angela looked on for the source of the pungent smell. A small cabinet and clothes hamper in the corner were the only places she had not looked. The smell almost knocked her over when she opened the hamper.

160

Using a clean towel from the cabinet above, she pulled each piece of clothing out and dropped them to the floor. The smell gained strength the deeper she dug. The last items in the hamper were a blouse, a bra, a pair of pants, and a pair of panties.

The outer garments obviously belonged to Marina as they matched the description from the reports and what she remembered from the brief glance she got of her. Most of the blood was dry and cracked, but a few spots were hydrated by the warm moisture inside the hamper; those spots were giving off the sickly odor. Her arm brushed another towel hanging on the back of the door as she stood up to get add a little distance between the source of the smell and her nose. It was significantly wetter than the ones in the hamper, as if the shower had been used very recently.

"Joe, I found something."

"Good. I'm coming up empty."

"It looks like Marina was here, and not very long ago. I found these clothes buried in the hamper."

"We can take that back to the station for the lab to test; they should be able to see if it matches Marina's. We can also have the EMTs confirm if this is what she was wearing when they patched her up. It looks right to me, but I didn't get a very good look at her."

"I guess she made it home, but I wonder where she is now."

"I don't know, and I don't know how to find..." Joe stopped before he finished his sentence, looking like he had an idea. Joe walked to the phone in the kitchen and looked at the handset, obviously satisfied to find what he was looking for. He pressed the redial button and listened for the phone to connect. He hung up after the person on the other end identified himself.

"What are you doing?"

"That was the bus station and I'll bet that's where she went when she left here."

"Then she could be anywhere by now."

"Let's hope someone at the bus station remembers her. I'll put in a request with the phone company to get her phone records for the last twenty-four hours; maybe that'll shed some light on her destination.

She probably had to make some arrangements before she went to the station."

Joe and Angela found a paper bag in the kitchen to carry the clothes in and left the apartment. The damage to the door was very minimal, and it actually locked when they shut it.

"I don't think Marina is in any immediate danger, and it's unlikely that anyone else knows where she went."

"I bet you're right," returned Angela. "I want to find out if this blood is Marina's or if it belongs to the John Doe. I think there's too much here for it all to be hers."

The detectives headed for the bus station first, feeling the trail was getting hotter and they were finally getting closer to Marina. As long as she used her real name, they would be able to find out where she went. It would also verify the last time she was seen and the physical condition she was in at that time.

Father Samuels spoke to his congregation, but his voice sounded hollow. The parishioners looked on, listening intently. The priest looked strange, but no one was sure of the reason why. His eyes were bloodshot, and he perspired heavily even though the chapel wasn't overly warm. It appeared his mind was somewhere else, and worried wherever it was. He could see the scrutiny in the eyes watching him with looks of concern.

He cut his sermon short, turning the pulpit over to one of his assistants and excusing himself to his chambers. He felt overwhelmed and a sense of guilt worked its way into his mind. He didn't feel right about teaching God's word ever since he took the killer's confession. His heart no longer drove his desire to preach the Word; it was too busy fighting with his mind, trying to figure out what to do. He tried to read scripture, but it no longer calmed him and actually made him feel worse. He lit a small candle on his desk, watching the flame dance above the wax. It was graceful and pleasing to look upon, but he hastily extinguished it when he sensed that it might foreshadow his afterlife.

Thomas called the precinct during his break at the shelter to talk to Angela and Joe about the killing in the alley. He remembered more about what happened with the extra time to think about it. He had to leave a message, but he informed the receptionist he would be at the shelter most of the day.

The bus station teemed with people milling about. It was a true melting pot of cultures, races, and ages. The people sitting were mostly involved with newspapers, books, cell phones, and iPods. The pair approached the counter designated for information.

"How can I help you?" asked the clerk.

"We need to find out one of your passengers' destinations," started Joe, displaying his badge.

"I'm not allowed to give out that kind of information, but I can get my supervisor for you. She may be able to help you."

The young man walked into a room behind the counter. After a few minutes, he emerged in front of a woman that looked to be in her late sixties. She wore wire-rimmed glasses, pulled to the end of her nose, and her gray hair was bound into a tight bun at the back of her head. It was probably long enough to reach the middle of her back if she ever let it down, but she didn't look like the type capable of letting in down. Her expression was rigid, looking like a junior high school teacher after one too many problem students, and her smile, if you chose to call it that, looked like she swallowed a mouth full of alum. The clerk moved aside to help the next person in line.

"Hello, I'm Mrs. Doris Riley, the station manager. How can I help you?"

"We need to know where one of your passengers was going," stated Angela. "She probably came through here in the last six or eight hours."

"I wish I could help you," offered Mrs. Riley in a placating tone, indicating that she didn't really mean it. "I can't give out that information. We keep our customer's information confidential and it is the sole responsibility of the ticket buyer to inform all parties of their destination. It would be a liability for us to do that."

It was obvious that Mrs. Riley was telling them the bus company's policy verbatim. She kept her stance, acting prim and proper, obviously a stickler for rules and regulations. Joe started to say something, and then he thought the better of it. Angela took charge, surprising her partner.

"We can get a search warrant if necessary, but it will be much simpler if you give us the information now and I can guarantee that it will be more pleasant."

Joe was shocked.

I must be rubbing off on her.

"That's what you'll have to do then, young lady. Don't think you can come in here and intimidate me with that badge of yours! I'm not afraid of you youngsters that think you're 'all that.' I don't play games either."

Mrs. Riley turned and walked back into her office, closing the door behind her. Joe thought Angela was going to jump over the counter and throttle the old lady.

"Come on partner, we'll get what we need. Let her act smug now. She'll be begging us to play nice when we come back with a warrant."

They checked their on-board when they got back into the car. A message prompted them to check in with the precinct, so Angela made the call as Joe pulled out of the parking lot. It usually meant the news was pretty bad if they wouldn't send it in an e-mail.

"Central, this is H23."

"Yes, H23, go ahead."

"Update please."

"You have a message to call a Thomas Gianelli regarding your case. He said he could be reached at the Hope Shelter most of the day. Would you like the number and address?"

"Negative, I already have it. H23 out."

"I guess we can swing by the precinct to get the warrant for Mrs. Goody-too-shoes, and then go by the shelter," said Angela.

"That sounds like a good plan to me."

Julie readied herself for work. She felt like she needed to go in, even though she wasn't really up to it. She was distraught about her roommate, but she thought occupying her mind until she knew something solid would help. She also thought it might be a bad idea to call in the first day after a promotion. She left earlier than she was used to since she was working one of the club's satellite bars. She wouldn't have a barback working with her to help with the set up.

She called for a cab and finished getting dressed. She still had to wear costumes to work, but she didn't have to be as flashy as the wait staff. She chose a pair of leather pants, a suede tunic, and a pair of knee-high leather boots. She thought the outfit made her look like a thief, and the thought of being someone else was appealing; everything would be okay if she could wish herself to be someone else.

She gave up on her makeup after the third time she made it run with tears, and her eyes were swollen to the point that no amount of make-up would conceal that fact she'd been crying anyway. The cabbie honked as he pulled up in front of the lonely apartment.

Joe and Angela walked into the Hope Shelter.

"Looks like a pretty good setup," said Joe. "I really think it's a good thing to help out the less fortunate."

Angela sat at one of the tables as Joe went to the serving line to buy them a cup of coffee. Her ankle was holding up much better, but she didn't want to overdo it.

Joe exchanged a few words with the attendant by the coffee pots and then he walked away with two cups of coffee, looking disgruntled. He approached the man wearing a tie and jacket at the end of the line who was most likely in charge of the food services, if not the entire shelter.

"You in charge here?" asked Joe.

"Yes, I'm the shelter's administrator. What can I do for you?"

"Well, I went over to the buy these cups of coffee and the line attendant wouldn't let me pay for it. She sent me down here to talk to you."

"That's because the food here is free, Officer. Everyone is welcome. The food you see here is all donated by various organizations throughout the city to benefit the less fortunate."

"I see, but I can assure you I'm a long way from 'less fortunate.' How about I handle it this way? This is my donation since you kind people gave me and my partner a cup of coffee on a cold winter day."

Joe handed the administrator a small bundle of money and walked away. The administrator accepted the money, not knowing what else to do. He was pleasantly surprised when he discovered that the bundle was a one-dollar bill wrapped around two one hundred-dollar bills.

"What did you say to him, Joe? He looked pretty happy after you walked away."

"I made a donation to the cause."

Angela hesitated before she complimented him. She wasn't sure how he would react to her acknowledging his softer side.

The two sat in silence while they drank their coffee, waiting for Thomas. Joe asked for him when he first went to the serving line. The attendant said he was working in the back and they would send him out when he had a free moment.

"Hello Thomas. You wanted to see us?" asked Joe as Thomas was finally able to approach the detectives.

"I've been thinking about the alley. I realized earlier today that I actually heard three screams instead of two. I heard the woman, then, I assume, I heard the man as he died, but I heard something else while I was still inside my...house. I remember seeing someone's shadow heading deeper into the alley. I think I was expecting to see someone else because of the first scream, but I only realized it subconsciously. I dismissed it as imagination at the time, but on recollection, the woman was also looking off in that direction when I first saw her."

"Are you absolutely certain?" asked Angela. "The other officers checked out the rest of the alley and found nothing. There was no evidence that anyone broke into one of the buildings as a way out either. You know that alley is a dead end."

"Yes, I'm positive. I just wasn't sure at the time, probably because of the shock of the situation."

"If you don't mind my asking, what did you do before you ended up here?"

Angela intended to ask the question before when she got the hunch that he was more than he seemed to be. Each time they had a conversation, her suspicions grew stronger.

Thomas hadn't been asked that question for a long time, which was how he preferred it. He didn't like remembering, but he couldn't completely hide all of the clues to his past, even with the intention of keeping it hidden. He let out a sigh that sounded like a mix of regret and indignation.

"I was a counselor at a drug rehabilitation clinic after I graduated from the University of Michigan eleven years ago. I have a Master's Degree in Psychology. I couldn't find a job back home, so I came to New York and signed on with the Charter Plains facility in Brooklyn. The job was very rewarding and it was the avenue that led me to my wife.

"When I first met her, she was coming in as a patient, hooked on cocaine. I got her through rehab and she managed to stay clean. She came back to the clinic to visit me after she finished the program and we became friends. The rest is history, as they say."

"But how did you end up living on the streets? Surely you don't have to live like this forever, especially with a college degree."

Thomas took a deep breath. He mentally prepared himself for the memories he was about to express.

"About five years ago, my entire life fell apart. We were starting a family. The doctors said the baby was stillborn because of residual traces of cocaine in my wife's system. The drugs caused a deformity in the heart that the doctors couldn't repair. We would have had a baby boy. The valves in his heart were misshapen, not allowing blood to flow correctly. The operation necessary to repair the damage was far too strenuous for him to survive it; he would have died during the operation anyway."

"I'm so sorry, Thomas," said Angela.

"We were heartbroken, as you can imagine. I started to question the doctor's explanation, so I went to see him alone to dig a little deeper. It turned out that my wife used cocaine off and on the entire time she was pregnant. The "trace" in her system was less than a month old and it was much larger than residual.

"I got home from the doctor's office to ask her what was going on and I found her on the bathroom floor, lying on her back, dead from an overdose. She left a note saying she couldn't live with the guilt of killing our son and lying to me. That's when I cracked. The stress was more than I could take.

"I stopped going to work and stopped paying my bills. All I did do was sit at home and drink whiskey. I fell into the same trap of addiction that she battled, just with a different drug. As you can imagine, it didn't take long for me to lose everything, but I didn't care anymore. I ended up here because I couldn't bury my need to help people. This way I can do as much as I feel I can handle without the responsibilities of your world."

"So, you're just here by choice," said Joe, a statement instead of a question.

"That's the way it is out here sometimes. It's easy for people to see us on the streets and assume we have no real value to society. They don't think that any of them chose to live this way. It's pretty easy to think that bad things can't happen like that when it hasn't happened to you personally. A lot of people end up here, far more than you would expect, but all they need is a little encouragement and a chance to get back out. Give them that chance is what I try to do."

"I think you're doing a great thing," said Angela. "I also owe you an apology for not expecting much either. You're quite right that it's easy to judge someone else when you have no idea what their situation really is."

"If everyone could understand that, Detective Benson, none of us would be here."

"Do you think you can come back to the Precinct with us?" she asked, changing the subject to something more comfortable for her.

"Am I under arrest?"

"Not at all, we just need to get your statement formally."

"Sure, let me go ask my boss. I don't think he'll mind."

Thomas went back into the kitchen, looking for the administrator.

"I never expected that," said Joe.

"That's what he meant about human nature. I asked him about his history because something nagged at me about him. Some of the things he's said, his word choice, and even the way he carries himself made me think he didn't belong in the streets. He tried to play it down, but he slipped often enough for me to realize that it's an act."

A few minutes later, Thomas emerged from the back area in his regular clothes. The three left the shelter, headed for the 42nd Precinct, when a call came across the radio.

"H23, come in."

Angela picked up the radio's transmitter.

"H23, come in Central."

"We have a 10-73 at Pier 39 on the beachfront."

"10-4 Central, H23 in route."

"Sorry about this Thomas, but we've got to work this call. It looks like you're along for the ride," apologized Joe.

Julie was surprised the club wasn't very busy; it usually swarmed with people from open until close. She guessed the crowd was at about half of its normal size. She had a chance to talk to some of the other bartenders because of the lull in business. She never got the chance to say anything more than her drink orders when she waited tables. The mini bars had dedicated wait staff to keep the service quick, so they never mixed with the regular waiters and waitresses.

"I'll bet it's because of that 'Hook Guy' – the whole city is scared," said one of the shot girls as Julie approached the main bar.

"Who's the 'Hook Guy'?" asked Julie.

"You don't know? What planet do you live on?"

The shot girl walked away to answer a call from a patron.

"Don't take her too seriously. She couldn't beat a box of rocks in a game of Scrabble unless it was restricted to three letter words. I'm Donnie, and you are?"

"Julie."

"Are you new?"

"No, I've been here for a few years, but I just got promoted to bartender over at the Bastille. We've probably walked past each other before and just didn't notice each other since everyone dresses up."

"It's nice to meet you. Shot girl Wendy was talking about the serial killer that is stalking the city. The news said a killer is loose and he uses this hook-like weapon to kill his victims, then he mutilates them."

Wendy came back to the bar to fill the order, rolling her eyes with a look bordering disgust for Julie. She made a slashing motion with her hand like she was wielding the grisly weapon as she walked away. Julie felt her throat constrict as her thoughts went back to Ellen. Several new scenarios entered her mind, none with happy endings. She went back to the Bastille cautiously, trying to draw as little attention to herself as possible, and slipped into the small storeroom behind it. She couldn't stop her tears, and she didn't want anyone to see her.

"Good evening, New York, it's time for the WJNY evening news," said Denise, looking into the camera. "I'd like to begin the broadcast with a retraction concerning last night's top story. We discovered some of the information we received was actually falsified by an unknown source. The police department issued a formal statement to the press which I'd like to present for you now."

Denise shifted her gaze to a different camera after she saw the signal. She held her papers gingerly, trying not to let on how badly her wrist hurt to support any weight whatsoever.

"The New York City Police Department is currently working on several homicide cases, and in a city this size, it is not uncommon for some of these cases to have similarities. A special investigation is being conducted that does involve more than one homicide, some of which were reopened, but we have not at this time established a solid link between any of these cases. The theory of a serial killer has been discussed, but that is always a consideration when similarities are discovered. We are simply following our standard procedures and this in no way means a serial killer is stalking our city. It only means we are utilizing thorough investigative efforts and covering all the bases. We do not have a suspect being referred to as the 'Hook Man'. We are asking for the public to contact their local police precincts via the non-emergency numbers if they have questions. We've also established a link on the city's website to offer FAQ answers to help keep the phone lines available for emergencies."

Denise looked up from her notes.

"That's the report from the NYPD. Here's the website address for those of you that need it."

The web address displayed across the bottom of the viewer's screens.

"The police are asking all citizens of New York to go about their daily routines as normally as possible. They advise a common-sense approach. This request is not due to the special investigation they are conducting; they simply want you all to be careful. A citywide panic will only get more people hurt. We will continue to give you all of the breaking news as we receive it. We added a link on our website to the police's web address as well."

Denise finished the rest of the broadcast as usual, but her eyes, watching the station manager gloat, kept shifting to a point beyond camera three. He was smug over the fact he'd gotten his way with Denise, he was still on the air, he was still going to cover the serial killer storyline, and he managed to get Jamison off of his back, too. She didn't acknowledge his outwardly victorious mood. After the newscast was over and the cameras were off, Denise left the studio to go to her office. Jack was waiting in the hall as she passed.

"That was nicely done. Did you really get a statement from the police?"

Denise didn't respond and she kept walking to her office. He grabbed her shoulder and spun her around to face him.

171

"It's not wise to ignore me, and you shouldn't play these stupid games either. You already have one strike against you. I've been keeping an eye on Stephanie from the mailroom. She's got what it takes. You might find yourself traded in for a newer model."

"I'm a busy woman and I already did what you asked. What do you want now, Jack?"

Jack pulled her into a storage room and locked the door. In one quick movement, he yanked opened her shirt and pulled it down her arms, exposing her chest and binding her arms behind her back. He twisted it into a knot, tying her wrists together and putting unwelcome pressure on her already hurting joint.

"To the winner goes the spoils," he said as he manhandled her.

Thomas sat patiently in the squad car, watching the waves lap against the sand. For most people, it would be a very serene way to spend some time. For Thomas, it was more a mockery of his life. He wanted serenity and consistency, but he couldn't commit to the first step to get it. It was so easy to help others, yet it was virtually impossible for him to help himself. He knew encouragement and a chance was all it took.

The car was parked on the beach, facing the pier, which extended from the boardwalk out nearly two hundred feet over the Atlantic Ocean. All of the attention was focused under the pier among the pilings. The radio buzzed off and on as the dispatcher issued commands and waited for the various units to respond. Thomas didn't understand the ten-codes the police used, but he could tell how severe an incident was by the amount of radio traffic.

"Ten-sixty-five, respond to H23, they have confirmed two."

"Ten-four, Coroner Examiner is in route."

Thomas realized that the call came from one of the officers at the scene before him. H23 was Joe and Angela's unit number he heard them use. He deduced that the "two" must mean two bodies.

Joe and Angela came back to the car, both needing a break from the wind and the snow. The air coming off of the Atlantic was extremely cold, making the temperature on the beach considerably lower than the rest of the city. It made Angela's ankle hurt, but the sensation was far less than any other time since she hurt it.

"Looks like we've got two more John Doe's," said Joe. "If this is the same guy, he works fast."

Joe passed Angela the digital camera he took the picture with. The view screen showed a two inch by two-inch photo of the victims. Thomas caught enough of a glimpse of the little LCD screen to see that one of the bodies was missing a head. His stomach twisted nervously as realization latched onto him out of the blue.

"Can I see that?" he asked. His skin went a pale, pasty white.

Angela turned towards him. "What's wrong Thomas?"

"The camera...please" was all he could say through the thickness taking over his throat. His fear was confirmed when Angela held the camera up so he could see it clearly, unsure if she should actually show him. He frantically worked to open the door, but the handle didn't work from the inside. Angela got out and opened his door just in time for him to lean out and throw up.

"What's wrong with him?" asked Joe across the vehicle's interior.

"Most people have trouble with severed heads, Joe, but this seems like something more, like maybe he knows one of the men in that picture."

Thomas progressed from actual sickness to semi-violent dry heaves and the intensity lessened from there. His gag reflex relaxed in turn. He leaned back into the car, sideways with his feet on the ground, when he was back in control of himself.

"The men in the picture are friends of mine from the street. Their names are...were...Todd and Freddy. They always ran together and I noticed the other day that they weren't around. They were always around when it was time to eat, so I asked about them. It had been a couple of days since anyone saw them. I even checked their places, but they weren't there either."

"Can you take us to where they lived?" asked Angela. "We might be able to find something there."

Thomas nodded in agreement, unsure if it was safe to open his mouth. He turned back onto the seat and Angela shut the door. He gave directions that led them to Beggar's Alley.

173

They walked to Joel's hut first, finding nothing that would help them. Thomas' stomach settled enough for him to speak comfortably when they approached Freddy's box.

"He's got a flap cut in the side of the box that opens into that building. I checked it out but I didn't find anything out of the ordinary. It looks like an abandoned motor pool garage. I think he was just taking the tools one by one and pawning them off, but you might find something more useful."

Joe crawled through the window. He told Angela to take Thomas back to the car and wait while he took a look. He didn't want Angela to hurt her ankle again, and he didn't want to leave Thomas or the car unattended.

The inside of the building was just as Thomas described it. He checked all the rooms, not skipping anything, making sure the building was empty. The room-by-room search didn't yield anything helpful, so he proceeded to the office off of the main garage.

"Thomas, have you ever considered getting back into society?" asked Angela.

"It's crossed my mind a few times, but I can't seem to bring myself to do it."

"Why not?"

"I don't know if I want to, or if I'm ready. I get a lot out of my life the way it is now. I don't know if I want to deal with society's rules, red tape, and other strings."

"That sounds like a pretty weak answer. All you want to do is help, right?"

"Yeah, that's right," he returned, with a little stronger tone.

"Have you ever considered how much more you could do if you had some influence over a bigger spectrum?"

"What do you mean by a bigger spectrum?"

"I mean you could make a bigger impact and help a lot more people if you got into some type of organization that does that kind of work. You would have no trouble getting a job like that. You have the credentials, you have the work history from the clinic, and you have a perspective from the street, which makes you more valuable and more experienced than most anyone out there. How many people do you suppose that fight to help the homeless have ever lived that way? I know some will live on the street for a week or so trying to validate themselves, but they aren't there because it was the only option left for them. That's not desperation, and the experiences they have aren't the real thing."

"I never really thought about it that way, but then, I haven't thought about a lot of things since I stopped caring."

Thomas looked down at his lap. He was wringing his hands and unable to look at Angela directly.

"I think you should consider it, if I'm not being too bold. It's a funny thing with people that say they don't care when they are only trying to convince themselves."

The desk in the office was covered with carelessly scattered papers. Joe knew Thomas hadn't done it because he said he didn't touch anything in the office, and the thin layer of dust covering the pages confirmed it. Joe thumbed through the papers, periodically checking his watch to see how much time passed. He didn't want to stay too long since they still had so much to do.

The papers identified the building as the Thornquist Corporation's Central Garage and Motor Pool. Thornquist was a large import-export company with customers in several countries around the world, shipping and receiving just about everything the law allowed, and probably a few things it didn't. Most of the pages were shipping manifests with some type of error on them, like the wrong box was shipped to the wrong place. A slightly more arranged stack of papers rested on one corner of the desk that contained past due bills and statements from collection agencies. Some of the letters were from the New York Port Authority and the city, which caught Joe's focus.

The past due bills ranged from four months late to almost a year past due. The official letters stated the company was in foreclosure, and the stack also contained letters from the bankruptcy court. The warehouses were locked down and the contents would be sold at an undisclosed date to cover some of the company's debts. Joe read on, getting a more official insight on the company's plight. The business going belly up made front-page news for a few days at first.

Several interoffice memos were printed from e-mail. Apparently, the owner's son, Alan Thornquist, took over when the father fell ill. He invested a large chunk of the company's capital into several high-risk stocks. The plan would have more than quadrupled the company's worth if it worked. Unfortunately for Alan, it didn't, and he lost almost everything he invested. The company was devastated, but it managed to survive. From the look of some of the memos, many of Alan's decisions were unfavorable, but no one could stop him. He learned nothing from his first stock market failure, so he borrowed large amounts of money from several of the banks with which Thornquist did business.

The second quest into the market was worse than the first. Although he didn't lose everything, he lost enough to bury the company. The company's capital was too low to cover the basic operational costs, which lead to large layoffs and pay cuts, crippling the Thornquist work force. The lack of help made it impossible for the company to meet it deadlines and keep all the shipments going, which led to many customers taking their business elsewhere. The drop in revenue led to more layoffs, putting the company into a downward spiral that made recovery impossible. It appeared that several long-time customers kept using the company, but only out of respect for the father, Richard.

Richard Thornquist was a shrewd businessman. He started the company in a run-down garage, working long, hard hours to give his customers the service he promised at a price that was better than the competition. It didn't take long for word to get around and his customer base grew. He soon branched out, shipping for the entire state of New York, instead of just parts of the city. His keen eye for quality and strong work ethic kept the company growing until it played on the world stage. Twenty-two countries around the world were home to Thornquist shipping depots. The fleet contained everything from bicycles to Boeing 727s, and Richard never lost control. He set up each location as a separate company under one umbrella, and he kept the controlling stock in each one. He branched out to other countries instead of expanding within the US to keep from falling into an anti-trust problem in the states. He welcomed competition, and he could always manage to outwit it.

Alan was nothing like his father. He was a get-rich-quick kind of man with no intention of doing any work himself. He got into the market hoping to make a lot of money so he could sell the business and its need for constant tending, problems he called it, while he lived the jet-set lifestyle. Alan's total lack of business sense destroyed the it in less than two years. It took Richard almost fifty to build the Thornquist Empire. Luckily, Richard passed away before the company was totally destroyed.

Joe found an iPad in the top desk drawer and a cable to connect it to a desktop computer. The cable was still plugged into it, like it was accidentally forgotten. Alan's name was engraved in the cover, so he guessed that the office used to be Alan's, or at least one that he used often. The battery was dead, but a wall adapter was in the drawer as well. Joe plugged it in to find that the building still had power. The wall connection gave the device enough power to operate, so Joe used the stylus to look through the electronic appointment book.

It contained several meetings and appointments with bankers, stockbrokers, lawyers, and customers, but none of the comments typed by the appointments looked favorable. One name, a Mr. Sayer, stuck out. There were never any notes by his entries, and his meetings were usually at very strange times and places. The number of meetings also seemed odd, as Alan met with him twice a week, every week, for several months. Joe pondered if Sayer might be an old, eccentric customer that demanded a lot, but gave the company ample business for its time.

Joe flipped on the computer, which surprisingly had no login or password requirements, and accessed the company's customer files. He tried to cross-reference them with the iPad to find Mr. Sayer, but that name wasn't in any of the files.

Jack led Denise back up to her office after the rough session in the storeroom. He hadn't completely satisfied his desire. The physical acts were over, but he still needed to assert his control. He was careful, like always, to not leave any bruises that could not be easily explained away if they appeared anywhere they could be seen while she was dressed. He kept has hand around her tender wrist, but he didn't squeeze it this time; he only kept himself in a position where he could.

He poured them a few shots from the Vodka he made her keep in her desk. The alcohol renewed his vigor. He pulled Denise to him and unzipped her skirt again.

"What do you intend to do if Jamison doesn't agree with you?"

Denise didn't want him to touch her, but she knew an outright denial would not get the desired results. She tried to make him think of one of his other conquests to put the attention off of her.

"I don't care what that blowhard piece of shit has to say. I know what he can and can't do, and he can't shut this station down. I'll be damned if I'm going to do anything to make his life easier. Cease and desist my ass! I don't care what he needs and I don't give a damn if his life is convenient or not!"

Denise just offered a little smile as she stood up and pulled Jack to his feet. She started undoing his belt and rubbing lightly against him.

"That's more like it," he groaned.

Jack left the office before Denise finished putting her clothes back on. Her skin was sore and tender in several places, but they would not have a mark. Jack figured out early on exactly how far he could go without leaving a bruise. He was rough with her normally, but the physical reprimands were severe when he felt betrayed or threatened.

After she finished dressing and freshening her hair and makeup, she left the TV station for the night. She was bound for somewhere other than home. She got what she needed so she would not have to endure him again.

Joe looked at his watch again; over half an hour had passed since he entered the office. He knew he needed to get back, but he felt like something in the files would help them with the case. He powered up the printer, but the ink cartridges were dried up. He looked in the middle drawer of the desk and found a flash drive at the back. A quick explore showed the portable drive had more than enough space to save copies of everything he wanted to look at later.

"Thomas, wait here for a minute. I just thought of something that I want to go check. I should be back before Detective Anderson."

"Okay."

Gianelli was relieved to see her get out of the car. He enjoyed her company, which surprised him, but the recent topics for discussion made him uneasy. He had been content with his life, but now he was facing all the same internal struggles that he worked so hard to bury.

It's always the same. I get my life where I want it and I go and screw it up trying to help someone.

Joe exited the garage through Freddy's box, carrying the flash drive in his pocket. He returned to the car to find Thomas dozing off in the back seat. He woke up when Joe got into the car and shut the door.

"Where's Angela?"

"She said she wanted to go check on something. She said she'd be right back."

"How long ago was that?"

Joe looked at his watch, even though he knew it had no bearing on the events.

"About twenty minutes, I think."

"Which way did she go?"

Thomas pointed deeper into the alley. Joe got out of the car and starting walking that direction, instructing Thomas to stay put until he got back, as if he had a choice. Joe couldn't decide if he should be worried or angry, but Angela knew better than to go off alone.

Angela walked backed to the car as Joe started looking for her. She went to ask some of the other alley folk if they saw or heard anything suspicious. Thomas couldn't hear what they were saying, but he could tell Joe was very angry. The exchange looked very much like a father catching his daughter sneaking back into her room through the window after spending most of the night at some boy's house.

"Why did you go off like that when I asked you to stay put?"

Angela wasn't sure how to respond. It was the first time she'd seen him this angry.

Chapter Twenty-One

The protector entered his superior's chambers as silently as possible. He padded softly through the room, navigating easily through the pitch-black darkness, as the heavy wood door swung shut on silent hinges. The stone floor and walls defined what was used as a private study for the senior priest when it was still in use. The wooden bookshelves built into the walls remained, unable to offer anything to the occupants save the echoes of emptiness. The small fireplace, set into the stones in one corner, was devoid of any warmth, serving only as a resting place for a thin layer of gray ash. The cold, heartless spaced conveyed its sadness for the warmth that once called it home.

"It's just past sunset," indicated the servant as he reached his destination.

"I know. I've been awake a few moments, contemplating the night to come."

The servant dismissed himself with a silent nod, off to prepare a simple repast. The master exited behind him, bound for the barren room that once served as the church's chapel. The altar he knelt before was a simple design in red oak with very little ornamentation. He spoke his thoughts aloud.

"Oh, Heavenly Father, I pray to thee that I survive this night, as I have for all the others before, for you can truly understand my mission and its necessity. The balance must not be lost; thus, I will not allow the Books of Kalanak to fall into the wrong hands. I pray that you forgive me for I cannot spare the rod along the way. In your name I pray, Amen."

The goliath rose and turned, leaving the altar behind him. He entered what was once a common room and ate a humble meal with his servant before entering the night.

Joe and Angela got back into the car without any more words. Angela focused her gaze on the tan, rib textured fabric upholstery covering the inside of the passenger door. Joe looked gruff, but he never took his eyes off of the road. Thomas sat silently in the awkwardness, unsure what reaction he might get if he spoke. His thoughts drifted back to his murdered friends.

As Joe worked through the evening traffic, the hard edge slipped away from his expression. He settled back more comfortably into his seat and released a small sigh. The tension in his shoulders slipped away like a discarded coat as he turned to look at his partner.

"I'm sorry for being such a jerk back there, Angela. I think I was a little too hard on you. I was just...worried...about you. I couldn't handle it this time if something bad happened to you."

That was the second surprise in one day. She composed herself before she looked back at him.

"It's okay, really. I know better than to go off alone like that, and it wasn't respectful."

I wonder what he meant by "this time."

She did feel that he had been a little too strict with her, but she realized he was masking his concern and not sure if testing the waters any more extensively was a good idea.

She quickly changed the subject, not knowing what else to say about it, and not wanting to discuss the altercation any further, asking "What did you find back there?"

"I'm guessing a lead on the murder of Thomas' friends. The company that owned the garage also owned a huge warehouse on the docks. The bodies were underneath the pier that runs up to that very warehouse. It looks like several people have been in that garage recently. I wonder if the killer is looking for something there or if it's a hideout?"

"It sounds like a good possibility," she answered. "He may have killed two people because he was trying to protect something. This is the first double homicide we've come across, but it fits the same MO. We just got lucky that Thomas could identify them."

When they reached Precinct, they took Thomas to get his formal statement, leaving him alone in a waiting room while they went to attend to other duties.

Joe went to his desk to check his voice- and e-mail. He wanted to get all of the most recent information available concerning the investigation.

Angela visited the judge's office to check on the status of their search warrant for the bus station. The county clerk stood to hand the signed warrant to the detective as she entered the office, remembering her from earlier in the day.

"That was quick."

"The judge got to it right away. Anything remotely connected to the serial killer case is being marked high priority and worked immediately. The whole department is on edge, but that's not a shocker with the city in such a panic. Don't tell anyone where you heard this, but I saw a copy of a memo from the mayor come through and they're talking about closing all the non-essential businesses in the city and mandating curfews until the case is solved."

"You're saying he wants to declare martial law?"

"I don't think that's exactly it. He doesn't want to militarize the city, or involve the National Guard or anything that extreme at this point, but he does want to curb the amount of people out and about during nighttime hours. Everyone needs to be in their homes unless it's absolutely necessary to be out. He said in the memo that this will be very hard to enforce, but he hopes some of the citizens will voluntarily observe his requests."

"I don't know how much good that will do."

"I think he just wants to do what he can to minimize the threat to the people. If we do have a serial killer, this will make it harder to be successful. He can reduce the media's involvement at the same time without anyone calling foul since everyone has to do it."

"I didn't realize it was that bad," responded Angela.

"It doesn't seem that bad, but you have to step back and take in the whole picture. Since the news got everyone worked up with this 'Hook Man' story, the number of calls increased tenfold. It is getting difficult to even communicate internally at times because the switchboards are constantly overloaded. 9-1-1 service is only operational about sixty percent of the time and the uniformed police units are running ragged with more false alarms than anything else. They have to work every call and a lot of them are nothing more than people's imaginations."

"How do you manage to find out all of this? We don't get this much info down the pike at the Precinct, and we are the police."

"I guess you could call it a perk to working here. Judge Terrence is on the City Council, so he's consulted about almost everything. We see a lot of things as they pass through the office that we wouldn't know about otherwise."

"Thanks for the info. Your secret is safe with me. I don't like being in the dark either."

"No problem."

Angela left Judge Terrence's office, bound for the lab to check on the results of the tests ordered on Marina's clothes.

Joe scanned through his e-mail, reading only at the ones marked urgent. One item in particular from Captain Bishop caught his attention. A body turned up in Central Park, and another homicide unit that was immediately available and close worked the scene since it was in such a public area. The police wanted to avoid initiating a circus with the media or the general public. Luckily, the section of the park where the body was discovered saw little foot or bicycle traffic even when the weather was good. The full report from the other homicide team was attached to the e-mail, so Joe printed it while he continued through the other flagged correspondence.

Angela read the lab results as she walked back to her desk, stopping cold about halfway through the report, almost causing a collision with an officer from Narcotics.

"Sorry," she offered offhandedly. What in God's name is going on?

The report stated that the blood on the clothing was broken down and identified, and approximately seventeen percent was type O negative. Marina was a universal donor, so that made sense. The other eighty-three percent could not be identified at all, other than that it was blood. Six percent could be differentiated from the rest when viewed under a microscope. This meant the blood came from three separate sources, not just the two that were expected. Since the lab technicians had never seen anything like it before, the samples were sent to a Federal forensics lab for another look.

When Angela made it back to her desk, she exchanged her new information with Joe, and he relayed the high points from his e-mail. Their frustration was unspoken as they realized they just kept ending up with more questions and no answers. Going back to the bus station was the most logical move since Marina's trail wasn't completely cold and her importance to the case kept increasing. As they made the trip to the bus station to get what they needed out of Mrs. Riley, they discussed the Central Park death in more detail, trying to brainstorm some sense into it.

The bus depot was still busy, but not like it was during their first visit. It was fairly easy for the detectives to work their way through the terminal. They went back to the same counter as before, and Angela asked to speak to Mrs. Riley directly before the clerk got out a word.

The manager emerged from her office and the pleasant look on her face melted away, replaced with one of aggravation and disgust, when she saw the detectives at the counter.

"I assume you have your warrant. Unfortunately, the information desk just closed for the day. You'll have to come back in the morning."

Angela sensed Joe bowing up his chest, so she gently put her hand up in front of him, silently indicating that she would handle it.

"I really wish that was my problem, but the criminal element doesn't observe works hours, so neither do we. This warrant gives me the right to any information you have that I might deem helpful, and lucky for you, I didn't wait until the wee hours of the morning to have the added pleasure of waking you up and forcing you out of your warm bed. I am choosing to show some decency and remain civil with you. I strongly suggest you get the information we need about Marina Makovoz quickly."

Mrs. Riley took a visible double take, shocked and surprised by Angela's aggressiveness. She accessed the terminal on the counter, looking put out but newly respectful.

"It seems I'm having some trouble..."

Angela cut the older woman off mid-sentence. "I've got all night, so you should probably get that trouble fixed. I'm not leaving until we have what we need."

Mrs. Riley went through the motions to reboot the system, much to the chagrin of the other patrons. The process shut down everything in the depot, not just the information workstation. No one could see when buses were due to arrive or depart, or even purchase tickets, until it all came back online. A barrage of dirty looks and mumbled comments were directed at the epicenter of the disruption. Business returned to normal in just under four minutes, ebbing away the waves of aggression and frustration since everyone could get back on with their lives.

"It looks like we sold a one-way ticket to a Ms. Marina Makovoz this morning. Her destination was upstate New York, Albany to be exact. She is scheduled to arrive at 3:00 PM today. I can verify she boarded the bus on this end, but I have no way of knowing if she stayed aboard all the way."

Angela's face took a harder edge. The bus manager spoke up quickly to explain the discrepancy was not within her control.

"If she chooses to disembark at a different stop, the driver will issue a reboarding pass for her. The passes are generic and do not identify the passenger specifically. The bus will depart as scheduled, even if some of the reboards, as we call them, remain outstanding. This happens a lot more than you would expect. We do perform counts at each stop, and those tallies are turned in at the end of the day. We can determine how many people did or did not make the entire trip by working the returned reboards, but we do not have the ability to identify those travelers with the exception of children under eighteen that travel alone. If they absolutely have to get off of the bus, they are escorted to and from the vehicle by local personnel."

Angela turned to walk away without acknowledging the older woman's help. Joe watched her leave, sensing greater depths to her dissatisfaction as she took several steps. He turned back to the counter and Mrs. Riley.

"Thank you for your help," he added with a nod of approval as he turned to follow his partner.

"I didn't think you had it in you," commented Joe when he caught up, well out of Mrs. Riley's earshot.

"I can be a bitch when I have to be, even though I don't like acting that way. At least she knows I'm game if she wants to play hardball!"

"Easy Trigger, you got what we needed. You need to rein in what's really bothering you a little before you hurt yourself."

Angela turned to Joe, unsure of what to say, but looked incredulous all the same. He spoke again before she managed to formulate a response.

"I've been down this road before. I don't know exactly how you feel, but I can still sympathize. I know there's more upsetting you than just

185

the investigation. Give yourself a little time to work through whatever that is. I want you to understand that I'm not making any demands here; I'm simply offering advice that only comes with wisdom."

They got back in the car and Angela faced forward. She lowered her head slightly as the heat of her anger went from open flames to undying embers. She organized her thoughts and cleared her throat, afraid her voice might break otherwise.

"You're right, Joe. The exchange with Mrs. Riley…reminds me of someone."

Joe waited in the silence as she gathered her thoughts again, knowing she just needed someone to listen.

"No, that's not quite right. It wasn't the conversation, but the way I handled myself. I've been on Mrs. Riley's end before. I told myself I would never act that way. I'm mad at myself for that."

Angela looked up and out the passenger side window at some point far away that only she could see. It took her a few minutes to firm up her resolve a third time. Joe took his turn when he sensed she was ready.

"It hurts more when it's someone close."

Angela turned to him, wondering how he was so good at reading her thoughts. His face confirmed that he was just making a good guess, more like he had a personal experience to relate to than being omniscient.

"My father and I had a falling out several years ago. I was reaching for my independence and being headstrong. I wanted to do things my way and he wanted me to do things his way. We couldn't even agree to disagree. It had to be his way or else. So there I was, painted into a corner, and I found myself hating him for it. I tracked the wet footprints all over the little of our relationship that was left, scarring it beyond repair. I just put Mrs. Riley in that same corner, even though I swore to myself I would never do that to anyone."

"That's a hard place to be, without a doubt, but I can tell you this," advised Joe. "It takes two to argue and harbor bad feelings, so the fight with your father wasn't all your fault. I also know that you won't let that happen again because you learn from your mistakes. The problem is that you are too hard on yourself when you make those mistakes. Without mistakes, we have no way to learn, no way to better ourselves. Mistakes are only bad when we don't learn from them."

"Thank you for that, Joe. It really means a lot to me."

"I've got your back, Angela," he returned, clearing his throat before changing the subject. "We don't have the time to get upstate tonight, so we'll have to leave early in the morning. We can handle a few things at the office tonight and get some rest so we'll be fresh tomorrow."

She turned her head to resume gazing out the passenger window, thankful he steered the conversation to a more mundane course. She wasn't ready to share the tears brimming in her eyes that were sure to fall with one more act of kindheartedness.

Marina stepped off of the bus, looking around nervously and searching for a payphone to call a cab. She wanted to get to her sister's house as quickly as possible. She was already over four hours late due to mechanical problems with the bus. She was frightened, disoriented, and nervous from thinking about hours of her life that she could not recall. The trip was long enough for her to do a lot of questioning, but the answers continued to elude her.

Joe and Angela had dinner delivered to the Precinct so they could work without interruption. They got all the information they had about the case together on the tables before them so they could go over everything at once, hoping something was hidden there and making sure they didn't overlook anything.

The information Miles O'Toole already gathered proved invaluable, so they tried to follow his train of thought. Angela pulled up the older logs, combing through them to check all the homicides for the past several months. She found a piece of the puzzle there.

"Joe, take a look at this."

"What is it?"

"I've been back tracking through the logs. Out of the hundred or so homicides in the last six months, I'm seeing a trend. I found it by cross-referencing the homicides and the medical records of the victims because of that Medic Alert bracelet and the gut feeling I got from the doctor. Nineteen of them were single young women with diabetes and all patients of the same doctor. Can you guess who that doctor was for all of these cases?"

"Arkits."

"Exactly! Our doctor is somehow involved in all of this. It's almost like he's acting as a supplier for the killer. It's typical for serials to stalk a particular type of victim. I guess this guy has weird tastes for victims so he had to enlist help. It fits the theory."

"But why is Arkits involved? What would he gain from it? What's his motive?" asked Joe.

"Maybe the killer is rich and eccentric, thinking he's above the law. Money can get some people to do almost anything."

"I'll get a warrant in the works for his bank records to follow the money to see where it leads. What about the other homicides? Do they have any connection?"

Angela turned back to the monitor as she answered. "I set up a search profile query in the database to isolate all of the homicides during the last twelve months by age, sex, and medical info. It'll take a while for it to finish compiling."

"That's great work, partner! Let me buy you a cup of coffee while it's running."

The detectives walked to the break room, letting the motion reinvigorate them from all the sitting and intense studying. The coffee dregs they found there were strong enough to eat the bottom out a coffee mug, quite suitable to keep them awake and going for another few hours.

Ann Arkits walked into her husband's study. He was working late, like most nights recently, making phone calls and working on patient charts. He sat at his desk, facing the window in the wall opposite the door that overlooked the immaculately landscaped backyard.

Unbroken snow followed the gentle slope of the hill, ridged on both sides with rows of manicured boxwoods that concealed the trunks of symmetrically planted rows of oak trees. The path that wound down the slope from the house was clear, as always, due to the warming lines hidden in the concrete foundation underneath the cobblestones. Midway across the yard, the path meandered to a small covered gazebo housing comfortable chairs and an iron fire pit.

The walkway continued on from the far side of the gazebo that sat closer to the eastern edge of the vast lawn, back towards the north-to-south centerline, ending at the building that enclosed their in-ground pool and hot tub. The solarium style windows twinkled in myriad colors as the light from within refracted through the water droplets the moist, warm air created on the inside of the glass.

The desk lamp gave off a warm glow, competing only with the fireplace and the computer's screen saver as the light sources for the doctor's study. Herds of flying cattle moved across the flat screen at different speeds and angles, with the occasional "moo" thrown in at random intervals. The only other noticeable sound was the slight crackling of the fire burning in the fireplace to the left side of the desk.

"Charles, are you coming to bed anytime soon? It's getting awfully late."

He sat in silence, not indicating that he was aware of her. She could see the silhouette of his head over the crest of his high back chair.

"How many times have I told you to take it easy? You always fall asleep down here and you end up with that terrible pain in your neck, or your back, and I get to hear you complain about it for the rest of the week. You're not even awake."

Ann turned her husband's chair to rouse him. Her hysterical scream echoed through the house when she saw why her husband didn't answer.

His shirtfront was red with the blood that recently poured from his throat, still pooling on the chair in his lap. The front half of his neck was gone. Ann could see the stark whiteness of two of his vertebrae through the deep, red, ghastly wound. A shard of metal, pushed through the opening and into the back of the chair, shunted through one of the exposed vertebrae and prevented his body from slumping forward.

A voice from behind her, unfamiliar and threatening, caused her to wet herself as she stumbled and fell, seeking escape. She didn't see anyone else when she entered the room, but the killer was obviously still in residence, awaiting her arrival.

"Mrs. Arkits, I'm so terribly sorry about your husband." The bitterness of the voice was delivered in a sickly-sweet tone.

Ann looked around frantically in her flight, trying to locate the intruder, but she saw no one.

"He decided to squelch on a business deal. I take my arrangements very seriously."

The deep, rigid voice shifted to a more mocking chord.

"I simply could not allow it to go unpunished. How does that saying go? If you let one break the rules, you have to let them all?"

Ann's scramble continued across the floor. Her hands and knees were unable to find purchase now that her husband's lifeblood ran across the hardwood flooring, making the contact slick. She gained her feet once her hands landed on one of the plush Chesterfield style accent chair, giving her the leverage she desperately needed. She sprinted towards the front door.

The solid mahogany door would not open at her request. The deadbolt was still in the locked position, as it should have been at such a late hour, but that reasoning was not at the front of her mind. She grabbed the brass handle to disengage the lock, but it wouldn't budge. She froze, staring at the thumb turn in confusion, when her head sharply snapped backward. The assailant grabbed her ponytail, using it as a lever to pull her away from the door and throw her backwards to the floor. She screamed, not only from the pain, but the realization that she was fully airborne, flying through her front hallway, thrown as if she was nothing more than a child's rag doll. The abrupt jolt against the floor knocked the air from her lungs, allowing only a barely audible hiss from her mouth as she slid to a stop. She was fifteen feet down the hall, looking up at the beveled glass and brass light fixture. She saw her assailant for the first time as he walked to her and leaned into her field of vision.

He was very tall and well built with definable muscle structure. His jet-black hair was uncut, hanging just below his shoulders in the back and framing the ashen pallor of his face. His features were sharp and chiseled, like his countenance was carved from actual stone. The most striking attribute was his eyes. A wide ring of luminescent crimson circled the small, not quite human pupils. The shape fell somewhere between human and that of some other large, predatory creature. The red irises glowed in the darkness, not from reflection but from within, highlights of color that resembled red bolts of lightning against a darker maroon canvas. She could see his teeth as he spoke, lined behind virtually black lips, although she was too terrified to comprehend anything he said. They harbored no resemblance to human incisors, bicuspids, or molars, but all came to sharp points, some of which had small serrations obviously designed to facilitate rending flesh from prey. The canines, much like big cats, were noticeably longer than the rest, sporting tips so sharp that it didn't appear that nature alone could hone them.

Ann backpedaled away from her demonic-looking attacker, rolling to her hands and knees to hasten departure, trying to cover the ten feet to the back door to flee across the back yard. Complete terror stole all of the fight from her, along with anything in the realm of reasoning. The thought never entered her mind that she might not be able to unbolt the lock, or that turning her back on the intruder might prove to be a bad idea.

He grabbed her by the shoulder, piercing her skin and puncturing the sinew underneath. The pain was intense, burning with an unnatural fire, as she felt her clavicle shatter under the mammoth pressure of his grip. He dragged her back up the hall to the study's threshold, hurling her body in an underhanded motion with the ease of a softball pitcher. She saw the ragged chunk of bleeding flesh and bone that was once her shoulder fall from his hand at the apex of her trajectory.

Her body rotated head-over-heels until she was virtually vertical, the victim of a ghost wrestler satisfying violent crazy spirits chanting "pile-driver" when she made contact with the desk. Her chin caught the edge, whipping her body onto the desktop on her chest. The momentum carried her and everything else on the desk over the front edge and onto the floor before the picture window.

Ann shook uncontrollably as she tried to get up, feeling only fear, thinking only survival. Shock didn't allow her to realize that her right arm was completely unresponsive, attached to her body by a few unbroken tendons. Another trail of blood trickled from the gash below her jaw. With a wild cry of unrelenting defiance, she hurled herself at the large window. Her ability to shatter the glass was never in mind; her thoughts were not organized enough to cipher that possibility. Her attempt was that of a fly trapped within a glass jar, simply rushing headlong to what it sees as freedom, regardless of the personal cost, but unable to reason why that freedom cannot be obtained.

Her good shoulder bounced off the plate glass, deflecting with a resonant thump, and twirling her back to the wood floor. She slid face down to the open space between the desk and the hearth of the large fireplace.

The killer's foot bore down on the small of her back with tremendous force. A loud crack shot pain through her entire body. The sensation in her legs lasted a few short seconds before it dissipated entirely. She pulled herself along the floor with her left arm as it was the only limb still responding to her commands. The intense pain in the rest of her body above her waist washed through her in wave after wave of agony, sharp pains separated by deep aches.

"I'm impressed by your conviction, but it's really is quite fruitless. Your husband chose to break a deal that could not be broken. He knew the consequences, but as your kind so often decide, they would not apply to him. I've had enough entertainment for one night. It's time for you to die."

The attacker grabbed one of Ann's limp legs, lifting her entirely off of the floor. She flailed her good arm wildly, hoping to grab onto anything that might save her. She couldn't reach anything and doubted her ability to maintain a grip on anything if she did. She could see out into the hall, but everything was shifting in and out of focus, so she wasn't sure. She landed back on the floor, face first. She felt her good arm being pulled behind her back and bound to what she assumed was the eviscerated flesh of her right arm, wrenching that shoulder from its socket. The tie was then extended to her ankles.

Her back was suddenly very warm. She was on her side facing into the room, lying on the large Persian rug. The fire still raged in the fireplace behind her. She could see the reflection of the flames flickering off the smooth, lacquered side of the desk. Her husband's body was no longer in the chair; only the blood and the metal shard remained. Her mind was foggy from the pain and her throat was very sore, dry, and scratchy, as if she burned it by drinking scalding coffee.

I must have passed out.

Some of the smoke from the fire was drifting back into the room, carrying a horribly foul stench with it. She was having more trouble drawing breath as the smoke thickened, continuing the caustic damage in her throat.

"Goodbye Mrs. Arkits."

The killer lifted her with the wire binding her limbs, sending more sharp waves of pain through her dislocated shoulder and arm. She saw the carpet move away from her face as she swung up and back towards the desk. When her momentum stopped and reversed direction, she realized how her life was going to end. She landed on the smoldering remains of her husband, surrounded by the roaring flames. Her skin blistered as it burned. Her vocal cords were so aggravated from screaming she could only make hoarse mumbles until the fire stole the small amount oxygen she needed for that. Never ending sleep came to her as she blacked out the second time.

chapter twenty-two

"Trokar, we need you in the terminal."

"What is it, Viktor?"

"It's Bjorn. He's…requesting you."

Trokar entered the main terminal to find the young Bjorn herded into a corner by the others.

"What's wrong Bjorn?" asked Trokar with a sarcastic tone as he breached the semicircle of followers that watched with interest. He knelt beside the afflicted youth, just out of arms reach. Bjorn lay huddled on the concrete floor, curled into the fetal position, facing the corner formed by two of the terminal's tiled walls. The clothing he had not discarded during the preceding violent rage clung to him from a sour smelling sweat that covered his body and dampened his hair. Tremors riddled through his limbs, interspersed with jerking shocks as if he was recently shot with a taser.

"It's the pain Master! It is…more than I…can bear! Help me."

Trokar stood and began pacing between Bjorn and the others bearing an expression of frustration mixed with anger.

"You were warned of this Bjorn. You were told what would happen if you exceeded your limitations. You are beyond the point of no return, not that I would help you recover from such stupidity even if I could. You have to pay the price."

Bjorn's voice was laced with desperation as he asked, "You cannot make it stop?"

"The pain will stop itself soon enough, you fool. You turned far too many at one time, maintaining no control over your bloodlust. Even we must observe moderation. The metamorphosis links you to them all until they reach maturity. They depend on your essence to provide the strength they lack to survive the change. I am very disappointed. I had such high hopes for you in the beginning."

Trokar stopped his pace and turned back towards the onlookers. They cleared a path for him as he crossed the terminal to return to his chamber.

"What shall I do with him?" asked Viktor in a low voice as Trokar passed.

"Leave him," he returned quietly. "The show is almost over, but it is valuable for the others to see it through to the end. They will learn far more from his example."

Angela answered her cell on the fifth ring, fumbling it open and getting it turned the proper direction. It was just after three in the morning.

"Yeah," she uttered, still closer to sleep than awake.

"It's Joe. I'm really sorry about the time, especially with the day you had, but this is bad. I'll be there to pick you up in twenty minutes." The speaker fell silent as the call disconnected. Angela got herself out of bed, moving about with the precision of a baby deer walking on a sheet of ice. She could tell from Joe's tone that his apology was sincere, and this was an odd hour to be awake for him as well.

Satisfying sleep continued to elude her more and more each night. Exhaustion proved far easier to handle than the internal fight to obtain slumber and face the dream. It grew worse each night, more difficult each time she woke. Waking brought fear, sadness, confusion, or a combination of all three. It began when they took the case, but a nagging at the back of her mind felt as though something else was fueling the mental fires. She felt clarity in that minute span of time that starts when you open your eyes and ends as you truly wake. Everything made sense, only to be immediately replaced with the thick fog that allowed no recognition of the place you just left, or the bearings to find your way back. It seemed as though someone was toying with her mind, letting that brief flash of understanding linger just long enough to torment her with the knowledge of what she was repeatedly denied.

Joe honked, announcing his arrival when he pulled in front of her brownstone. The timbre rolled through the air with the essence of a fog horn, the air's moisture bouncing and amplifying the sound in all directions. A few windows illuminated and one angry voice rang in response. A break in the clouds drifted overhead, letting bright beams from the full moon illuminate the path from the building to the car.

Angela emerged wearing jeans, thick socks, hiking boots, a baggy sweatshirt sporting her collegiate alma mater that concealed a thermal long john top, a form fitting black leather bomber jacket, and a baseball style cap with a Chicago Bears "C" stitched into the face. Her long black hair was pulled through the opening in the back of the cap, obviously designed for women with ponytails, as it fit her correctly. Her badge hung from a lanyard around her neck. Her firearm sat cradled in the holster under her right arm, although it wasn't obvious under the jacket. She didn't bother with makeup, but she didn't really need it. The Tomboy look was a stark contrast to her office attire, but it suited her just as naturally.

She walked slowly, but more steadily than she had since the accident. A mix of ibuprofen and acetaminophen, coupled with the small warming pack nestled between her sock and the concealed elastic wrap on her ankle and lower leg, removed the fangs from her injury and from winter's bite. The pain was much easier to manage now that the swelling was reduced. The thick lotion she rubbed into her skin around the wounds before she dressed contained lidocaine, that numbed the areas enough to allow uncomfortable, but unhindered movement. She discovered the trick was avoiding any hard jolts or allowing the joint to twist too much.

"Morning," she muttered as she got into the car. "I really hope this proves to be necessary."

Exhaustion clung to her, trapped beneath the thick syrup of sleep deprivation, as she settled into the passenger seat and buckled the safety belt. She was unsure if Joe slept at all either, since he was still wearing the same clothes from the previous night. His five o'clock shadow was sitting closer to eleven, but other than that, he was ready to go.

Joe handed her an insulated cup, before he pulled away from the curb, of mocha latte with frothed milk and hazelnut syrup from an open-all-night shop dedicated to the worship of Arabica beans. She wasn't coping well with repeated nights of sleeplessness, but the aroma from her favorite brew, and the fact Joe remembered the mixture, eased some of the pain. He let her enjoy a few sips before he spoke.

"We've got three dead kids."

"What?" she asked, jerked into full awareness.

"It looks like our serial may not be working alone. Narcotics got wind of a rave party uptown and they decided to bust it. They got a lot more than they bargained for."

"What is a rave party? I'm not familiar with that term."

"It's a kind of drug party catering to rich kids. They all get together somewhere, and cocaine, meth, LSD, or some other hallucinogenic is handed out at the door. Once inside, the kids get high and everything happens from orgies to overdoses."

"Doesn't Narc usually handle ODs?"

"Yeah, but these kids didn't OD. To say they were slaughtered like cattle, or even drawn and quartered, would be inadequate descriptions from the info I was given. This was a brutal, primal bloodbath, meaning this investigation is about to get way out of hand."

Bjorn huddled in the corner, cursing and screaming as he thrashed about. His plight no longer held the attention of the audience, who had already dispersed back to their routines. Some of the more recent turns shifted their line of sight in his direction for quick glances, none of them watching outright, save one. Arin, the youngest, stood entranced at the situation unfolding before him, appearing neither afraid nor anxious. He casually walked to Viktor, holding his gaze on the stricken outcast.

"What is wrong with him?" asked Arin, using a firm but quiet voice.

"He did that which the Master expressly forbade. Our gifts are miraculous, but they are not free of rules. Breaking them brings on a heavy price, life itself."

"I don't fully understand what's happening to him."

Viktor motioned for his protégé to sit on one of the benches.

"We have all been granted seeds of power that give us abilities unknown to mortal man, but they need time to grow."

Viktor made it a point to infect older victims, but something about the child enthralled him. The boy of fourteen watched as his parents were drained for his master's sustenance, seeing without reaction the carnage just beyond his reach. He merely looked on as their cries of pain diminished and the attacker turned to him to finish the family of three. Shock and fear did not overcome what the boy truly felt, which was curiosity.

"I turned you about four months ago, and since then, you have changed physically and mentally. Your body and mental activity grow stronger every day, much beyond that of the mortal age you left behind. You only lack the wisdom. These changes are extremely strenuous, at times exhausting, which I'm sure you have realized. What you don't see is that more of your burden rests on me. We are…linked by this power until you reach maturity, your body siphoning power from mine so you can survive the metamorphosis."

"So, the metamorphosis is hurting Bjorn?" asked Arin, looking back into the terminal's corner.

"He is already mature and no longer becoming. The link is the source of his pain. He turned too many at once, giving more power to them than he can sustain. It seems manageable when you have power for yourself and power to share. Fate is realized when what you share runs dry, leaving just your life force, and by then it's far too late. Once he dies, all of his other immature turns will see the same end, although it will happen to them much faster. I'm surprised he has lasted this long."

"Couldn't you kill some of his line to take off some of the pressure?"

"Absolutely not!" roared Viktor. "You would do well to remember that in only a few special circumstances are we allowed to kill our own kind! Even if we could, it would not help him. The bond is unbreakable, releasing only when the turn's strength surpasses the master's shared energy. Killing them would have the same effect as attacking Bjorn directly. Abusing our power yields nothing but its loss."

Arin's expression changed to one of understanding as he asked "how long will you and I be linked?"

"It can vary, but usually several months. Your body is transforming, radically changing your needs and abilities along the way. The constant is the increase of your power; it's…intoxicating."

Viktor looked content as he spoke, contemplating his own birth and ascension.

Bjorn's screaming settled as he slipped between unconsciousness and convulsions, each longer and more violent than the last. His body shook visibly between attacks while white froth bubbled from his mouth. His eyes rolled back in the sockets, making them appear as open windows to a black soul.

"Bjorn let the power control him; he succumbed to the thirst."

"How often does this happen?"

"More than Trokar would like. His line is very long with only a handful coming to this end, but he despises failure."

"Could he have done anything for Bjorn?"

"In truth, yes, he could have ended Bjorn's life to save him from some of the suffering, but that's part of his punishment. We will be dispatched to destroy the rest of Bjorn's immature turns soon. They are not at fault for his mistake, thus Trokar allows us to save them from the end Bjorn must endure."

"The punishment is meant to be ours as well," added Arin. "Trokar meant for Bjorn to serve as an example to the rest of us."

"You are becoming wiser than your years, Arin."

A demonic scream came from Bjorn as a seizure raged his body, physically bouncing him along the concrete floor, completely airborne at times. The successive impacts audibly broke bones and knocked chunks of flesh loose from his limbs.

A slight smile touched Trokar's lips as he felt the tension building in the others. This event would leave a lasting impression on the young ones far more powerful than any words could convey.

Bjorn's last breath escaped in an unholy scream. His body fell, limp and lifeless, to the floor. The carcass and the discarded pieces around it gave off a thick, smoky stench that curdled the air. The tissue dissolved, leaving only a blackened skeleton. The deterioration seemed complete when the bones themselves crumbled into a fine black powder. The slight breeze that constantly wound through the terminal swept the remains away, leaving behind nothing but a dark stain.

One of Bjorn's turns, Ferrok, stood watching indirectly from a distance. He was unsure of what happened, and absolutely clueless to what was about to happen. He never saw the attack coming.

Mekune and Damok bore down on him from the darkness, rending his body limb from limb, ripping out his heart and lungs. Within seconds, he was reduced to a bloody lump of blackened flesh. Trokar approached the remains and spoke, barely above a whisper. Only he knew what the ancient words meant, or the power they held. All the pieces of Ferrok's body dissolved quickly, starting with his amputated heart, leaving nothing behind. There was no trace he ever existed aside from memory.

Trokar commanded Viktor, Mekune, and Damok to follow him as he left the subterranean terminal to deal with the others.

chapter twenty-three

Kattalin lead Keith by the hand from the frat house, across the snow-covered parking lot, to a car parked near the back edge of the area. Between the thick forest at the far edge of the grass and the curb bordering the pavement stood an imaginary line that students tried not to cross. Upper classmen warned freshman about classmates being dragged off into the trees and never heard from again. The stories were older than anyone's memory could prove, so the haunted line was generally avoided by all, freshman or otherwise.

Keith's black Dodge Challenger R/T was easily visible against the wintry backdrop. It was his graduation present when he finished high school that June. He dared the danger of the woods to protect the showroom condition of the car, as very few spaces along the back edge were ever utilized.

His parents weren't extremely rich like one would expect. He was from a middle-class family that believed in the value of hard work and knew how to save their money. Those traits were passed down to Keith and he honored them well. He let a lot of the typical high school life pass him by, using the time to study and work. He was the fourth to cross the stage during the graduation ceremony; that accomplishment earned him a full scholastic scholarship. Between the money he saved and what his parents had stashed away for his education, they were able to buy the car outright for him with money to spare. He was able to spend a little of his own to add the extras he wanted to make it uniquely his. He collected pictures of the revamped muscle car since the first preproduction images hit the Internet, and he knew it was what he wanted.

The downside to his efforts was the simple fact that he had little to no time for the opposite sex that equated to virtually no knowledge of about women. He was smart enough to know that most of the things his big brother and his friends told him were guesses or outright fantasy. That left him with only one indicator, hormones.

"Come on, Keith, hurry up. I'm ready right now."

Keith saw Kat the moment she arrived at the party. Even with the cold outside, she braved the weather and wore a black leather halter, matching leather mini skirt, and deep red thigh high leather boots. He heard several lewd names for the footwear mumbled from other guys around him. Although he didn't approve of the word choices, he had to agree with his hormones that the names were apt. Her midriff was exposed, revealing tight abs. Her dark chestnut hair was tied with a ribbon of red, into a ponytail that hung almost to her waist, to match the provocative footwear. Her arms and shoulders were covered by a trendy leather half jacket in the same hue. Her deep green eyes literally glowed in contrast.

To his surprise, she looked directly at him and cut straight through the crowd to introduce herself. She pushed past several jocks offering the same old pickup lines, ignoring the jeers she got as she made her way to the "geeky bookworm."

She was very outgoing, but not enough to be overly aggressive. They talked for a few minutes, and that turned into whispering, which led to a little heavy petting before they slipped out of the front door to find some privacy. A couple Keith's friends saw them slip away. As they were in the same boat when it came to women, they followed after a minute or so, hoping to get a personal peek at whatever was about to happen

Keith and Kat pushed through unbroken snow that was as deep as their knees at times to reach the car. He unlocked it with his remote, pulling a small chirp from the horn as the parking lights flashed. She went right for door, opened it, and pulled him into the back seat behind her. He started to ask her what happened next, but she only shushed him and pushed him back against the seat. She worked his belt off before he got halfway settled.

"I want you so bad," she whispered into his ear as she unzipped his pants. She untied her ribbon, releasing her locks, to let them fall forward to conceal her face and shroud his now exposed mid-section. Her enthusiasm gave way to aggression, putting an edge of fear on his excitement. He never imagined his first time would be anything like this, or with such a beautiful woman.

"Oh, wow! Ungh!"

"What's wrong?" she asked in a playful tone.

"Your hands are really cold."

"Well, it's cold out here, but just you wait. I'll have you absolutely dripping in a minute."

"Arrgh! What are you doing?"

The expectation of pleasure turned into excruciating pain. She tilted her head up, finally exposing her face. Trails of blood trickled from the corners of her mouth and down her chin. The exquisite emerald of her eyes was gone, replaced with empty blackness.

"Feeding!"

Her expression turned completely feral. She buried her fangs into his thigh, pressing him down into the seat with strength unnatural for a girl her size, not allowing him to push her away. He passed out as his femoral artery supplied more blood than he could stand to lose.

"Virgin blood is so sweet," she whispered as she lifted herself off of his dead body. Her chin, neck, and upper chest glistened with his lost lifeblood. She got out of the car and walked over the imaginary line towards the trees.

The euphoric sensation that followed feeding melted away too quickly, replaced with a more awkward rumbling in her stomach. It mutated into a painful churning, the likes of which she had never felt. She put her hands over her stomach and noticed her smooth skin losing its healthy color, darkening to gray like ash.

"Kattalin?"

She turned back towards the car, looking for the one that called her name.

"Who...Trokar...what are you doing here?"

"I know why you feel this pain. Come, my child, I can help you."

She mustered her strength and stood up, forcing herself to walk to him even though the pain was almost unbearable. He was strong, and she wanted to appear strong to him. She held back her tears, but the effort was exhausting.

When she reached him, he put one arm around her back in a comforting embrace. He placed his other hand over her chest and pressed down hard. Her mouth opened wide in a silent scream as a flash of light surged from the under his palm, bursting into an eerie wave of green that encompassed her entire body. The light died and her body was gone. Her vacant footprints were saturated with the still lukewarm blood she'd just drawn from her victim.

"What the hell?" yelled Josh as he approached from the fraternity house. R.J. held out his small digital video camera, capturing video, intent on taping some candid mementos for Keith.

Trokar jumped skyward, disappearing into the gray swirls of snow laced wind. Another dark green flame erupted from the ground. It gave off no heat, but the stained snow returned to a pure, bloodless white.

Josh and R.J. broke into a sprint. They didn't know what just happened, but they knew it wasn't good and they couldn't see Keith. Josh reached the car first, throwing up when he saw his roommate through the open door. He straightened up from his doubled over position after two heaves to find himself alone. R.J. was right behind him, out of his direct sight for less than ten seconds, but now he was gone, vanished without a trace. Now alone, Josh felt his fear fester, ready to pop like the second coming of Mt. Vesuvius. A sudden crash behind him made him jump, providing a focal point for his trepidation.

He turned to the now destroyed roof of the car to see R.J.'s mangled body, cradled into the huge depression in the metal, as if he fell from a very high place. Window glass was scattered around the car, shattered outwards from the pressure of the impact.

He ran as hard and as fast as he could back through the deep snow, bound for the fraternity house. Instinct replaced rational thought, urging him to find a place to hide, anywhere out of the open. Halfway to the first row of parked cars, cold fingers closed around his neck and lifted him into the night sky. It happened fast enough to blur his vision. He felt another cold hand grip his chin just before his head turned sharply to one side. Before he blacked out, his eyes focused for half an instant as he looked down, seeing the school logo stitched onto the back of the jacket he was wearing.

One of the front tires popped as the second body slammed into the front left side of the hood, fully destroying the Challenger. The upper half of it lodged into the area that once held the windshield, while the lifeless legs folded over the top to rest on R.J.'s corpse. Glass and blood graced the snow around the car in a wide perimeter, sprinkled all around like diamonds and rubies on white felt.

Joe and Angela arrived outside a small warehouse in the business district about 3:45 in the morning. Rave parties were held in this area often since the district was almost devoid of life at night. It was anything but deserted now. Emergency vehicles of all types were parked around the building, lights dancing in a morbid Christmas-like display. Several uniformed police units set up barricades around each door so no one unwanted could gain entry. Three coroners waited for clearance to remove the bodies. Members of the Fire Department stood ready, assisting where they could.

The detectives produced their badges at the main entrance to get inside, but weren't prepared for what they saw. The warehouse was mostly empty, apparently cleared for the party. Makeshift lounging areas were all about, some consisting of card tables with chairs, others just twin mattresses pushed together on the floor. Everything was damaged to some degree, leaving splintered wood and bunting everywhere. Virtually every visible surface was covered in varying quantities of blood.

The three dead bodies were spread awkwardly in the center of the interior space. The severity of the injuries ranged from deep gashes to decapitation. Two of the bodies, one male, one female, were stripped naked, while the third was completed clothed. The two naked corpses showed injuries on, in, and around their sexual organs. Entrails hung from gaping holes in their stomachs and sides.

Angela closed her eyes and doubled over, trying as hard as she could without avail to keep from vomiting. Joe patted her on the back and asked her if she needed anything, offering her a handkerchief and looking very pale himself. The intense shock of the scene stilled him utterly; the only thing keeping him from shaking with convulsions. Angela regained her composure after a hard five minutes with help from some fresh air outside.

Two other Homicide units arrived that were put under Joe and Angela's direction by Captain Bishop. The six detectives swept over the scene, taking pictures and notes and collecting evidence. They found several remnants from the drug party in the form of paraphernalia, but nothing that put them any closer to the killers. After the scene sweep, they inspected the bodies in teams of two, to measure the size of the wounds and look for any obvious patterns.

Joe and Angela took the headless male. He was still clothed, but they found nothing to help identify him. He had no tattoos or piercings, no birthmarks, nothing. They could only hope for a dental record match.

The bodies were designated as John Brown, John Blonde, and Jane Blonde by the detectives for lack of anything other to use. Once the teams finished, the coroners moved the bodies to ready them for transport to the morgue. The cadavers were tagged and transferred to gurneys. One of the medical examiners was pulling a white sheet over Jane Blonde when Angela grabbed his arm to keep the face uncovered. Something was pulling at her memory that she couldn't quite recall. She started to let his arm go when it came to her.

"Oh my God, Joe, this is Kelly Richardson!" she exclaimed.

"Are you sure?"

"Completely, even though she changed her hair color since the DMV photo we found was taken."

Joe looked more closely, imaging her face without blonde hair framing it and the small lacerations chicken-scratched across the skin.

"You're right!"

Angela turned to the MEs on hand.

"During the autopsy, can you determine if one or both of the male victims was diabetic? You should find that the young lady was."

Several news crews arrived while everything happened inside the building. The Captain ordered roadblocks at every street and alley in a half-mile radius. The press was not allowed to see the warehouse or what was going on, in, or around it. It was almost nine in the morning before the last of the procedural protocols reached completion.

A Sanitation crew diligently followed behind to clean up all traces of the incident. Lines of people, waiting in or around their cars, formed at all of the roadblocks. The police weren't allowing anyone into the area until it was cleared by the Commissioner himself. Several of the stranded motorists were getting irate because they couldn't get to their place of employment, nor have any chance of working back through the pileup to go anywhere else.

Commissioner Jamison stood near the barricade at the warehouse's main entrance, watching the activity around him and wondering what he was going to do. It would prove impossible to keep the incident under wraps for any length of time. The families of the slaughtered kids would be looking for them soon, and the rest of the partygoers could be anywhere, telling everyone what happened.

Police helicopters were dispatched to keep the air space above the warehouse secure, as press teams were trying to fly over to get a look. The police would be bombarded with calls and complaints about the situation until everyone reached their required level of dissatisfaction. Jamison could only imagine the uproar. He already talked to the Mayor and the Chief of Police, discussing the need do something to satisfy the public at large until the perpetrators were apprehended. The case was escalating faster than the police could keep up. Growing ever impatient, the press waited just beyond the barricades, looking for an exclusive story as hungry lions stalk prey.

"This is Denise Rigsby, reporting live from the warehouse district for WJNY, Channel 17. As you can see from the commotion around me, something major happened here, but at this time, we have no idea what that something is. Several emergency vehicles have passed us, but the police aren't allowing the press access and they aren't making any comments so far. We have seen small groups moving back and forth between the vehicles and one of the warehouses near the center of the block, but all we can identify are law enforcement officials. I get the impression they're moving something, or someone, and trying to keep a lid on it."

The broadcast switched to the in-studio anchor.

"Denise, have any of the vehicles left the scene so far?"

"No, so far we have only seen an in-flow of police. There were already three ambulances on scene when we arrived and a few unmarked vehicles."

The cameraman pulled the view back to envelop the whole scene, angling the camera skyward to show the news copters hovering in place, held at bay by the police pilots. He shifted the shot back to Denise for her closing remarks.

"We will keep you posted as the situation develops."

As the feed was faded out, the cameraman swept the crowd, giving watchers a good visual feel for the anger and frustration seeded within the group. Small fist fights broke out that required police intervention here and there, stretching the officers on hand extremely thin. Even without audio, the overall sense of fear was almost palpable.

The detectives finished up and headed for the Precinct. They were both completely exhausted. It was only midmorning and they both had a full day's work under their belts.

"Joe, that was about the worst I've ever seen. What kind of sick bastard can do something like that to another human being?"

"I'm guessing just one, and unfortunately, it's the one sick bastard we're trying to find."

"We've got to check out Dr. Arkits and we better do it right away. I'll bet dollars to donuts he's brokering people's lives. I just can't figure why. He's already a doctor, so I don't see money being a motive."

"I'm not having any luck figuring him out either Angela. My gut instinct tells me we aren't going to like the answer. This is turning into something much bigger than we're ready to handle. We're up to five bodies that we know are connected to the case, and the only possible living witness is still at large."

By the time they got back to their office, Captain Bishop had already ordered the creation of a task force dedicated to the case until the killers were stopped. He put the group under Joe's command, and he only had to answer to the Mayor, the Commissioner, and the Captain himself. The department shifted to alert status, meaning that all shifts were twelve hours instead of eight and all overtime had blanket approval. The current shortage of manpower only made things worse.

All officers and detectives were instructed to make no comments to the media. All questions, complaints, and comments involving the case were to be routed through a special number and website. The force was about to get its money's worth out of the PR Department.

International flight 1603 touched down at La Guardia airport just after nine in the morning, Eastern Standard Time. The Boeing 747 taxied to the gate after its smooth landing, at which point almost all of the passengers stood up to retrieve luggage from the overhead bins and turn on their cell phones. A cacophony of compartment latches mingled with rushed and overly loud conversations. One man, sitting next to the window just behind the wing, sat calmly, immersed in his own thoughts. He rose once everyone else disembarked to comfortably exit the plane.

Joshua Stone walked up the gangway into the main terminal to find the bulk of the crowd had dispersed. The line of people waiting to board the 747 for the return transatlantic flight were herded off to one side in a serpentine, rope laced path. A pair of plain-clothed police officers waited at the carpet-to-tile edge between Gate 9 and the main corridor that connected all the gates, holding a sign that read Detective Stone.

Stone exchanged greetings and left the airport headed for the 42nd Precinct, as it now served as the headquarters for Detective Anderson's task force. The meeting Stone was slated to attend started at nine, but the flight delay and snow-slowed traffic would force the meeting to begin late.

CHApCER CWENCY-fOUR

Commissioner Jamison opened the meeting.

"You are aware of the brutal series of killings in our city. The number of new homicide investigations that are positively linked, or appear to be linked, has increased at an alarming rate. All of you were chosen to be a part of this task force based on your skills and abilities. We needed our best, and here you are. This task force was developed to deal exclusively with this outbreak of violent crimes. Most of you know Detective Joe Anderson, or his reputation, and with the help of his partner Detective Angela Benson, he will take the lead of the group. They have both been working this case since day one."

Jamison paused to wet his throat with a sip of black coffee.

"Before I turn the meeting over to Joe, I'd like to make you aware that we have a guest in route from Scotland Yard. Duty Sergeant O'Toole spent several hours researching the information gathered thus far and discovered this advisor may prove invaluable to the case. Now, I'd like to give the floor to Sergeant O'Toole for a few moments to fill everyone in on what we know until our guest arrives. Miles."

"Good Morning. As the Commissioner said, I've looked into this case for a few days, and I noticed a handful of previous homicides with mutilation as a common thread. Most of you received a copy of this information, so I won't go into detail about it. If you didn't get a copy, see me after the meeting and I'll see that you do. Since this morning, we've reopened twelve cases that are linked, and four units from Homicide are working them."

Joshua Stone slipped into the back of the meeting room unnoticed at 9:20. All eyes were on O'Toole; his eyes were consulting the notes on the podium. Three large LCD screens hung behind the duty sergeant, displaying the NYPD logo. The room itself was quite large, rising slightly from front to back to offer an unhindered view of the front of the room, much like a university lecture hall, designed to hold at least a hundred people,. He took off his hat and sat down along the back row while Miles presented his information.

"The Department is severely under staffed, as you all know, but we cannot let that temporary handicap prevent us from stopping this killing spree. We have officially put the department on an alert status and you know what that means. I have no doubt you can all see the need in this case. These murderers are working extremely fast."

One of the officers in the audience raised his hand.

"Yes."

"I thought we were just looking for one serial killer, but you said 'murderers.'"

"That's a good observation Officer Fleming. We now believe we are dealing with a small group of killers instead of just one, even more reason to prevent this case from drawing out. This task force was organized on such short notice due to events that occurred in the small hours of this morning and it verifies the existence of more than one killer.

The screen over his left shoulder was swapped to display the image of the logo for a map of the warehouse district. A red "X" glowed in the center of the map.

"Narcotics got a tip about a rave party last night. It took place where you see the mark on the map. When they arrived, they found much more than narcotics. Three dead kids, a lot of blood, and an assortment of drug paraphernalia littered the scene. The kids were slaughtered like animals.

"We are doing everything we can to preserve the confidentiality of this case, but there are several party attendees unaccounted for at this time. We estimate at least fifteen to twenty people were at that party, and I'd guess that at least a few of them know what happened. The amount of blood and corresponding spill patterns suggest that some of these kids were hurt when they left the warehouse. We've already put calls out to the local hospitals and clinics, especially the closest ones, to watch for any admissions or ER visits with strange injuries.

Half a dozen green "X" marks appeared on the map, highlighting the locations of the medical facilities nearest the warehouse.

"No thanks to the press, the city as a whole knows something happened last night, but they don't know exactly what and that makes them all the more dangerous. The rumors will be far worse than the truth; if this goes public before we solve it, we'll be dealing with a panic we won't be able to control and we'll have a snowball's chance in hell of finding the killers."

Miles tapped a button on his laptop computer, activating the two remaining screens. He used a laser pointer to go over the displayed information.

"As you can see, we have a total of forty-four homicides in the last eight months that fit our profile at an increasing rate of incidence; all but thirteen of them happened in the last week and a half. We are finding dead bodies like they are going out of style. There may be several more we don't know about, and these numbers don't reflect the three from this morning.

"In this data set, two distinct groups can be formed, and two of last night's rave party victims fit into it. The first group consists of several types of people, but they all are under the age of forty-five and all died from mutilating attacks centered on the upper body, with a special interest in the neck area. We suspect this focus is primarily strategic on the killers' part. Death would be quick, quiet, and messy. The most extensive amount of mutilation occurs after the victim's death and it appears that the same murder weapon was used in all of the attacks. The media released an artist's rendering of the weapon."

Miles tapped the spacebar, replacing the map with the weapon graphic shown to the public by one of the local TV stations.

"Although this drawing is contrived purely from an artist's imagination, we don't think it is very far from accurate. I can't recall ever seeing anything of this nature before, so we are guessing the killers designed and built the weapons themselves, which fits into the serial profile."

"How many do you think we're dealing with?" came from the crowd.

"We're guessing three or four. After analyzing this data, we discovered that some of these homicides happened almost simultaneously in locations too far apart for one killer to commit. Unless one man figured out how to be in more than one place at one time, he's got help."

Miles advanced the presentation. He took in the entire audience and noticed Joshua sitting in the back, offering a slight nod of acknowledgment.

"The third victim from last night fits into the second, smaller group of only seventeen victims. The severity of mutilation in this group is much more extensive. Some of them were decapitated, some were completely dismembered, and in most of these cases at least one vital organ was missing, primarily the heart."

"Why did the connection between these prior cases go unnoticed for so long? It seems like something this bad would have set off some alarms before now," queried another voice from the group.

"I honestly don't know why, but that very thought crossed my mind when I crunched this data. My best guess is that the short amount of time we're dealing with, in conjunction with the nature of some of the victims, made it a little less obvious."

"What's the nature of some of the victims?" came from another part of the room.

"A large percentage was homeless, and unfortunately, it's an easy demographic to miss. I've already proposed a few changes to our system to help fix the issue. Now, we need to get to this."

The police artist's version of the murder weapons filled the other two screens.

"As I said before, the press' idea of a murder weapon looks very close to what we believe to be true. Our artist drew two different weapons, as we feel two separate weapons are being utilized. Some cases only show evidence of one or the other, while some show that both were used, which also supports our theory of a small group of serial killers.

"Serials working together is a very rare occurrence, but it does happen, and it establishes a whole separate range of problems. Most serial killers follow a very specific pattern, seldom wavering from it, but with more than one we have to deal with a blending of mental processes. This blending effect makes it harder to predict what will happen next. With that said, I'd like to turn the meeting over to our guest advisor. Some of you have probably heard of Detective Joshua Stone before as his reputation precedes him. He is a highly recommended criminal psychologist, and he has more solved homicides under his belt than any other member of Scotland Yard. Joshua."

Stone left his seat and approached the podium, descending the gentle slope of the center aisle. He carried his hat in one hand and a briefcase in the other. He was in his late forties, but he appeared to be a little younger. His hair was dark brown, except for small patches of silver interrupting the color at his temples. His thick mustache that almost concealed his upper lip was the same color. He was average height and appeared to be in excellent physical condition except for a slight limp in his left leg. He spoke with an accent that bordered cockney.

"Good morning. Thank you for the introduction, Miles."

Joshua opened his briefcase and removed a folder full of papers. He arranged it on the podium as he started.

"Miles and I go back a few years. We lived in the same village in Ireland when we were very small. I was sad to see such a fine Officer serving anywhere besides the Yard, but that's our loss. Time is of the essence, so I'll get down to business."

Stone flipped through the stack of papers. The officers in the audience that knew Stone, or of him, whispered to each other.

"I must warn you that this case is going to get worse before it's over. I can issue that warning because we dealt with a very similar chain of events at Scotland Yard, and to be honest with you, we never stopped the killers. The homicides we tried to solve stopped just over ten months ago, which isn't very long before they started here. It is my belief that the same group migrated across the Atlantic and started anew here. The problem is we have no idea why."

Joshua flipped a few pages into his packet, scanning the information he wanted to present next.

"I've spent the last few years of my life following this group, trying to find answers and stop the killings in England. One would expect to have more answers by now, but this troop doesn't leave many clues. I have managed to come across some pretty unbelievable things, which dictates that I begin with a little history."

Joshua produced a flash drive from his jacket pocket and plugged it into the laptop. A graph popped up on the screen. It showed the number of matching cases against a time line, and the average was remarkably consistent.

"My research led me further and further back. I found other incidents that almost exactly match, some of which date back much farther than I expected. If you'll notice the span of dates, the oldest is just over four hundred years ago."

A hush swept across the audience. Some did not accept what they heard and others wondered if they heard correctly.

"I can see the shock on some of your faces. I was just as mystified when I compiled the hard facts. A few other interesting discoveries presented themselves as well."

He tapped the keyboard, replacing the graph with an animated map of the world. A red dot appeared over central China and a line worked across the country, creating another dot in western China, and so on. The line progressed across the map, moving west. A counter at the bottom of the screen, labeled year, started at 1594 and increased as the line grew longer.

"This power point shows the locations of the cases I have found. As you can see, the progression steadily moves west across the continent of Asia, then to Europe, and ultimately here to New York. This evidence suggests the same group of killers slowly worked through the world for over four hundred years. We know this can't be possible, or can it? I think Occam theorized it best when he said that whenever all the possible explanations are eliminated, whatever remains, regardless of its impossibility, must be the solution."

"Then what do we do?" came from the audience.

"We have to accept what is left as the truth. I did not allow myself to accept what I found for a long time, but I now whole-heartedly believe what I am about to tell you."

Joshua set down his papers and leaned slightly forward against the podium, his notes unnecessary for the explanation, and needing to take some weight off of his left leg.

"As I investigated further, I found that the killings themselves weren't the only commonalties. The stories and theories surrounding the homicides started to follow a pattern. Most of them could be easily dismissed as myths or legends, but one stood out against the rest. At the time this began, lines of communication were relatively nonexistent over large areas, especially so from country to country. I found it strange to see the same myth pop up in several different cultures that had no contact with each other, and that particular myth coincides almost perfectly against this global progression."

Stone set the laptop in motion, and the screen scrolled through a series of drawings and sketches, some of which were obviously very old.

"These drawings depict a creature that is capable of doing exactly what you're seeing here and what we couldn't stop in England. Different cultures have different words to describe this creature, but they all mean roughly the same thing. Some translations call it the taker of life, some call it a demon, and some refer to it as unholy. Modern man calls it a vampire."

A wave of movement and whispered comments washed through the audience.

"I know exactly how you feel. Remember, I refused to believe it at first, just like you are doing now. I didn't want to accept what the evidence suggested was the truth."

The murmurings continued to work through the group, drawing attention away from Stone.

"I think we need to listen to what he has to say. We don't know what we're dealing with and Mr. Stone has a lot more experience with this than any of us," intervened Joe. As a much-respected senior officer of the force, he hushed the crowd.

"As I was saying," resumed Stone, "I didn't want to believe it either. Vampires are creatures novelists and movie makers conjured to scare us as children, but my own childhood made this myth tangible, even though I didn't want to believe."

Joshua removed his jacket and unbuttoned his shirt to expose his right shoulder and upper back. A large scar ran across his skin, almost eleven inches in length, from the shoulder and across his back towards the back of his left leg.

"As a child, I was attacked by…something. I have this scar and others that run down the back of my leg. The trauma of the experience blocked the whole episode from my memory for several years. My foster parents told me I was attacked by a wild dog, which satisfied my curiosity until I saw a similar wound on one of the victims. I never questioned that a dog could not inflict such a wound. With the help of hypnotic therapy, my mind finally released the memories of the event. I investigated my own injury, trying to find a link. The doctor's account of the attack only produced more unanswered questions."

A copy of the doctor's report filled the screen with certain lines and words highlighted by the software.

"According to the report, I was unconscious when my foster parents took me to the doctor, and I mumbled something they couldn't understand. The doctor made my parents wait in another room while he tended to the wounds. As you can see, the doctor could tell that a dog wasn't to blame, even though that's what they claimed. No one else saw the attack, so my fosters either assumed or made up an explanation that they could accept. The wounds were too deep to be a bite, and they didn't react as such. The doctor identified the source of the wounds as unknown."

The screen went black as an audio track prepped itself to be played.

"As I said, hypnosis found the answer. I couldn't remember what happened, and no one could fill in the blanks. This recording is from the session when my therapist worked through the mental block."

Stone hit a key to start the audio sequence.

"Joshua?"

"Yes."

"I want you to think about the night you were bitten by the dog. You were hurt very badly, and your foster parents had to take you to the hospital. Do you remember?"

"Yes."

"Can you tell me what happened?"

"No, and I know I don't want to know."

"Joshua, I really need to know what happened. Don't forget that you are safe now; you're just remembering what happened. It's not real this time, okay?"

"Okay."

"You can start at whatever point you want to."

"I'm playing out behind my foster home, chasing fireflies. They are all in the woods behind the house."

"How far from the house are you?"

"I'm not sure, but I can't see it. The fireflies are gone now."

"Where did they go?"

"I don't know, but I feel scared. I think someone is hiding in the woods."

"What are you going to do?"

"I'm running home. I feel like someone is chasing me, but I can't see anyone. I'm scared."

"Don't be scared, you're just remembering."

The child's voice didn't answer in acknowledgement, but his rapid breathing was audible.

"What's happening Joshua?"

"Who is he? Why is he chasing me? He doesn't belong here."

"Did you say 'he' Joshua?"

"A man is chasing me. He's right behind me, trying to catch me. He keeps swinging his arms out, trying to grab me and drag me down. I want to get away from him."

"What does he look like?"

"Something is…wrong...with him."

"What's wrong with him?"

"He looks sick."

"How does he look sick?"

"He's very pale like he's sick and his eyes are wild. I need to get away…ugh!"

"What happened Joshua?"

"He got me on the back. His fingers cut my back. It hurts, and it burns. I can't run as fast. He's going to catch me!"

"No, he won't Joshua. He's not really there. It's just a memory. You're completely safe. Can you continue?"

"He hit me again in the leg! His fingers are stuck in my thigh! He's squeezing! It hurts! I'm falling down! I can't get…"

"Burbank!"

The safe-word stopped the commotion and Joshua fell silent. The therapist's voice continued, giving the exact place, time, and date. She added that Burbank was a code word she established at the beginning of the session to immediately pull Joshua out of the hypnotic trance and restore the memory block. Trauma of such a high severity offered uniquely high risks if repeated as it could further the damage.

"Joshua?"

"Yes."

The voice sounded adult and calm.

"How do you feel?"

"I'm fine. What happened?"

"I think we found what you've been looking for."

The recording stopped, and Stone continued.

"I wanted to be absolutely sure about what happened to me. The session you just heard was with the third therapist I saw, and none of them were aware of each other. Each time a therapist wormed through the mental road block, the story was the same. I have since been able to resolve the emotional damage and restore my memory of the event."

A picture replaced the blackness on the screen. It was a drawing of a man.

"This face is the face from my memory, and I think he is one of the killers."

"How can that be?" asked one of the officers. "If you were a child and the attacker was a grown man, he'd be too old now."

"That would be the case if we were dealing with a normal man. I've gone through several texts and personal accounts of vampire claims and sightings. I even went to the University of Oxford to discuss the findings with some of the professors there and we came up with some answers."

Joshua handed out copies of a small booklet titled A Study in Vampirism.

"This booklet contains all of the information we managed to collect, but I'll just summarize what it contains."

Joshua opened a large text he pulled from his briefcase. The text carried the information from the booklet as well as many of his notes and photographs.

"Most cultures see the vampire as nothing more than a myth, and Americans have adapted them into popular entertainment icons. Let me assure you, this isn't movie magic."

The audience's demeanor ranged from curious to nervous.

"Vampirism is a disease that is transmitted through direct contact with bodily fluids. The disease actually attacks the victim's blood cells, breaking them down at the cellular level. For all intents and purposes, the victim clinically dies. Without a supply of living blood, the victim will eventually die in the true sense of the word, and this is the motive behind the attacks you've seen. The mutilation serves as a front to disguise what they are actually doing. As Sergeant O'Toole mentioned, most of the attacks focused on the neck. They strike there because it is an easy target and the jugulars supply a large amount of blood in a short amount of time. Once the blood is ingested, the necessary elements are utilized as fuel."

"How does that work?"

"We're not completely certain. It's almost like a person dies when they become a vampire, but they don't. I looked over the information about your cases on the flight over this morning. The John Doe autopsy Dr. Palmer performed a few days ago was a dead vampire, for lack of better terminology."

"How can they die if they're already dead?"

"The disease makes certain genetic changes to the host, and these changes cause physical and mental changes that somehow allow them to cheat death."

Dr. Palmer stood up to ask a question.

"Mr. Stone, if this disease allows the victim to cheat death, how did one end up on my exam table?"

"From what we've discovered, a vampire can be destroyed, but we don't know exactly how. We have found three to date, but they were nothing more than skeletons. You were lucky to find one so quickly."

"If you don't know how to kill them, what are we going to do?"

"That's a good question. We think we have an answer, but we haven't had the opportunity to test our theory. It seems the disease utilizes the victim's heart as a type of conversion chamber since the concentration of the infection is heaviest there. We think destruction of the heart via removal or any other means squares the deal with Death, but the problem we've faced is getting close enough to do it. One of the physical changes that we know of is enhanced strength and conventional means will not stop them. It is very much like a drug user high on PCP. They can take several bullets and act as if nothing happened. The theory is based on our findings from the past several years, and the cases you're working seem to follow suit."

Joshua pulled Miles' graph back onto the screen.

"I think this second group is all dead vampires with the hearts removed."

"Why didn't they all fall apart like the John Doe? Something like that would cause quite a stir," asked Dr. Palmer.

"We think it is somehow related to the length of time the victim suffers from the disease. Once the disease can no longer support itself, it dies, and the body seems to catch up to what should have happened to it."

"How is that?"

"Let me give you an example. If a person was infected with the disease a week ago, he was clinically dead since that time. If he truly dies, the body will return to its correct state as if the disease never occurred. The corpse would look normal at that point, but the autopsy would yield senseless results. Now, assume the infection took place thirty years ago. What do you expect would happen, using what you've learned here today?"

"The body's rate of decay would accelerate to compensate for the borrowed time."

"That's right. If you recheck your John Doe now, that process would be finished, and you can determine the actual date of death, or more appropriately infection, fairly accurately."

"What can we do to stop it?"

"From a medical standpoint, we can do nothing, but contemporary medical knowledge deals with living tissue. Vampires are a completely different ball game."

Joshua flipped through his book, looking.

"Moving on a bit, let's talk about the cases at hand. We rendered several drawings of murder weapons as well and most of them are very similar. We believe, however, that these weapons don't exist at all. The attacks are done by hand."

Another wave of shock rolled through the crowd.

"As I said, the disease makes physical changes to the victim. Outwardly, the changes are subtle, but they're there. Vampires develop sharp, talon like claws in the place of their finger and toenails, and these claws, in combination with their enhanced strength, produce the results you've seen."

"If you haven't been able to test your theory, who figured out that removal of the hearts works?" asked Angela.

"That's another good point, and one I've contemplated for several months. It seems the only thing powerful enough to kill a vampire would be another vampire, but that doesn't make sense. Vampires killing their own kind would be counter-productive to their proliferation as a species. It could be blamed on a territorial instinct, but our evidence suggests that they tend to work in groups, and that would also work against their survival instinct."

"Who do you think it is?"

"I'm not sure, but I personally think there's something else out there."

"So you are saying we have more than one supernatural killer running around," said Joe.

"I'm not positive of anything, but the evidence suggests a natural predator exists."

Joshua paused a moment, allowing a break for more questions. The room remained silent until Joe broke the tension.

"Why did they come here?"

"That's another question we have yet to answer, but my instinct tells me they are looking for something. Let me show you."

Joshua returned to his world map.

"As you can see, the progression is slow but continuous. The group never appears in the same place twice, which makes them harder to catch. We can't get very close before they're gone, and all we have is what they leave behind."

"Do they have any weaknesses?"

"The only one we are fairly sure of is sunlight. I don't know if this is a true weakness or if the disease makes them photosensitive, but we don't have any accounts of sightings or attacks during daylight hours. I think most of what we believe to be weaknesses, like holy water and the cross, are nothing more than movie filler. The stake through the heart may have some truth, based on how we believe the disease works."

"I don't know of anything that can't be killed with a big enough gun!" said one of the S.W.A.T. team members.

"That sounds very easy, but landing the shot is more difficult than you think. I've seen cases where an entire clip of bullets was unloaded and the vampire didn't fall. The disease apparently gives them heightened agility as well because I never thought dodging a bullet was possible, but the facts are there."

Joshua closed his text and again leaned against the podium.

"As introduced, I am here as an advisor for these cases. My intent is to aid your investigations with advice and suggestions, but I will not interfere with your protocols. I will remain here at headquarters as a resource because I feel I can do the most good that way. This group must be stopped. Aside from the obvious threat they pose, we could also be faced with a pandemic with no cure. The victims that are not killed for food are still infected with the disease and they will continue to spread that disease. At some point, the spread will progress, completely out of control, as more and more people are infected. We have no idea what will happen when their source of food is gone, but it will mean an end to the human race as we know it."

The crowd fell silent for a second time as Joshua took an empty seat at the front of the room. Joe took the floor.

"Thank you, Detective Stone. Your presentation was very informative and enlightening."

Joe turned his attention to the audience.

"Okay people, we've got a job to do. We will step up all the patrols, especially at night. I have all of you reassigned into two-man teams if you don't already have a partner because I don't want anyone working alone out there. We also need to focus on the areas where we see large groups of homeless people. I also want all of you to learn that booklet from cover to cover. We don't have a chance if we don't know what we're dealing with out there. Captain, do you have anything else?"

"Yes. As I said before, we are on alert status, which means hourly radio checks from all units. I don't want any heroes out there. If you get in a tough spot, call for backup. I've put together a list of the officers that I want assigned here to headquarters. Once I call the names, the rest of you are dismissed to your duties."

A beat cop entered the meeting room, almost out of breath, with a desperate look on his face.

"Captain, you need to see this while everyone is here."

"What is it?"

"This was discovered earlier this morning."

The officer handed Bishop a flash drive. He hooked it to the laptop. It contained one video file, and the operating system asked what the user wished to do.

"An officer with campus security found this in the parking lot this morning at the University. He was making his normal rounds and found a car that was severely vandalized sometime during the night, and there was a lot of blood, but no bodies. This digital file was copied from a digital camera almost buried in snow about thirty feet from the car. He called 9-1-1 right away."

Bishop clicked the mouse to initiate the media player. The movie popped up on the large screen behind him. The angle pointed directly at the ground, and the person with the camera was running, feet breaking into the frame at even intervals. The camera was then dropped, as the image rolled over and stopped. The new angle showed a black Charger, sitting alone in a snow-covered parking lot. The camera was obviously lying on the ground, and the lens zoomed in to autofocus on the car, bringing it into clear view. The top was crushed inward, almost half the distance to the top of the dashboard. A leg hung out over the edge, draping over the driver's side door. Red smears of blood stained the glass of the driver's side door.

The jolt to the ground, or the water melting out of the snow, somehow activated the microphone on the camera as a slight breeze was suddenly audible.

A loud crash broke the calm as another body flew through the front windshield, shattering the glass and actually rocking the car on its shock absorbers. A large man landed on the hood from above, reached out and grabbed the two obviously dead bodies and carried them into the sky as he flew away.

The crowd could not believe what they were seeing. A wave of shock and awe worked through the group.

The man returned within a few moments, pulling a third body from the car and disappearing into the night.

"The scene doesn't change through the rest of the recording," offered the officer that delivered it. "It ran until it used up all the space in the camera's memory."

The demeanor of everyone in the room changed, at varying rates, to one of unified fear and disbelief; the nightmare was real. Without a doubt, they knew what they were up against.

Bishop broke the silence by announcing the list of eight officers he wanted retained at headquarters. Joe and Angela were a fourth of that group. Joe approached the Captain once the room cleared.

"Captain, why do you want us assigned here? Angela and I have the most time on the case, and you need every available officer out there to fight those things, not to mention the leads we need to follow."

"You'll have to assign those duties to another unit. I want you here because you've been on the case since the beginning. You two know the most about it."

"What about Marina? We still need to find her?" asked Angela.

"What do you have?" asked the Captain, looking at Angela but not making eye contact.

Angela crossed her arms. "We know that she went to Albany by bus yesterday morning, and we need to check with the station there to find out if anyone saw her."

"I'd send a uniformed unit to check it out," returned Bishop, looking back at Joe when Angela pulled her jacket more tightly around herself.

"Understood," answered Joe, even though his displeasure with the order was written all over his face.

The Captain and Commissioner left the room to allow the task force to settle in. Joe turned his attention to Stone.

"I don't know what it is, but my hunch tells me you're on top of this. I didn't want to believe a word you said, but I can't see anything else that could be the truth."

"That's how I felt a few years ago, Detective. I absolutely refused to accept what I found, but I didn't make any headway on any of the cases until I realized that Occam might be right."

"I'll go check on that warrant for Dr. Arkits," said Angela after they got back to their office from the conference room.

"Okay, I'll get a unit to head upstate to find Marina. I want her here. I think she's a big piece of our puzzle. If Stone's suspicions are right, she may have seen whatever preys on these bloodsuckers, and that may be our only chance to stop them."

"Agreed. I'll be right back, and please don't say 'bloodsucker', that's too creepy."

The Sanitation crew finished up inside the warehouse and the city workers slowly dispersed, leaving nothing to indicate what happened in their wake. The roadblocks were removed, but the police kept the warehouse secure, and the press continued to push for information. Denise finally packed up and went back to the station when she realized she wasn't going to get anything newsworthy by conventional means.

She made a few phone calls when she reached the TV station. She wanted the scoop on what happened in the business district. Regardless of what most people thought about her reporting ability, she wasn't bad at it. There were better journalists out there and she did take shortcuts to reach the top, but it didn't mean she was totally devoid of talent or desire. She wanted the exclusive to prove a point to herself, and it would insure that Jack stayed off of the offensive for a while.

To get what she wanted this time meant taking a few of those same shortcuts. It also meant knowing the right thing to say at the right time to the right person. She dialed the number to reach the right person. She knew it was always the right time and she wouldn't have to say much either.

ChAPCER CWENCY-FIVE

The door buzzer pulled Julie from sleep. She sat at the kitchen table, still wearing her thief outfit, facing a now cold hot toddy. She tried to stay up after work, hoping to get some word on Ellen, but dozed off, unable to resist sleep any longer. The buzzer chimed a second time. The wall clock indicated it was just after eight in the morning.

"Yes," said Julie into the microphone.

"Ms. Romanowski, its Officer Hernandez and my partner. Can we come in?"

"Yes, just a moment."

Julie was instantly awake with anxiety and nervousness. She didn't know what she was going to hear, but at least she'd know something. Julie let the police into the apartment offering them comfortable chairs and drinks. Their expressions were somber, and they kept their posture very proper, politely refusing her hospitality.

"Miss, you might want to sit down," said Malcolm.

The life, all that was left of it at least, visibly drained from Julie's face. She knew what was coming next, and her body started to tremble uncontrollably as she collapsed onto the couch.

"Ms. Romanowski, we need you to come to the morgue to identify a body discovered by a window washer on a rooftop downtown this morning."

Julie's expression changed slightly, curiosity woven into the sadness.

"Why would she be there? Ellen is afraid of heights."

"I don't know. We think it might be your roommate, but we have to have a positive identification. We'd like to take you now if it's not too inconvenient."

"Okay, let me change and grab my purse."

Julie's curiosity didn't hold long, giving way to depression.

Angela walked into Judge Terrence's office to see the same secretary working behind the desk.

"Hi, what's new today?"

"You haven't heard? Judge Terrance is furious. The media and the public have called nonstop all day. Last night's fiasco caused a huge uproar and everyone wants answers. He's getting hit especially hard because he sits on the city council."

"We were afraid of that. The press got there early and kept pressing for answers. We were worried that they might fill in the blanks on their own."

"Yeah, and the morning news didn't help. All the stations broadcast what they could, and most of them had live coverage of the police keeping everyone out of the area. The press is having a field day, saying were infringing their rights. The kicker came about an hour ago."

"What do you mean by kicker?"

"Channel 17 released the news that three kids were killed at a drug party last night and the police are refusing comment or release any kind of statement."

"Crap! This just keeps getting worse. How did they find out? We had the area locked down!"

She turned and went for the door, wanting to share the bad news with Joe.

"Do you want your warrant?"

"Yes, thank you. I forgot what I came down here for when you told me the news."

Joe was furious, to say the least, when he heard. They were in their meeting when the news hit so they were hearing it second hand. He called Captain Bishop to make sure he was aware of it and asked him what course of action he wanted them to take. The fact they had an information leak in the department was obvious, and the damage was already done.

The Captain was just as mad as Joe, and he said he would pass the info along to the Commissioner. Joe told Bishop they needed to make a short run to Arkits' office. They had a strong lead that could help the case and no one else was available to make the visit. The Captain grudgingly agreed, so Joe went back to get his partner.

"Let's go talk to the doctor and get on this lead. I'm getting tired of coming up empty handed and I can't stand being cooped up in here."

Joe and Angela left the Precinct, headed for the doctor's office.

"I thought that was too easy on the phone," she said as Joe worked through the late lunchtime traffic. "It didn't take him any time at all to give me an answer that killed the lead we had, no pun intended."

"Well, he can't keep us out of it now. We'll tear his office apart if we have to. I hate it when people lie to me."

Tatianna knocked on the door to her guest bedroom before she entered. Marina was still asleep, in the fetal position and trembling visibly.

"Marina, what's wrong?"

Marina woke with a start, her hair and nightgown soaked with sweat. Tears ran from her eyes.

"I don't know. I woke up at home covered with blood, but it wasn't mine and I can't remember what happened. I was going to the market, and then it was the next morning and I was at home. I don't know what happened in between."

Tatianna held her sister, rocking her back and forth, having no idea what to do or say.

Joe and Angela approached the front desk in Dr. Arkits' office.

"How can I help you?" asked the receptionist. She was a young woman, probably no older than twenty, with blue eyes and sandy blond hair. Her sweater was too tight to be considered professional and she looked somewhat put upon to look away from her copy of Cosmopolitan.

"We're here to see Dr. Arkits," said Joe.

"He's not here. He left yesterday for a four-week vacation in Cancun."

"Must be nice," added Angela. "We can still check the records if he's here or not."

"I'm sorry, but I can't let you do that without…"

"A warrant," finished Joe, as he set it across the article she was reading about sexual positions.

"Very well, help yourselves."

She motioned to the shelves containing the medical charts of all the doctor's patients. Both shelves ran parallel to the reception desk, hiding the second shelf behind the first.

Joe and Angela looked for the chart on Kelly Richardson first to verify Arkits lied about the medic alert bracelet. The receptionist made phone calls as soon as the detectives were out of her line of sight. Angela noticed, but she just kept watch through a small break in the charts. She could see the secretary's hands as she kept hanging up and redialing, like she kept getting a busy signal or an answering machine. She would glance over her left shoulder every few seconds to see if either officer came back from the records area, but Angela was behind her to her right.

Angela moved beside Joe. She needed a distraction so she could use his redial trick to find out whom the receptionist was trying to call so desperately. The chart for Kelly Richardson wasn't on the shelves.

"Does the doctor keep charts anywhere else?" Angela asked aloud from behind the charts.

"He usually has some in his office, but it's locked. I don't have a key."

Joe asked which door led to Arkits' office. Once identified, he disintegrated the lock with his service revolver and walked inside. The receptionist bolted like a scared rabbit at the sound of the gunshot, taking refuge in the restroom in the lobby. It disturbed no one else. The office was empty since the doctor was on "vacation."

Angela walked straight to the phone, seeing it had a history log. As she suspected, the girl tried to call the same number repeatedly. Angela hit redial, jotted down some notes, then hung up and went to join Joe.

"I don't see any records in here either, Angela. I think the secretary is giving us the run around, but she should persuade easy enough."

He purposely spoke loud enough for the petrified receptionist to hear, even through the locked restroom door.

"I think she may be in on it," added Angela. Joe stayed at the door to make sure the secretary didn't try to slip away.

"She was trying to call Arkits at home. That's an odd place to call when he's in Cancun."

"How nice is that? This will be very interesting."

"Wait a minute," whispered Angela, "maybe we aren't looking in the right place," pointing at the PC on the desk.

She sat down and switched on the computer.

"He said something on the phone about recently converting to a new system. Maybe what we need is in here."

"Can you get into his system?"

"Yeah, I'm pretty sure I can. He's got some security, but I've hacked tougher stuff."

"You?"

"Yeah, I spent a lot of time on the computer when I was a kid and took some classes as electives in college. I taught myself how to hack as a way to get back at a professor that embarrassed me in class every chance she got."

"You? What did you do?"

"I sent a candid photo of her, that she was stupid enough to keep on her computer at work, to all of the departments via e-mail. She had some kinky hobbies that apparently involved another woman, so I used it as payback and deleted her hard drive. I heard she resigned from embarrassment."

"Wow! I didn't know you had it in you, partner. I'm impressed."

"Well, I was young and dumb, and lucky they didn't decide to press any charges against me, but I appreciate the compliment. The school was trying to get rid of her for some of her public behavior, but they didn't have enough to do it."

Joe decided to go collect the receptionist as Angela sliced through the doctor's defenses, having little trouble getting around the passwords. The doctor apparently didn't expect anyone to hack his computer since the security in place would only be useful in keeping mild curiosity at bay. Most of the files looked normal, and she was about to stop looking when she decided to check the file structure. She found a discrepancy.

The file sizes and the amount of available drive space didn't add up. With a little digging, she found a large section of files were hidden on the hard drive, buried in several layers of sub directories, and they were more heavily guarded. As she drilled down to view the files, the computer would create another hidden directory, copy the files contained in it to that directory, and delete the files from the prior directory. The target directory was always empty when it displayed. Angela had hacked this type of security before, so she knew what to do to get around it. Otherwise, she could have spent eternity not finding anything.

"Miss, are you alright?" Joe asked as he knocked on the restroom door. "I need to ask you a few questions. Miss?"

The door remained closed, the room behind it in total silence. He tried the handle, checking that it was actually locked.

"Miss, if you're okay, let me know, or I'll have to shoot out this lock to help you."

The door opened immediately. The receptionist was terrified at the very thought of a second report from the pistol. She was deathly afraid of guns, and the unannounced discharge sent her to the edge of hysteria. She went to one of the chairs in the back corner of the lobby's waiting area and sat down. Joe followed her.

She was a petite woman, wearing too much makeup, and she was obviously uncomfortable. She trembled as she fidgeting in the chair. She would not make eye contact with Joe. He recalled the name from the plaque on the front desk.

"What are you trying to hide, Crissy?"

"What do you mean?"

"You tried to call Dr. Arkits at home several times when we started looking through the records. Why would you try to reach him there so desperately if he's in Mexico?"

Crissy obviously didn't realize the detectives could see her from behind the shelves, but she knew she was caught. The expression on her face confirmed it.

"I just thought he should know. He is very protective about his business, and he always drills me about keeping everything confidential and never giving out any information. I don't want to get in trouble."

"You didn't answer my question. Why did you call him at home if he's in Cancun? You told us he was gone. Would you like to change your story?"

Crissy leaned forward, putting her head in her hands and letting her knees support the weight, still trembling.

"Yes. They really are leaving for Mexico, but not for a few days. Dr. Arkits wanted everyone to think he was gone so he'd have a few days of peace before they left. He said I was the only one to know he was still in town."

"Don't you think this is pretty important?"

"He was very detailed with his instructions."

"Do you know a patient named Kelly Richardson?"

"The name sounds familiar, but I can't place it."

"Does your boss have anything to hide?"

She realized that she stood the chance of being in far more trouble if she didn't cooperate.

"I don't know. He acts strangely about it, the confidentiality I mean. He's been a lot worse about it lately."

"Have you noticed anything else strange?"

"He's been keeping some odd hours. I noticed a drop in the number of patients he sees and he works more nights. I don't know what he's working on that's taking so much time, especially when he's seeing less patients. Look, I just don't want to get in trouble and I really need this job. I'm a single mother. He already fired two other people from the staff without any justification or reason. It's like he's paranoid."

"Okay, that's all I wanted to know. Let me get your full name and personal information. We may need to contact you again."

Joe wrote down the answers to the questions when he heard Angela call him from the office.

"Did you find something?"

"Yes, and it's a pretty big piece of this puzzle. He's got some pretty fierce security on some of his files. The easy stuff I hacked at first was probably a ruse, but I've dealt with this type of security before. A weak program is installed, letting the user easily access what appears to be everything and they are tricked to stop looking. The strong security is usually never tampered with because they don't every go that far. Take a look at what I found."

Angela pressed a few buttons and a file opened on the screen. Joe looked on as Angela explained.

"This spreadsheet contains several patients and their medical information. The numbers identifying them are in a uniquely different format from the regular charts. None of the people in this spreadsheet have regular records with the other charts. Two particular columns caught my eye. The first identifies the patient as a diabetic and the second shows the next of kin. A few of the names are highlighted, one of which is Kelly Richardson."

"What do you make of it?"

"It's a checklist and all of the highlighted entries are almost identical in those two columns. They're all diabetics and they don't have any immediate relatives. I want a copy of this. I wonder how many of these names fit our list at the Precinct, or were identified by Miles."

"I'm betting all of them. We should pick up Arkits on the way back. This makes him an accessory, at the very least, and he bridges the gap between the killer and the victims. I'm glad we got that warrant."

"Definitely, but who's he an accessory to?"

"I'm hoping he'll answer that question."

"Let's take a look at his organizer. We might find something in there, too."

Angela flipped the electronic pages while Joe looked on.

"Wait a minute, go back a page."

Angela did as he requested, wondering what he saw.

"There, that meeting scheduled at 2:00 AM. That's an odd time for an appointment and there's no name."

"That could be the person he's supplying."

"Can you check and see if he had, or if he's got, any other meetings like that?"

"Yeah, I just have to sort it that way."

Angela hit a few keys and the electronic calendar switched over to a year-at-a-glance format. Any meetings between the hours of midnight and 6:00 AM highlighted.

"Go back to the first one."

Angela queried the appointment and opened the electronic marker. It identified a phone meeting with a man named Alfred Sayer. They spoke at 3:30 in the morning."

"Who's Sayer?" asked Angela.

"I ran across that name at the old Thornquist garage. Alan Thornquist met with a man named Sayer several times and they were always at odd hours, too. The first meeting between them happened the same night at 2:00 in the morning. Mr. Sayer must be one of the killers."

"It sure looks that way. Let's keep digging. He used a ruse once, this could be another one."

Angela turned her attention to the computerized address book. The name Sayer was listed in the section labeled "S." One phone number was entered by the name, an international number. Angela jotted the number down in her notes.

"I don't think he would keep the name of his partner in crime like this. He's smarter than that. This might be a code name or someone else entirely."

"Okay, let's go get Arkits. I'll bet he has the answers we need. Crissy?"

"Yes sir."

"What's Dr. Arkits' home address?"

Crissy looked in her Rolodex and gave the address to the detectives.

"Thank you," said Angela.

"Do to the nature of this case you'll have to stay in the city until further notice in the event we need to speak to you again."

"Yes sir."

Joe and Angela left the office, bound for the home address.

"It looks like Arkits lives in the suburbs, in a very nice neighborhood I might add. His practice must be doing very well, even losing patients. It'll take us almost an hour to get there."

"Why don't you call and check in with headquarters. They need to know what we're doing out here and I want to see if they have anything new. The Captain wasn't very happy that we were going into the field, but he didn't have a choice."

Angela called in as Joe asked. They found out about the rooftop body and missing persons calling in a young lady to attempt identification. It was suspected the deceased was her roommate, who was listed as kidnapped, but they needed a positive ID on the body to proceed. Another eleven bodies were also discovered; all of them homeless people from all parts of the city.

The sun set as the detectives arrived at the Arkits' home. The street of the upper-class neighborhood was lined with oak trees and antique street lamps. All of the homes were very large, sitting on spacious lots. The soft light radiating through the crackle glass globes cast a pale amber tint on the snow, making the borough all the more inviting.

The doctor's house, a large Victorian gothic in style, sat back from the street behind a large front yard. Two windows were alight along the porch that that ran across the front of the entire house. Smoke from the fireplace rose gently into the cold night air from the chimney on the left end of the house. The brick driveway circled around a large fountain with a trio of winged angels as the centerpiece. Joe stopped the car at the base of the steps that led onto the porch. All of the intricate trim was flawlessly painted white. Several Adirondack rocking chairs sat along the porch, offering several quaint places to sit and enjoy the landscaping when the weather permitted.

Joe rang the bell after they walked to the front door. Their footprints were the first to disturb the snow in front of the house. The garage, and more commonly used doorway, was most likely on the backside of the house. Joe rang again when no one answered. Angela noticed the current copy of the New York Times resting on the front porch, wrapped in a plastic bag. Joe chose to knock on his third attempt.

"Do you smell that?"

Angela caught wind of it a few seconds after Joe. The light wind shifted direction, drawing the fireplace smoke around the front side of the house.

"Yes, what is that? Oh God..."

Angela wrinkled her nose, her expression one of recognition and disgust.

Joe drew his revolver and kicked the door open upon identifying the smell for himself. The stench rolled out of the house when the wooden door frame yielded to Joe's second kick and it almost knocked them over as they crossed the threshold. They broke apart to search room by room, covering their faces in an attempt to reduce the horrible odor and smoke they inhaled.

Angela stopped mid-sweep, freezing without a word.

Joe sensed her hesitation and stopped.

"What is it?"

"I'm going to be sick. Look in there, in the fireplace."

Joe turned to look at the firebox. The remains of two burnt bodies lay on the iron grate. A menagerie of charred chunks that would fit together to make an entire corpse lay broken in the fireplace and on the tile floor, still smoldering. The second body mostly intact, resting atop the remains of the first. The arms were still bound behind its back with a length of cable that had thus far survived the heat from the flames and white-hot embers. Joe's face lost its color. Angela doubled over and went to her knees, retching in small spasms. The smell seemed stronger once they saw the source.

"Oh my God! Who are we dealing with?! They were still alive!" Angela, being overcome with the need to vomit, heaved again and started coughing.

Joe leaned over, supporting his upper body by putting his hands on his knees. He took the deepest breath he could with the putrid smell of death lacing the air. He moved to Angela and helped her to her feet so they could get back outside before they succumbed to the smoke or lost the last traces of their sanity.

Joe got his partner to the nearest rocking chair. He stayed on his feet, breathing in the clean, crisp winter air in long draws. After several breaths, he could breathe normally, but the acrid fumes had already burned his throat, leaving a caustic feeling and a lingering remnant of the ashy vapors.

Angela took shorter, faster inhalations. She was on the verge of hyperventilating. Joe knelt it front of her and took her hands in his, calling her attention to his voice.

"Angela, look at me. Focus on my voice and my hands. It's okay. You've got to slow down your breathing."

He felt her grip tighten slightly in acknowledgement.

"I'm not going to say that I've seen worse than this because it would be an outright lie, but we will get through this and catch these twisted bastards. We're in this together and we're both going to be okay. I want you to slow down and try to take a good deep breath."

Angela focused on her partner like he asked. She drew on his strength and slowed her breathing. It got easier as the smoky smell gave way to the normal scents of winter. Joe wiped the tears running down her cheek with a handkerchief from his pocket as she calmed herself down.

"That's good. You're doing just fine. Now, we've got to get this cleaned up, quickly and quietly. If the people in this neighborhood get wind of this we will never get this case solved. A lot of the people that live around here are very influential downtown, and we're already having enough trouble as it is because of the press."

Angela nodded as she rebuilt her composure and got complete control of herself.

"They sure don't cover anything like this back at the academy."

"That's the honest to God truth. Are you okay now?"

"Yes, I'll be okay. Thanks Joe."

"No need for that; I know you'd do the same for me. And don't worry about what just happened; that's just between us."

Angela stood up and gave Joe a heartfelt hug. She felt him return the gesture in a loving, fatherly way. She backed away and straightened her coat as he walked back down the steps to their car. He called the necessary parties and instructed they use a quiet, staggered approach to minimize attention on the house, and to pull around to the back for cover from the street.

The driveway that went around to the back of the house was lined with thick evergreen trees that would give them cover from any curious onlookers. Joe pulled the car around to park it out of sight in front of the garage while Angela waited on the front porch. The cold air helped her mind focus and the stench to lessen, even though she could still smell passing wafts of the odor.

"We've got to go back in there. Can you handle it?" asked Joe as he came around the end of the porch.

"Yes, I can go back in there now. It won't catch me off guard this time. I've never seen that before and I sure hope I don't ever again."

"I think the odds are in your favor on that one."

They went back into the house to start working. He gave her the extra handkerchief he carried so she could cover her nose and mouth. They used the small cloth squares as air filters to protect themselves from further smoke inhalation and to lessen the smell.

The bodies, black and scorched with a slick, sticky appearance, were too extensively damaged for immediate identification. The one on top rested towards the back on the fireplace, wedged between the remains of the other body and the heat plate on the back wall of the firebox; what was left of the fragmented body rested directly on, through, and around the iron rack. It looked like the lower body was put into the fireplace before the fire was set, and the second body was thrown into the flames later. Closer inspection revealed that the ankles of the intact body were bound, but not with cable. The power cord from one of the desk lamps was used instead. The victims had no chance of escape. The fractured body appeared larger than the other one, so they assumed it was the doctor. They would have to wait for the dental records check to have a positive identification.

"Good evening, Detectives."

Dr. Palmer entered through the back door, the first to arrive.

"I told you our paths would cross again. The Commissioner wants me to get the first look at any more bodies we find. What do we...?"

His sentence trailed off when he looked at the fireplace. He didn't appear nauseated, but his expression strained with emotion when he looked.

"I see. What happened here?"

"We're not completely sure yet," answered Joe. "We haven't found any evidence of forced entry, and it doesn't look like anything is missing. We found signs of a struggle in the office and out in the hall by the front door, and we found a lot of blood around the desk. I'm guessing the killer attacked Dr. Arkits in there and moved the body in here."

"Who did you say?"

"Dr. Arkits."

"Dr. Charles Arkits?"

"Yes."

"My God, I went to medical school with him! We graduated in the same class. He pursued keeping people alive while I focused on figuring out why they died."

"Were you close?" asked Angela.

"We kept in touch, usually seeing each other at social functions. He was at the luncheon I attended the other day, just after the autopsy you attended."

"Was he okay?"

"Now that you ask, he did seem a little nervous. What is this all about?"

Joshua Stone entered the room. Bishop felt his presence would also prove beneficial.

"We're not positive," started Joe, "but it looks like Dr. Arkits was a type of broker for the killers. Benson uncovered a heavily guarded file on the computer at his office that isolated many of his patients, most specifically if they were diabetic and without any immediate family."

"Why would he do that?" asked Palmer.

"I think I may have the answer," interjected Stone. "We've seen this type of pattern before, and as unpleasant as it sounds, we believe vampires develop tastes, just like you might enjoy steak over chicken. Vampires prefer certain qualities in blood, and in this case, the doctor supplied diabetics for one of them because it likes the way a diabetic's blood tastes. We've seen these tastes range from alcoholics to anemics."

"That puts a whole new light on last night's slaughter," said Joe.

"Yes, it looks like one or more of them prefer a victim with some form of narcotics in their system. As morbid as it sounds, the killer probably gets an extra high from whatever drug the victim used."

"In last night's incident, the drug of choice was a designer."

"We saw other types of patterns in England as well, like gender, hair color, age, and sexual maturity."

Angela shuddered at the thoughts running through her head as the three men spoke. She had the mental picture of a menu, displaying people like entrees, with the killer picking the flavor he preferred as off handedly as the soup do jour or a bottle of house Chardonnay.

"That does make sense," said Palmer. "We have a hard time accepting it because it's beyond our realm of understanding for someone to be killed for that purpose. We've always been on top of the food chain and never experienced playing the role of prey."

"It's difficult for the hunter to accept that he's become the hunted," added Stone. "That's one of the main reasons we are in a state of denial about a vampire's very existence. In many ways, they are superior to us."

With that, the small group dispersed to their duties. The other requested parties trickled in slowly, just as Joe ordered, diligently working the crime scene to get it inspected and cleaned up as quickly as possible. Luckily, everything looked normal from the street.

"Jamat, I will be back late. I suspect this night will be busy."

"Why is that?" The question was delivered with a heavy Austrian accent.

"I've noticed activity and traces of them in the same general area for several nights. They're spending a little too much time around the docks and the warehouse district. I have a hunch I will see them tonight."

"I advise caution Daxxe. I suspect you will be outnumbered."

"It won't be the first time. I think they have located one of the books. It is not their nature to stay is one area so long."

"I pray you are right, and that you reach it first. I also expect you to be careful. Your life is far more valuable than that book. He can't possess them all as long as you walk this earth."

"I will be careful."

Daxxe took his leave and Jamat began his nightly ritual.

"Come out come out, wherever you are…"

Casey hid underneath a car in the back corner of the parking garage. He was sleeping on the top landing of the least used stairwell when someone woke him with several hard kicks to his side. He landed a lucky punch as he flailed in defense and managed to run out onto the seventh floor of the parking facility.

The man that attacked him was obviously strung out on something and looking for a fight. Casey encountered this kind before; he just had to wait him out until he got bored and moved on, looking for someone else to bludgeon in his drug induced stupor.

"Aw, come on out. I'm just foolin' with ya, I don't mean no harm."

Casey held his ground, knowing better from his prior experience. At this hour, no one else would be around anytime soon and no one would hear him if he called for help except the violent druggie.

"I know you're still here. I can smell your sweat and your fear."

Stefan worked through the vehicles slowly and carelessly. He knew exactly where to find his prey, but the game was too much fun to cut it short. He hit some of the hoods and fenders just to make noise. A large SUV took one of his shots to the front driver's side fender, setting off the alarm.

Casey heard a loud, shearing rip and the alarm fell silent, followed by thud and more footsteps. He laid flat on the concrete on his stomach so he could look under the parked cars. He saw booted feet walking away from a broken black box with wires dangling from one side.

This guy is totally stoned. I need to get out of here now.

He waited until the footfalls came from the far side of the parking level and he made a break for the closest stairwell. He wanted the longest head start he could manage to get away. He looked over his left shoulder when he was a few feet from the exit, trying to locate his assailant. He tripped and fell to the cold concrete floor, rolling hard into the wall to the left side of the door. The booted foot in his line of sight was responsible for the tumble.

"Howdy pardner!"

The stoned drugstore cowboy's boots were pointed with metal capped tips. His jeans were black denim, matching his jacket. His western style shirt was a deep red that matched the band around his black Stetson. A partially destroyed toothpick hung from the side of his mouth.

"Where're you off too?"

"I don't want any trouble. I don't have any money on me."

Stefan laughed, stepping on Casey's wrist to keep him pinned to the floor.

"Ungh! What do you want?"

"I'm just having a little fun."

Stefan reached down and grabbed Casey's pinned wrist, using it to lift him off of the floor altogether. Casey started flailing, and Stefan squeezed down hard, crushing the bones in the wrist and lower forearm.

"Aagh!"

Casey felt himself drop to the floor. He scrambled to his feet and ran blindly, looking for a way to escape.

A sharp blow to the back of his left shoulder spun him down, out of control. He hit the bumper of a pickup with his face, knocking loose two teeth. His broken wrist throbbed unbelievably as he reached out to break his fall. Blood ran over his lips from the open sockets, forming a crimson string from his mouth to a growing pool on the floor.

"What do you want?" forced the homeless man between arcs of pain and sobs.

"Endorphins, you pathetic little mortal."

"What?"

Casey couldn't immediately comprehend the unexpected answer. More blood dribbled through his teeth.

"I really like the way it tastes. Your brain releases them into your bloodstream in response to pain and fear, and boy do they make the blood sweet. It's a real rush!"

He kicked him in the ribs again. The force of the blow lifted him off of the ground and hurled him to the middle of the throughway. The metal tip of the boot punctured his skin.

Casey tried to get up and felt another sharp pain under his left arm. He knew some of his ribs were broken. The point of impact seared with pain intense enough to blur his vision. His hand returned red when he reached back to feel the wound. He felt light-headed, like he was floating, when he looked up and saw the clouded sky. He was on the top of a building, laying on the tar and pebble roofing material.

"Ah, welcome back. Now we can get started."

Casey's ribs wouldn't allow him enough air to produce a sound, and barely enough to remain conscious. His attacker grabbed him by the arms, lifted him up, and held him out over the ledge. He looked down, realizing that the roof didn't belong to the parking garage. He was far too high up to see the ground through the fog settled below him. A stronger wave of fear grappled his senses.

"That's it. You have to be awake or it's just no fun."

Stefan let go. The fall lasted about thirty feet before the rope tied around his ankle jerked him around 180 degrees and slammed him into the glass side of the 38th story. He hung helplessly as Stefan hovered down beside him.

"What are you?"

"You've been a lot of fun, pard, so I'll make the end quick!"

Stefan grabbed him by the neck and sunk his teeth into the strained flesh. The burning outmatched the pain from his ribs, arm, and newly dislocated hip. Blood loss made him so weak that his muscles went limp, forcing his body to lose its rigidity. He dangled in the cold, the only movement spurred by the weather.

Wind tore across his face, pulling him back to a fuzzy state of consciousness. He felt like he was falling, but all he could see was a dull shade of gray all around him. The air was cold and wet, with a slight salty scent. He heard a few far-off noises that sounded like a mixture of foghorns and car engines. He landed on his back at a sharp angle that knocked the breath from his lungs. He slid for several feet and started falling again. He was able to make out one of the large supports of the Brooklyn Bridge as he fell away through the fog. He was still trying to catch his breath when he hit the water. It pushed the little air he managed to draw from his lungs as he went under. He instinctively gasped for air, pulling icy sea water into his lungs. He blacked out as he sank through the dark water.

Daxxe perched atop an office building overlooking the warehouse district where he could see most everything except the shoreline. A cold breeze blew off the Atlantic keeping him downwind from anyone that might be in the warehouses. He waited patiently for several minutes, airborne the instant he picked up their scent.

"Why are we wasting our time?" asked Dimitri. "We could be feeding right now."

"Don't you ever think about anything else?" asked Viktor. "The Master wants us to find a special package. He knows when it arrived here, but he doesn't know where, and that is why we have to look for it."

"How will we find it?" asked Arin.

"It is marked. I do not know how, but we will know it when we see it. Now, get started, we only have a couple of hours before we'll have to hunt."

They moved to the next row. Trokar expressly forbade them from opening what they found, and he even gave specific instructions that Viktor was the only one to even touch it. The cautious nature they observed made the searching itself long and tedious. It was their third night searching in the same warehouse.

Daxxe watched the three break apart at the door, only recognizing one of them. He touched the scar running across his chest, remembering when Viktor gave it to him. The other two were very young, probably recent turns. Daxxe planned his movements as he slipped through the skylight.

Dimitri started where he left off the night before, scanning boxes and moving them aside if they concealed other crates from view. He hoped they would find some more bums; he enjoyed a snack while he worked. He slowly moved crates this way and that, putting them back as he found them if his search yielded nothing. He reached out to move a crate when he stopped cold. A strange scent drifted by him.

A hand closed around Dimitri's throat, forcing him to the floor before he could react. The claws found purchase, piercing the cold flesh of his neck and crushing the windpipe. He tried to strike back, but he lacked the strength of his adversary.

Daxxe flexed open his free hand to a striking posture and thrust it deep into the vampire's chest, cutting through flesh and bone, drawing out the blackened heart. The undead lasted long enough to see the organ before his eyes as he died the second time.

Daxxe's lips moved silently in an unknown tongue, making the heart burst into an unnatural, intense green flame. In a matter of seconds, the fire burnt itself out, leaving his hand empty and clean. He brushed his cleansed fingers over the still eyes to close the lids in final sleep as he bowed his head.

"May God have mercy on your soul."

He leapt into the air to make his next move.

The darkness in the warehouse was complete, but it offered Arin no hindrance. His night vision developed early for him, allowing him to see in the blackness as though it were daylight. He felt a strange, new sensation. It went away as quickly as it came and was just as quickly dismissed. He rounded a stack of crates and picked up the smell of old blood and something akin to smoke. He followed the trace of odor, not sure of the source, and found Dimitri's lifeless body in a broken heap on the warehouse floor, sans his heart.

"Vik…" escaped his lips before a sharp pain pierced his back and forced silence. The pain bored through his torso and into his chest. He looked down and saw a large clawed hand back into the gaping hole left in its wake. He blacked out as he felt his body lift into the musty air.

Viktor jumped over a stack of crates in time to see Arin's lifeless body land on the floor and slide into a row of stacked crates. He knew the body was thrown and that he was not alone. Only one enemy possessed the ability to strike at him in such a way.

Viktor felt Arin's pain rack his body and diminish through the death-severed link they no longer shared, just as he had felt Dimitri's demise. He moved cautiously, listening and trying to pick up the scent of his adversary.

Daxxe watched through the skylight and waited. He didn't want to confront Viktor yet. His importance to Trokar made him far more valuable alive.

Viktor took his leave when he realized Daxxe was gone. He was weak, trying to stifle the pain of losing two fledglings. He needed to feed to regain his full strength; he had no intention of facing off against Daxxe with anything less.

Daxxe chose not to follow, knowing it would be pointless. Viktor was Trokar's best henchman and his reputation preceded him in death and life.

Viktor was a hunter/tracker in mountains of Austria before he was turned, known to the locals only as Jäger. He was a very successful outdoorsman in all arenas, making good profits from furs and gaining more wealth from gambling. He had a sharp mind and a knack for efficiency, always thinking ahead and planning for contingencies. The combination made him a very dangerous and difficult adversary.

Jäger was known to all undead as the only human to ever single-handedly take down a mature vampire. The astonishment of the act overcame Trokar's anger at losing one of his best followers, so he turned the hunter, christened him Viktor, and awarded him his second in command. Many in Trokar's clan were vehement about Viktor's ascension, but the fear of their master held their tongues.

With a small bottle of healing salve, Daxxe tended to a small scrape on his forearm where Dimitri connected in the throes of death. He reserved the use of healing spells for more significant wounds. Using magic to heal small wounds was a useless waste of power and time. With the small gash closed, Daxxe took to the air, letting the wind rushing inland from the Atlantic carry him westward over the city.

Viktor returned to the terminal before the others, approaching Trokar's tenebrous chamber with a body over his shoulder. The young girl was awake, but staying unnaturally calm. He knocked and carried her inside. He placed her on a stone dais at the back of the room, locking her wrists and ankles in iron shackles that were bound in the rock. He ripped away what was left of her clothes and released his influence over her, allowing her to panic.

"What are you doing to me?! Help! Someone help me!"

"Your screams are wasted here. The Master will attend to you soon."

Viktor left the chamber, locking the door behind him. Lying alone in the dark, the girl kept calling for help. A column of stark white light from an unknown source slowly illuminated her bound form, making it impossible to see anything in the darkness that consumed the rest of the room.

"You have nothing to fear."

The voice came from the darkness beyond her feet.

"Who's there?"

She pulled at the manacles binding her on the altar, but she couldn't free herself. The chains rattled with her trembling.

"I have been called the Taker of Life and you have been chosen."

Trokar stepped into the light at the girl's feet, looking at her body. He slowly ran his hands over her frame, inspecting her. She fought back, but he didn't stop until she stopped begging and pleading, her spirit broken. Trokar walked to the head of the altar, gently stroking the hair back from her forehead. She cringed at the coldness of his skin, warmed only by her resentment.

"Poor child, it's better this way. The end is quite nearer than you think."

She caught a glimpse of his teeth, drawn by fang-like canines. He bent over her and sunk his teeth into her neck, allowing blood to pump out of the puncture wounds with each beat of her heart. She could feel the warm fluid run down her neck and shoulder, pooling underneath her as his mouth closed over the wound and drew her blood into his mouth. Dizzy and light-headed, the room spun and she felt more and more nauseous as he drank more and more. She blacked out, losing the fight to stay conscious.

Trokar licked the last of the blood from his lips as he approached his table and picked up one of the texts to continue his studies. The two very special books he lacked were all that separated him from his goal. He spent the next two hours working incantations through his mind.

A low moan escaped the girl's mouth, breaking the darkened silence, as her consciousness returned. She sat up, finding herself on a large stone altar. Chains hung from each corner, bound to the stone on one end and supported hand and ankle cuffs on the other ends. She was covered with a thin gown that looked like it was made of gauze. She could almost see through the material, and every inch of her body that would not been seen with clothing was covered in a variety of designs, all interlocked, like a massive tattoo. As she reached to touch it on her thigh, she saw the entire design glow a dark red visible through the fabric. She felt it sink into her skin as the light faded away.

She didn't recognize the room, or even know how she got there, but she felt comforted. She slid to the edge of the dais. The movement washed a wave of dizziness over her, making her think better of it.

A man, judging by size alone, approached her wearing a thick, black robe adorned with embroidered symbols, some of which appeared to be Celtic. He lowered his hood to look her. She could see him, but she wasn't disturbed by his appearance.

"Who are you?"

"I am your savior and Master, at the very least."

"And why I am here?"

"Because I want you here. You have a decision to make about your future."

"What do you mean?"

"At this point, you belong to me. In exchange for your servitude, I gave you a very powerful gift. That gift is yours, regardless of what happens, but what you decide to do with this gift, or what it does with you, rests in your hands."

"I don't understand."

"You lack the means to control it. If you choose to pledge your loyalty to me, you will be taken care of from this point on, but if you refuse my generosity, you will be turned out of my community to fend for yourself. I will offer only this as a forewarning – if you decide to turn away, you will meet a very painful and violent end. Make your choice."

"I will stay here with you, as that is the only real choice."

She wasn't sure what drove her, but she found herself attracted to her benefactor. She was drawn to the sharp angles on his face and his air of complete superiority.

"Here, you can put this on. I'll arrange for more later."

He mumbled a few words in a language she didn't understand. A tingling sensation ran over her entire body like pins and needles, slowly becoming visible as a dark blue aura. It brightened to a lighter shade, heightening the feeling to the point of pain. It briefly localized over her neck before dissipating. Trokar walked into the darkness, saying only that she was now known only as Shayla. She followed him into the void, not wanting to be away from him. As she walked, she realized she couldn't remember anything before waking on the altar, but the thought amounted only to mere curiosity.

"Stay here, I will come for you at my leisure."

Trokar left through a large wooden door. She heard the lock engage as darkness consumed the room.

"Viktor?"

"Yes, Master."

"Show her around and keep an eye on her. I will be most disappointed if anything happens to her."

"Understood."

Trokar went for Shayla, bringing her out into the main terminal. She squinted her eyes at the light, finding it uncomfortable; she waited for them to adjust. Viktor led her around the large room, allowing her to explore her new surroundings as the others looked on. Trokar returned to his chamber.

"She's a pretty one," said Mekune, eyeing her.

"She belongs to Trokar. Remember that or you'll end up like Ferrok."

They ventured farther into a more secluded part of the terminal, backing into the shadows. He chanced a quick kiss, but she held on, kissing him back more deeply.

"Be careful! No one can know!" he whispered sharply. She gave him a coy look and bit his lower lip as she backed away from him.

Viktor finished the hasty tour, returned Shayla to Trokar's chamber, and stalked off to his quarters, bound for his hammock.

ChApter Twenty~Six

Father Samuels slid the portal open between the confessionals.

"Forgive me Father, for I have sinned."

Samuels went rigid. It was the killer, returning as promised. His voice was unmistakable and forever imprinted on his mind.

"Father?"

"I'm here."

"I have killed two this night, and I pray for their souls."

Father Samuels sat in silence, trembling, unsure what he should do.

"Father?"

"Why have you done this? I cannot and will not absolve you of murder!"

"That is not the reason I have come. I pray that their souls be forgiven so they will have safe passage into the afterlife. I'm not here out of concern for my own. I will face my penance when my time comes."

"How can you be so bold? How dare you come into a house of God with this arrogance? God is just…His justice won't sleep forever." Samuels fell silent after recalling the wisdom of Thomas Jefferson. He sat for a few seconds to collect himself. "You should be suffocating in humility, begging for your forgiveness."

"I know you don't understand; you cannot understand. I wish I could tell you the truth Father."

The door opened and Daxxe slipped away, leaving Samuels alone in the confessional. He felt hopeless and lost, adrift on a sea of confusion and despair with no land in sight.

"No, you fool!"

"Why not?"

"Have you already forgotten what happened to Bjorn? I should let you turn her just for the pleasure of watching you succumb to the sickness."

Mekune was furious with the carelessness of his recent turn.

The young girl, barely a day over sixteen, lay on the snow-covered football field. Pieces of her running suit fluttered across the hidden tick marks, scattered by the wind. A fight with her father led her out of the house, hoping to run off her pent frustration, to the high school track that circled the football team's practice field,.

A man and a younger woman stood over her, arguing. She couldn't make sense of the words or of what was happening. She remembered running around the track, and then she was face down in the snow, in pain, racked with sore joints and muscle cramps. Scores of tiny scratches, all of them barely trickling with blood, covered her skin everywhere she could see through a swarm of cuts in the clothing. The fluid was warm for a quick second before the wind chilled it, making it more uncomfortable.

She felt bruises on her body, and the ones she could see appeared to be in the shape of fingers or a hand. She could tell by the size of the imprint that the woman gave them to her. She felt very weak and scared when more of her memory returned, mentally reliving groping.

She felt sick to her stomach, but the desire to get away overtook the ill feeling. The argument consumed her attackers, allowing her to slowly move away. They didn't notice her as their confrontation grew more and more heated. She didn't look back.

"Mekune, I know what I can handle!" Natasha yelled in defiance.

"No, you don't! You will not disrespect me, insolent child!"

The report of the slap across her face snapped in the crisp air. Small rivulets of dark, still warm blood formed along the scratches left by his claws.

"How dare you strike me! I'll have your head!"

Natasha lunged at Mekune, going for the throat. Her hand was less than an inch from him when her forward movement abruptly stopped. She screamed in anguish. His punch landed squarely on her chest, reversing her momentum and sending her flying towards the end of the field. Her breath exploded from her lungs as she fell and slid to a stop on the cold ground, curling up in a fetal position in the snow. Her eyes opened wide as another intense wave of pain washed over her.

"You are lucky Trokar isn't here to see this. He'd break his own rules to deal with your insubordination."

Natasha didn't understand what was happening. The pain didn't pass like she expected, which brought an emotion theretofore unknown to her, fear. The throbbing sent sharper and sharper pulses of pain through her body. She tried to get up, only able to get to her knees. A burning sensation, like that of an overworked muscle, began building deep in her core.

Mekune bent over and clutched his stomach. He looked as though he was hurt, although Natasha knew her attacks were unsuccessful.

"Damn you for this!"

He finally dropped to his knees to ride it out. She was unaware the blow to her chest ruptured her heart and she was bleeding out slowly on the inside. The magical connection between master and servant sent the same pain into Mekune.

Tara reached the edge of the schoolyard, clear of the violence at the center of the field, and finally gaining her footing. She couldn't see the center of the field through the falling snow, and she didn't want to see. The cold numbed her cuts, allowing her to move more easily, and the bleeding stopped. She couldn't go home like this, so she ran to her best friend's house, looking for somewhere to find descent clothes, warmth, and a shoulder to cry on. If she was very lucky, she might be able to take a shower. She couldn't talk to her father, especially after their argument, and she had no intention of going home unless it was to get her things.

By the time she rounded the corner to go to Kirsten's house, she felt something strange boiling up within her. She stood, under the street lamp, realizing that she no longer felt cold. The pain from her injuries subsided as well. She picked up a handful of snow, rubbing it over her arms to wipe away the dried blood. She found no marks on her skin, and the bruises were gone as well. All she did feel was a hunger, an unnatural craving she couldn't pin down.

Marina woke with the sun. Beams of light filled the room with a warm glow. She startled when she realized someone sat in the chair next to the bed. Tatianna had dozed off keeping an eye on her, trying to maintain her vigil through the night.

"Tatianna?"

Marina spoke softly, but her sister still woke instantly.

"Are you okay, Marina?"

"Yes, I'm okay. I didn't mean to scare you. You look a lot worse for wear. Have you been in that chair all night?"

"Yes, I just wanted to watch over you. You've been asleep since yesterday morning. How do you feel?"

"I'm actually pretty good for right now."

The ring of the doorbell broke the conversation. Tatianna went to see who it was while Marina dressed. She entered the kitchen, stopping when she saw Tatianna sitting with two police officers.

"Marina, these men are here to see you."

She looked shocked and confused.

"What happened?"

Tatianna directed her question more towards the police than her sibling.

"We're not at liberty to discuss the case, ma'am," said Officer Dupree, "but we need to take Marina back to New York."

"Did she do something wrong?"

"Ma'am, as I said, I can't discuss the case. Ms. Makovoz, can you get your things, please? We need to take you back."

"Yes, just a moment..." Marina wasn't sure what to do. She didn't know why the police were here, how they found her, or why they needed to take her back to New York.

"What is this all about? You can't just take my sister away without some type of explanation. That's the way of the Old Country, not here," argued Tatianna.

"Ma'am, your sister is very important to a case we are working. Here is one of my cards; you can reach me anytime. We'll let you know what we can as soon as we can."

Marina returned to the kitchen carrying her small overnight bag; then the police excused themselves and led her out of the apartment. Tatianna could see the worry on her face as they took her away.

"Marina, the car is right out front. Marina?"

Marina was standing still, almost in a trance, when Emilio spoke to her.

"Are you okay? Have you seen a doctor about your neck?"

Marina wavered slightly as she tried to focus on Emilio's words.

"What's wrong with my neck?"

She reached up to touch it, checking. Malcolm and Emilio exchanged glances, unsure how to respond.

"It's okay, ma'am," said Malcolm. "Let's get on the road. We have a pretty good trip in front of us, but we can make it back before dark if we get going."

From her window, Tatianna watched them walk to the squad car, seat Marina in the back, and put her bag in the trunk before pulling away.

"We just got a call from Dupree. They're bringing Marina in," reported Joe.

"Good, maybe we can get some answers now."

"He said we might have a problem, but he didn't want to say why until they got here."

"I checked my e-mail while you were taking that call. Dr. Palmer positively identified the bodies of Charles and Ann Arkits. Most of Charles' teeth were broken or missing, making the process of identifying him much harder."

Angela offered Joe the hard copy of the report.

"Did he give us anything that might help us find their killer?"

"He said the front of Arkits' neck was ripped out, like some of the other victims, but his wife's body wasn't mutilated at all. Her injuries were internal, mostly deep tissue bruising, fractures, and three of her lumbar vertebrae were completely crushed."

"It doesn't say anything about a struggle here."

"No, he didn't, but his opinion is that the killer beat her, possibly to death, before she was thrown...into the...fire..." Angela stifled a wave of nausea and chills at the memory.

Joe glanced over the report a second time. "Stone must be right about the enhanced strength. It would take a lot of localized force to break one vertebra, not to mention three."

"Forensics finished their report, too. The blood in the office matches Charles' blood type and we were right about the killer attacking him first."

"Do they know when Mrs. Arkits died?"

"Palmer estimated an hour or so after her husband. I'm betting she was upstairs when the killer attacked him. The killer could have taken his time if he got the jump on Charles. She probably came downstairs, surprised the killer, and ended up dead like her husband. Palmer said she wasn't burned as badly as her husband. She might still be alive if she'd stayed upstairs. Do you think we could be dealing with a copycat? The MO is a little bit different this time."

"Instinct tells me no, but that doesn't rule it out. Arkits was too involved with the other cases, and I'm not a big believer in coincidence. I'm putting my money on a problem with whatever deal they worked out. Why else would the killer take out his supplier? It doesn't make sense, unless they disagreed about the deal."

"That's a sound argument and I'll bet your right. I hope we get some answers from Marina, and maybe she knows how the mysterious Mr. Sayer fits into it all."

The drive from Albany passed slowly. Marina sat in the backseat of the police car, watching the world go by. It looked very pretty covered with a white blanket of snow. The trees were devoid of leaves and entombed in a coating of ice. Marina thought about how different it all looked in the winter, everything buried in a layer of pure white, leaving no evidence of what lay beneath.

Malcolm drove, not being able to go much faster than thirty-five miles per hour. The snow kept falling, keeping the roads in bad shape, forcing the plows to run twenty-four-seven to keep up. In some spots, the piles of snow on the roadside were taller than the cars. If the snow didn't let up soon, it would rank as one of the worst winters in New York's history.

As he drove, his thoughts drifted to his son and the police academy. He was still having second thoughts, unsure if he wanted his son to follow in his footsteps. When he finally pinned a word on it, the word was "afraid". He was afraid of what might happen to his son in the line of duty. It wasn't the same world, or the same police force, when he joined after the military. People were much more creative when it came to hurting other people.

Emilio rode quietly, working on paperwork because he didn't want to disturb Malcolm, considering the road conditions and the seriousness on his face. Every so often, he would check to see if Marina needed anything, or if she needed to stop for a few minutes. He worked through the paperwork twice, reading and rereading it all to see if they missed anything.

A pair of officers left the 42nd Precinct, bound for the alley where Marina was originally discovered, dispatched to find Thomas Gianelli and bring him in. Joe wanted him readily available when they questioned Marina since he found and helped her, and they wanted her to be as comfortable as possible. To their knowledge, she was the only living witness associated with any of the homicides.

ChApTER TWENTY-SEVEN

Father Samuels left St. Christopher's to take a long walk. He needed time to think, away from his duties and away from the church. He found it impossible to deal with his newfound sense of guilt within the hallowed walls. He devoted his life to helping other God-fearing people face and overcome their challenges by offering support and His teachings, but he was at a loss for how to overcome his own internal struggle.

The bitterly cold air had little effect on him as he walked. The areas beneath his eyes were grayish-black due to lack of sleep, and his eyes were glazed over. He looked this way and that as if driven by confusion and paranoia. He studied the city and its people as he walked, assessing his responsibility to it and them.

News of the recent killing sprees reached the church by way of outside media and the parishioners touched by the violence. Evening mass grew in size nightly as more and more people turned to God for answers. They also felt safer in numbers since the killings were no longer localized in the slums.

The fact that Father Samuels had not placed his piece in the puzzle is what troubled him the most. He spent hours going through his texts, searching for anything that might render some direction, wishing he could turn to Stephen for the answer.

Snow fell as he walked. Some of the flakes were the size of golf balls, limiting his line of sight and making the street and the city feel smaller. He could only see a short distance through the white curtain, and the number of cars and other people out and about lessened with each passing moment. He walked without a particular destination in mind to allow for unhindered time to think and pray.

Thomas heard noises outside. He didn't recognize them, but they sounded very close. He peered out of a small hole in his corrugated wall to see two police officers standing out in the center of the alley talking to each other.

"It's supposed to be right here somewhere. Detective Anderson said the fire escape missing its pull-down ladder was the landmark we needed to find."

Officer Temple pointed at the metal fire escape attached to the exterior wall of the building that made one side of Thomas' urban cove.

"I don't know. It looks like the ladder is gone down there, too."

Officer Davis shielded his eyes with his hand as he focused on another fire escape farther down the alley.

"The snow is coming down too heavy to be sure. It's all starting to look the same."

"We can't go back without Gianelli; Joe said we have to bring him in."

Thomas shrunk away from the peephole very slowly and quietly, wondering why they wanted him so badly.

What if they think I did it? Or what if they just need a scapegoat?

He waited several minutes until their voices slowly trailed off, hoping the two policemen wouldn't look his way. They moved deeper into the alley. He needed to get out, suddenly feeling trapped and claustrophobic. He looked down the alley cautiously, seeing no one. He saw two sets of tracks in the snow where they stopped to talk, and where they turned to walk farther into the alley. He headed out, stepping into their footprints as he left. If they didn't see him flee, the ruse would prevent any later accusations. He needed time to think about what he should do.

Malcolm pulled off of the street into the Precinct's garage, parking on the top floor. The horrible weather and extended working hours filled the garage to the brim. He went to the trunk to get Marina's things while his partner helped her out of the car.

They escorted Marina to a briefing room on the fourth floor. It was a small cinder block room, painted entirely gray. A small table sat at the room's center. A large mirror was built into the wall directly behind the table. She was instructed to sit in the single chair that faced the mirror. Two empty chairs waited on the opposite side. She knew from the rash of crime dramas on primetime TV that someone would be watching her from the other side of the one-way mirror.

Emilio made a final attempt to get her anything before they left the room, but she politely declined. She sat in the hard wooden chair with her head down and her hands in her lap, focusing on the metal loop built into the tabletop to restrain prisoners. She could not bring herself to face the faceless behind the special glass.

After what felt like an eternity, a man and a woman entered the room, sitting down in the two vacant chairs. The woman seemed somewhat approachable, but the man made her very uncomfortable.

"Marina, my name is Angela Benson, and this is my partner Joe Anderson. We're detectives. I'm sure you already know why you're here and we're glad to see you're okay. Is your neck okay today? Did you see a doctor?"

Marina sat, dumbfounded, like she hadn't heard, or didn't understand the question.

"Marina, are you okay?" asked Joe.

Marina spoke without looking at them. "I'm...sorry, but...I don't know what you're talking about. The men that brought me asked me the same question."

Angela and Joe adopted a confused look.

"Are you okay?" Angela asked, sensing her unease. Marina tried very hard to remain still, but the trembling in her limbs and voice was impossible to hide.

"I...I am very nervous...and scared."

Angela got up and walked around the small table to squat down next to Marina at eye level.

"You have nothing to fear, Marina. We're here to help you. This isn't a good cop bad cop sort of thing."

Angela could tell Joe was making her more nervous.

"Joe, can I handle this one?"

The question surprised the senior officer, but he complied without comment or complaint. He left the interrogation room and entered the observation room next door.

"Okay, now it's just the two of us. Does that help? Do you remember what happened?"

Marina made eye contact, feeling a safe connection on some inner level. "No Miss, I have no idea what you're talking about. I wish I knew what was going on, but I don't. Did whatever happened…happen a couple of nights ago? I can't seem to remember anything from the other night, and I woke up at home with blood all over me, but it wasn't mine." Tears welled up in her eyes, ready to gush out at the slightest inclination.

"I know you're scared, and a little confused. If you can give me a moment, I'll be right back."

Angela went into the observation room to find Joe standing at the glass.

"We've got to get to the bottom of this. She is completely mortified in there, and I think she's telling the truth. She has no idea what happened to her."

"Mr. Adams?"

The intercom resting on the corner of his large desk buzzed.

"Yes?"

"There's someone here to see you."

"I'm too busy right now. Make an appointment."

Adams office door swung open before his finger cleared the intercom. He protested until he saw the badge.

"What can I do for you?"

"You have the right to remain silent. Anything you say can and will be used against you in a court of law. You have the right to any attorney. If you cannot afford an attorney, one will be appointed for you. Do you understand these rights I've given you?" asked Captain Bishop, as he placed Adams' right wrist in handcuffs.

"What's going on? What am I being arrested for?"

262

"Is this your voice?"

Commissioner Jamison pushed the play button on the digital recorder in his right hand.

"It's about the serial killer story we're covering. The Commissioner just called and told me that we can't run it anymore, but I'll be damned if I'm going to ruin our ratings for his convenience."

The Commissioner stopped the playback.

"You are under arrest for hindering an official police investigation, inciting a riot, recklessly endangering the public as a whole, and assault and battery."

Captain Bishop walked Jack out of his office, and Jamison followed. Denise stepped off of the elevator as it opened in front of them. Jack tried to burn her down with a glance, but she didn't shy away, her fear gone.

"It looks like you're damned alright," she whispered as they passed.

The workers in the office broke out into laughs and cheers as soon as the elevator doors shut, taking the tyrant away. In one motion, Denise removed her only predator and made many allies, one of which was the assistant station manager, Phillip Winslow, who she walked to immediately.

"Phillip, I think we need to run these stories by the numbers. I want the exclusives so bad I can taste it, but it's getting dangerous out there. Everyone is in a paranoid panic, and the whole city is a powder keg set to blow. This media circus "Journalism Jack" wants us to run doesn't help matters. I don't think we want to take responsibility for lighting it."

"You're right Denise. I tried to warn Jack, but you know how he is about these things; he wouldn't listen. You did a brave thing, standing up to him like that."

"I just couldn't deal with him anymore. Everyone thinks I'm the village idiot, only hanging around to give the men folk a piece of ass. I realize Jack hired me because of my looks, but I'm not stupid – I've got a degree for God's sake, and I've learned a lot along the way. I just want to start over, on the right foot this time around."

Denise stood up straight, making sure her clothes were arranged properly. Phillip noticed that she wore an ankle length skirt, a high neck blouse, and a jacket, not fitting too tight or too loose. Her hair was fixed conservatively. She put her glasses on and extended her right hand.

"Hi, I'm Denise Rigsby, and I'd like the job of anchorperson for the evening news."

The words sounded corny, at best, but Phillip understood her intent. He was, to say the least, impressed. Denise's makeover didn't cost her any of her appeal; it actually intensified it, which is exactly what the station wanted and needed.

"As acting station manager, I give you the job."

Philip reached out to shake her hand to close the deal when he noticed a purplish-yellow ring around her wrist.

"What happened? Are you okay?" he asked in a low voice.

Denise bowed her head, ashamed and embarrassed. Resolutely, she faced the question.

"That was a gift from Jack. I'm sure you were aware we were...involved. It was nice at first, but it turned into something else."

Denise drew her hand back, letting the jacket sleeve slip over the bruise. Phillip caught her hand in mid-motion, being careful not aggravate the damage. He didn't baulk at the injury, but his body language suggested sympathy and understanding as he gingerly held her hand and looked at her wrist. His touch conveyed comfort and concern.

"I think you'll do just fine. Let me buy you a cup of coffee and we can discuss the particulars."

The journalists left the office bound for the cafeteria. Denise expected sour looks from the rest of the staff, and she could already imagine the gossip. To her surprise, the glances cast her direction harbored little to no resentment, as though everyone understood.

Word travels fast.

Angela returned to the interrogation room.

"Marina, could you come with me?

Angela led Marina to a room converted into a makeshift psychologist's office. A chaise lounge rested at the center, and a table with three chairs stood to one side.

"Please, have a seat. Marina, this is my partner, as you already know, and this is Joshua Stone. Mr. Stone is a detective and a criminal psychologist, and with your permission, he'd like to try hypnotic therapy to find out what happened the night of the 27th. It won't hurt in any way. We would like to help you, and we need your help."

"I guess that's okay. I don't know what else to do to find out what happened to me."

Marina's expression couldn't disagree more. She was scared, and even though she wanted to know what happened, she was more terrified of the truth.

Angela squatted to be at eye level with her again. "Marina, I give you my word that you are completely safe here with us, and we mean you no harm. If you don't want to do this, you can tell us."

Marina relaxed slightly at the words. "I believe you Angela. I want to help."

"Okay, thank you, Marina. Detective Stone will handle the therapy. Do you have any questions or concerns before we start?"

Marina simply shook her head to the negative, but she was now holding eye contact.

"It'll be fine Ms. Makovoz. I promise this won't hurt a bit, and you probably won't remember it at all. Please, lie back and make yourself comfortable. We are only trying to help."

Marina did as Stone instructed. She didn't fully trust him, but they had not done anything so far that would indicate their intentions were not honorable, and she felt comforted and protected by Angela's presence. She knew most of her fear of the policemen was rooted in stories she heard as a child in Russia about the KGB and their methods. This was the first time she had dealings of any kind with police in America and had no idea what to expect.

Stone pulled one of the chairs up to the side of the chaise and took a shiny gold medallion from his pocket. It hung on a length of matching gold chain and it appeared to be very old. He swung it back and forth before Marina's eyes.

"Marina, I want you to focus on the medallion as it moves. Let yourself relax, and empty your mind of everything except my voice and the medallion. As you relax, you will feel warm, comfortable, and calm."

Joe and Angela stared in amazement. Neither of them really believed in hypnotism, yet they were watching it firsthand. Marina's muscles released their tension all at once and she looked totally at peace.

"You will start feeling sleepy, don't try to resist it. This sleep is welcome, comforting, and safe. I will count backwards from five, and when I reach one, you will be completely at peace, feeling asleep, but able to communicate with me. You will remain in this state until I say the word bergamot a second time. When you hear that word, you will also forget everything we've talked about from this moment until then, as though it never happened. Do you understand?"

"Yes."

Marina's voice was alarmingly lifeless. Joshua counted backwards, completing the trance.

"Marina, can you hear me?"

'Yes."

"I'd like to start with a few basics."

Joshua asked several questions about Marina's personal information to ensure the hypnosis was working.

"Marina, do you remember the a few nights ago when you went to the market for groceries?"

"Yes."

Father Samuels walked for several hours, realizing his path took him to the Bronx, and by one particular building many times, even though he didn't consciously decide to go there. He finally walked up the first three steps and paused. He glanced back down at the street, as if to make a final consideration before committing himself.

He continued the climb to the front doors. Each step felt as though it shrugged off a part of the weight resting on his shoulders. The words "46th Precinct - NYPD" embossed on the stone face under the soffit, three stories above the street. The glass header above the main entrance displayed the correct precinct number, the 42nd, and the address, 830 Washington Avenue.

Julie sat in the waiting room, crying uncontrollably. She held her face in her hands and kept to a quiet whimper, but tears escaped through her fingers and down her forearms. The police brought her here after the stop at the morgue where she identified Ellen's body. There was no anger, and the denial phase gave way to grief at once. She could see her friend's lifeless body in her mind, and she knew the memory would haunt her for the rest of her life. Ellen's skin was ashen, frigid to the touch, and the left side of her neck was all but destroyed. Her body was stripped and cleaned, lying on a hard metal table, looking more like an experiment than her friend.

She dropped to her knees on the cold tile floor and wretched, unable to handle the intensity of her emotions. A female officer was called to help her and escort her to the Precinct. Something was said about a safe house, but Julie didn't hear most of it and comprehended even less of what she did. Her world was a maelstrom, spinning out of control, and she didn't know what to do to stop it.

"Dad! Dad!"

Tim yelled from his bed, the covers pulled up to the bottom of his eyes.

"What is it son?"

Max rubbed the sleep from his eyes as he entered his son's room and turned on the light.

"There's a monster in my closet."

"Tim, we've been through this before. There are no monsters in your closet. Your imagination is just playing tricks on you. Nine-year-old boys should know better."

"But Dad, I saw it! It was real!"

Max let out a small sigh, realizing the battle was already lost. He wouldn't call his wife to get help as he was manning the boat alone while she was gone on a business trip.

"Okay, Tim. I'll check, but this is the last time."

Tim nodded and looked at his father in awe for his bravery.

Max opened the closet door, looking back at his son.

"See Tim, all clear."

The fear in his son's eyes was the likes of which he had never seen. He turned to look at the source when the door slammed into his chest, knocking him against the wall and to the ground, robbing the air from his lungs.

"Dad!"

In a blur of movement, Tim's monster lurched down on Max, finishing the job before turning his attention to the boy.

"What will you do now, Timmy? Daddy's not here to save you now."

Timmy sat, trembling, unable to move or comprehend until Nicol moved towards him. He leapt to the floor, darting for the still open window. To get away, he could crawl out onto the roof and climb down the tree in the front yard, just like he did when he and Sam slipped out on their adventures. A cold hand clamped around his calf, pulling him back into the house.

"Help! He's got me!"

Tim screamed at the top of his lungs before he was pulled back into the house.

Nicol silently flew into the night sky after he fed.

268

"Marina, tell me what happened that evening, starting around five in the afternoon. Tell me everything until you got onto the bus headed for your sister's house."

Marina's voice sounded strange as she spoke. Her accent was almost gone, as if someone else spoke through her. Her gaze was utterly blank as her lips moved, more like a machine than a human being.

"I got home from work just after five o'clock. I didn't have anything in the cupboard I felt like having for dinner, so I decided to go to the market and get whatever looked good. I don't have a car, so I walked. It's only a few blocks. I bought what I needed to make a small batch of pelmeni and started home."

"What happened next?"

Marina's expression changed to a look of distress. Her voice trembled with an unusual timbre.

"I want to go home, not down the alley. Why are you calling me this way?"

"Who is talking to you Marina?"

Joe and Angela listened intently as Joshua took notes. Angela already set up a digital recorder to capture the session.

"I don't know. A voice is…in my head, making me go down the alley. I don't want to go, but I can't stop myself."

"Go on."

"I'm walking down the alley. It's dark. There are trash cans on both sides. Some of them are knocked over. I can smell rotting garbage. I can't see the street or hear any noise from it because of the snow and wind, and it seems much colder now. A man is standing in front of me, and I feel I should be afraid, but I'm not. He's telling me to come closer. It's his voice inside my head."

"What does he look like Marina?"

"He is very large, but not overweight, just well built. He's dressed in black, and his hair is pulled back into a short ponytail. His skin is very pale, like he's sick. He has a scar across the left side of his face. His eyes are sunken into his head, and they look like they're…on fire."

"What do you mean they're on fire?"

"They are red with fire."

269

"Can you see flames?"

"No."

"Are they glowing?"

"Yes."

"What else do you see?"

"He is reaching his hand out to me. His hand looks strange. The skin is a darker gray than his face. The fingers are…pointy…on the ends. I drop my sacks and walk towards him, but I don't understand why. I'm scared and want to run away, but I can't."

Marina stopped speaking. Tension wrinkled her forehead.

"What happened next?"

"I put my hand in his and he smiled. His teeth are sharp and pointed like his fingers. He's holding my hand gently, caressing it."

She stopped again, straining against the memory and the request to relive it.

"It's okay Marina. You are safe, this is just a memory. What did he do next?"

"He moved my hair to one side and bit into my neck."

Her expression went placid.

"I'm not scared anymore. The pain feels good. I feel like I'm floating."

"Did anything happen after that Marina?"

"Yes."

"What happened next, Marina?"

"I was knocked to the ground. I'm afraid again."

"What knocked you to the ground?"

"It was another man."

"What did this other man look like?"

Stone's attention was locked on her words. They needed this for the case at hand, but her answer could finally provide support for one of his theories and unlock another part of his past.

"He's very big for a regular man. His skin is light gray, but not sickly looking like the other one, even though his hands look like the same. His eyes are afire, too, but they are yellow. His ears are pointed on the top and he has thick black hair on his head, like a mane."

"What did the second man do to scare you?"

"He didn't do anything to me. He attacked the other man, hitting him several times until he fell to the ground."

Marina stopped talking, her face twisted with a new horror.

"Go on, Marina. Remember, you're safe here."

"I am scooting backward in the snow, trying to be quiet. The snow is melting and soaking into the back of my jeans. The gray man is a demon. He grabbed the other man's chest and ripped out a large piece of it. I don't want to see, but I can't turn away. He said something I couldn't understand and then there was a flash of green light. His hand was empty and all the blood was gone. He looked at me for a second before he quickly turned and looked up the alley. He walked off into the snow and all the fear trapped inside of me burst out all at once. I started screaming as loud as I could, but I didn't have the strength to move. I just sat in the snow."

"Okay, let's talk about something else Marina. Tell me about the first birthday party you remember."

Marina's face calmed instantly as she recalled the story. Joshua went to the detectives, speaking quietly. "I needed to give her a break. Even though she was safe, she felt like she was back in the alley, in immediate danger. Too much trauma could have permanent negative effects on her psyche." Joshua let Marina go on about her sixth birthday party for almost ten minutes, feeling that was long enough for her body to recover from the episode.

"Marina?"

"Yes."

"Can we go back to the alley?"

"Okay," she answered, her demeanor becoming darker.

"What happened after the gray man left?"

"Another man came into the alley. He looked scared and confused, and he asked me something, but I didn't hear it. He put his jacket over my shoulders and ran away."

"Did he come back?"

"Yes, after a few minutes. He sat with me until a police car arrived."

"Okay, Marina, I want to jump ahead a little bit."

"Okay."

"Do you remember the ambulance?"

"Yes."

"Do you remember running away?"

"Yes."

"Why did you run away?"

"I was scared. I wanted to get away from the dead man and I didn't want to be there if the gray man came back."

"What happened when you ran out of the alley?"

"I was running home, and I started feeling lightheaded again, like I was floating. I felt like something pulled me off of the ground and carried me into the sky very quickly, but my vision was blurred and dark. I'm not sure what's happened."

"What lifted you up?"

"I think it was the gray man."

"How did he do that?"

"I don't know."

"Where did he take you?"

"Home."

Joshua was lost for words for a moment, not expecting that answer. He looked at Joe and Angela, seeing a similar expression on their faces.

"The gray man took you home?"

"Yes."

"Did he do anything once he took you there?"

"He put me on my couch and put a pillow under my head. He was looking at the side of my face or my neck. He was being very gentle."

"I thought you didn't want to see the gray man again."

"I was scared of him at first, but he didn't hurt me. He doesn't scare me anymore. I think he was trying to help me."

"Why do you think he tried to help?"

"He looked at my neck where the other man bit me. It hurt and burned."

Marina put her hand on her neck, covering the spot where the wound was inflicted.

"What did he do?"

"He rubbed his hands together quickly." Marina mimicked the motion. "He said something that I didn't understand. I don't know if he was barely audible, or if it was a different language. His hands started to glow and he put them around my neck very gently. The touch was very soft and warm, and it felt good. The glow went away and my neck didn't hurt anymore."

"How did it not hurt anymore?"

"It just didn't hurt anymore, or burn or anything, like it never happened."

"What happened next?"

"I must have fallen asleep."

"When did you wake up?"

"The next morning."

"Do you remember what happened then?"

"I got scared."

"Why did you get scared?"

"I had blood all over me, but I didn't know where it came from."

"You didn't remember what happened the night before?"

"No."

"What did you do?"

"I took a hot shower to try to get clean. It made me sick to my stomach. I didn't know what happened, and I didn't know what to do. I decided to hide at my sister's until I could make sense of it all."

"Marina."

'Yes."

"I want you to pretend you're sitting in a ski lodge in the Rocky Mountains. The sky is clear, and the ground is covered with fresh snow. The fireplace behind you is keeping you warm as you look out the large picture window, enjoying the scenery. You can see the skiers coming down the slope, and the lodge is full of people taking a break to warm up. Can you do that?"

"Yes."

"Good. A waiter approaches the table where you're sitting, and he asks you if you want something warm to drink. What would you like to have?"

"I'd like a mug of hot chocolate with little marshmallows."

"The waiter suggests a cup of Earl Gray."

"Why does he do that?"

"He tells you it's popular with the skiers because they like the flavor of bergamot, bergamot."

Marina blinked slowly, closing her eyes for several seconds before she opened them again, as if waking from a deep sleep. She looked calm and rested as she turned to look at Joshua.

"Are you going to hypnotize me now?"

Daxxe worked rooftop to rooftop, following a recent turn, waiting for the opportune moment to strike. The older female tracked a man that looked to be in his late forties. She picked him up his scent after he spent two hours drinking in a local all-night coffeehouse, and she felt like a warm up. She was unaware Daxxe shadowed her as he stayed downwind at a high vantage point.

Daxxe prepared to dive off of the ledge for his prey when he felt something, something new. He felt it pulling him towards the suburbs, only a few minutes away as the crow flies. He memorized the scent of the man and adjusted his course to go into the residential area.

He lit next to a goal post, looking out towards the center of the football field. A body lay crumpled near the fifty-yard line, unmoving. A set of ruts moved away that turned into footsteps at the curb. To his eyes, the tracks glowed.

What is this?

He followed the path. Closer inspection revealed pink drops marking the snow for the first several feet. The scent identified them as blood. The drops grew smaller in size and farther apart the farther he went. He followed the illuminated trail at a distance as quickly as he could, not allowing himself to be out in the open as he approached the houses of the neighborhood.

The lots were very large, with many trees, providing ample cover. The tracks followed the sidewalk to a street corner; then they worked across a lawn and back through the houses, staying close to the walls. They led to one of the larger homes. A barn sat on the back of the property near the rear fence. The barn door stood cracked open a few inches. He entered through the door near the barn's crest that accessed the hay loft.

A young blond girl stood beside one of the stalls, looking at the horse standing within it. Tears ran down her cheeks, soaking her destroyed running suit and the large piece of burlap she found and wrapped around her for warmth. Upon seeing her, Daxxe understood the path he followed to reach her.

She turned and looked at the slightly open main door.

"Who's there? I know you're here. I don't mean any harm. I'll leave."

Her words were replaced by sobs as she backed into a corner and slid down into a sitting position.

"That won't be necessary, little one."

Tara jumped at the voice, being suspicious of someone else's presence, but not yet convinced someone else was there. She said nothing, and she didn't move; she was too scared to move.

275

"You are not in trouble or in danger; of that you have my word."

She looked up. The voice came from the darkness of the hayloft. She trusted the voice, but she couldn't fathom why. She saw two eyes reflecting much like that of a cat or a dog, but the two yellow orbs were much too high to belong to a domestic animal.

"I'm guessing that you've had a pretty scary night with what happened out there."

"How do you know that? Are you one of them?" A tidal wave of fear started to surge within her, building to burst through at any moment.

"No, I'm not one of them, but I do know what happened to you. I know you are very scared and confused, and you don't know what to do now. I mean you no harm."

"How can you know what I'm thinking? Why won't you show yourself?"

"It is better this way, for now. Let me explain to you first."

To her surprise, the desire to know the how and the why overpowered everything else in Tara's mind.

"Okay, if you wanted to hurt me, you would have done it already." She sounded as though she was trying to convince herself.

"That's right. You're very smart for one so young, but you're also different."

"How's that?" Her words trembled hearing his voice, labeling her "different". This faceless voice could see her innermost feelings.

"You have always been smarter and stronger than your friends, and most of the other people you know for that matter. You're honest without fault, which makes you stand out against the rest, and it costs you friendship with some. You tend to feel like an island unto yourself with no one to turn to, no one to understand. That's what you and your father fought about, isn't it? He called you a freak, said you were different, and it hurt you deeply."

Tara only nodded her head in agreement, unable to speak over the lump in her throat. The feelings she could not voice were just spoken to her. Tears welled in her eyes and she put her face against her drawn up knees.

"You are different for a reason. Your family line reaches back many, many years, and you've inherited a special trait from that line on your mother's side. Your father is incapable of comprehending it. If your mother were alive, she could help you as I am helping you now."

"I never knew her."

"I know. She died when you were only an infant. Your father never learned of her secret."

"What...secret?" she asked, looking up towards the hay loft again.

"Long ago, powers that I will not attempt to explain left marks on this world. You carry one of these marks."

Tara dropped one side of the burlap sack, examining herself, searching for a scar, a birthmark, or something of the like.

"It's not that kind of mark. It's inside you, on your soul. You have two choices. You can explore this mark, or your life can go back to the way it was before you were attacked at the school."

"I want to go home, but..." she looked up at the ceiling of the loft, but her sight was searching much farther away than that.

"But what, Tara?"

"I want to know, but I don't think I'm ready. Can I change my mind later?"

"It's not the best option, but yes, you can. Close your eyes."

When Tara opened her eyes, she was standing beside the school track, wearing her running suit. Her watch told her it was almost five in the morning as she wiped the sweat off her brow and took several slow, deep breaths. She held a cord, leading to small amulet hanging on the end.

It was round, made of a gray stone, and hanging on a length of black leather cord. The face bore a cross that was familiar to her, but she wasn't sure of its origin or denomination. The symbol was raised from the smooth face of the medallion. She liked the way it felt when she ran her thumb over it. She was surprised to find that it was quite warm, even though it hung exposed to the elements. When she took a closer look, she found the back held an inscription carved into the polished rock in a language she had never seen before. She could only wonder what the words meant.

She didn't know where it came from or why, but she knew in her core that it was very important and a time would come when she would discover its use. She placed it around her neck and let the amulet fall inside her shirt. She could feel the warmth of the stone against her bare skin, and it seemed to make the winter not so cold.

The snow near the center of the field was disturbed. She was aware of it but she wasn't sure why she noticed it. She jogged off in the direction of home with a clear mind. The anger she felt towards her father had vented away with her exertion. She knew she was different, and for the first time in her life, she felt good about it, freak or otherwise.

"Excuse me, miss," said Harold as he passed her to sit down in the subway car.

"You're fine. Have a seat," she returned, making the offer sound sultry.

He thought about her offer, accepting it since no one else was riding in the car. If his wife saw him with this younger, attractive woman, he would never hear the end of it, but what she didn't know couldn't hurt him. And he was just sitting.

"I've never seen you out this way before. Are you new in town?"

"Yeah, I just moved here. It's kind of scary down here. I've never ridden the subway before."

"Well, you really need to be careful. There are a lot of folks out this time of night that would love to take advantage of a pretty lass like yourself."

"You wouldn't be wanting to take advantage of me, would you?" she asked in her sultry tone.

Crystal leaned forward just enough to show a little cleavage.

"I'm a married man, Miss." Harold was taken aback by her promiscuity, but it also intrigued him.

"No one will know." She put her hand on his thigh. Harold stood up, putting a few feet between them.

"Miss, I'm sorry if I've in any way given you the wrong impression."

He looked at his watch, avoiding eye contact with her. He boarded at the last stop in the metro area, and it would be another five minutes before they reached the next stop. Crystal stood up, keeping the distance between them at a minimum, even though Harold kept backing away. His stomach lurched with the acid in his stomach. He knew he should have skipped those last two cups of espresso.

"Maybe you are the one that should be more careful." Harold's eyes opened wide as he looked up at her. He caught a glimpse of her face just before the lights went out. Her expression changed to slightly sinister and her canines lengthened visibly.

The stretch of track they were traveling had a small dead spot in the middle where the power that ran the car transferred from the downtown station to the one in the suburbs. The momentum of the car carried it through the transfer area, but the lights darkened for about fifteen seconds until the car regained power. She was so close he could feel her breath when the car went dark.

The subway car rolled to a stop at the next terminal, empty. Two of the windows on the outside of the car were broken out and a few droplets of fresh blood ran down the glass and the side of the car.

ChApTeR TweNTY-eiGhT

Father Samuels didn't realize his walk lasted all night until he saw the clock behind the front desk.

"Good afternoon, sir, oh excuse me, Father. How may I help you?" asked the Desk Sergeant, noticing the white collar.

"I need to talk to someone about the recent killings in our fair city."

"Okay. If you'll have a seat over there, I'll get someone for you."

Samuels sat in one of the indicated chairs to wait. After a few moments, a burly man with salt and pepper hair, looking like death warmed over, approached him.

"Father?"

"Yes."

"How can I help you?"

"I've come to talk to someone about the recent killings in our community."

"Let's go to one of the briefing rooms upstairs, we'll have more privacy that way."

Joe led Samuels to the room they used for roll call. It would be empty for another half hour. Joe offered a chair and a soda or coffee, which Samuels politely refused as he sat down.

"What do you need to tell us, Father?"

"It took me quite some time to come to the decision to do this. As a priest, I am ordained to listen and console parishioners regarding their sins by way of confessional. The confessors, for the most part, are anonymous, but I will occasionally recognize a voice. The point is not so much what I hear or who I know, but the fact that it's all kept under the strictest confidentiality."

"I understand."

"Late a few nights ago, a confessor entered my church." He paused, contemplating this last chance to change his mind before it could not be undone. "I am about to tell you something I am sworn to keep a secret. I pray for my own soul."

"What is it Father?"

"This man confessed to me that he killed another man. He was very confident about the fact he did it, although I did sense some remorse."

"What did he say?"

Joe was curious about the priest's predicament, but he didn't yet see how it connected to the case.

"He said he was on a mission, and that it meant he would have to kill others. He swore his intentions were pure, even after I reminded him murder was the most damning of all sins."

Joshua and Angela entered the room, planning to attend the morning briefing, as Samuels spoke.

"That supports the serial killer theory we've established," interjected Stone. "Even serial killers need an outlet for how they feel. This man sounds as if he is regretful of the act after the fact, but the regret isn't strong enough to make him stop."

"Do you have any way to identify him" asked Angela, sitting in one of the available chairs. "I apologize. I am Detective Angela Benson, Father..."

"Samuels. I never saw him. I only know his voice. He said he would return each time he killed one of them, to pray for their forgiveness and their safe passage into the afterlife."

"Has he come back to the church?" asked Joe.

"Yes, last night. He said he killed two others. I got angry with him and I think he left before he was ready."

"Thank you, Father. That should help us at least understand the killer a little more," said Angela. "We can keep an eye on the church to make sure nothing happens to your parish, and maybe we'll get a chance to catch him."

"As hard as it is for me to accept what he's doing, I don't think he means any harm to me or the church; he would have done something already if that was his intent."

"Very well, but we'll keep loose surveillance. We will not intervene in any way unless it is absolutely necessary; on that you have my word," said Joe. "Here, take one of my cards. If you need anything at all, please call us."

"I will. Thank you."

Samuels left the briefing room alone, telling Joe he knew the way out when he offered an escort. He saw a young girl in the next room as he left. She was crying, and by the look of her, had been for quite some time.

Julie saw a priest leave. His eyes were full of sympathy for her as he passed. She started to call to him, but she remained silent, watching him leave with mixed emotions. She questioned God for what happened to Ellen, and that issue of trust transferred to His follower.

Samuels entered the next room. He saw Marina when he came in, but he didn't have the opportunity to speak to her. Marina worked at the church, and she never missed work, except for the last few days. He wondered what happened to her, and now she was sitting in a police station. He walked into the room to see her when he knew no one was looking.

"How are you Marina?"

"Oh Father, I'm so glad to see someone I know. I'm okay now. Thank you for asking."

"Are you in some kind of trouble?"

"No, I don't think so. Something happened to me a couple of nights ago, but I don't remember any more than that. It sure seems like they really want to talk to me."

"Do you know what it's about?"

"The only hints I heard have something to do with a body in an alley, but that's all I know."

"Where have you been? I haven't seen you at the church."

"I went to my sister's house because…"

Marina's voice fell off as a puzzled look crossed her face.

"What's wrong Marina?

"I can't remember why I went to see her. I remember waking up in her guest room this morning, but I don't remember anything from before since I left work the last time."

"That's unusual, Marina. Are you okay? What can I do to help?"

"I don't know what will help."

282

Marina's eyes welled with tears as her resolve against the fear deteriorated. Growing up in the USSR gave her advantages to dealing with fear, but not at the current intensity. Samuels knelt before her and put his hands on her shoulders.

"I hope the police can help you, and I'll be around if you need me. You don't have to go through this alone."

He hugged her and left, knowing he wasn't supposed to be in the room with her. He felt better since he told the police what he knew. He stopped questioning himself and his faith, feeling like he did the right thing to set his life right again.

Life is a series of tests. How well you score shapes the person you become.

Samuels walked out of the Precinct, headed for his church.

"Julie, can we talk a minute?"

"Sure."

Angela sat down as Julie tried to quiet her sobs.

"The other officers told me you had some questions when they told you they needed you to come in. I'm here to answer those questions if I can."

Angela put a hand on her shoulder as an offer of support while Julie collected herself.

"I wanted to know what she was doing on the roof of that skyscraper. She's afraid of heights; she would never go up there."

"We are assuming her assailant took her there."

"Wouldn't that be difficult, I mean, if she were still…alive? Wouldn't someone notice a body being carried through the building? How did she end up there?"

"Those are all good questions and we've got our forensics team checking it out. I agree that it's an odd place to find a body and I promise we'll tell you as soon as we know."

"Thank you...for helping." Julie began crying uncontrollably again. Angela held the girl, not knowing what else to do, and not wanting to sit without doing anything.

"What's going to happen to me?"

"We want to take you to a safe house."

"Why? What about my job?"

"We don't want anything to happen to you. We think Ellen's assailant confronted her in front of your apartment, meaning he may know about you. He can't come back to finish the job if you're not there. We'll send a unit out to get some of your things, whatever you think you need, and we'll post a unit to watch the apartment. If the assailant does come back, we'll have a chance to catch him without putting you in danger. As for your job, we already contacted your boss, and he was very receptive to what we told him."

"What did you tell him?"

"We told him you were assisting the police department in a very important case, and you had no choice in the matter."

Julie pondered the detective's words for a second. "You said 'he'. How do you know Ellen's attacker was a man?"

"Actually, we don't know if it's a man or not; that's just my take on it." Angela covered herself well. She didn't intend to give anything about the killer. She was surprised Julie picked up on it in her current state. She felt it would be best to keep as much as possible under wraps until the case was solved.

"Here's one of my cards. You can reach me directly at the number on the back. If you aren't able to use the phone, one of the officers acting as chaperone will be able to contact us. We've almost got the safe house set up, so I'll be back in a few minutes to get you." Angela gave Julie a supportive rub on her upper back and left the room.

The wind lashed out at the priest as he walked, colder and more brutal than he expected, blowing snow that stung his skin and made walking difficult. His time inside the police station changed his resolve, and with it his short-lived ability to ignore the severe weather.

He stopped at a deli for a quick breakfast and spent the day visiting homeless shelters along his route. The light gray of the clouds faded away as the unseen sun set for the day. He approached his church and saw a large man wearing a dark cloak enter the chapel.

He was immediately curious and suspicious as he didn't remember the parishioner. Samuels had a good memory for people and faces, and a man of that size would be memorable. The same man left the church within a couple of minutes, walking off in the direction from which he approached. The odd behavior further fueled the priest's curiosity, so he followed, knowing a man that large would likely have a deep, possibly scratchy voice.

The man walked quickly, gaining ground on Samuels. He jogged to the corner to a long side street to close some of the distance when his line of sight was broken. The street before him was empty. The man was gone.

He looked in all directions, unable to see anyone. The snowfall thickened with nightfall, coming down in larger flakes, cutting visibility by the minute. The priest looked down at his feet, hoping he would be able to feel them again when he got out of the weather, when the idea struck him to follow the footprints in the snow. If he started right away, he could follow the tracks before the new snow hid them completely.

The tracks were easy to find and see, and they were very large, just like the man. The shape seemed a little odd, but that didn't perplex Samuels nearly as much as the fact the man was barefoot.

How can anyone handle this snow and cold without shoes?

With fired curiosity, he followed the tracks down the street about fifty feet when he stopped in shock. The tracks ended in the center of the street. The snow farther on was undisturbed, as if God himself reached down and snatched the man up.

He headed back to St. Christopher's with nothing more to follow. Samuels entered his church, cold and empty handed. He wanted to know if anyone saw the man he followed, but no one within the holy walls could help. The early evening mass began just before the man entered, allowing him access to the church without being noticed in the shadows along the walls.

He went to his chamber to warm up, making himself a cup of coffee and turning up the space heater by his desk when he caught a glimpse of something out of the corner of his eye. An envelope rested on his desk pad. It was blank, but it wasn't there when he left the day before. He sipped his coffee and warmed his frozen toes as he contemplated opening it. He didn't lock his door, but no one entered his chambers without permission. As he reached the bottom of his cup, his feet lost the last of the effects of the cold. He picked up the envelope and opened it.

It contained a simple card with the words "Thank You" printed on the outside. The interior read, "Forgive me, Father, for I have sinned." Samuels stopped reading, frantically looking around to assure himself he was alone. He knew the killer left it, and he was convinced it was the man he tried to follow.

He calmed down as he read farther on, realizing Marina had left the card, not the killer. She thanked him for all the things the church did for her, and she felt badly that she hadn't yet offered her thanks.

The church helped her get into her new apartment and get on her feet again. She lived in a run-down tenement building in a bad part of town when she answered an employment ad for the church. She wanted to make it on her own, but everything didn't work the way she wanted it to. Jobs were scarce and she slowly slipped into financial hardship. Samuels sensed her purity, so he offered her a job assisting him personally with his studies. She had first-hand experience of religion in Russia, one of the few places he never got the chance to visit. As her life started to turn, she was able to move into a nicer apartment closer to the church, and volunteers from the congregation helped her move her belongings.

chApCeR CweNCY-NINe

Daxxe descended on the warehouse district, knowing his prey wouldn't arrive for a few hours, which gave him a chance to look around. The building's front bore a sign that read "Thornquist." He slipped through the open skylight he found in the west end of the building's roof. He overheard Viktor say the object they were looking for was marked, and although he didn't know what mark they sought, he knew he would recognize it when he saw it. He looked for almost two hours before luck played its hand.

A small crate, tightly sealed, rested on the bottom of a pallet. The pallet was pushed against one of the building's walls, only allowing a small face of the crate to be seen. It bore a small symbol burnt into the wood face, four double-ended arrows forming an eight-pointed star within a circle. The symbol was from the old language, and only a very small group of people would recognize it for what is truly was. He quickly freed the crate and caught the scent of one of Trokar's minions as he readied himself. The smell was still faint, giving him enough time to conceal his find.

Daxxe worked his way down one of the aisles, picking up a second distinct scent. Both were getting stronger. He was about to leave the warehouse when two stacks of crates beside him toppled. He jumped back the direction he came from when something struck the back of his legs, catching him by surprise and dropping him to his knees. A second blow found the back of his head, but he rolled with the hit and found his feet quickly. Viktor stood before him, holding a steel pipe.

"Well, well, if it's not the avenging angel. I owe you for Dimitri and Arin."

"Was that their names? I lose track when there's so many."

Viktor jumped at Daxxe, instantly enraged. Daxxe dodged the attack, raking through the flesh on Viktor's back as he passed.

"Your temper is still getting the best of you. I'm disappointed in you, Viktor."

A lasso of steel cable looped over him and tightened, pinning his arms to his sides.

"Not temper, distraction."

Mekune yanked the cable tight as Viktor rushed Daxxe again, striking him hard. Viktor's claws drew blood as they tore into his chest, and the force of the blow hurtled him backwards. Damok struck him on the back of the head with another length of pipe, putting him into an out-of-control head-over-heels spin through the air that knocked him out. He crashed into stacks of crates, causing them to fall on top of him. Mekune pulled the unconscious body out of the rubble with the steel cable.

"No Mekune!"

Viktor held his hand out, palm open as he spoke.

"We are finished. Trokar's package is not here, and we've searched top to bottom. Set the building on fire. Not even the 'mighty' Daxxe can survive an inferno."

Mekune and Damok did as they were instructed. They poured flammable chemicals they found in some of the crates all around the building and over several of the crates stored inside. They locked down the east skylight and went to the roof via the west one.

"Do it," ordered Viktor as he disappeared into the frozen night.

Damok threw a container of kerosene he fashioned into a Molotov cocktail through the skylight after he lit it. Mekune sealed the skylight and they both leapt to the street to find their next meal.

Officer Miller rolled slowly through the warehouse district with his partner Jon Salowski. Several new patrols overlapped in the area since the rave party slaughter.

"Miller! Stop the car!"

"What is it?"

"Look over there."

Jon noticed a glow in one of the warehouses, the glow of flames. He jumped out as soon as the car stopped moving, moving to the trunk.

"Grab the assault rifles; we're not taking any chances."

The two officers moved on the building as a pair.

"David, you go around that way. I'll go left and meet you on the other side."

"Alright, but be careful, and no heroics."

288

The two broke apart as planned. Jon turned the corner at the back of the warehouse and saw two men walking away from the building.

"Police! Halt!"

One of the men stopped as the other disappeared into the darkness.

"You! Stay where you are!"

Jon walked towards the remaining man slowly, trying to watch him and keep an eye out for the runner.

"Don't move! Keep your hands where I can see them. I have you in my sights, and I will fire if you move! What are you doing out here?"

Damok turned and walked directly towards Jon. The assault rifle barked a single report. His rating as an expert marksman placed the bullet in the attacker's left knee, as he intended to disable, not kill.

Damok's smile widened as he advanced, never slowing.

"Oh holy…"

Jon discharged seven bullets on semiautomatic. All seven found Damok's torso, but they had no effect on him. He kept coming. Jon stumbled backwards, switching the weapon to full auto. The distance between them was twenty feet and closing. The muzzle flash highlighted the attacker's face, allowing his razor-sharp teeth to be seen in the eerie strobe light effect of the discharging ammunition.

Jon pulled the trigger back and held it fast, clearing the rest of the hundred rounds in the magazine in seconds, and almost every slug found its mark. He backpedaled, trying to get away, and fell to the slushy pavement. Damok was right on top of him, unaffected by the storm of hot steel.

David heard the assault rifle's reports and broke into a run. Jon didn't lose his cool, which worried him. He rounded the corner to find Jon sitting against the back wall of the flame-engulfed warehouse.

"Jon, what happened?"

He was pale, and the rifle's firing pin clicked rapidly. His knuckle was white on the trigger, holding it down, trying to fire bullets that were no longer there. He trembled visibly.

"It's not possible."

"What's not possible, Jon?"

Miller was at a loss about what happened. Jon was talking, but not in response to him. The shock would have to wear off before they would get anywhere.

David checked the area, finding no evidence of the attacker. He also found no blood, which he expected to see. The clicking stopped, catching his attention. He turned to see Jon looking at him, back in the real world.

"I dumped a whole clip in him and he just kept coming. I know I hit him with all of those bullets, like over a hundred friggin' rounds! Did you see him? Stone wasn't kidding!"

"No, I didn't see him, but I know you're not reckless with a weapon. I believe you."

David helped Jon to his feet and they walked towards the spot where Jon originally opened fire. An unmarked squad car screamed into the alley, responding after hearing the gunshots. The driver squealed to a stop roughly thirty feet from Jon and David, lighting up the entire alley with the car's headlights. Shell casings littered the asphalt, shining like a string of brass Christmas lights. The heated metal melted the snow, and little streams of steam drifted up through the halogen beams.

Jon and David stopped dead in their tracks once they got a closer look. Several slugs lay on the pavement closer to the car. All showed impact damage, proving that they hit something, but the slugs where clean. A barrage like the one that occurred tended to leave behind a corpse, or at the very least blood and bone fragments.

"Jesus! What is that guy made of?" asked David, at a loss for an explanation.

Jon took a couple of small plastic bags from his pocket. He put his hand in one and used it to pick up all the casings and slugs he could manage without defiling the evidence. The snow already cooled them enough to be handled.

"I want forensics to check this out. This just isn't possible."

David relayed the story to the plain-clothed team as they walked up; they radioed it into headquarters and called for the fire department, even though they all knew the building was beyond saving.

The heat inside the cavernous warehouse increased steadily as the blaze spread quickly over the flammable solvents. The crates, being extremely dry, caught fire quickly. Several boxes of emergency flares ignited explosively as the flames crept over them, causing the fire to spread faster. A stack of jumbled crates near the heart of the blaze shifted slightly and fell aside, redirecting that part of the fire away.

Daxxe removed the lasso of cable from his arms and stood up, unable to apply very much weight to his right leg. When he was thrown into the stack, a large crate fell from the top, corner first, directly on his thigh. It left a deep, ragged gash. Blood trickled down his leg, over his knee, and onto the concrete floor. He spoke a few words as he searched the area around him. He lost his bearings during the fight and needed to find the crate.

The spell made the symbol on the small crate glow like a beacon, making it easily visible. He grabbed the crate and leapt into the air, gliding over the flames to the closest skylight. A hard push against the updraft from the flames made him accelerate quickly. He ducked his head and burst through the glass in a spray of crystal shards.

Striking him across the head and shoulders, Mekune yelled "Damok!" at his counterpart, forcing him to open his eyes. "What are you doing? We are not indestructible!"

Damok's shirt was torn to pieces from the array of bullets that passed through it. Mekune examined the bullet holes finding no evidence of the injuries.

"They are mere mortals. Someone has to show them that we are superior and keep them in line."

"We will in time Damok. Trokar has told us many times that we are not quite prepared for an all-out war with the humans."

"Then why did he do nothing about our little warehouse buffet the other night? Viktor spoke nothing of it either."

Mekune stood in silence, not having an answer. Trokar only confided in Viktor, and he guessed they must have some larger plan in the works.

"I don't know. Uuntil recently, Trokar always cautioned us away from direct contact with the humans unless we were feeding. He didn't want undo attention called to our kind. I overheard him talking to Viktor the night of the party. Viktor was concerned and asked how we should be disciplined."

"Yes?" Damok stood up effortlessly, all of his wounds vanished.

"Trokar said it didn't matter because the end was almost here. I don't know what he meant, or what end he's talking about."

"Daxxe, what happened?"

Jamat queried as his master limped across the belfry.

"Things got out of hand."

"Out of hand! You call this out of hand! You look like absolute hell. From the look of you, I'd guess you almost didn't make it back."

"I didn't waste the time or energy to heal myself. The situation heated up too quickly."

Jamat made a gruff noise, denoting his disapproval, and helped Daxxe to his chamber.

"Which Book did you risk your life for?"

Daxxe settled into a heavy wooden chair, offering no response.

"Well, which one?" Jamat's voice was harsher as he inspected the injuries.

"The symbol of Chaos is burnt onto each face of the box. No one else would take any particular notice since they probably don't know what it means."

"Are you intending to open it, or keep it around as a footstool?" Jamat's sarcasm further defined his mood as he tended the wounds. He easily aggravated when his master took unnecessary chances.

Most of the damage amounted to nothing more than simple cuts and light burns, but the gash in the leg concerned him.

"I don't think I can help you here."

Daxxe merely nodded in acknowledgement and thanks. He spoke silently as he rubbed the palms of his hands together slowly. Jamat heard nothing, but he knew the chant of healing well, after seeing his master use it so often. As the tempo and speed of motion increased, his hands took on any eerie blue glow. The illumination grew, making his hands look as if they were engulfed in blue flame, but it didn't offer illumination to the area around it. The light appeared bound, as though it was trapped in his hands. He placed them on both sides of his leg, making his thumbs touch over the worst part of the injury. His fingers touched on the backside of his leg, closing the ring. The glow faded slightly as he took his hands away, but the glow stayed wrapped around his leg, pulsating randomly at first, finally settling on a steady rhythm. As the light faded away, so did the black tinged break on his skin. The injury was completely gone.

"Now, let's make sure this was worth it." His limp was gone as he approached the wooden box.

Angela tossed and turned for several hours before she gave up and got out of bed. The dream was even more intense, but all the harder to remember. She had the vague impression she was fighting something, or for something, and that winning the fight meant everything.

She got dressed casual in jeans, a white blouse, and a dark blazer, and donned her heavy coat. She clipped her badge at her waist, grabbed her keys and purse, and went for a drive. The roads were bad, but the traffic was sparse. She didn't have a particular destination in mind, but she found herself sitting in a parking lot, looking at an out-of-place train depot and four train cars. The signs were lit up, as where the dining areas inside. She locked her car and walked onto the platform.

"Welcome back, Ms. Angela and fellow Texan."

Flip came up beside her, moving a hand truck full of supplies from one of the freezers in the box car to the kitchen car.

"Good morning, Mist...eh...Flip. How are you?"

"I'm good as ever, but pardon my saying that you look like you've been rode hard and put away wet. When's the last time you got some sleep?"

"It's that obvious?"

"Well, no, but the neon sign floating over your head, flashing 'Sleepless in New York', is a dead giveaway."

Angela laughed. It felt good.

"Why don't you come on inside and pull up a seat while I whip you up some breakfast."

"Thank you. I'd like that."

Flip unlocked the door, allowing them access to the inside. He closed and locked it behind them as the diner didn't open for business until six.

Angela chose a booth across from the center of the bar. She could hear Flip whistling in the kitchen as the aroma of fresh coffee filled the car. He came out with a large steaming mug of it, along with creamer and a little metal table caddy that held the other condiments for the table.

"I made that a little stronger than normal. I can get an ice cube if it's too stout."

"I think it'll be fine. Thank you for your hospitality."

"No thanks needed, my dear. You get started on that and I'll have some breakfast out in a few minutes."

She sipped her coffee and watched the snow fall outside the window. She didn't realize how hungry she was until a mélange of savory smells drifted from the kitchen. When Flip returned, he carried a large tray and a collapsible stand to set it on. It was piled high with food. He started setting it all out on the table and sat down across from Angela.

"Wow! I'm impressed. It all looks and smells so good!"

"Let's worry a little more about how it all tastes."

They fixed themselves plates from platters laden with bacon, sausage, thick country ham, Western omelets, biscuits, gravy, and grits.

"This really reminds me of home. Mom used to fix breakfast like this on Sunday mornings." She took a few bites and said, "you are an excellent cook."

"Flattery will get you everywhere, my dear."

They ate over idle chit chat until they were both miserably full, leaning back slightly on the seats.

"I'm not sure I'll be able to eat for a week."

"That's good. It's just like the sign says."

Flip pointed to a hand-painted sign hanging on the wall behind the bar. It read 'If you don't like the food, Flip's to blame. If you leave hungry, it's your own damn fault.'

Angela laughed when she read it.

"Now, why don't you tell me what's on your mind."

Angela felt no reservations about talking to Flip. She told him everything she could remember about her dreams, the stress about the case, and her worries about being Joe's new partner. Flip listened, nodding and offering consolation when needed. When she was finished, he threw her for a loop.

"You really do look like her."

"Like who?"

"I know Joe hasn't said anything. He probably never will, and you can't let him know that I told you. Actually, you'll have to take this to your grave. Can you handle that?"

"I don't understand."

"Joe was married once, to a real catch of a woman. Her name was Michelle and they were truly in love. They had one child, a daughter they named Celeste, and you are a spitting image of her."

"Joe's never told me about his family. I thought he lived alone."

"He does. Nineteen years ago, a drunk driver hit the car Michelle was driving. She had just picked Celeste up from school and they were going to meet Joe for dinner during his break. He was a beat cop then. They never made it. Celeste would be about your age if she was still alive."

"That's...that's so sad."

"It was a real shame, and it almost broke Joe. He was ready to throw in the towel."

"You mean he wanted to quit being a cop?"

"No, I mean that he was going to put his service revolver in his mouth and pull the trigger. That's how I met Joe. Tom went by to check on him and he didn't know what to do, so he called me. It took me almost two hours to talk him out of it and let me have his gun. Counting you, a total of four people in this world now know that."

"I just can't see him doing that. He's got such a strong sense of worth and a solid personality. I don't quite understand why you're telling me this."

"You will, but we've got to cover a little ground before we get to the point. I imagine you're worried that Joe picked you as his new partner because you look like his daughter, but that's not the case. Joe never saw you until you met. He's a good, honest cop, and he was a good husband and father. He knows his business, so you don't need to keep worrying about that."

"Did he tell you about our little talk?"

"He didn't have to. I could tell you felt insecure the first time I met you."

"It seems I read just like a book these days," she said, halfheartedly throwing up her hands.

"No, not like a book, like a rookie, but it's nothing to be ashamed of. We all go through it, but we're getting away from the point. Joe gave me his gun that night because I told him that I knew Michelle and Celeste would want him to go on so he could protect people, and maybe save some lives from other drunk drivers and the like.

"He became absorbed in his work, pulling double shifts and never taking a day off. He lost himself to it, and somewhere along the way he forgot what it meant to be alive. At least until he met you, that is."

"Sorry, but that's still sounds a little creepy."

"It's not like that. When he met you, he saw what Celeste could have been. He knows you're not his daughter reincarnated or anything weird like that, but it reminded him of what it was like when he had a good life with a purpose. You reminded him that he needed a goal, and that's why he acts more like a father than a partner sometimes."

"How do you know all this?"

"I know because I know Joe and we talk all the time; he's a horrible cook so he ends up eating here more often than not. What he needs is to help you become a great detective and succeed. To him, this is a second chance of sorts to set some things in his life right. He'll always be there for you, through thick and thin. I think he sees a little of himself in you, too.

"He was too hard on himself at first, and that brings me to the point. You've got to slow down and look at things in the right perspective. You can't afford to waste time second guessing yourself. All that will do is bring something bad down on you when you least expect or need it."

"I guess I have been a little too wrapped up in things."

"It's not a bad thing, but you need to be able to tell when you're doing it. This case already has everyone wound tighter than the spring in a doomsday clock, so adding tension only makes it worse."

"I see your point. I'm borrowing worry."

"Exactly; and another thing, it's okay if you don't always know what to do. It's better to realize that you don't than do something for the sake of doing it. That can prove disastrous."

"I see what you're saying." She nodded to herself. "I already feel better. I'm sure the wonderful breakfast helped, too."

"I know you do. You've got a good head on your shoulders."

"Thanks Flip. You always seem to know the right thing to say. I imagine that's why I ended up on your doorstep."

"I'm glad to help, and I'm just speaking from experience. I've been down this road and I'm just imparting some hard-earned advice and wisdom. It will still hurt to make a mistake, but as long as you learn from that mistake, it's okay."

"Thank you for everything, Flip. I better get going or I'll be late for work."

"Come back anytime, my dear."

Angela turned to leave, but she paused at the door. She walked back to Flip and gave him a hug first.

"I really feel much better now."

She stepped out onto the platform, taking in the brisk winter morning. The sun was just starting to give enough light to see by and the day already seemed brighter than any from the last few.

Jon and David pulled into headquarters at five-thirty in the morning, recalled for the rest of their shift because of the attack. A skeleton crew remained at the central base of operations around the clock because Joe felt it was absolutely necessary. The officers rotated the duty so no one worked an insanely long shift repeatedly.

Jon and David were debriefed and dismissed until the following day. Jon changed into his S.W.A.T. sweats and headed for the forensics lab. He knew he wouldn't be able to sleep until he had some answers.

"Morning Jon," said Greg, one of the lab techs. "What can I do for you today?"

"Aren't you here kind of early? It's not even six in the morning."

"Yeah, it's because of the shift rotations. They want someone here all the time."

"I need you to take a look at these. They're a couple of hours old."

Greg picked one of the bullets from the bag with a long pair of forceps.

"What were these fired at? There's almost no impact damage."

"I can't really say, but that's why I'm here. Just do what you can."

Greg's mind was already working to solve the mystery of the bullets.

Jon left the lab, headed for home, realizing he couldn't do anything but wait. The night's events left him exhausted.

His apartment was a mess, looking very lived in. He side-stepped around two piles of clothes, not remembering which one was clean. He crawled into bed, untwisting the sheets so he could be under the covers and tried to sleep. His mind did not want to cooperate, and it kept replaying the night's events like a song stuck on repeat.

Jon woke for the fifth time, drifting into the same dream when he managed to doze off each time. He could see the face of his attacker bearing down on him, hear the guttural growl, and see the teeth and the fiery eyes. He gave up the battle and got up, going to the kitchen for a glass of water. He downed the second glass before he realized how thirsty he was. The cuckoo clock on the dining room wall announced it was nine in the morning. He made himself a pot of coffee and went to the living room to lounge on the couch. He switched on the television to catch a few game shows, looking for something mindless, for a lack of anything better to do.

"Viktor!"

"Yes, Master?"

"I want you to get some information from our friend at the police department."

"What do you want to know?"

"It appears that a female cop named Angela Benson is the one that called Arkits. Arkits felt I might reconsider my decision to conclude our business dealings if I knew he talked to the police. I need to know what they know. If they get too close, we'll have to handle it."

"Understood."

Viktor immediately called one of the police stations, relaying orders to their insider. He wanted the answers by sunset.

Angela drove herself to the Precinct just after nine in the morning, fearing for her beloved Ford Mustang the entire way. If was a gift from her father before their relationship collapsed, but she still thought of him fondly for it. She grinned at the thought of him telling her that wouldn't have to clean up after it, and she would get more than one horsepower.

She managed to sneak in a little more sleep after she went home from Flip's, albeit still restless. His words of encouragement and advice put some of her fears to rest where Joe was concerned, but it did nothing to help with the dreams.

Her nights were becoming more and more restless as the dreams grew in intensity. She would wake, trapped in twists of the bedclothes, dripping with sweat. The images left strong impressions in her mind, but they faded away whenever she tried to focus on them or even remember them, like they had a mind of their own. She managed a little peaceful sleep about an hour after she got back home. She was thankful for the later start she was allowed on the task force. Her sleep deprivation showed, but she was still able to function on just a few hours. She found her partner in the central briefing room.

"Morning, Joe. Do we have anything new this morning?"

"Actually, we have something very odd."

"What is it?"

"After the rave party, as you know, we alerted the local hospitals and several doctors to keep their eyes open for any admissions that might fit that profile. So far, we've gotten six calls."

"What's going on?"

"All six cases are almost identical. Luckily, they're all at different hospitals, but all six started in the emergency room. From appearances, they were suffering from the initial stages of drug overdose, and the blood tests all contain a specific blend of narcotic. On the molecular level, the blends are identical, confirming all these kids were at the same party. The weird part is that all six have fallen into deep comas. They were all almost unable to communicate, or hardly walk for that matter, when they were admitted. The doctors are running every test they can think of so far, and they administered counter agents for the narcotics."

"And nothing is helping?"

"No, not yet. They don't seem to be getting any worse, but they aren't getting any better either."

"They've got to figure it out; those kids may be able to identify one or more of the killers."

"I know. We're hoping the doctors can find a way to pull them out of it. Even so, we still have to worry about the narcotics. These kids may be strung out too far to remember anything. Some of them may have permanent brain damage."

"Has anyone made the connection between these kids and the killers?"

"No. We've instructed each attending doctor to keep everything quiet for now. These kids probably have powerful and influential parents that we can deal with individually, but they could blow this all out of the water if they get together. It's been hard enough handling the parents of the kids that were killed. That fiasco started last night when the news got out and those kids hadn't come home. The Coroner only had the body you identified as Ms. Richardson confirmed at that time. The other two were confirmed earlier this morning. To make things worse, one of the girl's was the Mayor's daughter."

Angela was shocked, partially because the Mayor's daughter was involved in such seedy dealings, and partially over the amount of heat the force would receive over it. Everything found a way to go from bad to worse.

"Has he been notified?" asked Angela.

"Not yet, but the Commissioner said he would take care of it. He's got to be the bearer of bad news two times over."

"Why's that?"

"The Mayor will be completely separated from the case. His interest is now on a very personal level that could jeopardize the safety of others on the task force. As much as I can understand his pain and his need to avenge her death, I know we can't risk that kind of liability."

"I hadn't thought about that. Who will act as the interim?"

"The Council will most likely assume control. I think that may be better anyway, having several opinions instead of one."

"I'll bet you're right. What about the boy?"

"His name is Shane Willis; both of his parents are high-dollar lawyers. I can't even imagine how bad that's going to be, but the other girl belongs to Deacon Trass."

"Well, that's just great!" she returned with a knowing look.

"Yeah, we'll have to deal with his army of goons now, too. If they find these guys first, we'll have a real bloodbath on our hands."

"Is there any way to keep him out of it?"

"I highly doubt it, he's too well connected. We're going to have to stay ahead of him and we better make sure we don't get in his way."

"Do you think he'll do something stupid?"

"It wouldn't matter. We wouldn't be able to lay a finger on him anyway."

The phone in front of Joe rang. His expression was intent and focused until the end of the call, and his mood lightened as he hung up the receiver.

"What happened?"

"We just got another eye-witness; one of the kids that showed up at the City Hospital is coming out of the coma."

"Let's go."

Captain Bishop fell in step behind them as they entered the hallway.

"Joe, we just got this in. Another victim was found this morning in one of the restrooms in a subway terminal by a maintenance man with the Transit Authority. The victim's name was Harold Nicholas."

"How did you get an ID so fast?"

"Luckily, his wallet was still in his back pocket, and from the report, it looks like this wasn't a robbery. The wallet, and the rest of the room, was soaked with his blood. The maintenance man noticed a small pool of liquid just outside the door. He called us as soon as he realized it was blood. We're not sure if the killer was already gone or not. This is the first time we've discovered a body with any kind of identification. The area was swept immediately and cleaned up; that's a very busy terminal with a lot of foot traffic. Luckily, the restrooms are usually closed for a little while in the mornings for cleaning, so no one thought anything of it.

"They are really getting brave. Why are they branching out and getting out of their patterns? It's like they aren't even trying to hide anymore."

"I don't know, Joe, but I sure don't like it. To make matters worse, the Mayor is even against us since he's out of the loop. His heartbreak turned to hatred and he's been on the rampage ever since. It's harder to get things done with our own ranks divided."

"I hear you. We'll be back in a bit; we've got a lead we have to handle personally."

A small crowd stood on the sidewalk in front of the house as Sarah pulled into her driveway. She couldn't imagine why so many people were there or what they were looking at. She got out and walked to the small group, curious. She caught a foul odor floating in the air just before she reached the gathering. She looked at the house, following the gaze of the onlookers, who focused on the window to her son's bedroom. She noticed right away the large number of flies passing through the open window in both directions.

Sarah fumbled for her keys as she ran to the front door. After several unsuccessful attempts to disengage the lock, she finally got the front door open. The stench gagged her when she breached the threshold, almost forcing up the peanuts and soft drink she ate on her flight. Some of crowd moved a little closer.

"Max! Tim! Where are you? I'm home!" She yelled her greeting as she entered, but it elicited no response. She double-timed up the stairs, tripping and crawling when necessary to reach Tim's room. She fell to her knees, retching, screaming, and crying when she got there. Flies were everywhere, desecrating and crawling all over the bodies of her dead family, working in time with their maggot cousins to decompose the dead flesh.

A man standing with the group outside called the police on his cellular phone when he heard the scream, knowing something very bad was inside the house.

The childless widow stumbled back out onto the porch a few minutes later, racked with a combination of hysteria, confusion, and fear. Tiffany, the next-door neighbor and one of Sarah's best friends, come over when she saw Sarah's car parked outside. She came to investigate when the commotion caught her attention. A police car pulled to the curb about a minute later, responding to the 9-1-1 call. He saw the two women sitting on the front steps, crying and rocking back and forth, in front of a semi-circle of onlookers that looked despondent.

"What happened here?" He wrinkled his nose at the smell drifting out of the front door.

Sarah tried to speak, but her voice failed her. She started trembling so violently the officer thought she was going into a seizure.

"It's…I don't know how to say this. She just got back, and…go upstairs, second room on the right," answered Tiffany.

The officer went upstairs to investigate, aware that he was about to handle the aftermath of something with no present danger at hand.

"You sent for me, Boss?"

"Yes, come in. Thank you for coming on such short notice."

"Anything you need, Boss. We're family."

Trass smiled. Luigi was family, but not in the normal sense of the word. He worked for Deacon Trass as a part of a vast, underworld empire that ran most of the illegal enterprises in NYC. Trass had his hands in virtually every industry throughout the city in some form or fashion, regardless of its legality. Luigi had been in Trass' employ for eight years, progressing up the family ladder. He was one of the best hit men in the country and his loyalty to the organization was unprecedented.

"Luigi, I need you to do something for me."

"Consider it done, Boss. What is it?"

"It's about Tracy."

Luigi's expression went sour. He and Tracy were somewhat involved. Deacon was aware of their relationship, and he trusted Luigi far more than his own daughter.

"What happened?"

"Tracy's with Dr. Mason right now. She went to one of the drug parties in the warehouse district with some of her friends and something went wrong."

"Excuse me for asking, Boss, but she didn't OD, did she?" he asked, concern on his face.

"No, she didn't. I've asked her not to go to parties like that, but she's as stubborn as her old man. The morning after the party, she showed up at a hospital in Queens. One of our people recognized her and called us. We went and got her, but she's in a coma."

"A coma, from what?"

"Mason's not sure yet. We've brought in the best doctors money can buy, but they don't know, and our friends with the police department don't have enough information yet either. I don't know what happened but she is getting worse. I want you to find out what drugs were at the party and how they got there. I'll bet she got a special cocktail, and I want the supplier in my office as soon as possible."

"I'm on it." Luigi left with a look of intensity rarely seen by anyone but the mark.

Trass called the private medical center he owned and staffed. He employed the best doctors in their respective fields, and paid them well, for around-the-clock services. He didn't like to lose his men, but he couldn't afford to have them in public hospitals. He protected and paid his family well for their loyalty. Anyone found to be disloyal would have no use for medical attention.

"Yes."

"It's Deacon. How is she?"

"She's the same," answered Mason, "but I don't know how long her condition will hold. I'm afraid she's getting worse. We're doing everything we can to keep her comfortable, and we're working around the clock to find out what's wrong."

"Have you learned anything new?"

"We know it isn't the drugs reacting with each other, but I can't rule out the designer. We've flushed her system pretty well to get the drugs out, but something is still affecting her. I'm checking with our friend in the Coroner's Office."

"Why the morgue?"

"He's got the best access to information since they need everything for autopsies. I want to see if anyone else presented with the same symptoms. Maybe another doctor has uncovered a solution."

"Thanks, Doc. Keep me informed."

Deacon hung up the phone and rubbed his eyes, not sleeping since Tracy fell into a coma. Her mother died of cancer eleven years earlier, and he didn't want to lose his little girl, too. He spent his life providing for them, and they meant everything to him. He built his empire from the ground up, and he was devoted to keeping it viable, but family always came first.

Luigi headed for his ride, furious, but maintaining control. He never lost his temper, which was one of the reasons he was so dangerous and so feared. All of his jobs were executed with unrivaled precision, regardless of anything the mark might say or do.

His solid black Ford Excursion was a huge four-wheel drive. A custom grille protected the front, and a solid steel bumper protected the rear. The frame was heavily reinforced, to the point he could punch a hole in a brick wall without scratching the paint. The limousine tint covering the back and side windows concealed a mobile armory and a very high-tech computer system. He could access virtually any computer network in the world with an Internet connection, allowing him to locate almost anyone or anything within minutes. His armory contained all of his weapons of choice, ranging from throwing knives to sniper rifles that could fire over a mile without making a sound.

He drove to the roof of the parking garage across the street from Trass' business office to have a clear satellite connection for his onboard system. A retractable privacy panel stood behind the front seats, and with the press of a button, the driver's seat rotated and the panel compressed to the passenger's side. The driver's seat then slid backwards and the panel resealed. The computers automatically came online, and the lock boxes for his arsenal opened with the assistance of a hydraulics system.

The alarm system was almost too advanced to be called an alarm system. It offered contingencies for almost any attack; the glass was bulletproof, the body was armored enough to withstand a bazooka blast, the tires were solid-filled so they couldn't blow out or be shot out, and the door handles were connected to a separate power source set to deliver 440 volts to anyone that shouldn't be opening the doors.

Luigi accessed the police department's computers first. He could get in and look around undetected. He found the case file and studied it. Another case was linked to the one he was reading, but he focused on the task at hand. Narcotics found several illegal substances, but only three of them were designer drugs. He cross-referenced the drugs with his own system to see who received shipments of them in the last six months. Most dealers didn't sell the designers because they were easier to track and more expensive to buy. The system produced four names, one of which was Deacon Trass, narrowing the search to three.

Luigi checked Dr. Mason's file on Tracy to see what was in her system the night of the party. The initial blood test run by the hospital showed marijuana, cocaine, and the designer drug named Desert Spice. Spice, as it was called, was a new narcotic in the states, containing hallucinogenic drugs found in plants in the outback of Australia. It was also laced with LSD. The drugs were mixed and ground into a fine powder that could be snorted like cocaine or free-based like heroin. The purity of the mixture made it highly addictive and very dangerous.

One of the remaining suspects was a problem Luigi personally handled two months earlier, leaving Tony Sarducci and Al Vanetti. He decided to pay a visit to Vanetti first.

Lenox Hill was one of the largest health facilities in the city. Joe and Angela entered through the emergency room doors, quickly finding the room they wanted.

Two police officers stood guard outside one of the private rooms close to the hospital's emergency department. The detectives displayed their badges as they approached, gaining entry to the room. A young woman lay on the bed. The attending physician and his nurse stood by as two of the floor's RNs secured the restraints on her wrists, ankles, and waist.

The doctor looked at Joe and Angela as they entered. "Can I help you?" His tone indicated he was slightly irritated.

"I'm Detective Angela Benson. This is my partner Joe Anderson. We're with Homicide."

"I see. I'm guessing you need me to tell you again what I know," returned the doctor after requesting the patient's chart, which the charge nurse hastily fetched.

"This young lady presented at roughly seven this morning. It is unknown if she was capable of speech or just choosing silence. The attending doctor described her as lethargic, physically and mentally impaired and borderline delirious due to the influence of some type of drug. She was admitted on doctor's orders and examined. She was completely unresponsive to stimuli and severely dehydrated. They started a lactated ringer IV, took blood samples for a complete CBC workup, and performed a general examination. We haven't found anything so far that contradicts narcotic substance abuse. She slipped into a comatose state at approximately nine-thirty."

"How long was she actually out?" asked Joe.

The doctor's tone lightened as he considered the question.

"It wasn't very long at all, really, and it's one of the strangest things I've ever seen. At first, we believed she simply passed out, which is fairly common in substance abuse cases, but it only took a few minutes to confirm she was comatose."

Angela looked at the young girl as the doctor spoke. She was a very attractive blond, probably seventeen or eighteen years old. She was lying deathly still in spite of the restraints. The bedclothes were tangled about her legs and floral print hospital gown was stuck to her skin with sweat.

"Why do you have her restrained?" asked Angela. "She looks...tranquil."

"When she came around, she thrashed violently and pulled the IV out of her wrist before the nurses could get control of her."

"Did she say anything?" asked Joe.

One of the nurses answered. "I wouldn't say it was speaking. She moaned and mumbled, but we couldn't make any sense of it. She looks much worse than she did earlier this morning."

"That's because she's losing blood," said Joshua as he entered the room. "You need to give her type O negative blood and I'd suggest stronger restraints."

The doctor and nurses looked at Stone as if he walked in with his head on fire. "Sir, she doesn't have any injuries or internal bleeding. She doesn't need any blood, and those straps have a seven-hundred-pound test. We are taking every precaution," responded the doctor.

"Doctor, I would whole heartedly agree with your assessment of the situation if you had any idea what you are dealing with."

The retort was met with a chagrined look until the girl moaned, catching everyone's attention. She rolled back and forth as far as the restraints would allow, as if she was having a bad dream. Without warning, she opened her eyes and tried to sit up. Her feral gaze focused immediately on the straps. She pulled at the restraint confining her right arm, pulling it taut. It looked tight enough to snap, but it held fast. The tension in her right bicep built as she held pressure on the restraint, becoming audible.

"Nurse Beckham, administer a shot of Thorazine, quickly!"

The nurse retrieved the drug as the girl looked at the doctor and screamed, pulling harder against both wrist restraints. The edges of the strap holding her right arm started to fray, individual strands snapping, sounding like guitar strings breaking. The doctor and both nurses approached the bed with the retrieved injection.

"We need to administer the Thorazine directly. It will work much faster undiluted."

The charge nurse approached the bedside. "This won't hurt a bit, dear."

The doctor and the other nurse each took an arm and held them against the mattress, pushing the girl down on the bed. In the blink of an eye, the girl pulled her arm from the doctor's grip, shredding the strap in the process. She grabbed the charge nurse by the wrist and pulled her onto the bed. The downed nurse started screaming.

The doctor and the other nurse hesitated from shock for half a second, then managed to pull their coworker away from the patient, but not before the damage was done. Blood soaked the young girl's face and chest. The charge nurse bled profusely from the hole where her right cheek used to be. The other nurse rushed her away to get the injury treated as the girl lay back in a sudden, quiet calm. She licked her lips clean and quickly fell asleep.

"What the hell just happened?" barked the doctor to no one in particular.

Joe and Angela stared at the girl blankly, as if they were deciding if what happened really happened. The entire incident took less than thirty seconds.

Joshua stood at the window, his face resting in the palm of his hand. He shook his head back and forth slowly as he looked up and out the window. "She is in the advanced stages of the disease. Every so often, for reasons unknown, the disease will progress at an exponential rate. I suspect one of those jumps is what we just witnessed."

"What 'disease' are you referring to?" asked the doctor.

"Vampirism," returned Stone stoically.

"Did I wake up in the wrong world this morning? Do you expect me to believe that this girl is suffering from vampirism? There's no proof that the disease even exists. Are you a quack or something?" The doctor's tone was turning demeaning, his control deteriorating under the higher level of stress.

"You no longer have the luxury of catering to that belief. I told you to give her blood to avoid any unnecessary complications. You didn't listen, and now you have an infected charge nurse missing a cheek. She will be calm for a while, which gives you the chance to get her properly sedated and restrained. I would double the dose of Thorazine and you need straps with a minimum test of 2,500 pounds." Stone then left the room, saddened, bound for anywhere he could get a cup of coffee.

"Is he serious?" uttered the doctor, shocked, looking at Angela and Joe.

"That he is," returned Angela, speaking softly. "I'm sorry we weren't able to tell you before, but this incident puts you on the 'need to know' list."

"I'm the treating physician and I was never on a need to know basis! How in the hell am I supposed to treat a patient if I don't know what's wrong…"? The doctor's face turned red and the veins on his forehead bulged visibly. The quick rise in blood pressure cutting his words short as he sat down and lowered his head between his knees.

"Dr. Hogan," said Angela, from the name on his ID badge, "we aren't trying to keep you from doing your job, but we can't allow this information to spread unchecked. Can you imagine the pandemonium if the general public even had an inkling about this?"

Joe moved by the closed door and stood against it to restrict entry. The doctor leaned back in the chair to look out the window, staring silently. "I'm sorry for the outburst. I can see the need to keep this quiet. The city's already on edge with the 'Hook' murders. If the public starts to think this killing spree is somehow spreading a new disease, we would have complete chaos."

A light knock rapped the door behind Joe. It was Joshua, holding a cup of coffee. Joe let him in and resumed his post at the door. "Dr. Hogan, I'd like to offer my apologies for earlier because you weren't informed of the situation. Your charge nurse is resting comfortably. They've stopped the bleeding and a plastic surgeon will be consulted to repair the tear. They have started antibiotics and other protocols I shared with them."

Joshua turned his attention to Joe. "Both of the nurses are convinced the attack was a result of the narcotics in her system. I told them that the drug is synthetic, and it causes very violent side effects. They think the added security is part of a Narcotic's investigation and they believe the blood loss is also a side effect."

"You're good," said Joe.

"I like to consider myself cautious," replied Stone. "It's easy to play the attack off as a bad trip, and that won't call any undue attention to the case regardless of how far the story spreads."

"Why did you want me to give her blood? And why type O negative?" asked Dr. Hogan with his composure restored.

"The disease uses the host's blood like a fuel. The blood is consumed internally and that metabolic process creates the need for more. It doesn't seem to matter how the blood gets into the host's system as long as it gets there. The tendency for those suffering from the disease to select an oral method of replenishment is probably psychological. I said type O negative because it's a universal donor, as you know. She's still somewhat human, so that's the safest route to take."

"I see," said the doctor, shaking his head from side to side. "I'm still very skeptical about all of this. Vampires aren't real."

"That's what most people believe. I can't make you agree, but I can give you a lot of hard evidence to support it."

"Assuming that's the case, how does the disease work? Is there a cure?"

"We don't know. If a cure exists, we haven't found it yet. I'll get you a copy of a study that explains the dynamics. For now, we should probably get her strapped in and lock down this room. As I said earlier, she's in the advanced stages, so I don't know how long this lull will last."

Angela looked over at the young girl, amazed at how much better she looked now than before the attack. She slept peacefully, and the correct pallor returned to her skin. The drying blood on her neck and chest started to crack as her chest moved up and down with each breath. The doctor approached cautiously, but the girl didn't wake. The syringe of sedative still lay on the bed by her leg where it was dropped during the attack. He emptied the contents into the girl's IV line before using the call button to request the additional dosage and the stronger restraints.

"I need to clean her up a little, could you gentlemen step outside?"

Joe nodded and followed Joshua out of the room. Angela sat in the now vacant chair at the foot of the bed. The doctor went to the small bathroom inside the room to get a small basin and a sponge. He filled the basin with warm water and grabbed a couple of towels.

He removed the soiled gown after placing towels over the patient's private areas, gently cleaning up the dried blood as much as possible for the short term. He grabbed a new gown from a cabinet in the room to replace the soiled one.

"What's that?" asked Angela as the doctor repositioned one of the towels.

"What?"

"That," said Angela, pointing at the girl's chest, "on the bottom of her left breast."

The doctor looked down, discovering two small puncture wounds in the soft flesh under the shadow of the towel.

"We didn't see that before. It looks like a spider bite."

"I agree it's a bite, but I don't think a spider did that. Whatever, more likely whoever, bit her wanted to conceal the wound. Those punctures wouldn't be visible if she wasn't prone."

"I'm going to go with a spider on her chart, based on what you all have told me. I still don't think I believe this, but the chart doesn't need to advertise a problem."

Hogan put the gown over the girl and asked Angela to help support her neck to get it tied behind her neck. He then pulled the towels from under the gown. He changed the top sheet on the bed for a fresh one and pulled it up over her legs and torso.

"You have an excellent bedside manner," offered Angela as she walked to the door to motion for Joe and Joshua to come back in the room.

"She has two puncture wounds under her left breast, like her attacker didn't want the wounds to be seen," commented Angela. "Why would they try to be discrete with just this one? They didn't seem to care with…"

Angela dropped the rest of her comment, remembering that the doctor wasn't aware of the connection to the other killings. The look on Joe's face changed to alert Angela of her fumble as she realized she was about to slip up. Hogan didn't see Joe's look, and he didn't seem to realize what Angela said. He was busy writing in the girl's medical chart. The doctor excused himself to check on the sedative and restraints.

"Sorry," offered Angela, after the door shut behind him.

"It's okay, he wasn't listening," said Joe, "but that's a good question. What do you think Joshua?"

"I'm not truly sure, but this may be the first time a turn, which is the term we use for someone changing, has occurred in captivity. Once the disease sets in, the site of infection will disappear, so she's not completely through the process. This could be completely normal for them, or they may be creating a diversion for us."

"If this gets out, I'd say they pulled it off. We won't be able to do anything if the city panics about this," said Joe.

"Yeah, but this feels new for this case. Why would they need a diversion?" asked Angela.

chapter Thirty

Malcolm opened the back door of the unmarked police car for Julie. He and Emilio were assigned to escort her to one of the safe houses the NYPD had access to use. To insure the safety of the witness, it was up to Malcolm and Emilio to decide which one. Once she was secure, the officers would call in with a location number, which would only give headquarters the phone number to contact the house, but not the address. It was necessary precaution to keep the charge truly safe.

The "house" the officers chose was actually a loft style apartment in an upper-class neighborhood. It was built with its own alarm system and the building offered closed caption security cameras throughout the parking garage, hallways, stairwells, elevators, and lobby areas. The garage, located underground, was secured with automatic gates that required an access card and a personal code to gain admittance. The fact it was below ground also made it easier to stay out of sight when transporting the people they were charged to protect.

Malcolm pulled Julie's belongings out of the trunk along with two overnight bags that she knew weren't hers.

"Are you going to be staying with me?" she asked uncomfortably.

"Yes ma'am. The apartment is a two-room setup. You'll have the bedroom that has its own bathroom. We'll share the other room that's on the opposite side of the living area. We'll be with you until this is over."

"Don't they need you to help find Ellen's murderer?"

"They can spare an officer or two when the situation warrants. If they really need us at the station, they'll have us split the duty here so you aren't alone."

They walked to the elevator to ride up to the ninth floor. The apartment building stood fifteen stories high, but from the tenth floor up the apartments got progressively larger and more expensive, exceeding the needs of the Department.

The apartment was very plush. Hardwood floors ran throughout with large area rugs placed strategically to offer comfort and protection for the floor. The furniture was contemporary in style, very comfortable, and appeared new. The apartment was also one of the few in the building that didn't have a balcony.

The architectural design on the outside of the building was very decorative and appealing as well. Two columns ran vertically from the ground to the roof on each side of the main entrance on the building's face, robbing four apartments on each floor of their outdoor terraces, which was why this loft lacked one. The proximity to the elevators was of more import than a balcony.

The kitchen was stocked and ready for use. The bathrooms sparkled, and they had a variety of soaps, shampoos and the like, just like an upper-class hotel. The closets even had a small selection of clothing for men and women in varying styles and sizes. A charge could come with nothing and still be relatively comfortable.

"Your room is right over there, ma'am," instructed Emilio. "We'll be in that room over there. That door is useless for now; it connects this apartment to the one next door, but we won't need it for just the three of us. You'll find a two-way radio on the nightstand and we'll have the other one. We'd appreciate it if you'd leave the channel open at night; that makes it work like a baby monitor."

"Why do I need to do that?" Julie was still on alert, cautious of ill intent, real or imagined.

"It's only a precaution. We probably won't need to use it, but it's there just in case."

Julie looked around the living room. She felt cozy and uncomfortable at the same time, like she was staying with a favorite relative in a house she'd never been in before. She peeked into the other rooms, but only with cursory glances. She realized just how tired she truly was now that most of the excitement was over.

"Guys, I'd really like to get something little to eat and get some rest."

"Okay, we can order in or you're welcome to raid the refrigerator."

"I can fix something here. A piece of toast or a bowl of soup would work just fine."

She walked into the kitchen in search of her meal.

"Just let us know if you need anything else," added Mal.

Julie decided on a piece of peanut butter toast and a can of soda. She took the quick meal to her room and closed the door. She felt better to be alone, but it wasn't enough to shake the feeling that she was more a captive than anything else. The discomforts of being out of her element only made her feel worse. She ate quickly and got into bed, forgoing a shower. She left the light on in the bathroom, knowing she would be scared if she woke in the middle of the night and couldn't see her surroundings. She stared at the radio on the night stand for several minutes before she reached over and switched it on.

"Can you hear me out there?" she asked softly.

"Yes ma'am, loud and clear. Try to get some rest. Malcolm is going to take the first watch."

She found some comfort in the response and she leaned back into the pillows in silence. She hoped against hope the police would find the murderer soon. She wanted justice and the freedom to mourn for her friend without interruptions.

Jon stared blankly at the television. A game show contestant jumped up and down, screaming and hugging the host because she won a new car, but Jon didn't seem to notice. He was exhausted, but he couldn't get to sleep. Beads of sweat dripped from his brow, running down his face, leaving the collar of his T-shirt soaking wet, even though the temperature was comfortable. He had the phone answered and to his ear before the first ring had a chance to finish.

"Yes."

"Jon?"

"Yes."

"It's Greg, from the lab. I've got the test results you wanted."

Jon pulled from his diminished state. "What did you find out?"

"None of the bullets looked like they hit anything from the initial inspection. Under the microscope, we found several fine scratches, and almost all of the bullets had the markings. Several of them also showed variation in the overall shape, implying that some of them impacted against something. The residue we found in the microscopic scratches confirms impact."

"What's this residue made of?" asked Jon.

"We don't know yet, but we're analyzing it now. We know it's the only evidence that you did hit your target. I don't have any idea what you were shooting, but I can't imagine anything surviving that many hits."

"Thanks."

Jon hung up and sat for several long moments in a state of shock and denial. He had proof he shot that man with over a hundred rounds, and it didn't even slow him down. Jon picked up the phone to make a call.

"Forensics, this is Greg."

"It's Jon again. Will you call me when you get the results on the residue on those bullets?"

"Sure thing, Jon. We should have the analysis completed in the next couple of hours.

Joe and Angela left the hospital. The young girl, whom they still hadn't identified, slept the entire day. They waited to no avail in the hope she would wake up. Her body consumed all the blood the hospital supplied, but the consumption rate increased slightly as the day went on. The sedatives appeared to have the desired effect, but she would become restless if the bag supplying her with blood sat empty for any length of time. Three restraints now bound each arm and leg securely to the bed with heavy bolts. The restraint system, originally designed for PCP addicts, seemed like overkill. On three prior occasions, PCP junkies managed to release themselves from double restraints, hence leading to the addition of the third.

Joe gave instructions to one of the uniformed officers standing guard in the hall before they left. Only five people were allowed access to the room; that's Joe, Angela, Joshua, Dr. Hogan, and the primary nurse he designated to care for the girl in his absence.

Joshua conferred with Hogan before they left as well. He explained that the disease also made the patient highly photosensitive to natural light. The allergy was so volatile that it could kill the girl. The reaction would happen at the cellular level, resulting in thousands of damaged cells. In response, Dr. Hogan left orders to keep the blinds tightly shut unless it was dark outside, and he wrote in the chart that she was highly allergic to sunlight. He also ordered a strict regimen of sedatives and pints of type O negative blood as needed.

Joe checked on the other cases as they left the hospital. None of them had changed, all still deeply comatose and unresponsive to treatment. He returned to collect his partner.

"I wonder if there's something special about that girl."

"What do you mean, Joe?" asked Angela.

"She's the only victim from the rave party that's shown any signs of life. Why are the others still comatose?"

"I don't have any idea, but it would help us if we knew. I wish we had her name so we could get some information about her. She could have a special medical condition that's changing the way the disease affects her or something like that, possibly something that could become a treatment. We'll have to put missing persons on high alert, and with luck, we'll find out who she is without letting anyone know we have her."

"Right, but we've got to get through this quickly. Can you imagine being one of the parents of one of those kids?"

The detectives rode in silence back to the Precinct. The day's continual snowfall deepened the drifts by over a foot.

Daxxe pushed his claws into the pine, getting a solid grip. The wood splintered into pieces as he pulled the top off, revealing a silver metal box inside. The box was overly heavy for its size and it looked like it could take a direct hit from a nuclear warhead and remain sealed. Daxxe pulled the box from the rest of the crating material. It was completely solid, void of a handle, lock, or hinges, and an inscription adorned what Daxxe knew was the top of the box. The words were engraved in the old language.

"What does it say?" asked Jamat.

"It's a warning. It says the power contained within is unfathomable," he returned, looking up from the inscription. "It's the Book of Chaos. The incantations written on its pages are more powerful than the other four books combined. It's by far the strongest of the five."

"Why is this one so much stronger?"

"These spells were used to sunder the Old World. Kalanak himself had trouble controlling the flow of power once the spells were cast, oblivious to what happened. That's why Trokar wants it so badly; he wants this power."

"How do you open it? I assume you intend to do so."

"I'm not exactly sure, but I know it's magically sealed. I just have to find a way to break through the spell."

"I'll leave you to it then, but don't overdo. Tonight you need to rest."

Daxxe examined the box's aura, studying the structure of the spell sealing the case. Once he understood the spell's architecture, he could dismantle it piece by piece until the lock yielded.

Jamat entered Daxxe's quarters several hours later, just after sunset, to find him studying an antiquated book. The metal case lay on the floor, opened, next to the remains of the wooden crate.

"Why does my mind tell me that you haven't slept?"

"That's because your mind knows me too well, old friend. I don't think it's been opened since the sundering. The pages still smell of the old magic."

"What's that, in the case?"

Jamat indicated a small bundle of parchment, still secured in the lid of the metal case.

"It's a part of Kalanak's Journal. I don't understand how it survived the sundering, unless it was tucked inside the Book of Chaos when everything happened."

"What are you going to do with them?"

"I'll destroy the Journal, but I have to put the Book in a safe place. I cannot allow Trokar to obtain it. He could destroy this world with it."

"Do you think he'll come for it?"

"I'm not sure if he can. If he could sense the Book's magic, he would no doubt already possess it. I know he can't sense my presence, but we still have to be careful. His resources run deep, which I fear will put me, and ultimately you, in more danger."

"That is why I'm here. Regardless of what happens, you gave me an extra six hundred years to live in this the world. I know it cannot last forever, but I am thankful for all I've seen and done during that time."

"You have always served me well, and we've made it a long way with nothing more than hope and luck at times."

Marina sat patiently in the interrogation room, even though she'd been there overnight. They got her a cot and made sure she had plenty to eat and drink, trying to make her as comfortable as possible under the circumstances. Several different officers and detectives stopped in to check on her, so she knew she was never forgotten.

She guessed they were deciding how they were going to handle the hypnosis session and how long they would detain her. It gave her plenty of time to think and reflect, but she couldn't hack away any of the barriers blocking the hours she lost. The harder she tried to remember, the more euphoric she felt, which kept her from focusing her concentration.

A message was left for her that her sister called during the night, but the delivering officer didn't disturb her sleep. She wanted to call her back, but the police wouldn't let her, stating that it was not safe for her to do so.

Joe and Angela made it to the Precinct just after dark. The snowfall slowed, flakes not much bigger than grains of sand because the temperature dropped significantly, actually making it too cold to snow. The slush on the streets turned into jagged peaks and ruts, forcing Joe to wrestle the steering wheel to keep the car going in the right direction.

Most of the day staff already went home, leaving the Precinct with a skeleton crew. They checked on Marina before they went to the rooms designated for the task force.

"How much longer do we need to keep her here?" asked Angela of Captain Bishop when they entered the conference room.

"We got an artist to put sketches together from her first session with Stone, but we need to verify them with her which means another hypnotic session. Stone wanted to give her a good break before putting her under again, and he's trying to figure out what's keeping her from remembering."

Joe noticed Bishop's eyes shift from him to Angela's body. The show of disrespect bothered him, but it bothered him more that he never noticed it before Angela called attention to it. Joe made a mental note, watching Angela wrap her jacket around herself and cross her arms, visibly uncomfortable.

"Angela, why don't you go check on Marina, I'll finish up here."

"Yes sir." Angela got the way out of the room that she prayed for, and she took no time exiting. Joe opened the door for her and closed it behind her as she left; the closing of the case wasn't soon enough.

"Ed, we need to talk."

"What's on your mind, Joe?"

The use of first names identified the conversation as personal instead of business. Bishop sat down and poured them both a small drink from a bottle he kept in his desk for certain occasions. It was against regulations, but it was overlooked unless it became a major problem.

"It's been a long time since you've worked in the field, hasn't it?"

"Yeah, it has."

"Do you remember what it was like having a partner?"

"It's been a long time Joe. Is Benson not working out? I can have her reassigned."

"No, she's coming along fine, and I'm taking a pretty strong liking to her. You remember that, too, don't you? That knowing that someone's got your back?"

"Yeah, it's a nice feeling." Bishop sipped his scotch, paying a little less attention to what was being said.

"How far would you go to protect your partner?" asked Joe.

That caught Bishop's attention. "That's kind of an odd question. You know we all do whatever it takes."

"That's what I thought, but I just wanted to be sure."

Joe's glass still sat on the desk, untouched.

"What's this about Joe? That's pretty expensive scotch."

"Since we agree on this," started Joe, leaning forward to lessen the distance between them. "I know you'll understand when I tell you to stop eyeing my partner like a piece of meat. She's a good cop and a good person, and she deserves better from you than being treated like eye candy."

Bishop's jaw dropped. He was taken back and unsure what to say or do. Joe pushed his glass of scotch back across the desk, spilling some across the top as he stood up.

"I'm going to assume we're at an understanding here. I don't want to have to talk to you about this again and I can assure you it won't be pleasant if it comes to that, Sir."

Joe left the office, bound for his desk. All he could do was wait. He knew Bishop would react fairly quickly, regardless of what he was going to do, and Joe had no idea if he'd pushed too far. He didn't care if he had, but he was unsure of the ramifications from the confrontation.

Bishop sat motionless in a state of shock. On one hand, he was amazed that Joe confronted him so boldly. On the other, he knew he was caught. He wasn't in a position to retaliate as he couldn't afford to have the accusation come to light. There were other female officers on the force that might step forward with a little push of courage.

He wasn't having the best rapport with his significant other to boot, and an issue like that would surely hurt that relationship. His fiancé worked at the 17th, and she had several friends throughout the department.

"What was that all about, Joe? Don't get me wrong though, I did want out of there."

"We were just catching up on old times, enjoying a nightcap," he played off. "How's Marina?"

"She's okay, but she's tired of being cooped up in there. I told her it wouldn't be much longer. Stone wants to be careful dealing with her psyche; he doesn't want to leave any more psychological scars."

"How would he do that? She's not aware of what's happening when she's hypnotized."

"He admits he has no idea what's keeping her conscious mind from seeing what happened, but he doesn't want to tamper too much without a good understanding of what happened to her mind in the first place. If he pushes her too far, she could be trapped in a hypnotic state, she could lose touch with her subconscious, she could even go completely crazy."

"Does he have a plan?"

"He has one that he thinks will work. He wants to construct a grid of safe words and backdoors in her mind before he asks her any more questions dealing with the mental block to make absolutely certain he can pull her back to reality if something goes wrong."

"When is he going to try again?"

"He's almost ready now; he doesn't want to make her spend another night here."

"Do we have clearance to put her up in a safe house for a while?"

"Yes, and I think we should house her with the Romanowski girl."

"Why is that?"

"Well, she already knows Dupree and Hernandez, so it would be more convenient, and it'll keep us from diverting two more officers from the case."

Joshua entered the conference room reading a text.

"Are you ready to do this?" asked Joe.

"Yes, I think so. I want to have all the crisis management rules for dealing with hypnotic shock fresh in my mind if something goes awry. Angela, would you be so kind as to go get Marina?"

"Sure thing, be right back."

Joshua situated the room like it was for the first session, also requesting a heart monitor, smelling salts, and ice water.

"What are those for?" asked Joe.

"I want to have a little fore warning if I start to lose her. The heart monitor will be my indicator because her heart rate will jump considerably if she starts to go into shock and it'll give me a couple of extra seconds to start the fail-safe protocols to pull her back. It will do far less mental damage if I can keep her together. If not, it'll affect here much like a computer that's turned off while still performing a task. The machine isn't damaged, but it takes a few extra, specific steps to restore it to its original state. In a person, it will render them unconscious for a few moments until the mind can reboot, and it'll likely do actual damage, corrupting her software, so to speak."

Marina entered the room behind Angela. She looked nervous, but not fearful.

"Are you ready, Marina?" asked Stone.

"I think so. Will this help me?"

"That depends on how everything goes, but I think it will. We have to find out what happened to you. Please lie down on the couch and make yourself comfortable."

Daxxe positioned himself on a dark ledge of the tenement building overlooking the 42nd Precinct. The spell of finding he cast on Marina before he left her in her apartment allowed him to find her again. He needed to make sure she was okay. From his vantage point, he could see through several of the windows on all of the floors of the police station. One window allowed him to see her. She laid on a chaise lounge, and an older man sat next to her with his back to the window. Another man and a young woman stood off to one side, the woman the attention of his focus for several moments.

He cast another spell, verifying his suspicion. The woman walked away from her partner and to the window, looking directly at him without seeing him, even though he was in plain sight.

She carries the gift.

An ally within the police department would prove very useful. A few more words of incantation set his plan in motion. She walked away from the window, exchanged a few words with the man she stood beside, and left the room.

Daxxe recognized Stone when he turned his head enough to display his profile. Their paths crossed many times since they hunted the same prey, and Stone's presence required more caution. Stone was aware of him, only lacking solid proof of his existence.

Angela stepped out onto the front steps of the Precinct a moment later. She looked up and directly at Daxxe, still not seeing him. She didn't know for sure why she kept staring at the empty ledge, but something in her mind pulled her gaze to that spot. She could easily see the ledge held nothing, but she stared on, as if she might miss something by looking away. The spot she focused on didn't look quite right to her, but she was amiss as to why.

Daxxe took a long look back at her, casting a spell of finding on her while she stood there. Something in her gaze was intriguing. He leapt into the cold air and disappeared into the night.

Without reason, Angela's need to look at the ledge slipped away, and the vacuum it left behind filled with bitterly cold wind and skin stinging sleet. The weather didn't bother her when she stepped out, but she immediately went back inside when she realized how cold she really was. She dismissed the event and blamed it on her lack of sleep. She went back to the conference room to find Joe and Joshua standing in the hallway, Marina on the chaise, appearing to sleep quite peacefully.

"I just finished setting up my safety grid. I've got five different safe words and two fail-safe protocols established. I've decided to keep her unaware of this session as well."

"Why's that?" asked Angela.

"She still knows what happened, on a subconscious level, and it gets harder and harder to fool the mind, even with the power of hypnosis. If I keep trying to subdue that part of her mind, it will start to resist, and that resistance could cause several severe problems. Her subconscious will try to find a way to retake control during the session."

"What is she doing now?"

"I've got her conscious mind resting while her subconscious absorbs all of the precautions I put in place. I've found it beneficial in the past, and the subject tends to respond better. I'm going to give her a few more minutes. I need a cup of coffee, would either of you like something while I'm headed that way?"

The detectives politely refused and Stone went on his way.

"Where did you go?" asked Joe.

"I just wanted to get some fresh air."

Angela didn't want to say anything about what happened. He would probably think she was losing her mind if she tried to explain the pulling sensation she felt. She didn't want Joe to have the opportunity to doubt her, and she wasn't up for any wise cracks that would surely follow if she told the truth.

"Okay, let's get this going," said Stone as he returned, coffee in hand. They went back into the conference room, assuming their original positions. "Marina, can you hear me?"

"Yes." Her voice was again monotone and lifeless, and the tempo was a little slower than normal, making her sound robotic.

"What are you doing?"

"I'm sitting on my parent's front porch, watching the rain."

"Marina, I need you to help me for a little while. Can you do that?"

"Yes."

"I need you to take a look at something for me. I have a picture that an artist drew for me, and I want you to tell me if it's the gray man you saw in the alley."

"Okay."

Joshua handed the artist's rendering to Marina. She didn't open her eyes until she had the drawing before her face, and she looked at it for a few seconds without speaking. Her eyes were dilated from having them closed, but her pupils didn't respond to the light. Neither did she. She then closed her eyes and laid the drawing on her lap."

"That's him."

"Do you know who or what he is?"

"No."

"Do you have any idea where he might be since he helped you?"

"No, I don't know where he is, but he has the means to find me."

"What do you mean?"

"Before he left me at my apartment, before I fell completely asleep, he said something about watching out for me and protecting me. It was important to him that I was safe."

"Did he tell you anything else?"

"He said we might see each other again, if the others came for me."

"The others?"

Marina shifted her weight, becoming visibly uncomfortable. Joshua leaned back to whisper to Joe and Angela.

"This is where it starts getting tricky. I'm striking at whatever is preventing her from remembering. Her heart rate jumped by almost twenty beats per minute when I asked that question. I have to be very careful."

Stone turned his attention back to Marina, the lull allowing her heart rate to slow slightly, but not back to its original state.

"Go ahead Marina, it's okay."

"The others are much like the...the man, no, thing...he killed in the alley. He said they didn't want people to know about them. He..."

Marina's heart rate jumped up another thirty points. Her eyes popped open, darting her gaze around the room, looking terrified, as though she instantly went blind. Her eyes were still dilated and then rolled back in her head.

"Daydream!" barked Joshua. "Daydream!"

Marina rose up, arching her back like a rope connected to her stomach was drawing taught. Just as quickly, her eyes closed and she fell back onto the couch. Joshua held the smelling salts as he watched the heart monitor. Her rate peaked very high, but not to the point of causing physical brain damage. Her rate slowly decreased back to normal and Joshua passed the smelling salt before her face. After about a minute of inhaling the pungent odor, Marina released a low moan, turning her head away from the smell. The tension in her body relaxed and her heart rate returned to normal.

Joshua leaned back, finally releasing the breath he held. "That was very close."

"What just happened, exactly?" asked Joe.

"She started to slip into neurological shock. I asked her mind to do something it's already been told it can't do. In a normal situation, the mind shuts down to regroup. Outwardly, she would zone out for a moment, or possibly pass out for a short while, while her mind essentially erased the few minutes of high stress and she would wake up unaware of it. Hypnosis puts the mind and body in an unnatural state, forcing it to wait for external stimuli to provide instruction and guidance. If the mind shuts down that way while she's hypnotized, it will still wait for external stimuli to tell it what to do, but when it shuts down, it can't receive anything externally, keeping the subject in limbo indefinitely. The fail-safe protocol I initiated with that safe-word released her from the hypnosis enough to receive the external command before her mind shut down."

Marina opened her eyes, slowly looking around the room. She visibly aged over the last few minutes, and fear rested behind her eyes. They could tell her memory was fully, or at least partially restored, and she trembled as she sat up under the weight of the burden she now carried. Joshua handed her the glass of ice water he already poured, which she drank it quickly and asked for more.

"Thirst is a common side effect of hypnotic shock in most people. No one has managed to figure out why, but it almost always happens," offered Stone as Marina drank the second glass. "I hoped this wouldn't happen, but it's not completely unexpected. We will have to set up more aggressive counseling for her soon."

Angela sat down beside Marina, offering what comfort she could. "Are you okay?"

"Not really."

"You'll be safe here. We're making arrangements to put you up in a safe house for a few nights."

"He'll still be able to find me."

"Who?"

"The gray man."

"I think it'll be okay, Marina. You said yourself that you felt he was trying to help you, so I don't know why he would try to hurt you now."

"I'm still afraid. I saw what he did to the other man, even if he didn't turn on me. That doesn't mean that he won't try to hurt me next time. How can I take his word after seeing him murder someone?"

"You said that the other man was trying to seduce you to go where you didn't want to go, and the gray man stopped him. Why does that frighten you now?" asked Joshua.

"The other man wasn't hurting me or threatening me. I walked to him, even though I didn't want to. That could have changed when I reached him, but the next thing I knew I was sitting in the snow. The gray man was walking away and the other man was dead. Wouldn't you be afraid too?"

Marina started to cry. Angela held her and slowly rocked her back and forth as Joe and Joshua left the room.

"Why is she reacting so differently now?" asked Joe. "She wasn't afraid of this 'Gray Man' before."

"This is the first time since the murder that her mind has actually had all of the pieces to the puzzle, and she has to deal with all of it all at once. I'm guessing that whatever prevented her from seeing the truth also left her with a false sense of security, and the vampire that tried to attack her had her entranced. Some of those effects may still be running around in her head. Most of this will pass, given a little time. The forces that worked against each other are suddenly on the same side and she needs a little time to work out the details. I can't do anything more for her here. She will need rest and then counseling as I said earlier. I've got to get some things together for tomorrow's briefing. Can you two take care of Marina?"

"Sure, we'll get her to the safe house. See you in the morning."

Stone was already gone. He was the closest he had ever been to proof from another source for his natural predator theory. He didn't know who or what this 'Gray Man' was, but it was working towards the same goal.

"Al, Tony, thank you for coming," said Trass.

"As if we had a choice," said Al Vanetti, looking cross at Luigi.

"Now, now, let's not get started on the wrong foot. I respect the fact you're both busy men, but this won't take long. I just have a couple of questions."

Al looked very put out and had trouble keeping still. Tony sat very calmly and respectfully.

"Tony."

"Yes, Deacon."

"How long have you brought Desert Spice into the city?"

"I started about six months ago, going through the channels and getting permission from your office before I started. I know how strict you are about your business ventures."

"That's very good. I seem to remember approving that, now that you mention it."

"Al, how's it going? How about you, same question?"

"A couple of months."

"Two months? Are you sure that's all?"

"Yeah, give or take a month."

Trass' expression lost its fatherly qualities, taking on a hard, chiseled edge.

"Give or take a month, let's say we give. I think it's more because you've been selling since March."

Al's expression lost its confidence, but he didn't change his story. "Boss, I'm not selling, I just let out a couple of samples, you know, to test the market."

Trass stood up behind his desk, slamming his fist down on the leather desk pad, making Al flinch. He kept his voice low and even. "All transactions go through me and they're all approved personally by me. Did you honestly think I wouldn't find out about your little side venture?"

"Boss, I just passed along a few samples, nothing for profit."

Trass glanced at Luigi, starting him in motion. He set a brown envelope on the desk in front of Al, who looked at it questioningly.

"Open it!" demanded Trass.

The envelope contained photographs of Al and some of his men completing various drug deals. "These can be explained, Boss, we weren't selling Desert, we were…"

The door to the right of Trass' desk opened. A young brunette woman in a tight fitting, one-piece leather outfit walked in and set a small vial on the desk.

"Al, you do remember Sandra, don't you?" Sandra was in one of the photographs, the one with Al handling the exchange personally. Al's expression grew more worried. Tony was looking very worried as well, even though no animosity was directed at him.

"Don't hurt my feelings and tell me you forgot me," she said as she leaned down, pouting with a sparkle in her eyes, and setting the vial on the table in front of him.

"Boss, I'm being straight with you. I didn't sell her Desert Spice! That was nose candy. She's hooked on the stuff, buys it from me all the time."

Sandra straightened up, shaking her head side to side as she pulled the hem of her too short skirt down to smooth out the wrinkles.

"Al, I'm going to give you the benefit of the doubt."

"Thanks, Boss."

Two shots rang out from the Glock 9mm Trass held under the desk. The bullets splintered the modesty panel and shattered both of Al's knees as they hit their targets. He fell from the chair, screaming and trying to cover the wounds with his hands. Trass walked around the desk, stood over Al, and pressed down on his neck with his foot.

"Shut up, Al! I really detest screaming, and you need to take this like a man."

Al's screaming reduced to a whisper.

"That's better."

Trass removed his foot.

"Now, this is for not following my rules."

Trass kicked his right knee.

"And this is for lying to me about selling Spice!"

He kicked the left knee, and Al did everything he could to keep from screaming again.

Luigi showed Sandra and Tony out of the office as Trass knelt beside Al. They had seen enough for the example to stick with them.

"I've known you for a long time Al, so I'm going to go against my normal way of thinking and ask you again. How long have you been selling Desert Spice?"

"Ten months!" he strained through clenched teeth.

"Better answer, and why didn't you get my approval?"

"I...wanted to make some extra on the side. I've got a lot of debts..."

"That doesn't give you the right to operate outside of my rules. When was your last sale, and to whom?"

"One of my guys sold...to a punk kid...a few days ago. He wanted...it...for a party."

"Really? Was the punk kid, by chance, the Senator's son?"

Al didn't answer right away, but he nodded yes within a few seconds.

"Do you know why I brought you here?"

Al shook his head no.

"My daughter is in the clinic right now. She attended the rave party that the Senator's boy bought the drugs for. She's comatose and I'm certain it's because of Spice. The doctor's say they don't know, but they can't find a reason why we she's not coming out of it either."

Al's body went rigid and he opened his eyes wide. "Boss, I'm sorry. I didn't...I mean..."

"This is not acceptable, Al. You know how I feel about family and loyalty. Luigi!"

Luigi reentered the office carrying a tool bay men used on the docks. It was a long, fiberglass rod with a very large, barbed steel fishhook mounted on the end. Fishermen used it to drag large catches aboard ship and move them around on the docks. Luigi swung the hook over his head, planting it deeply in Al's left shoulder. Al screamed in agony as Luigi drug him out of the office through the side door.

"Consider it done," was all Luigi said as he closed the door.

Trass sat down at his desk and picked up the phone.

"Nikki, be a dear and call someone to clean up the mess in my office, and cancel the rest of my appointments for the day. I don't want to be disturbed, and please order me a new desk."

Deacon turned his high-back leather chair to face the picture window behind said desk. His office consumed the top floor of the downtown Manhattan building. He had an excellent view of the city and the ocean from his northern facing window. A single tear rolled down his cheek. Some of the pain found the chink in his armor.

ChapterThirty-one

Father Samuels woke with a start. He was leaning forward at his desk with his head resting on the leather desk pad. His back ached sorely when he straightened up in the chair. Apparently, he'd been asleep for quite some time. A blanket hung over his shoulders that he had not put there, so he knew someone was watching over him. Marina's card still rested on the desk next to his empty coffee cup, and a small plate with two bagels and a muffin now joined it. One of the staff must have left it for him if he woke up hungry.

A popping sound caught his attention; the sound the floor towards the back of his office made when it bore weight. The desk lamp's light didn't reach into the darkness in that part of the room.

"Is someone there?"

He stood, looking into the void, seeing nothing, but feeling the presence of someone else in the room. He started to adjust the lamp, but thought better of it.

"Is someone there I said?"

"Yes, Father."

Samuels fell back into his chair. It was the voice from the confessional.

"Oh, God."

"Don't be frightened, Father. I intend you no harm."

"Then why do you hide in the darkness?" He trembled as he spoke, giving him a pseudo lisp.

"Seeing me would not be beneficial to either of us; of that I can assure you."

"Why me?"

"You are a true man of God. I can see into your soul. It is untainted."

"How can you..."

Daxxe cut the sentence short.

"How is of no consequence. Why is the more appropriate question."

"Very well then, why?" Some of the fear was ebbing away, replaced by curiosity and anger.

"I, like you, am doing God's work. We don't use the same means, but the ends are the same."

"Is that how you justify murder?"

"You aren't in a position to understand the nature of the tactics I must employ. I don't have much time. I have a request."

"Are you out of your forsaken mind? What would that request be, out of curiosity?"

"You will find a book on the shelf by the door. You will know which one because you've never seen it before. Take the book to the New York Downtown Hospital, room 526. You will find what you need on the forty-ninth page. This must be done before dawn, or it will all be for naught."

Samuels sensed that this directive was extremely important, and he couldn't shake the conviction that he believed what he heard, even though he knew he shouldn't.

"What am I supposed to do?"

The voice didn't respond. The presence was gone.

Samuels walked to the office door and turned on the overhead light, finding the room empty except for himself. On the shelf, he found a book bound in black leather. The leather showed wear, but it was still in very good condition. Lettering, inlaid in gold, graced the cover, but he couldn't read the words. The writing was in a language completely foreign to him. He flipped through it, finding it was all written in the same foreign script, except for page forty-nine. That single page, out of roughly two hundred others, was written in Latin. He closed the book and left the church with it, feeling an overwhelming urge to fulfill the request, even though he had no clue why.

Father Samuels walked through the main entrance of the medical center and approached the information desk. He was unfamiliar with the hospital and needed to get directions to Room 526. After a brief visit with the attendant and the information desk, he boarded the correct elevator and rode to the fifth floor. The sign mounted on the wall opposite the elevator bays indicated the room he sought was down the hall to the left. A police officer stood guard in front of the door.

"Excuse me, Officer. I'd like to see the patient in that room."

"I'm sorry, Father, but I can't let anyone in the…"

The officer's words fell off in silence and he stepped to one side, assuming his stance, as if no one else was in the hallway. He looked directly at the other side of the hall as if the priest was not there.

Samuels walked into the room unhindered, and the policeman moved back in front of the door as it closed.

What was that?

The room was very dark. All the lights were off except for the one in the bathroom, but the door was pulled to so only a small sliver of light cut across the white tile floor and matching wall. The room carried the scent of antiseptic cleaners. It startled him when the automatic sprayer shot a mist of citrus air freshener in the otherwise quiet room.

He passed into the main section of the private room. A few indicator lights glowed in the wall above the headboard. The electric green display showed the girl's blood pressure was 120 over 80 and her heartbeat was slow and steady. She appeared to be sleeping, but it was too dark to tell. A small digital clock rested solitarily on the nightstand beside the bed.

He went back towards the door and noticed a dimmer mounted next to two wall switches. A slight clockwise turn brought the room lights up enough to see by without waking her.

She rested peacefully on the bed, even though her ankles and wrists were secured in buckled leather cuffs bound to the bed frame with what seemed an overabundance heavy duty straps. A half-empty IV bag slowly fed blood into her system while its mate dripped a clear liquid into the central line, probably supplying normal saline or glucose of some variety. He knew this was a pretty standard setup for a blood transfusion from his time volunteering for the Red Cross and the Peace Corps during the Korean War.

He also realized that the room was oddly spartan. He saw no personal effects on any kind. There wasn't a single "Get Well" balloon, stuffed animal, or even a card. It was strange for such a young, attractive girl to be utterly forgotten by the outside world. He felt the urge to go get her something from the gift shop he saw in the lobby, but he doubted they were open at this hour. He figured it would be even less likely that he would be able to get back into the room as easily a second time. He decided he could arrange for something to be delivered on his way out or he could call it in when he got back to St. Christopher's.

336

He moved the reasonably uncomfortable green upholstered chair from under the window to a spot beside the bed. The cushions were overly firm, but that was probably due to the fact that it could be unfolded to double as a single cot for someone that chose to spend the night with the patient.

The girl was still asleep and totally unaware of him. He risked a peek at the medical chart handing in the rack on the bed's footboard to at least find out who he was charged to help. It identified her as Jane Doe, which gave credibility to the starkness of the room. The brief opening doctor's note was extremely difficult to decipher. The handwriting was almost cryptic, but he was able to piece together the facts that she was recently admitted without any identification and she was unable to provide any information to the hospital staff. The word unable was underlined twice, giving it emphasis and making him wonder what it signified.

The clock changed to five-thirty-seven in the morning. Sunrise was only about twenty minutes away. He opened the book to page forty-nine, remembering the warning, and read aloud.

The abandoned terminal rocked with noise, music, and unnatural screams. Nikola returned from feeding to find the main area swarming with his kind and their newly acquired prey.

Trokar sat to one side, yelling to the crowd.

"Eat, drink, and be merry! Our time is at hand! Relish it!"

The entire room looked as though it was alive as bodies surged this way and that. Some of the clan violated their victims in all manners while others simply drank their fill. A small stack of lifeless corpses steadily grew off of the platform where the tracks once ran.

A small group near the boarding area laughed loudly.

"What's the matter, boy? Don't like an audience! Do it and we'll let you live!"

A young couple stood, both naked and trembling, trapped within the ranks of five vampires. Damok slapped the black-haired boy as he backed away from Mekune on the other side of the circle.

"What's the matter, you two loose the mood? I think we need to remind them of what they were going to do."

Nikola leapt within the circle, punching the blond girl hard enough to double her over. He latched his arm around her neck, forcing her to stay bent over.

"Come on! Here's what you wanted!"

Both of them broke down, unable to deal with what was happening.

Mekune took over. The black-haired man straightened and walked very awkward and rigid to Nikola, like a marionette with twisted strings terror in his eyes. He tried to stop, but his limbs wouldn't respond. He felt he was trapped in someone else's body, looking out through a filthy window. He watched his hands work of their own accord and grab the girl around the waist. He saw himself engage, but he couldn't feel anything. Mekune worked the strings for several minutes, making sure they lost all hope, before he issued his command.

"Now!"

Nikola punched again, claws extended. His hand went through the blonde's stomach and into her boyfriend's body. He pulled a handful of entrails from both victims back out through the hole and let them fall to the floor. Both fell, still joined and shuddering with pain and fear as the feeding frenzy began. Within a couple of minutes, two bloody, shapeless heaps of flesh were all that remained.

"Hey! You! Get aways from my car..."

The drunken young man slurred as he spoke. Another man stood beside the driver's door of a new, red Corvette, rattling the door handle and playing with the lock.

"Hey! I said for I told you to get away."

The drunk stumbled and he yelled the second time and again, stumbling picked up his unsteady pace. The parking lot was slick from the ice and snow, and the wind made balance even more difficult. The man trying to break into the Corvette didn't seem to notice the owner yelling at him. The car owner swerved closer and closer, finally pulling a small revolver that was tucked into his belt.

"I told you…"

Before the man could blink, the would-be-thief grabbed the owner by the wrist, took the gun, and slammed him into the driver's door. The frozen fiberglass worked as well as solid concrete. The owner slumped to the ground, knocked unconscious. A couple exited the nightclub in time to see the man fall to the ground.

"Wait here," ordered the young hero to his girlfriend. "Hey! What's going on here?" he added, as he walked towards the sports car.

"My friend had a little too much to drink, it seems. He still thinks he's sober enough to drive. He's too drunk to stand! Can you help me get him into the car?"

"Okay, sure thing. I've got a buddy that pulls the same crap, too. I've had to knock him out before to keep him off of the road." He relaxed, changing from would be hero to good Samaritan.

The thief opened the car door and pulled the drunk back a couple of feet so they could pick him up more easily, heaving the unconscious drunk into the passenger seat. He never made eye contact with the undiscovered hijacker. The young man's girlfriend walked to the car to join her boyfriend since there was no apparent danger. The hijacker thanked them for the help without looking up. They turned to walk away when their heads slammed together hard enough to knock them both out cold.

The Corvette pulled out of the nightclub's parking lot, headed towards the harbor. The rear of the car rode very low to the ground from the extra weight it carried.

The girl woke first and her head throbbed painfully. The edges of her vision held stars and she couldn't focus clearly. She discovered her hands were bound behind her back when she tried to touch her head in an attempt to lessen the pain. Another rope ran from her wrists to her ankles, which were also bound together. A gag that tied behind her head restricted her mouth. She looked about as much as possible, trying to establish her bearings. She was very cold and wet, pulling at the ropes as hard as she could when she realized she couldn't move.

Tears ran along her cheeks as she tried to scream through the gag. The last thing she remembered was looking at Billy, then the other memories started coming back to her.

It must be the man from the parking lot.

The scene suddenly made sense, even though her head hurt too much to think. She managed to roll over onto her back in the frozen slush and her face almost hit one of the Corvette's exhaust pipes. She was lying directly behind the car, almost underneath it, behind one of the rear tires.

She stopped struggling at the ropes and tried to calm down. She knew that outright panic would not get her through this, so she stayed motionless so she could listen and give her vision time to correct itself.

The cold numbed her body to the point the pain went away. She could hear the wind, but she didn't feel it passing over her. She leaned her head back, just being able to see past the car's rear quarter panel.

A tall chain-link fence, topped with barbed wire, stood about twenty feet from the car. Plastic inserts ran through the channels in the links, not allowing her to see beyond the fence. She could smell salt in the air.

The still hot exhaust pipe burnt the tip of her nose as she was pulled out from under the rear of the car. She couldn't see who was pulling her because whoever it was turned her sharply to drag her right beside the car. The momentum of the turn flipped her back onto her stomach. The ice on the ground pooled under her, drawing out the hem of her shirt, allowing the snow direct access to her skin, and the snow that piled up between her thighs dumped over her bottom and lower back as the pile grew. She lacked the strength to pull away from her assailant. Even if she could regain it, her positioning left her without the leverage to use it. She tried to keep her head turned to one side to minimize the contact to her face.

A small sliver of hope broke through her fear when she felt her feet fall to the ground. Her ankles were loose, but her wrists were still connected to her left leg. A cold hand grabbed her free ankle as she tried to draw it in. She flailed uselessly as the motions did not move her right foot. The grip holding it was deathly still. She felt a metal band lock around her right ankle, and then the left. Her legs were forced apart, spread at a large angle. Tears poured from her eyes as she thought about what could happen next.

340

The unexpected took her by surprise, although it didn't improve her situation. She found herself hanging upside down by the bar connecting her ankles with her head about two feet above the ground. Looking skyward, she could see the hoist supporting her weight. The pressure on her ankles was unbearable. She went rigid when warm breath crossed over her legs from behind her.

Intense pain burned like fire through her left leg, but she couldn't squirm away. The metal separating her ankles bit into her flesh, making movement even more painful, and throbs of pain washed through her in waves. She felt her blood running over her pants, covering her skin, making its way over her body until it dripped to the cold ground. She gasped for air as it moved over her neck and chin and into her nose. She could taste it as ran into her mouth, but she felt most of it drip away to the ground. The world went black.

Sleet, stinging her exposed skin, pulled her back to consciousness. The tail end of the Corvette swung inches from her head, tires spinning, looking for traction. The car shot away when the tires got purchase. She hung, weak and bleeding, slowly twisting in the air from the hoist holding her off of the ground. As she turned, she saw that Billy and the drunk suffered her fate as well, knowing they were already dead as she closed her eyes for the last time.

After the first few lines, the girl grew restless but remained asleep. Low moans escaped her mouth as if she was experiencing a bad dream, but Samuels continued to read. Her slightly disturbed sleep progressed to outright physical jerks and contortions until she rose as far as her body could move and tilted her head forward, eyes wide open, staring directly at him as if she already knew he was there. Her eyes were backed with a low orange like glow, and she spoke in tongues. The change startled and frightened Samuels, but he didn't turn away from the book. He was growing more and more afraid of what was to come, but it translated into an urgency to finish reading the pages scripted in Latin.

The luminescence in her eyes grew in intensity as he continued. She pulled at the straps holding her arms, fighting against the restraints. She appeared to be in a great amount of pain and trying to escape from the source, which she could not since it originated within her. She released a low, guttural scream as Samuels reached the middle of the fifty-third page where the Latin text stopped.

He looked up to see a pungent, sulfurous smoke radiate from the girl's body in light waves. It appeared to be seeping from her pores and it flowed most heavily from her eyes and mouth before drifting towards the ceiling. A spot on the front of her hospital gown dissolved as a stronger flow of smoke struck it from underneath on the left side or her chest. The thin cotton resisted the pressure of the smoke column until the smoke morphed into a deep blue flame and consumed a larger hole in the material. The fire gave off no heat and seemed to do no damage to her body, extinguishing itself almost as soon as it erupted.

The smoke made the room hazy and Samuels lightheaded. Halos surrounded the number on the clock's face and the indicator lamps. He looked back down at the book and blinked a few times, sure the smoke was affecting his eyesight. The effort did not change what he saw. The pages were no longer written in Latin, but the same strange language that graced all the other pages. He could no longer read the pages that he orated minutes before, nor could he recall the words he spoke.

The girl screamed at the top of her lungs, pulling his attention back to her. Her body arched high off of the bed with only her head, shoulders, and feet remaining in full contact with the mattress. She pulled through the upper restraints, freeing both arms, and rose to a sitting position. Samuels jumped up from the chair and moved back, unsure of what was happening or what he should do when the girl suddenly fell back to the bed in a lifeless heap. Her slow, labored breathing was the only physical indication she was still alive, but he chose to keep his distance for the moment. The heart monitor began to slow from peak levels that were almost double of what they were when he first entered the room. To his surprise, the incident did not trigger any alarms or automatic call routines that would summon a nurse from the station down the hall.

The smoke hanging in the air slowly dissipated, taking the acrid smell and the dizzying effects with it. The halves of the restraints still attached to the girl's wrists made a zipping sound as she brought her hands to her face, covering it. She opened her eyes when she felt the weight of them and heard the noise. Her face filled with fear and confusion as she looked around the room. She pulled the sheets up to cover her body, feeling very insecure when she realized she was in a hospital gown with a stranger in the room. She didn't understand why she couldn't freely move her legs until she saw the multiple straps running under the sheets from the sides of the bed.

"Where...am...I?" She spoke slowly with a tremble in her voice, as if she had to struggle to form the words. Her body still shook, but with tremors rooted in fear.

Samuels set the book down on the small desk opposite the bed and approached the girl, keeping his head down. Her fear was obvious, and he could tell that she knew as little about her predicament as anyone else. He also had no interest in making her, or himself, any more uncomfortable.

"Miss, this is the New York Downtown Hospital."

"How did I get here? What are you doing to me?"

Several scenarios ran through her head, none of them good.

"Child, poor child, I'm not sure how you came to be here, but I think the worst is over. I was...sent here...to help you. I mean you no harm."

She pulled the sheets up to hide the lower half of her face and started crying. Samuels backed away, looking for another gown for her to wear and to give himself something to do. After a few minutes, he found one in the bathroom. When he approached with it, she was reluctant to accept it until she saw he wore a Roman collar.

"Are you a...priest?"

The look on her face was hard to decipher. He wasn't sure if the realization was good or bad for her. It surprised him very little though, considering the vast number of the ordained brotherhood that took their commitments too lightly and took advantage of those that trusted them.

"Yes...yes I am. I'm Father Samuels, from St. Christopher's."

Jessica relaxed a little. She could see he was somewhat uncomfortable now that she took time to notice, which gave her less reason to doubt his story.

The room brightened somewhat with the first light of the new day, filtered through thick clouds and falling snow. It still seemed to comfort her even though it wasn't direct sunlight. She turned to face the shrouded windows. Samuels walked over and raised the blinds about half way, letting the golden rays pour into the room. The glow made the room fell warm, but it made the young girl absolutely beam, like she was absorbing and radiating the sunlight at the same time. She closed her eyes and basked in the bright rays. Some of her tears were now tears of joy, like those of a blind woman regaining the gift of sight and seeing the first sunrise of her life.

The sense of peace washed over him as well, putting him at ease for the first time in several days. He knew his immediate task was done, and felt much of his personal burden lifted.

"I'll go get a nurse. You should change out of that ruined gown," he said as he offered the new one he found in the bathroom. "They'll want to know what happened and I fear that we don't have a good answer for them."

She turned to him and nodded. She did not speak, but her warm smile offered her thanks.

He went to the desk to retrieve the book on his way out when he realized it was gone. He stood and stared for a few seconds at the spot he left it. It took him a while to realize that he would never know the "how", only left with the "why", and the only thing he could do at the moment was get someone with the hospital into the room. He realized how much more important the "why" truly was.

When the door drew closed, she slipped into the new gown and hid the burnt one under the mattress, not so much from the priest's instruction as the desire to stay out of any more trouble until she knew what was happening. She leaned back against the pillow, deciding against unstrapping her leg restraints, and started to think.

Viktor returned to the subway terminal, invigorated and practically intoxicated. The two men were reasonably unremarkable, simple beer drinkers, but the girl had a taste he truly savored. She must have drunk a high-quality red wine because she was very sweet and the effects of the alcohol worked on his system. He drained her as much as he could before he returned.

He terrorized pedestrians up and down one of the main drags in the stolen Corvette until two police cruisers laid pursuit. He led the chase through town and onto the Brooklyn Bridge. At the midpoint, he swerved the car hard to the right. The fiberglass offered no resistance against the railing. The front suspension caught, allowing the car's momentum to pop the rear off the ground, carry it over the edge, and the car plummeted into the dark water below, sinking very quickly. The police would spend all night dragging the bottom in search of a body.

Viktor laughed as he watched the police react below him. He enjoyed the scene from his perch atop the Manhattan tower for a few minutes before he headed back into the city.

Trokar was allowing the clan to cut loose and have some fun, and he realized his second in command needed a release as well. It would take the law at least a week to connect the car with the three bodies he left hanging like sides of meat at the shipyards.

The terminal was quiet when he arrived. The others were already passed out from their hunting and playing excursions. Their nightly outings were getting a little longer each time, but this night, they decided to dine at home where they could enjoy the sun's inability to shine on them underground.

Trokar followed his normal pattern, except for taking time to teach Shayla how to hunt and feed. They were never gone long as she had yet to learn the subtleties of prey. She killed and drank quickly as though she were dying of thirst. With time, she would discover the flavor she savored most and learn to relish in it. Trokar returned to his studies when they returned.

Viktor assigned two of the clan to continue looking for Trokar's missing crate, with the promise that they would be released for whatever level of debauchery they desired the following night. They had checked almost every warehouse and shipping facility in the city to no avail, which made them doubtful that the crate ever arrived.

Sayer set up the delivery, but they never received word from him, which was odd in itself because he always took great care in his duties to ensure the security of any of their shipments. Trokar believed something happened on the east side of the Atlantic. All they did know was it was supposed to arrive in New York via the Thornquist Import Company. If a mistake was made, it could be almost anywhere in the world.

Viktor settled into his hammock as the door to his master's chamber opened. Shayla, appearing to be in a very good humor, slipped out, quietly closing the door behind her. She danced around the terminal, careful not to wake anyone so she would not have an audience. He found the display odd because she danced in the same fashion as when he took her even though she shouldn't be able to remember. Personal history and individual habits were lost during the turn. He watched for several minutes, just as he did from the rafters of the theater where he found her. She retained all of the beauty that first drew him to her. Quite suddenly, she stopped, looked around, and ran back into Trokar's chamber when she heard some of the others waking.

Dr. Hogan checked Jessica's blood pressure manually and jotted it down in the chart after he arrived, even though the charge nurse has done it twice already. He also did a cursory examination, checking her pupil response and reflexes. He was beside himself at her recovery, although he didn't understand the "why" of it.

"This is amazing! She is completely alert and has no physical or mental impairment. I don't know or understand what caused her to fall into that coma, and I understand even less about her miraculous recovery."

"I don't know either. I was asked to come by to…say a few prayers for her and she just woke up." Samuels didn't want to disclose the rest. He was having a hard time believing it and he saw it first hand, but he saw no need in dealing with any of the doctor's questions that would surely lead to that which he knew he couldn't explain.

The girl identified herself as Jessica Stewart, the only daughter of Andrew and Louise Stewart. Her father held a seat on the state Senate, and her mother headed a local organization devoted to antidrug causes. The officer posted at the door called the task force headquarters to let them know she was awake, alert, and tentatively identified. He also added the fact that the priest somehow managed to breach their security.

Jessica opted to stop answering questions under the ruse of feeling light headed. More of her memories were returning, and she remembered the last place she was before waking up in the hospital. It was somewhere she was not supposed to be. She had no desire to offer explanations to her father, but her mother's wrath is what concerned her the most.

Hogan ordered another vast array of tests on her, wanting to be absolutely certain the she was truly okay. He also needed time to formulate a story. His doubt in Stone's theory all but waned, but he realized he would have to keep the other doctors and nurses in the dark about the true nature of her illness while avoiding the pitfall of looking like a bumbling idiot. The moderate amount of confusion created by people coming and going for other reasons allowed him to handle a few tests of his own. He drew a few vials of blood when he was alone with her in the room, pocketing them until he could go to a lab.

He checked her blood for any cellular defects, as the book Stone provided instructed. The study taught him what to look for if a person was suspected of infection and how to verify the patient was free of the disease.

Samuels used the confusion to his advantage as well, slipping out of the room and down the hall to the stairwell. He knew it would just be a matter of time before the questions were directed at him, especially since he had already been to the Precinct and would be recognized. He went down to the ground floor, looking for the best exit. He made a quick stop and slipped out of the hospital's front door. A wave of exhaustion hit him as the past few nights of excitement and sleeplessness caught up with him. He left for St. Christopher's as the dawn finished changing into day.

Joe and Angela got word of the girl as soon as they arrived, so they quickly checked in with the task force and headed for the hospital. According to the team, the night was unusually quiet, which they figured meant it was the calm before the storm.

ChAPTER ThiRTY-TWO

Julie woke feeling miserable after a mostly sleepless night. She was melancholy and uncomfortable being in a strange place. She entered the apartment's living room to find Emilio reading the newspaper and drinking a cup of coffee.

"Morning, can I get you a cup of coffee or something?" he asked, standing up when she entered.

"That'll probably help; you don't have to do that on my account."

"Do you take cream or sugar? Do what?"

"No, I need it black and very strong. You don't have to stand up when I come in the room. You are stuck here, just like me."

"I'll have it in just a second. Malcolm says my coffee is more like chicory on steroids. You will just have to get used to it. I take my manners pretty seriously, no offense."

"Okay, no problem. Thank you," she offered when he handed her to hot cup of coffee. "Where is your partner?"

"He went back to the Precinct about an hour ago. We've got another person involved in the case coming to stay here. We'll have plenty of room since this apartment connects to the one next door."

Julie looked taken aback. "How can someone else be involved in Ellen's death?" She also wasn't comfortable with the idea of another stranger being here.

"I'm sorry, but this is a little out of perspective for you. Ellen's death is part of a much larger case." He handed her the front page of the paper. "Series of Killings Sweep City" headlined the top half of the front page.

"Is this the 'Hook Man' stuff?"

"We don't have any proof that the Hook Killer actually exists. We discovered some very similar trends in recent homicides, and the evidence points towards the existence of a serial killer, but the press is having a field day with the gray areas."

"Is that what happened to Ellen? I mean an actual serial killer."

"It really looks that way. I'm very sorry for your loss, but that's why you're here. We're trying to keep you safe until we can apprehend whoever is behind this."

Julie excused herself to her bedroom. She needed to be alone, and she didn't want to break down in front of the officer. Emilio felt bad for her, but he was relieved she stopped asking questions. He preferred avoiding the subject. Her line of questioning would end up in a place that forced him to lie about what he knew to protect their case, and he didn't like to lie. He had already connected too many dots for her, but he felt the risk was low since she was in protective custody.

Mal returned a half hour later with Marina. They opened the adjoining door and showed her around the apartment. They covered the same basic ground rules they gave Julie the day before. They gave her another radio and asked her to keep it on channel two. Emilio and Malcolm would be able to hear both of their bedrooms, but they wouldn't be able to hear each other.

After the brief tour, Julie emerged from her room to get a second cup of coffee. Malcolm introduced the ladies, but the encounter had a very strained feel to it, catching Julie off guard. She didn't expect the new stranger to be here so soon. After the shortest of pleasantries, Marina went to the room designated for her to take a shower and attempt to rest. The two days she spent at the precinct really showed, even more so coupled with her anxious fear.

Malcolm moved his things into the second bedroom of the attached apartment so one of them would be in close proximity to their charges at all times.

The detectives entered Room 526 with Joshua Stone in tow, wanting to talk to Jessica before her family was notified. She was lying on her side, facing the wall and trying to enjoy what was left of the direct sunlight when they entered. It was obvious that she was almost in the fetal position.

"Jessica, someone is here to see you," said the nurse and she finished her duties and left the room.

Jessica offered no indication that she heard. She continued to lay motionless except for the slow motion of her breathing.

Angela tried to break the ice. "You sure have a pretty name, Jessica. Have you seen this yet? Someone sent you a nice gift." Angela indicated a large pink teddy bear grasping a small vase that held a bouquet of spring flowers. A small card rested like a tent on the desk in front of it with the words "Get Well" written in yellow across the face. That was nice gesture, wasn't it?" Jessica didn't move. "I know you aren't feeling very well right now, but we do need to talk to you for a minute?" added Angela as she sat on the bed behind the girl. Jessica rolled over enough to see Angela at her bedside. Tears clung to her eyelashes and left wet trails on her cheeks. Her eyes were very red from her extended outpouring of emotion.

"Can you take me home? I just want to go home."

Angela nodded. "Not just yet, but you're safe here. You're not in any kind of trouble. We just want to help you. Do you know why you're here?"

"I imagine something must have gone wrong at the party. I told Jake I didn't want to go, but he made me anyway. I told him my mother would kill me if she ever found out, and then she'd start to work on me."

Angela smiled, but held back the laugh. She appreciated the young lady having a sense of humor, but she didn't want her to feel alienated. "Who's Jake?"

"He's my...well...he used to be my boyfriend, but not after this." Her resolve strengthened a little as she spoke, obviously fueled by some deep seeded anger towards the boy. She rolled onto her back where she could see Angela and keep her head reclined on the pillow. Her eyes darted back and forth between Angela and Joe, not realizing he was in the room.

"I need to get some coffee," said Joe, deciding Angela's approach was still better.

"Why didn't you want to go to the party?" asked Angela after the door closed.

"I'm just not into that scene. I know better, but he thinks it's fly to get high. I didn't want any part of it, but I ended up there because I like him and I trusted him. He told me we would only stop by for a few minutes to make an appearance. He promised his friends he would and he promised me he wouldn't take anything. I told him I would ride along, but that I would wait for him in the car."

"How did he get you inside if you didn't want to go?"

"He tricked me, the jerk. We went to eat first, and he told me he had a surprise for me. 'A surprise like nothing I could imagine'. He blindfolded me when we got back in the car. I wasn't comfortable with it, but he told me that if I loved him, I would trust him. That sure won't happen again! He started driving and I must have blacked out. When I came to, he was lying on top of me, kissing my lips and neck and letting his hands wander all over me. He must have slipped Rohypnol into my drink and the restaurant. He's just like the others, just wanting into my pants.

"Music blasted from somewhere and the room flashed with multicolored lights, making the haze of cigarette and pot smoke in the air look like a rainbow. Jake unbuttoned my blouse and I felt a pain in my arm. I looked and some other girl walked away carrying an empty syringe in her hand, and she was like, totally naked. I tried to get up, but my arms were tied down, and then the room started spinning. That's the last thing I remember until I woke up here. Where's Jake? I want to give him a piece of my mind and tell him it's over."

An odd look came to Angela's face as she looked down at the bed.

"What?" she asked.

"Jessica, give me just a minute. I'll be right back."

She went out into the hallway to find Joe and Joshua.

"Do you think this is the same memory block problem you had with Marina?" she asked Joshua when she found him and her partner in the waiting room.

"It's very possible, but I don't see any reason why. Those kids were left for dead. Why would someone go to the trouble of keeping a dead girl in the dark?"

"Good point, but I don't know if we should tell her. She has no idea he's dead, or any of them for that matter, and she doesn't have any useful information from the party. Her memory seems to stop before the killers showed up. Whatever they shot her up with is probably the only reason she's still alive. It must have looked like she was already dead."

351

"How long can we keep her here?"

"I'm not sure, but I'm guessing not very long. Senator Stewart will come at us with everything he's got when he finds out. He's got a reliable reputation for being a real hard ass. The only thing we really have on our side right now is the timing. These kids haven't been missing quite long enough, but that won't last."

"What do you suggest we do now?" asked Angela.

"Let's go back to headquarters to check in and take a look at everything again. I feel like we're overlooking something and this is starting to spiral out of control. Some of the street cops were accosted by concerned citizens about doing their jobs and what was being done to protect the citizens of the city."

Angela nodded in agreement and walked back towards Room 526. "I'll go tell her that we have to help with a call and we'll be back to answer her questions later. I think someone should stay with her for a while after she finds out about Jake.

As the new night fell, Lefty walked towards Beggar's Alley after having a hot meal at the shelter. Joel was supposed to meet him, but he never showed, and it wasn't odd for Joel to end up doing his own thing. Joel's "own thing" usually consisted of a bottle of cheap whiskey and loud carousing. Only about half of the barrels in the alley were burning, but it normally teemed with life after the shelters served dinner.

Lefty wasn't sure what to do, especially with the Hook Killer running loose in the city. He didn't know if some of his street friends were hiding or something worse. A loud clatter caught Lefty's attention, making him jump. The noise came from somewhere deeper in the alley. It sounded like fighting and the commotion got louder as Lefty wrestled with his conscience over what he should do. Like always, it got the better of him, and he moved towards the sound, trying to be cautious. He could tell the scuffle was happening on the back steps of one of the businesses as he got closer. Two dumpsters separated him from the source of the noise, and his mind kept telling him to turn and walk away; it wasn't worth getting hurt or worse, but his heart would only let him do the right thing, so he peered around the second trash bin.

Joel lay at the top of the steps, rolling about wildly. He was obviously drunk, and the smell wafting off of him confirmed it. Three metal trashcans were knocked over, spilling their contents. Joel fought with the cans that bested him, determined to regain his dignity. Lefty trudged up the steps to gather his friend and make sense of the mess he created.

"Hi ya, Lefty my boy! What's up?"

"Come on Joel, get up, you're gonna wake up the whole block."

Lefty reached down with his good arm to help Joel to his feet.

"Hello, sir. What a fine weather we're having, considering the night."

Joel wasn't looking at Lefty, but into the alley, which seemed strange, even for a drunk.

"You've had way too much to..."

Lefty's words cut short as his face went unnaturally calm, a thin line of blood forming between his closed lips and dripping down his chin. Joel burst into uncontrolled laughter.

"That's just greats pally. Can yous do it again?"

Lefty's body slumped onto the steps and rolled back to the pavement. The man standing behind him looked at Joel, hands open with the fingers slightly curved, poised for the attack with a layer of fresh blood coating his fingers and palm. Joel walked down the steps, preparing to hug the attacker. His blood alcohol level spared him from the pain of the attack, even though it only lasted for a few seconds.

The first strike hit Joel squarely across the face, exposing his skull at the point of impact and ripping his right eye from its socket. The second hit gashed open his chest before his body landed next to Lefty's on the steps. The attacker picked up both lifeless bodies and carried them into the night.

Daxxe smelled much colder air moving into the city from the huge clouds rolling in from the ocean as he looked into Room 526. The blinds were half open, allowing him to see the young girl inside. Samuels had done well. He left to check on another that caught his attention.

The cell phone rang. The henchman accepted the call and waited for a voice.

"Luigi."

"Yes, Boss."

"It's my understanding that one of the other kids from the rave party recovered. I want you to find out how."

"Consider it done."

Luigi hung up the phone and tapped a button on his dash, starting the SUV's onboard computers that awaited voice commands.

"Yes, sir?"

"Assume vehicular control, destination, New York Downtown Hospital."

"Yes sir," responded the AI controller. The front windows automatically darkened so it would not be obvious the driver's space was empty as the driver's seat made its short trip to the console in the back. The computer piloted the vehicle via satellite uplink to GPS and a hypersensitive array of detection sensors helped with the finer details as Luigi accessed his system. He hacked the hospital's records to get a name and a room number. He noted that a gift was delivered to the room that morning, charged to the account for St. Christopher's Church.

After the quick trip, he stepped off of the elevator, bound for Room 526. He wanted to talk to the girl and her attending doctor, but the officer standing guard at the door blocked entry.

"This room's off limits, sir."

Luigi flashed a badge.

"Officer Saul Lewis, Narcotics. Bishop sent me down to ask a few questions."

The guard let him pass. Dr. Hogan stood at the foot of the bed, looking over the medical chart and talking to the patient, either answering questions or providing care instructions. He turned to look at Luigi as he entered.

"Yes?"

"I need to ask a few questions."

"And you are?"

"Saul Lewis, Narcotics."

"What can I do for you?"

"We're trying to get a clear understanding of how the Desert Spice designer drug induced her coma and how she recovered."

The girl sunk down into the bed a little at the name of the drug, recognizing it.

The doctor answered, "for starters, we can't confirm the drugs caused this. Our tests indicate that the dosage required to induce a coma would also result in very immediate death, but we don't know that for sure. Something else could have caused her condition, and something else we can't identify probably pulled her out of that state."

"Has anyone else been in here besides you?"

"Yes, the police allowed my nurses and themselves access. Oh, a priest was here the morning she came out of it."

"Who was the priest?"

"I don't honestly know, come to think of it. I don't remember anyone getting his name or how he got into the room either. He must have slipped away in the commotion when Jessica recovered."

"It looks like someone knows something we don't. Thank you, doctor."

Luigi glanced at the young girl as he left. She had curled back into a fetal position, keeping her face hidden as well as she could. The Narcotics Officer made her extremely uncomfortable. He stopped by the guard as he walked out.

"Hey, do you know anything about a priest being here?"

"Yeah, when I came in to relieve the night watch the other day, he reported no visitors, but Father Samuels came out of there and I never let him go in. I guess he could have slipped in when I went to the restroom, but that would be some pretty precise timing."

"Who did you say?"

"It was Father Samuels; he presides at St. Christopher's. I used to attend services there before my wife and I divorced."

"Sorry to hear that; things just go that way sometimes. Thanks for the info."

"Anytime."

Luigi walked towards the elevator; he stopped and turned around after he covered about half the distance.

"Oh, by the way, has anyone else asked about Samuels?"

"No, you and I are the only ones that even know he was here, besides the doctor and the girl."

Luigi nodded in acknowledgement and pressed the elevator's call button. That was just too easy. He dialed his cell phone as the doors shut.

"Boss, it's Luigi. I've got a lead on the girl that recovered and I should have some answers in the next couple of hours."

He listened to Trass' response and additional instructions.

"Consider it done."

ChAPTER ThiRTY-ThRee

The task force spent the day crunching data, and checking on the few new leads they had and trying to justify what they already knew. Joe and Angela looked most specifically into the mysterious Mr. Sayer, but they couldn't figure out how he pieced into the puzzle. They knew he had to be more than a coincidence, but they couldn't find anything about him to go on.

The clouds gave way to the sun for the first time in several weeks. The temperature stayed low, but not as bad as before. The local meteorologists didn't want to give the city more bad news, but they didn't have a choice. A winter storm warning was issued for most of the state, effective at sunset, because a huge storm was rolling in from the Northern Atlantic. Predictions called for at least a foot of snow and a ten to fifteen degree drop in the temperature. Record lows were anticipated statewide.

Luigi entered the Cathedral of St. Christopher's, the chapel mostly empty as evening mass already concluded. An altar boy attended the candles, making sure they were all lit or replaced if needed. The henchman stopped even with the front row of pews, knelt on one knee, crossed his chest in the air, and spoke a short prayer before he approached the teenage boy.

"Excuse me."

The altar boy almost jumped out of his skin, scattering a box of matches.

"I didn't mean to startle you." Luigi bent down and helped collect the spilled Diamonds.

"It's okay, sir. I just didn't hear you."

"I was hoping to have a word with Father Samuels."

"I'm sure he'd be happy to speak with you, sir, but he's not here at the moment."

"When do you expect him back?"

"I can't say, for sure, sir. He's almost always here to conduct evening mass. You could try again tomorrow night."

"Thank you."

Luigi walked back down the center aisle. He passed by the collection plate to offer his gift to the church.

Joe and Angela left headquarters to work a related call in the shipyards. Bishop wasn't happy about them being in the field again, but he didn't offer Joe many arguments since their discussion about Angela. From the tone of the information they received, the lull was over.

Stone advised increased caution at the crime scene. He was aware that the vampire's patterns were changing. He didn't have any idea why, but they were becoming increasingly bold in their attacks. It seemed as if they no longer felt the need to stay in the shadows and operate under the radar of law enforcement, which was new to even him.

The detectives arrived at a building that used to be a repair depot for freighters, just off of the harbor. Three bodies, two males and one female, hung suspended, upside down, from an overhead hoist used to move large ship parts. They must have hung undiscovered for some time, for the large pool of blood soaked into the snow beneath them was congealed from the cold and was covered with a light layer of snow. All three had clothing ripped to shreds and their inner thighs ravaged. This struck the detectives as appropriate for the crime since the femoral artery offered an ample supply of blood.

The sight was more than revolting. The shock value of the crimes had worn off for the detectives, but some of the others recently assigned to the case weren't so lucky. The rookie beat cop on the scene puked behind a squad car, trying to stay out of view, while some of the more seasoned officers, looking pale, shook their heads in disbelief.

"What do you think this is all about?" asked Joe of Angela.

"I'm beginning to think they are leaving this trail of bodies on purpose to keep us occupied, or they are challenging us to try to stop them."

"I can see that scenario. You might be right."

"And it's a pretty strong challenge. They could just be getting cocky since they keep getting away with it, too."

"The last thing we need is a group like this getting cocky."

Joe took pictures and Angela looked around the rest of the depot. She worked her way towards the back of the supply yard, walking down rows of steel racks holding ship screws and bulkhead plates. As she turned to work back towards the entrance, the yearning she felt at the hospital arose in her again. She almost convinced herself that it didn't actually happen the first time, but she couldn't deny it now. She heard a voice in her head calling to her. She needed to find out why she was being summoned and by whom. Nothing bad happened the first time that she felt it, so she justified to herself that she needed to heed the call.

She walked through a gate that allowed exit on the backside of the yard, and she found herself heading back into the city. As she got farther away from the crime scene, another voice, the one she knew as her conscience, reminded her how Joe reacted the first time she wandered off. In response, the longing to answer the call grew even more urgent, drawing her away from thinking about what she should or shouldn't do. She had no idea how far she walked, but the cold was starting to affect her. Her feet throbbed from the below freezing temperature and her almost recovered ankle managed to send sharp little pains through the onset of numbness.

The discomfort demanded more and more attention, to the point she was about to turn back when she caught a glimpse of something down the street. The thought of being that close to finding out some of the answers renewed her vigor. She hurried her pace to reach the corner. The street before her was empty, but the yearning was growing stronger still.

All of the windows in the building she stood next to were boarded up, lest one. She quickly ran the math in her mind, considering the distance and time, realizing that whoever she saw only had the open window as a means to disappear. Focusing on that unblocked casement told her what she sought was inside. She didn't know how she knew, but she knew. It wasn't just a hunch or a guess, she knew. When she saw the fresh tracks in the snow, she followed.

It took Joe almost twenty minutes to finish taking the photographs. He needed several angles of the bodies and all of the marks left in the snow. A couple of the footprints offered a good imprint of a shoe and a set of tire tracks were intact in a few spots.

He hadn't seen Angela for a few minutes, so he started looking for her. She probably got lucky and found something. His search was fruitless, just the same MO and evidence as most of the other murders tied to the case. He double-checked the car to make sure she didn't get out of the weather, but she wasn't there either. He asked some of the other officers working the scene, but no one recalled seeing her for several minutes. She was nowhere to be found.

Joe checked the rest of the yard. He didn't see anything that suggested that she went anywhere outside of the yard, but the increasing snowfall had time to conceal her movements. The thought entering his mind froze him in his tracks, something Angela said about the killers challenging them. What if they left these bodies as bait? What if they intended to hit them as hard as they could, just because they had the ability?

Joe hastened his pace. The depot was much larger than it looked. Several of the stored ship parts were enormous and required ample space for storage. He worked through several aisles of outdoor storage, but he came up empty. The only exit from the yard, aside from the large main gate at the front, was a small pedestrian gate in the back fence. It was locked by a large padlock closing a loop of chain.

Joe made a beeline for the car. Angela was gone.

Angela climbed through the open window, albeit slowly. Her ankle lasted until she got inside. When she dropped to the floor from the sill, the joint buckled, refusing to support her weight and toppling her to the floor. She drew her leg up and wrapped a hand around the tender joint. It was already swelling and hot to the touch, despite the cold. She managed to sit up and keep her ankle in front of her. She gently massaged it to try and stop the most intense waves of pain, and she looked around as she worked the joint.

From what she could see in the dim light coming through the window, it looked like she was in a movie theatre or a concert hall. She could make out a couple of rows of seats that tapered downhill from her position, but she couldn't see much more. The smell of dust and mildew was very strong, and it appeared no one had been in the room for a while. She got to her feet and gently shifted some of her weight onto her ankle. It hurt, but it held. She turned and started back for the window, feeling uneasy and deciding she was about to be in the wrong place at the wrong time when something moved at the edge of her vision.

In an instant, something bore down on her faster than she could get out of harm's way.

Shayla stepped into the twilight with Trokar. They moved through the night, exploring her new world. Several sights seemed familiar to her, but she was positive she had never seen them before. Trokar spoke as they moved through the night sky.

"Everything you see is ours for the taking. We are about to be in complete control and I will make sure it stays that way. Why do you feel strange?"

"How did you know?"

"It's not important, but I know what you need. I will show you, wait here."

Trokar set her down and leapt back into the night, disappearing into the darkness. Shayla sat to wait, perched atop the ledge one of the downtown skyscrapers, allowing her a view of the entire city. She watched huge snowflakes fall from above until the descending flakes were too small to see.

A new, intriguing smell floated on the breeze. She more than wanted to find the source, she utterly craved it. She turned around to see Trokar standing at the center of the roof, holding something that hung limply in his arms.

Luigi answered his cell phone.

"Yes."

"It's Trass; we've got some more news."

"What is it?"

"The police figured out some of their mysteries. I don't believe a word of it, but they must from the way they're mobilizing."

"What's their story?"

"Apparently, they are convinced a pack of, get this, vampires, is in the city. They think they ravaged the homeless people, and now they're going after everybody."

"What's the connection to us?"

"The rave party, three of the kids were murdered, and the MO matches a bunch of other cases they're working. They dismissed the notion of serial killers after bringing in an expert from England. I want you to shift your focus a little and check this out thoroughly. Something strange is going on here, and I want to know what it is. I think it'll get us closer to helping Tracy."

"Consider it done."

Luigi pulled into a restaurant parking lot for his lunch date was with one of Trass' people working in the police department. He couldn't have asked for better timing. The small bistro served the best pasta in the city and it catered almost exclusively to members of the underworld. The police could catch seventy percent of the city's most wanted list at one time if they had any idea who frequented the restaurant. A young woman sat alone in a booth at the back corner of the bistro. The lights were dimmed and she sat with her back to the room. The booth held a standing reservation for Luigi, and without one of his business cards, no one was allowed to sit there besides Deacon Trass himself.

The woman arrived early, before the regular patrons showed up. She didn't want everyone in the place to see her come inside in an attempt to shroud her identity, but unbeknownst to her, everyone in the restaurant knew she was there and they all knew what she was.

Luigi sat down across from his date. A glass of water and a cup of coffee arrived before his seat lost its chill. The staff knew exactly what he wanted, and when, and he tipped heavily when he received proper service.

"Hello, Sharon."

"Please don't use my real name Luigi. You know how I feel about that."

"Okay, I apologize. Did you order yet, Roxy?"

"No, I waited for you."

"Thank you. What'll you have?"

Sharon, or Roxy when she was undercover, produced a large brown envelope from her purse.

"I think this is what you need."

"What is it?" he asked as he pushed a smaller brown envelope across to her side of the table.

"It's the info you can't get on your own. Some of the systems within the precinct aren't networked for security reasons. Pay particular attention to the audio copies I managed to get from the morgue."

"I'm impressed. How did you pull that off?"

"Let's just say I still haven't got the taste out of my mouth."

"We all have our price, Roxy, and I'll admit yours is pretty steep. I wouldn't want to deal with that old woman either. Does she know you have these?"

"Of course she doesn't know. I drugged her wine. It took longer to work than I thought, but she was out cold long enough for me to make copies and return the originals."

"Did you cover your tracks?"

"Yes, you should know I don't make mistakes like that. She thinks I want to move down to the morgue and work "under her," as she put it. It's no secret she likes girls, but no one knows she accepts favors. You've seen her. Who would ever get that idea?"

"Excellent work, Roxy. I'll make a few recommendations of my own. You've proven your worth to the organization, and loyalty has its benefits."

Two steaming plates of manicotti arrived with a large basket of buttery French garlic bread. The scent was delectable.

"I took the liberty of ordering for you. You should try the house red; it'll cleanse your palate."

Sharon offered a coy glance that changed to a look of disgust, making Luigi laugh as they started eating.

Shayla approached Trokar. He held a young boy at waist level that couldn't be more than eleven or twelve years old. He was still breathing, but the breaths were shallow. A trickle of blood ran from the right side of his neck, dripping rhythmically onto the snow. She dropped to her knees as the smell of the boy's lifeblood hit her full strength. It drove her crazy. She scrambled across the tar and gravel roof to a position below him, catching the drops in her mouth. She rose slowly until her mouth closed over the wound, drawing all the blood from his body that she could. His color fallowed and she seemed to energize.

Trokar smiled as he set the body on the snow-covered roof. It was the first time she actually fed since she was turned. His power was strong enough to provide for them both. He let the need build within her purposely, knowing how much more exquisite her first time would be. She fed for almost ten minutes. When she was done, she felt warm and lightheaded, like she was drunk. She felt strong and renewed, and she realized it was the essence from the boy. She looked around for her mate.

Trokar sat on the building's ledge, looking out over the city, his city. He ran his plans through his mind as he waited for her to finish. She placed her hands on his broad shoulders after she walked up behind him.

"Oh Trokar, that was wonderful. I've never felt better."

"I am pleased."

"There's only one little thing; I'm still hungry."

Her eyes sparkled with a hint of mischief.

"Really?"

He turned to look at her, somewhat surprised. Human young offered the greatest amount of life force.

"Yes, but not for blood."

Luigi listened to both sound files when he got back to his vehicle. They contained preliminary reports and theories made by the performing medical examiners. The official, transcribed reports would not be ready for a few days, and he had no intention of waiting that long. The security on the transcription company's website was annoying at best.

He recognized the voice as Dr. Murphy's. According to the recording, the six teens that were in a coma had something else in common besides being at the same party. An unknown substance existed in their blood, but the doctors could not yet prove the etiology of their comatose state. They theorized that the unknown substance was more closely related to poisonous spider or snake venom. The reaction caused by the interaction of the two contaminants was also mentioned. Something invaded their systems and it triggered neurological shock. Once the body shut down, the cells started to deteriorate slowly. The problem rested in identifying the type and source of the neurotoxin. The vampire theory was the obvious choice, but no proof was evident of that either.

Luigi didn't need proof because he knew how Murphy worked. Murphy already said the answer, but he couldn't say it officially without physical evidence. Luigi made a call to Trass to update him on the situation, and to check on Tracy. After the short conversation, he checked his mobile arsenal. Big prey required a pretty big gun, so he chose a high caliber rifle. He preferred the faster firing time even though some of the other weapons packed more punch.

The rail gun Trass' development team built could kill anything walking the earth without making a sound, but it took too long to recover between shots. He changed into a set of black BDUs and loaded the pockets with the equipment he needed. It was less than an hour until sunset, and his prey only came out at night.

He instructed the truck to drive itself to one of the warehouses Trass owned since the incidents were most frequent in that part of town. He decided to use a new pair of night vision goggles, even though he hadn't had time to give them a test run. He stepped out of the truck at sunset, covered from head to toe with black fabric. His rifle of choice rested across his back, and pistols were holstered under each arm. Loaded magazines and clips filled almost all of the pockets in his pant legs. He held a sawed-off shotgun in his left hand, and two belts of shells formed an X over his chest.

"Lights, warehouse," he spoke into the small headset he wore.

The onboard computer executed the voice command. The cities power grid controller was automatically accessed and hacked. The warehouse went pitch black in just under ten seconds. He pulled the goggles down over his eyes and powered them up before he entered the building. The inside of the warehouse displayed before his eyes as if the lights still burned.

The new goggles actually showed real time and true color instead of the standard phosphorous green. He could adjust the sensitivity for differences in the amount of available ambient light and a smart chip in the goggles safeguarded against blinding. Bright flashes of light were filtered by the chip, allowing the user to see normally, a strong improvement over the prior models. Two buttons on the side of the goggles offered additional new options. One button changed the display to a thermographic scan; the other provided a view in a type of three-dimensional sonar imagery. Every image that passed through the goggles was transmitted via a wireless link to the system in the truck and recorded. Another added bonus was perspective. An array of transmitters housed on the goggles also mapped the area around the wearer. The data was deciphered and spliced with the line-of-sight images to create a fairly accurate three-dimensional model of the immediate area with the wearer always located at the center, much like a real-life version of a first-person shooter video game. It was essential to keeping the wearer from being ambushed or surprised, and it provided an excellent source for reference material if a location had to be revisited.

Luigi hoped everything would work as well on the move, or under fire, as it did during the trial runs when the unit was considerably still. He changed the channel on his specially designed iPhone and the police band transmissions emitted from the bud in his right ear. He could jump from channel to channel as needed using line-of-sight technology and a virtual menu displayed inside the goggles. He preferred to keep a greater distance than the perspective imaging could provide when it came to the police. He despised killing them, but it was still unavoidable at times. It worked much better to work around them.

After his recon of the building, he accessed the roof via an access port above a section of the catwalk that covered the perimeter of the interior. He positioned himself and waited, allowing him some time to play with the goggles.

I'll have to get the design team to look at these.

The goggles were apparently malfunctioning. One of the statues mounted on the roof of the bank across the street registered when he switched to the thermographic scan.

Almost two hours passed before anything on the radio caught his interest. Another unit was checking out a nearby disturbance at one of the docks. On the move, rooftop to rooftop, he was there in seven minutes.

"Don't move or I'll shoot!"

The officer yelled the command while his partner radioed in from the squad car. A man stood in the alley, in the sight of the officer.

"Put your hands over your head!"

The man remained motionless, not responding.

Luigi watched from a low rooftop.

"Do it!"

The cop was aggravated at being ignored, but the slight trembling on his hands gave his true feelings away.

The criminal moved suddenly and disappeared into the shadows. The cop pursued; Luigi switched to thermographic.

What's going on with these?

When he switched to perspective imaging, the computer-modeled image revealed a large man standing in the darkness against the back of the building, watching the cop approach. It was obvious that the cop didn't see him. Luigi switched back to thermographic, confused. The cop was still visible, but he now appeared to be alone.

The attack was swift and the cop never saw it coming. Luigi watched the cop's heat signature fall to a prone position on the pavement, fading quickly from a vibrant red to cooler hues.

What happened next disturbed him. The attacker slowly became visible on thermographic as the heat signature started at his head and seeped into the rest of his body. Luigi readied the assault rifle.

The other cop exited the car, calling for his partner. The attacker dropped the corpse's body and leapt into the air. It took Luigi by surprise, but it didn't affect his resolve. When the man was level with Luigi, he fired. The silencer stifled the report and all three shots hit their mark. The man didn't fall, but the force of the unexpected shots pushed him back a few feet before he turned his attention to the rifleman.

Luigi dropped the assault rifle and grabbed his shotgun. The flyer came within two feet of him when he pulled the trigger. The recoil knocked Luigi back a couple of steps from his off-balance firing stance. The force of the blast knocked the attacker back out over the edge of the roof to the snow-covered alley below.

Luigi holstered the shotgun and retrieved the assault rifle on his way to the building's edge. He knew he needed the higher firepower. A large space, devoid of heat, rested in the middle of the attacker's chest. The shotgun blast blew a hole almost a foot across through his body.

Luigi took off before the remaining officer understood what happened, and he heard the call for Homicide and the Coroner as he worked down the fire escape on the next building. He radioed a message of his own.

"Yes."

"It's Luigi. It looks like we better start believing; I saw it with my own eyes. We're not prepared to handle this, but I'll rectify that quickly. I got a lucky shot and took one of them down."

"I see. What do you need?"

"I'll get the information from the police department's network and I need your weapons design team at my disposal."

"I'll see to it, Luigi. Keep up the good work."

Luigi double-timed back to his SUV and got clear of the area.

"Dispatch, I've got an officer down and a dead perp. Get some help out here now!"

"10-4; units in the area are responding and the Medical Examiner is being located, over and out."

Officer Stevenson walked back down the alley. His partner was dead. At least the vampire that killed him was too. He had no idea who pulled the trigger on the bloodsucker, but he counted his blessings for it none the less.

"Captain, this just came in from the dispatcher."

Bishop read the transcript the office clerk handed him as he walked to the command center.

"It looks like we don't have a question whether Trass is in this or not," stated Bishop as he entered the room.

"Damn!" said Joe.

"At least they took one of them in the process. We need to issue a memo to the force to watch their backs. Trass' people won't avoid going through one of us if they feel like they have to. I don't want to take any extra chances. God knows we won't be able to finger Trass for anything."

Officer Richard Bachman parked on the street in front of the 42nd Precinct. He was early for his shift that started at six that morning. He got out of the car and went to the trunk to get his change of clothes. He was scheduled to pull a double. A loud thud directly behind him caught him off guard. He turned with his hand on the butt of his pistol. The mangled body of a man lay in the snow.

The remnants of his clothes were soaked red with blood and gaping wounds riddled his entire body. Bachman looked skyward, trying to figure out where the body came from, but a feeble streetlight and falling snow was all he saw.

He pulled the grisly body into the Precinct's foyer, trying to keep it out of sight in the event someone passed by. It was bad enough the snow on the steps shone with crimson evidence, but that could be explained if the body wasn't there. Once inside, he grabbed another officer to help with the corpse and immediately made his way to the task force ready room. He was making his statement when a call came in from the 113th Precinct in Queens; the same thing happened there.

The phone rang in room 1124 of the Ritz Carlton Hotel. Joshua Stone groggily reached for the receiver.

"Hello?"

He listened for a few moments as the caller spoke, but by the end of the conversation he was fully awake. "I see. I'll be there within the hour."

He disconnected the call and rang room service, ordering a pot of very strong coffee before jumping into the shower. He knew he was in for a long day and an even longer night.

A call was also issued to Commissioner Jamison. Joe coordinated the effort, spending the night at his desk, trying to stay awake if any word came in about Angela. So far, they hadn't heard anything and she hadn't reported in either. Worry, coupled with the lack of sleep, wore heavily on his stamina and his nerves. He kept running the events at the shipyard through his mind, hoping to remember anything that might be helpful.

chapter Thirty-four

"Jamat! No!"

Daxxe yelled as his protector bored down on his prey. The command issued just in time to lessen the blow from a killing stroke, but it still connected with the back of the young girl's head. The impact hurtled her to the floor and rendered her unconscious. Jamat looked towards his Master, askance.

"I led her here; she is important to us."

Daxxe lifted the girl's limp body in his arms gently and carried her deeper into the building. Jamat sealed the window before following his Master's path.

The darkness over Angela lifted as a thick fog over water on a winter morning. She was disoriented, confused, and her head throbbed painfully, not allowing her vision to completely focus. As her awareness recovered, she realized she was bound tightly to a wooden chair. A small table stood a few feet before her bearing only a beeswax candle. The luminaria gave off a slight scent of honey and just enough light to keep her from being in the dark. The flame's power didn't reach much beyond the edges of the tabletop.

She sensed someone else was in the room; but she didn't know where. She pulled violently at the ropes, attempting freedom, but only managing to break the skin on her wrists. The burning sensation coupled with the blood trickling down her fingers ceased her escape attempts. She tried to stifle the tremors starting to wrack her body. She had seen enough from the case to know what was coming next, regretting that she deserted Joe.

"Who's there? What do you want with me? I'm a police officer! They'll be looking for me!" she yelled, not as confident as she sounded.

The room remained silent. Even though her captor remained hidden in shadow, she could feel eyes upon her.

"Why are you hiding? Show yourself! Bastards!" Her scream trailed into silence. Tears rolled from her eyes as she succumbed to the fear.

Not like this…

"You have no reason to be afraid."

Angela jerked her head in the direction of the deep voice, squinting in the vain hope of seeing something.

"Who are you?"

"That will come later. Your wounds require immediate attention."

"Why are you holding me?"

"Always the detective, I see."

"You seem to know more about me than I know about you. Why are you dragging this out? Just kill me and drain me, right? Doesn't that happen next? I won't taste good, you prick! I'm not drunk, or diabetic, or..." Her defiance dropped to incoherent mumbling.

"I am not one of them," he started. "I apologize we had to meet this way."

Angela felt the presence of her captor go away. She heard no movement; yet she knew he was gone. She went through what she could remember. Concentrating hurt, but the ache was beginning to dull. She felt the tight, localized pressure of the knot swollen on the back of her head. The repetition of her memory slowly rebuilt a more solid but somewhat sketchy image of what happened in her mind.

She had seen her attacker from her peripheral vision. He was shorter than average in height with a very muscular build. She couldn't pinpoint why, but she felt he was of European descent. She gasped as another piece of the puzzle revealed itself. The attacker had hit her with a long sword. He must have used the flat since her skull was not parted down the middle.

Why a sword? She would have expected the butt of a rifle, or a blackjack, or a plain old two-by-four, but not a sword. The more she remembered, the less sense it all made. She heard a door ease open from somewhere behind her.

She could not see who entered, but the footfalls grew louder. She tensed when the footsteps stopped right behind her, which forced the ropes to cut into her already injured wrists.

"Ouch!"

"Be still, woman!"

This voice was different. The tone was harsher. The accent sounded Austrian.

She felt the man working with the ropes holding her arms. A sharp pain shot up her entire arm for an instant; then it was gone. She could move her wrists, but she was now tied higher in a position that allowed less body movement. The ropes bound higher up on her arms, almost holding her elbows together. If she sat still, the position was painless; leaning forward felt as though her arms were about to be ripped off.

"Stay still! I will fix your wrists."

"You hit me with that damn sword, didn't you!?!"

He walked in front of her.

What if they're the killers? How many more of them are there?

Her eyes gave away the fear she tried to cover with her harsh tone.

"Yes, the broadsword is mine." His tone softened a little. "For that, I am truly sorry. Fear not, the Master will come back soon." Angela's tension lessened.

Jamat fumbled through the pronunciation of the English language. He understood the language and grammar, but he had difficulty mastering it vocally. He had little use for it, but it was necessary from time to time.

He gently cleaned Angela's wrist wounds and dressed them with bandages. The ointment he used felt cool and it stopped the pain and burning on contact. Startled, her skin changed to gooseflesh when he walked behind her and parted the hair on the back of her head. She tried to pull away, paying the price in pain from both arms and shoulders.

Jamat said nothing as he checked the knot on her skull. The bump was solid and reddened, but it wasn't bleeding. He left the room, closing the door behind him. She saw shapes in the darkness when she felt the presence again. The candle, apparently of its own volition, went out, leaving the darkness unbroken. She started trembling again.

"Let me remind you that you have no reason to be afraid."

Angela heard what sounded to be a series of low whispers, and then her fear and tension started ebbing away.

"Do you feel better?"

"Yes, a little, but why does my welfare concern you, especially after your friend attacked me?" She shot a direct glare at him. "And with a damn sword, of all things! How much stranger is this going to get?"

"Right to the point, very good."

She couldn't see him, but she felt him. Her gaze followed him, but she was unaware she looked directly at him.

"Where the hell are we? Why are you holding me hostage?" She tested her restraints a little, knowing it would hurt if she pulled too much.

"We'll take one question at a time, I think. As for where, we are in the catacombs below the Cathedral of St. Francis. You met my servant earlier in the chapel above, and as for the latter question, you are not a prisoner or being held for ransom."

"Then why am I tied to this chair? I am losing feeling in my legs."

"It's a necessary precaution."

"This doesn't make any sense. What's going on?"

"You know much more than you realize."

"What does that mean?" she yelled angrily.

Daxxe walked about the room, keeping his eyes on her. Her gaze followed his path, even though she still didn't see him.

"Why do you move your head to and fro? What are you trying to see in this pitch darkness?"

"You, obviously."

"You don't understand the question. I realize your eyes don't see anything, but I want to know why you continue to look. I am making no sound as I move."

Angela wasn't expecting philosophy. She wasn't truly in the mood for it, but she went along.

"I guess I'm looking in the hope that I will see something."

"What if I told you that you are seeing and you just don't know it?"

"Okay, this is too much. Why don't you stop with the mind games and do whatever you're going to do with me, to me, whatever. My arms are going numb now, too."

"This is always hard at first, so I'll start more simply."

Daxxe moved in front of Angela, almost touching the table. She drew her head back slightly, aware he was very close.

"Which hand am I holding up?"

"How am I supposed to know that? I can't see a thing."

"You don't think you can see because you don't yet know how to look. Which hand am I holding up?" he asked more forcibly.

"I don't have time for this craziness." Anger and frustration were evident in her voice.

"You don't seem to be going anywhere. What can it hurt?"

"Okay, you're holding up your right, and your index finger is extended."

"That's very good, but now for the tough question. How did you know?"

"It was just a lucky guess." A hint of sarcasm was slowly working into the mix.

"Don't be so sure. How many fingers am I holding up now?"

"I'll go with three." She almost laughed out loud at the game her captor played. "You can say whatever you want to lure me in to this. I have no way to prove if you are telling the truth or not."

"That's true, but what was the other thing you noticed?"

Angela's doubts were now shaken. How could he know that?

"I'm waiting."

"You held up three fingers that time, but it was your left hand."

"Outstanding."

"I don't understand how I could possibly know that. I cannot see anything in here. My eyes can't adjust any more than they already have."

"You have a gift, Angela."

"What gift? What are you talking about? How do you know my name?" A subtle seriousness carried on her voice.

"The gift of which I speak passed down through many generations. It remains somewhat…dormant. There are many things you need to know first."

Daxxe spoke softly, almost under his breath. Angela didn't understand the words, but some of them had a familiar feel to her. A thin wisp of smoke drifted into the center of the room. Angela could smell it, but it didn't affect her ability to breathe. It smelled slightly of soot, but more akin to incense, not unpleasant. As it thickened, the room gained a certain amount of illumination from an unknown source, allowing her to see the outlines of the table sitting before her. She expected to succumb to the smoke, but her breathing was unaffected.

"What are you doing?"

"Your eyes know how to see, but I must teach you how to believe what they see."

The haze took on certain forms and shapes, but none of them lasted long enough to make a positive identification.

"Let me begin. Long ago, the world was a very different place. The powers of magic ruled the land, not giving way to what mortals dub science. The world was known as Talamhan, and a select few, known as magi, could control the power. It flows through Talamhan itself; the mage simply acts as a flesh and bone conduit to access, gather, and use that power to do his, or her, bidding."

The smoke took on a more solid form, laying out a landscape before Angela's eyes. The ground was very hilly, covered with hundreds of trees. A small clearing sat at the base of one of the hills, home to a small grouping of cottages. She could see people milling about, bartering or tending to their chores.

"Talamhan was a peaceful place for many years, but it could not last. Certain inhabitants desired control and power over all. They set out to take what they wanted, but the people would not follow, so they used the magic to create powerful beasts to enforce their commands."

A shape swooped down over the smoke village, moving quickly, immediately scattering the villagers. The shape returned, giving Angela a chance to see it. She realized it was a red dragon just before flame erupted from its mouth and engulfed the village. All of the cottages caught fire, and all of the scurrying villagers now lay motionless.

"This group of magi, calling themselves the Sect of Awakening, swept across Talamhan, taking control and leaving only death and devastation in their wake. The people of the land never knew war, so they were not prepared, or even aware of how to properly defend themselves against the vile magic. All looked to King Norack for help."

The scene slowly changed to a much larger city, its center holding a very large, beautifully adorned castle. To Angela's left stood a vast forest at the base of high mountains, and to the right, a large sea.

"Norack ruled his kingdom from the capital city of Chandrice. He consulted his advisors about a plan of action to save what was left of his kingdom. After several days of discussion, and the destruction of more villages, the Great War began."

Chandrice changed slowly before Angela's eyes, the beauty ebbing away as methods of defense appeared along with militia.

"Norack formed an army of normal men and magi loyal to the crown. The Sect moved ever closer with each passing day. The first few battles were costly learning experiences for the King and those that fought for him, and as a result, the King's magi, known as the Council of Norack, created stronger, more creative spells for battle. It wasn't long before the opposing sides reached a balance of power and neither could advance."

Angela watched the smoke theatre as battle after battle raged. A myriad of magical creatures and various villages rising from nothingness and dying just as quickly.

"The Great War lasted for almost a thousand years, neither side willing to concede. The kingdom and its people were devastated. Peace was no longer a familiar term, and no end to the fighting was in sight. The tide took an unexpected turn when the creatures the Sect created developed the ability to control the magic themselves. The servant quickly became the master and most of the Sect was destroyed, but it didn't stop there. These magical creatures redirected their attacks at Chandrice."

The haze lost all of its solidity for a few seconds as it reformed in the shape of a man, clad in dark robes with a walking staff at his side. His hair was a deep brown and his face was clean-shaven. A deep scar graced his left cheek.

"One of the King's most powerful magi had an idea. He was known as Kalanak, and he was very young for the range of his power. He was very adept at the arts, but many of the older magi feared he lacked the necessary wisdom. With Norack's blessing, the plan was set in motion. The Council pulled back, securing themselves deep within the King's keep, and all of the King's defenses were set to the task of defending Chandrice alone. The move took the band of creatures by surprise, ending the attacks for a short while, and Kalanak and the Council took advantage of the lull, working around the clock on a task that would ultimately end the Great War."

The smoke reshaped again, showing Angela a room full of magi working feverishly to fill hundreds of sheets of parchment with written incantations.

"They worked on a grand spell, the likes of which had never been seen."

The images of the pages slowly came together in the form of five books, called the Books of Kalanak, and each book was designed for a specific purpose; hence, each volume carried its own name as well. All of the images, except the parchment sheets, washed away from the smoky haze, collecting into five distinct piles. Each pile took the form of a book, and all of the covers were essentially plain except for a single symbol inlaid in gold on each cover. Angela saw each symbol before the smoke lost form.

"Descension, Death, Chaos, Order, and Life."

"What were they for?" Angela was awestruck. Her mind told her it was all trickery, yet in her heart, she knew it to be the truth.

"Kalanak's plan was to sunder all of Talamhan, with the exception of the capital of Chandrice. All else was to be destroyed and reborn anew, at peace. The innocents destroyed would be resurrected with no knowledge of Talamhan's true history as a means to insure a future without conflict. The plan was sound, but unbeknownst to Kalanak, it was doomed to fail."

"How so?"

The smoky theatre reformed into the image of Chandrice once more.

"When it was time for Kalanak to cast the spells, the flow of power through Talamhan was too great, worsened by the fact the magic worked against itself. Talamhan was utterly destroyed, as was

Chandrice, the creatures born of the Sect, the Council, and even Kalanak himself, only the Books remained."

Angela saw everything come apart before her eyes. The land engulfed with flame, leaving nothing but an ethereal haze in its wake. The land was barren, gray, and devoid of anything. It was flat and dead in all directions.

"What happened next?"

"The spells were already set in motion, and because the Books acted as the conduit, they were not destroyed. The extremity of the power unleashed greatly altered the desired outcome of the incantations. The world was still given life, but it was nothing like Kalanak and the Council envisioned. What you refer to as Earth was the end result. A world practically devoid of magic, and it's believed among my kind a power beyond our ancestor's scope played a hand in what happened."

"What is your kind?"

"We were born in the aftermath, in the visage of our ancestors, mage and dragon alike, sentinels of a dead past set to the task of protecting this new Earth."

The haze in the room faded away completely, leaving darkness in its place. Angela discovered she was no longer bound when she shifted her arms to give them some relief. The candle ignited just as it extinguished, and she saw him for the first time, standing just beyond the table.

His height came to just over seven feet and his frame looked to be made of all muscle. His skin held a medium gray hue, and his hair, lips, and claw-like nails were black as pitch. The pupils of his eyes were black as well, surrounded by luminescent yellow irises. The points at the top of his ears just poked through his mane of hair. Angela felt afraid, so she stood to ready herself, but she held her ground because his demeanor was calm and she did not feel threatened.

"Mortals refer to my kind as Gargoyles."

Daxxe offered a slight bow, allowing the tips of his wings to be visible over his broad shoulders.

Angela chose to remain standing, uncertain if her knees were now too weak to support her weight. She felt nauseated, and she put her face in her hands as she leaned forward, convinced she would wake from this dream. Daxxe put his large hand on her shoulder, his touch bearing a strange quality that made her feel better for reasons she didn't understand.

"You feel that sensation because of the gift."

Angela turned, looking him straight in the eyes. "How did you know what I was thinking?"

"I have many gifts as well."

"What is this gift of which you speak?" Angela wondered why she phrased the question that way; it wasn't her normal lexicon.

"As I said, Earth was almost devoid of magic, but bits and pieces of the power survived, and these remnants can exist in anything, or anyone."

"Are you suggesting I...?"

"I'm not suggesting, I am outright telling you."

"What does this all mean? Why have you brought me here? You need me for something, don't you?"

"Always the detective... What I need you for will help us both. Don't forget, I'm sworn to protect, and this place is in need of it."

"You're referring to the group of killers, aren't you?"

"Yes."

"Are they from Talamhan, like you?"

"No! They are nothing like me! They are the scourge of the earth."

Angela slowly moved a few paces away from him. The outburst rattled her. Daxxe was aware of her concern before she physically moved.

"I sense your fear, and your next question; my reaction requires more explanation."

Daxxe turned abruptly, focusing his gaze on the door. He mumbled something and the world was suddenly gone for Angela, and as she lost consciousness, she heard what sounded like an explosion. The thick wooden door shattered into a thousand splinters.

Daxxe grabbed the table, using the top as a shield. Some of the larger fragments broke through the surface, but they couldn't escape its grip.

The force slammed the table into him, knocking him to the floor as he tried to clear it from his line of sight, catching him off guard and taking his breath.

"Look what I found. Trokar will be pleased."

Mekune issued a silent call that only his kind could hear, and Trokar and Viktor entered within seconds.

"Well, well, we meet again," said Trokar.

Daxxe regained his footing, but his range of movement was limited by the size of the room.

Mekune advanced in a charge. Daxxe dropped to one knee, putting his head at Mekune's waist, throwing him up and over. The momentum, supplemented with Daxxe's strength, carried him into the back wall hard enough to crack the stone surface. He only managed to get a claw into one of Daxxe's wings as he careened over, but it tore a hole through it.

Viktor caught Daxxe firmly in the stomach before he could divert his attention from Mekune. The punch found purchase, breaking at least two ribs and doubling him over at the waist. Trokar's foot followed, catching Daxxe on the side of the face, knocking his upper body back upright. Viktor caught his arms in an attempt to hold him, but he underestimated his strength.

Daxxe flipped Viktor over his shoulders, swinging him hard as he went. Viktor hit the floor, square on his back, hard enough to bounce the broken pieces of table.

Mekune planted a flying kick into the center of Daxxe's back, pushing him forward, and a solid roundhouse kick from Trokar lifted his body from the floor, breaking another rib and worsening the already present damage. Blood spurted from his mouth. Trokar moved to finish him when he saw the true prize, the Book of Chaos, resting on a bookshelf to his left.

"Keep him busy."

Trokar went for the Book. Viktor and Mekune continued to batter the weakened Daxxe while Trokar retrieved the Book and started out of the room.

"That's enough. We must take our leave. Thank the dawn that you will survive another day."

"Captain, we've got to issue a statement and do something about Benson. She's not like this. She would have shown up or reported in by now if she was able."

"Joe, I understand the way you feel, but I can't authorize the release of that information. Can you..."

Joe already turned and left, expecting Bishop's response. Joe only wanted to cover himself in the chain of command, and now he could go to Jamison and get something done.

He felt very ragged and looked very poorly after spending the night at his desk listening for the phone and repeatedly checking email, hoping to hear from his partner. He battered himself for Angela's disappearance on top of it all. He held himself responsible as the ranking officer and on a more personal level. Several scenarios ran through his mind and he found himself coming back to the same one he had at the depot. This group of killers challenged the police directly, literally bringing the case to the department's front door, and now it looked like they successfully set a trap to add insult to injury. Joe approached Jamison, disregarding the conversation he was already having.

"Give me minute," said Jamison to one of the police lieutenants so he could talk to Joe. "I know what you're going to say and you're right. We put you in charge of the task force, so the decision is truly yours to make. I do want to advise caution though. We're already handling a lot of false leads and God only knows what will happen if Angela's face goes public. We'll get hundreds of calls that won't help us find her, but we'll have to work them all just in case it is a legitimate report. It'll turn her into an easy target, and it will put doubt in the minds of the people regarding our ability to protect them."

"I don't intend to do that, but I want to let the public know we're taking an even stronger interest in solving this case. I want stress put on cooperation from the public, and I want every cop, fireman, mailman, and dogcatcher in the city briefed on her. We've got people stationed at the local hospitals already, so they can ID her if she comes in hurt. I almost hope she was admitted somewhere as a Jane Doe because at least she'd be safe."

Jamison put his hand on Joe's shoulder, offering a consoling and understanding squeeze. "I understand and we'll do everything we can to find her. I want you to take a break. Go home and get cleaned up and get something to eat. I'll work at your desk just in case she reports in."

Joe felt his body release some tension. Jamison was not only his supervisor, he was a trusted friend. Joe knew he was right. He went to his squad car to get his overnight bag and headed for the locker room. He needed to get cleaned up and handle something personal before he would think about sleep.

He thought about what he should do and how the task force should proceed as he showered. The hot water soothed some of the ache from his tense muscles and helped clear his head. He let the steaming water run over him until it started losing temperature.

He knew they had to be careful since they had yet to discover if there was a mole in the department. If so, any information they issued to the force would also make it to the killers. It would hinder Angela's chance of survival if she was truly at large and publicly confirm that the killers slapped the department in the face.

Joe worked on a plan to find the leak as he dried off. He knew whom he could trust within the department, so he flipped through his mental roster of the officers on the task force and cross-referenced it with the officers that normally worked the first shift; there had to be a common denominator between the two. He got dressed and went to the car. His brain kept working for the entire drive, but it finally quieted when he pulled into a parking space along the curb. The sidewalk ran along a wrought iron fence, and he parked about four car lengths from an archway that spanned over the gate. Letters made of the same iron ran along the entire arch that read North Arlington Cemetery.

He passed several ornate headstones as he walked to the back corner of the graveyard. The snow had not been disturbed, and Joe felt the pangs of misplaced guilt for interrupting the sacred sleep of the inhabitants. The pureness of the virgin snow graced the hallowed ground. He stopped under the naked boughs of a large oak tree and turned to his left to look upon one of the larger markers. It was three plots wide and made of polished gray granite. The center face was blank, and would be until Father Time, or a thug with a lucky shot, punched his ticket. His attention focused on the left face that read "In

Loving Memory of Celeste Abigail Anderson." The dates showed that Celeste was nine years old when she died.

"I know it's been a few days Abby, but Angela's in trouble. I told you about her the other day; she's my new partner and she really reminds me of you. I kind of see her as what you could have become. What's happening now feels like it did when you and your mom died. I just don't want anything bad to happen to her, too, like history repeating itself. I haven't forgiven myself for that yet and I just don't think I can take it again. But here I am, babbling along again like normal.

"What I came to say is that you'll always be my little girl and Angela isn't taking your place or anything like that. She's not taking yours either, Honey."

He shifted his gaze to the right side of the headstone.

"I do hope I can right this wrong for myself. It's like I'm getting a second chance, you know. I would give anything to have you back. I miss you so much Michelle. It still hurts just as much as it did when I got that phone call 26 years ago. You know, I still can't go into our bedroom. It just doesn't feel right to be in there, or to lie in that bed, without you. I don't think I'll ever get used to that. I've kept Abby's room just like it was, too. I sit on the edge of her bed sometimes and just look at all of her things. Those memories don't hurt as much as they used to. I find some comfort remembering the happy times that we all shared.

"Well, I've got to go back to work now. Thanks for listening ladies. I won't wait as long to pay a visit next time."

Joe put his hands atop the frozen headstone and bowed his head. The cold stung his fingertips, but he would not pull his hands away until he uttered the same prayer he said for them every day since the day they died.

"Lord, please watch over my girls until you lead me back to them. I am trying to live as you wish, but I feel so lost without them. Please grant me the strength to make it. Amen."

He walked back through his tracks to the car, wiping the tears from his cheeks, feeling better when he got back behind the wheel.

By the second day, Julie and Marina found a little common ground and started talking to each other. Their situations were very different, but talking made them both feel better, and Malcolm and Emilio were both glad to see it. The situation was harder for the witnesses when it was uncomfortable, and it made their jobs harder. They could now comfort each other, decreasing the number of questions sharply asked of the officers, and their newfound outlet helped mask the fact they were essentially captives.

Malcolm and his partner had a laptop with Internet access that was secured in the room they originally shared when they first arrived with Julie. They could chat live or send email to the Precinct, and the system eliminated the need for an actual phone in the apartments, making them more secure. It was also a silent form of communication, so the witnesses had no idea the officers had access to the outside. The computer itself was installed in one of the cabinets in the bathroom, and the exhaust vent made enough noise to disguise the keystrokes. It was also impossible to establish the physical location of the computer from anywhere else. The gateway led directly to the NYPD LAN and the web was accessed from there. The IP address would show up as one of the Precincts so the Internet connection could not be discovered by a backwards trace. It would lead a would-be hacker to the police station.

Angela awoke, still in darkness, in a small closet-like room. She heard someone speaking in the room just beyond the door.

"You've always been weak," adding the word "Protector" as he spit.

She waited several long moments, listening for anything more, and once she convinced herself no one was around, she opened the door. Daxxe lay on the floor in the center of the room, badly injured, but his chest rose and fell with breath. She approached his body unsure of what to do, leaning down. A hand closed around her throat, releasing her as quickly as it came, and Daxxe slumped back to the stone floor. Angela stopped screaming.

"What happened?"

Daxxe forced himself to stand up, using one of the legs of the overturned table to steady himself.

"Trokar has someone inside your organization. You were likely followed by someone, which led them to me."

"I knew it! Joe and I knew a mole was in the department!"

Angela quickly helped support Daxxe's weight when he tried to walk, realizing he was barely able to stand, let alone move around.

"We cannot stay here. They will return after sunset to finish the job. We have little time."

"I'll get your friend. He can help us."

"I'm afraid Jamat can do nothing for us now. They took him by surprise as well and he's on his way to the heavens."

"What can I do?" Her voice was almost frantic. Even with the fear, she held to her oath to serve and protect, even though she wasn't sure what she was going to do. Being at a loss for what to do scared her even more.

"Jamat's body is at the entrance to the stairs of the bell tower. Go get his sword and the amulet from around his neck. I will stay here until you return."

Angela started to ask something.

"I'll explain later. Go!"

Angela easily found her way back up to the ground level of the church, which surprised her since she'd never seen the way. She did find Jamat quickly, but she wished she hadn't. His body was ravaged, torn limb from limb. Angela barely resisted the urge to vomit while she looked through the pieces to find what Daxxe wanted, quickly retrieving the items and going back down into the catacombs. Daxxe sat on the wooden chair when she returned, clutching a large, old and worn book. From her vantage point, she could see the large hole in his left wing.

"We have to get moving. The more distance we cover in the tunnels betters our chances of survival."

"What tunnels?"

"Tunnels run from these catacombs out underneath most of the city. Most of them converge here, but the outer ends are hidden. I don't think Trokar or his followers are aware of them, but I'll cover our tracks just the same."

He seemed a little stronger than before, but he still had trouble walking. He gathered a few items from the room, putting them into a knapsack made of some animal's skin, and instructed Angela to carry it along with Jamat's belongings. The bag's burden was much less than she expected as she threw it over one shoulder as they entered the tunnels, walking in a direction Angela couldn't determine. No lights lit the way, but Angela found navigation easy.

"It's your gift; it is no longer dormant within you."

"Would you at least let me ask the question first? That really gives me the creeps, knowing you can just rattle around in here whenever you want," she added, pointing at her head.

Daxxe let a small smile slip through his demeanor as he stopped walking.

"This is far enough; it'll only take a minute."

He opened the book he carried, reading from the pages. Angela didn't understand what he said, although bits and pieces sounded somewhat like Latin. She recognized the cover's symbol. It was the Book of Descension.

An unexplained gust of wind passed over them, rustling Angela's hair and disturbing the dust in the tunnel as Daxxe closed the book. The trek gave her time to think about everything, mull it over in her mind, but it was also tiring. She hoisted the sword over her shoulder when she noticed the tip dragging the ground. It didn't feel light at all. Daxxe turned his head towards her as she asked, "Where are we? And thank you for letting me ask first." Daxxe nodded his head.

"We are just east of the city. You should get some rest as it'll be light soon. We'll have to stay here until then."

"Why?"

"I have certain limitations, much like Trokar and his kind."

"Does the sunlight hurt you? A man helping us with the killings says that vampires are violently allergic to sunlight."

"It doesn't hurt me. My skin turns to stone when the sun shines on me to protect me while I sleep."

"How can you protect that way? Most bad guys don't take the day off."

"The evils my kind protects the world against have little power out of darkness. Now, get some rest. The questions will save until later."

Angela fashioned the knapsack like a pillow and lay down, setting the sword to her side with the handle close at hand. She closed her eyes, but she did not sleep, chancing the occasional peek to see what Daxxe was doing. Each glance found him doing the same thing, silently holding the amulet Jamat wore in life. At times he rubbed its surface or clutched it in his fist, casting occasional glances her way.

"Good evening, New York. I'm Max Green, signing on. We have several stories lined up for the evening news tonight, and here are some of the highlights."

Max, a very handsome man in his late twenties, started as Denise Rigsby's new coanchor because the station wanted to revamp the news and pull in more viewers from the female demographic. Jack Adams thwarted the prior attempts, primarily because he didn't think of it first. The changes had no opposition now that Jack was out of the picture.

"The police are still working feverishly to restore the safety of our fair city. According to the Commissioner, many internal processes were modified to increase the city's security and police response time.

Max shifted his gaze as the producer changed the camera angles.

"According to the police department, they have solid information that puts them closer to solving the mysteries plaguing our city. The department asks all residents to use a common-sense approach. Stay in your homes unless it is necessary to be out, and be cautious when you are out and about. They want to expend as many of their resources as they can on the case itself.

"In related news, one of the detectives very close to the case is reported as missing in action. The officer's name is being withheld for security reasons.

Max shifted his gaze back to the first camera.

"Another freak accident occurred very early this morning. For reasons unknown, the old Cathedral of St. Francis collapsed on itself just after dawn. No injuries were reported, as the church has been vacant for several months. The cause remains a complete mystery as there were no witnesses. No evidence of explosives or anything else that could have leveled the Cathedral was discovered.

Max closed with a heavy dose of charm.

"Join Denise Rigsby and myself at seven for all the details."

The cameras stopped rolling. Max hurriedly looked for a mirror to make sure his hair was in the right place. Denise shook her head from side to side as she watched from the wings. He is so full of himself. Thank God he's not in charge. She wondered how long he would actually last as she walked away from the set.

Angela woke groggily, unsure how long she slept. Daxxe was in the same spot, still looking at the amulet.

"You miss him, don't you?"

"Yes, he was my servant for many years."

"Tell me about him, please."

"I found Jamat in Austria late in the year 1352, after the Black Plague ravaged his village. Both of his parents were taken by the disease and none of the other villagers would take him in out of fear for themselves. I spirited him away during the night. He was not missed. The townsfolk assumed he perished like his parents. Like you, he possessed the gift. It's the reason the disease didn't take him. I provided for him and he learned from me in return. I taught him about his gift and showed him how to use it. When he reached maturity, he became my protector."

"He was *your* protector? I thought that's what you do."

"During the hours between sunrise and sunset, my kind needs someone to watch over them. Our bodies turn to stone with properties much like granite. Our skin becomes very hard, but it can be broken, which would destroy us. The vampires know this, but they need protectors as well. Some of my kind were lost to mortal men in the employ of vampires. We are the only true predators they have, as they are to us."

Daxxe paused for a moment, collecting his thoughts and remembering his friend.

"Jamat was my friend and my quest is a very solitary one. Others of my kind exist, but we are scattered throughout the world, rarely crossing one another's path. Most of my people are in Europe, but the different world cultures reflect our presence in other areas. We are very few in this land, thus Jamat was my only companion."

"I can relate. My best friend and I went to a summer camp when we were fourteen. We were wading in the creek when she slipped and her head hit one of the rocks on the bottom. She was in a coma for almost two months before she died. I was completely lost without her; we did everything together."

"Like you, I did all I could to help him. They outnumbered us and they knew they would have a better chance to get me by going after him. I let my guard down and they almost destroyed me as well."

"What will you do now?"

"I must continue my quest."

"Which is?"

"We can discuss that later. Night has fallen, and we have to find a new lair."

Daxxe sensed Angela's tension when he used the word we, but he said nothing of it. They walked a few hundred yards to an old wooden staircase rising upward. Daxxe went first, the old timber creaking loudly under his weight, but it held. Angela had no trouble following him. Her ankle was no longer swollen, or even cut for that matter, but she wouldn't be able to thank Jamat for it. Daxxe reached the top after what Angela counted to be four flights. Bitterly cold air rushed over them when he opened the door at the top, leading to a small building without a roof. The walls stood, devoid of any door or glass in the windows. From the look of it, they were standing in an old church or a schoolhouse.

"Where are we?"

"About 400 years ago, the Cardinal of St. Francis wanted to spread God's word as far as he could, so he established a small series of churches. He insisted the tunnels be constructed for the safety of the parishioners. At the time, attacks from the local Indian tribes were not uncommon, but they would not follow through the tunnels out of fear. This building is in the forest just east of the city. Two miles separates us from the beginning of the newest housing development in the suburbs."

"Are you planning to stay here?"

Angela shivered as the unhindered cold blew through her.

"No, this is too open, and much too difficult to defend. Back to the northeast is the sister chapel to the original St. Francis Cathedral. The tunnels do not connect it to the rest of the system, but I recently discovered its existence. I doubt Trokar is aware of it at all."

"Before we head out into the snow, will you tell me something?"

"That depends on what it is."

"If the vampires are not from Talamhan, where did they come from?"

Daxxe stiffened slightly, barely enough for Angela to notice, apparently wanting to avoid the question.

"They were born of evil, unforeseen by the magi of Talamhan. As I said, my kind was born of magic to protect the New World from evil and strife, whether it came from within or without. We never thought the evil would come from our own ranks. Some of my own kind grew tired of maintaining peace, desiring to rule those they were sworn to protect and defend, just as the Sect before them. As your scholars learned, history repeats itself. Our ranks divided and the conflicts followed. In 1743, one of the factions attacked a small village in Europe, wanting to establish dominance through fear. The leader of the faction decided he needed to leave a strong example of his power, and it resulted in the death of one of the villagers. He utterly dismembered the victim by tooth and claw while the other villagers were forced to watch."

Angela's faced paled.

"Soon after, the leader fell very ill, but on the very verge of death, he started to change. It is my belief the magic that survived the sundering of Talamhan was disrupted, altering the magic that created him. His physical form changed, resembling a more human-like appearance and characteristics, and many of the abilities he possessed as a gargoyle were altered instead of lost."

"Wait a minute, you're saying these vampires used to be gargoyles, like you?"

"Not all of them, just the first. He discovered quickly he could spread his disease to others and turn more into creatures like himself. He was already building his ranks by the time we learned of this ability."

"Who was the first?"

"Trokar."

"What did he mean about you being weak, back at the Cathedral? Have you fought before?"

"We've fought for hundreds of years."

His tone fell ever so slightly. Angela felt the subject wasn't worth pursuing for the moment.

"When are we getting out of here?" she asked, changing the topic of discussion.

"In a few moments, but you have to make a decision before we can go on."

Again, the we concerned Angela. She needed to get back to the Precinct to tell Joe what she learned. She had no idea what happened over the last twenty-four hours, or how many new corpses surfaced. She felt obligated to help Daxxe since she essentially led his enemies to him, but that sense of duty was wearing thin.

"What decision is that?"

"I am in need of a new protector, and that honor can only be accepted by those who possess the gift."

"Me," Angela said, pointing at herself. "I...just couldn't do that. I've really got to get back to my job and my life. They need this new information."

"I cannot allow you to take the knowledge with you."

Angela backed away, suddenly worried about her own welfare. His tone made her very uncomfortable.

"You will not be harmed. If you do not accept, you will wake up in the city with no memory of what I've told you or what you've seen. Stone won't even be able to make you recall it."

"And if I don't leave?" She also wondered how Daxxe knew about Stone, but that wasn't a priority at the moment.

"You will never be able to go back. Your life as Angela Benson will end, and you will start anew. In return, you will be able to see the past as if you lived it yourself, and you will live far beyond your normal years, not to mention learning to control your gifts."

The thought of accepting Daxxe's offer terrified her, worsened by another thought that entered her mind, a sense of excitement tingling beneath the fear.

"You will still work towards the same purpose, just in a different fashion. The life you chose is rooted in the traits you were born with, to protect, and this would allow you a wealth of power to do just that."

"But what about Joe and my family back home?"

"You would not be able to see them ever again. Until Trokar is destroyed, I must follow him, wherever that my lead. I cannot tell you that you will never be in danger, but you chose the life you have now because you were willing to risk getting in harm's way for the sake of others."

Angela flashed him a stern glance even though he was right, knowing she was unable to hide the truth from him. The more she thought about it, the more frightened she became. The fear was not just of the unknown, but also of her scaring herself by actually warming up to the idea.

"Think about it while we move on. We need to reach the chapel before it gets too much colder; your body can't withstand these extremes for long."

Daxxe led her out the north door into the fiercely blowing wind that bit her flesh with the pieces of snow and sleet it carried. He pulled a cloak from the knapsack after he took it from her. Angela didn't see it in the bag before, but she felt very warm wearing it. It puzzled her that it fit her perfectly.

Trokar rose slowly, careful not to wake Shayla, and went to sit at his desk. Four books rested before him, and he only lacked the first. That volume would allow him to sunder the world once more, into the image he desired. It would prove simplistic since so few could command the magical power coursing all around them. A smile came to his lips at the thought of ultimate power. He would rule with Shayla at his side, and Daxxe, along with the rest of his irritating kind, would be eliminated once and for all. He absently ran his finger over the symbol of Chaos embossed into the leather, tracing it repeatedly, unsure of the location of the Book of Descension. Many years of diligent study and practice would lead him to the last book.

He arranged the last three volumes in the shape of a triangle and placed the second book on top. The triangle supported the Book of Death without allowing it to touch the table's surface. A barely whispered incantation rolled off his tongue. He'd repeated it mentally thousands of times to insure the pronunciation and inflection were precise. The Book of Death slowly levitated into the air above the other three volumes as high as they were spread apart, forming the four corner points of an equilateral, three-sided pyramid. All the books began to move apart of their own accord, increasing the gap between each book to roughly two feet.

A blue arc of lightning ignited from the symbol centered on the back cover of the Book of Death, sparking and spreading to the other Books. The symbol on each spine and face began to glow, increasing in brightness causing the power to leap between the paired symbols on each volume until the symbols were no longer visible. The power discharged counterclockwise from each book in bolts of green, yellow, and orange, connected the spines to the faces of the next text in the circle. The power surged and all the lightning glowed in continuous red arcs, making each slanted edge of the pyramid visible.

The core illuminated with the same dark red light, forming a solid pyramid of light. Another image slowly coalesced in the core, becoming a recognizable shape. Trokar slammed his fist on the table, disrupting the spell, when the shape formed completely. The lightning flickered out and the Book of Death fell back to tabletop, partially hiding the crack now running across the thick wooden tabletop. The sharp report woke Shayla with a start, which irritated her, but she pushed her anger down and played her part.

"What troubles thee, my love?"

"He has the last book! He was in my grasp!"

"Of whom do you speak?"

"Daxxe! He has done nothing but get in my way since the beginning."

"What can you do?"

"I have to destroy him, once and for all. I hurt him very badly last night and eliminated his protector in the process. We'll go back tonight to finish the job. He couldn't get far in his condition."

Shayla went to him and sat down on his lap, facing him. "I love it when you're like this! I can feel your power running through me. It's intoxicating."

She kissed him passionately. He indulged in her before he went out into the main room of the terminal.

"Viktor!"

"Yes, Master."

"Get the four best of the clan. We leave in ten minutes."

"Yes, Master. Where are we bound?"

"We are going back to that vile little church. That pup has something that belongs to me."

Angela's thoughts drifted back to her childhood as they walked, recalling predominant memories. Some were unpleasant facts of life, like the last day she spoke to her father. Others were favorites that she truly cherished, like the first time she sat on her dad's lap and got to drive, which really meant steer the car home from the local ice cream parlor. She weighed the worth of what she knew against what she could know, and what she stood to lose against what she would gain, the detective in her analyzing and weighing the pros and cons.

The cloak's hood kept the wind from whistling by her ears, allowing her a reasonable amount of peace and quiet. Daxxe kept a few paces ahead of her. She could tell he was moving slower than he was accustomed to even though she couldn't match his long strides. She tried to use the footprints he made in the snow, but they were too far apart to benefit her progress. She fought through the deeper areas and jogged to shorten his lead when the wintry blanket was thinner.

He spread his wings to prevent the stronger gusts of wind from hitting her full force. During one of the more intense gales, that would have knocked her to the ground without the interference, she noticed the hole in his wing was gone.

They stayed on the fringes of the forest as long as they could, partially to stay out of sight and partially for protection from the harsher wind. The gusts whistled and whispered around the cold trunks, rustling the dormant branches and stirring the remnants of foliage. They crested a small hill and descended towards another small church.

The sister chapel was much smaller than the main Cathedral. The grounds were unkempt and the building itself stood in varying states of disrepair. Snow piled into large drifts against the north face of the church, completely blocking the main entrance from view. Daxxe approached the building's west side and entered through a service door built into that wall.

The inside of the church waited silently, undisturbed for many years. A layer of fine silt covered every exposed surface. The door was only open briefly, but the wind that managed to sneak inside lifted a cloud of dust into the stale smelling air. Motes hung in the still air after the door was closed and the breeze was stifled.

The stir attacked Angela's allergies, causing her to sneeze uncontrollably. The fit grew in intensity until she was almost coughing, tears welling in her eyes. Daxxe muttered another simple spell and Angela stopped sneezing at once. The dust cloud whisked away in the conjured draft, taking all the silt with it.

"How did you do that?"

"If you choose to stay, I can show you."

"If I do, what shalt do I do about everything else?"

Shalt? Why the hell did I say shalt?

"Everything is a very broad term."

"You know what I mean. You can see in my head, so you already know that I am worrying about my job, Joe, the case, my family, and…"

Daxxe raised his hand, ceasing her comments.

"If you stay, your life as Angela Benson will end; she will die for all intents and purposes. You will be reborn as a protector, namely my protector. It will be painful for you and the ones you leave behind, but it is necessary to engineer closure for that existence before you can proceed into the new one."

"How would you do something like that?"

"The details will be entirely up to you, but I would suggest something simple and preferably accidental in nature. If your death raises suspicions, the investigation that would follow would be a hindrance to us."

"I haven't given you an answer yet, so it's not us."

Daxxe grinned to himself, knowing her decision was made, even though it was up to her to say it and to convince herself that it was the right one. She sat on one of the cleaner pews, holding Jamat's sword and wondering what it would be like to wield such a weapon, especially since she had trouble lifting it.

chapter thirty-five

Jamison answered Joe's phone after the first ring, but it wasn't Angela as he hoped.

"Joe?" asked the caller.

"No, this is Commissioner Jamison."

"Commissioner, it's Stone. I've just received some new info from Scotland Yard concerning the Mr. Sayer that we are very interested in."

"He won't be gone long, but go ahead and tell me what you've found out. I can brief Joe and then we'll pass it along to the rest of the team."

"That sounds good. I'm getting ready to leave the hotel, but I didn't want this to wait. A body was discovered in Snowdonia National Park in Wales just over a week ago, but it wasn't whole; some his organs were missing, as well as one of his arms. The Yard assumed he was the unfortunate victim of a shark attack, until yesterday when the missing arm was found just south of Dublin, Ireland, near the city of Greystones. It didn't take long for them to realize it was all the same man, and the hand on the severed arm was frozen around the handle of a small briefcase."

"How did the body get so severely separated? Parts of the same man on opposite sides of the Irish Sea sounds a little farfetched."

"That's what the Yard thought as well, but their medical examiners confirmed the arm belongs to that body. It's theorized the freezing temperatures kept the body from decaying, meaning the body was dumped somewhere between England and Ireland, probably in the middle of the Irish Sea."

"Do they have any idea how long the man was dead?"

"No, they can't determine the time of death since the body was partially frozen, but the items in the briefcase provided some recent dates and positive identification."

"I assume it was Sayer."

"Yes, it was. Several documents and papers in the briefcase showed his name and his signature. One receipt in the bunch was for a ship chartered from Cardiff to Dublin."

"If he chartered the ship, didn't the ship's captain realize he was short a client about halfway through the crossing, or at least when they reached port?"

"The Captain must have been in on it somehow. No reports were filed in Dublin, and by the time they tracked the Captain down, he was dead as well. Apparently, he was killed in a pub in Dublin when a fight over the honesty of a poker game got out of hand."

"What about his crew? Surely he didn't charter alone."

"They don't have any leads there either. He apparently catered to members of the IRA and he didn't exactly advertise."

"Was there anything else of interest in the briefcase?"

"Actually, yes there was. They found a highly detailed shipping manifest and schedule. It looks like he was escorting something personally, and he was sticking to water and ground based transportation. He started in Stockholm, working across the Baltic Sea to Kaliningrad, Russia. He was there for a few days before leaving port for Copenhagen, continuing on to London, where he stayed for almost a week, before traveling overland to Cardiff. His final destination was New York."

"What was he escorting? And why all the short hops?"

"They don't have any clue as to the nature of the cargo. The Yard secured a copy of the shipping manifest from the charter he used out of Stockholm, and he didn't have any cargo with him at that time."

"Or it was small enough for him to carry."

"The Yard is following that possibility now. Another receipt in the briefcase came from an antique auction in Stockholm two nights before his departure. The Swedish Government is assisting with the investigation, so they should have something soon."

"Good, I assume they'll keep us informed. Thank you, Joshua. I'll pass this on to Joe and the rest of the team."

"Very good. I'll be joining you personally within the hour."

Jamison hung up the phone, finished jotting down the facts, and looked up as Joe topped the stairs and started across the room. It was obvious he was still exhausted, but he looked considerably better than he did before.

"Any word?" he asked as he reached the desk.

"Not on Angela, I'm sad to say, but Stone got some more info about the case."

Jamison relayed the facts and the mystery around Sayer to Joe.

"Let me double check a hunch," said Joe as he sat down across from Jamison, using the computer at Angela's desk to access the Department's intranet and Internet.

"I was surprised to find it, but the Thornquist website was still up the other day. We checked it out, mostly out of curiosity, and I remember a listing of their shipping centers online."

Joe looked through the website, navigating with the mouse. Jamison walked over to stand behind him to see what he was doing.

"Yep, that's what I expected."

"What's that?"

"All of the cities Sayer utilized have a listing. The name of the first manifest is different because Thornquist operated under a different business name in Europe."

"Looks like you need to go get Thornquist."

"Right. This evidence deepens the tie between Thornquist and Sayer, and Thornquist popped up too many times to be a coincidence. Angela mentioned the other day the killers' erratic pattern made it seem like they were looking for something, and I'll bet Sayer was transporting that something, he just never made it here."

"Very well," added the Commissioner. "I'll have Captain Bishop issue a subpoena for him."

Joe nodded his head in approval. His expression lost the small burst of life brought on by the conversation and the new evidence. It was hard on him not knowing what happened to Angela, and sitting at her desk made it worse. He went to the window and looked out at the frozen city, hoping for the best. Jamison excused himself quietly, knowing Joe wanted to be alone.

Jamison entered the command center just as Stone arrived. "Joshua, I briefed Joe on the new information you gave me. What about the hardcopies of the evidence?"

"It's already in route. I asked my friends at the Yard to make copies of everything and overnight it here, so we should have it in hand by nine in the morning.

"Excellent."

Thomas worked the serving line, handing out bowls of hot soup. He watched two uniformed police officers enter and sit down at the back of the dining room. They discussed something between themselves, and then one of them motioned Thomas to come to their table. Gianelli indicated he needed a minute, serving the rest of the line before he came out from behind the counter.

"Can I help you?"

"Mr. Gianelli?"

"Yes."

"Detective Benson asked us to come pick you up."

"What for? Am I under arrest?" asked Thomas, confused.

"No, sir. The detectives want you to assist the investigative team because your help has proven invaluable thus far."

"I see. I'll need about half an hour, if that's okay. I have to help break down the serving line and clean up."

"That's fine, we'll wait."

Thomas returned to the kitchen to finish his duties. He returned to the police officer's table almost twenty minutes after their first conversation, discarding his apron.

"Sorry guys, the mess was a little bigger than I thought. How long will this take?"

"I'm not sure, sir, but Detective Benson did suggest you bring an overnight bag."

"Okay, let me tell the boss I won't be here for at least a day or two. I don't want them to be short-handed."

Gianelli went back to the kitchen for a few moments before he left with the police. He had done well to avoid dealing with the deaths of Freddy and Todd, but the ride in the police car worked against him. He gave the police an address he needed to visit to gather some things along the way.

He could see the photograph in his mind distinctly, almost like he was seeing it again for the first time. He watched the other cars pass as he rode in contemplation. The inner sadness he felt hurt, but he was thankful for the pain, and he hadn't drunk since learning of their deaths. As much as he wished he could have helped them, the realization that he couldn't have done anything started setting in. Newly stimulated, his need to learn came alive, pulling him from his self-imposed exile from the world. He thought a lot about his ex-wife, and it was another welcome pain. He still felt that sadness, but it reminded him he was alive. The need to be a part of the real world, to help people, finally grew too strong to suppress. After the murders and their aftermath were over, he wanted to look into getting a real job and starting his life over. The lady detective hit a nerve that he felt ever since. He realized he was slowly turning a key in his right hand, and although he didn't remember taking it out, or even getting out of the police car, the sight of it solidified his decision.

The key mated to a lock at a self-storage facility he rented. He hadn't been to it in a long time, never before having a need. He paid the rent five years in advance and put it out of his mind. The ten-by-ten foot room contained all that was left of his old life. He pictured it all in his mind before he opened the door, and it was just as he left it. He had three boxes of books, all containing psychiatric texts and literature, and his college degree and high school diploma rested in padded envelopes to protect the glass and the frames. One box contained his memories, mostly small trinkets and photographs. The picture on the top was of his wife, right after she got out of the rehabilitation program and the next one from their wedding reception.

God, I miss her. She almost made it, and...I know now...it wasn't my fault. I did everything I could, but I couldn't do it for her. She had to want to be better; it's time to let it go.

Thomas put the key back in the zippered pouch strapped to his ankle and wiped the tears from his eyes. The world looked different to him now, and he saw the rungs he needed to climb.

Trokar and his selected clansmen left the subway terminal, making the return trip to the Cathedral. He put his fist through the corner of the brick wall of the building they rounded on their approach. Until that moment, they were unaware that it had been destroyed.

"The infidel is gone!"

"Are you certain?"

"He did this! He knew we'd come back for him and he has the last Book. He must be found. Look for anything that might lead us to where he went. I'll be back in my chambers."

Trokar leapt into the darkness and vanished, infuriated again by Daxxe's meddling.

Viktor issued commands to Damok, Mekune, and the others, as they looked through the rubble. Viktor surveyed the area from above while the other six dug through the building's remains. As he scanned across the fragments of brick and wood, he noticed Reist was missing, even though he was searching towards the back corner of the church only moments before. At that instant, Damok looked up from where he searched and turned towards the area of Viktor's focus. He started moving quickly across the rubble.

"Reist is dead; I felt it. Daxxe may still be here!"

The whole group converged cautiously towards the back corner. The building fell in such a way that high piles of broken concrete, interlaced with steel supports, staggered about the foundation, creating a virtual maze. They moved cautiously, ready to strike if necessary.

Bray stopped abruptly and turned to the others.

He stood between two piles of rubble, looking down at a large hole. Reist's body was lying at the bottom amongst shattered bricks and mortar. From the look of it, the ground collapsed under him, swallowing him and parts of the building. The large iron cross that once stood high on top of the Cathedral followed him down, severing his throat and separating his head from the rest of his body. The massive weight of the iron cross and its stone mounting only needed a little extra weight to exceed what the floor could support. It all came to rest in church's basement.

Viktor turned away when a recollection of his memory struck him.

"Wait, Reist may not have perished in vain."

"What do you mean?" asked Damok.

"What did he fall into? This is outside of the perimeter of the building. There shouldn't be anything but bedrock here."

Mekune jumped into the air and shot through the hole. After a moment, he floated back to ground level.

"It's a tunnel, from the looks of it, but it's sealed on both ends by fragments of the collapsed walls. It seems to run in that direction from here."

Mekune pointed his finger to the northwest. Viktor was the last to jump through the opening, disappearing seconds before a police car rolled past on the street. The entire area was sealed off to keep curious people from getting into it and from getting hurt.

Mekune walked past Reist's body to check the west end of the cavern-like area, the corpse already shrunken to less than half its original size. He almost reached maturity, but he served their cause well.

They started chipping away at the rubble, being careful not to bring anything else down on top of themselves. Damok moved a chunk of concrete near the ceiling, and a rush of cool, musty air ran over him.

"I found it! This passage must be how he got out of here."

"We'll try to clear it before dawn," added Viktor. "He may get another day ahead of us, but we don't know where this leads or how far it goes. I'll report to Trokar. Keep digging." He flew through the hole into the night air, bound for the subway terminal.

ChAPTER ThiRTY-SIX

Daxxe started towards the door of the small chapel and almost fell to the floor, catching himself on the back of one of the pews. A sharp crack echoed off of the walls, but the pew managed to stay intact under the crushing force of his weight.

"You're hurt a lot worse than you're letting on!"

"Yes, I am, but I will heal, in time."

"How do you expect to face them like this? They'll kill you for sure!"

"You're starting to sound like Jamat."

"I didn't mean…" Angela cut her words short. She didn't mean to bring up any painful memories.

"It's alright." She helped him move around the end of the pew to sit down, noticing a spot on his side that looked severely swollen. She chose not to chastise him for reading her thoughts.

"What can I do to help? I can't leave you like this."

Daxxe looked directly at her, his expression somewhat puzzled.

"Okay, I let the first one slide, but I asked you not to do that."

She paced back and forth in the row between the two pews. Daxxe had yet to speak.

"Okay, here it is. I want to help you, I really do, but I can't just leave my life. I have goals, and friends that will miss me. I'm…"

"Afraid." He interrupted. "You have always kept yourself in control of your life, living with a purpose in mind and making well thought out decisions. You know what you are doing, and you know how to get the others things you want from life. Or do you? A part of you has always wanted to break away, and that part has grown stronger as you've gone through life. Now, it even has a voice, but you don't want to listen to it."

Angela started to object, but she held her tongue.

How can I argue with someone that really knows what I'm thinking? He's right. I am afraid.

"What do you have to fear?"

"I don't know. The unknown, I guess. What if I make a choice now and it turns out to be the wrong one?"

"How can you truly live if you spend your time fretting over things that haven't happened yet? Risk is just another facet of life."

"I…I need time to think."

"Very well, but it will be light soon. At dawn I will become stone. If you are here at dusk when I wake, it is because you decided to stay. If you are gone, I will be able to find you and protect the knowledge I have shared."

She looked a little cross back at him, getting a little defensive. "And how can you keep me from saying anything when you're here 'stoned'."

"Because one of the spells I cast on you earlier won't let you share it. If you try to tell someone, they will hear mindless gibberish. If you try to write it, you will only make illegible scribbles."

"You did WHAT?" But her retort was too late. The sun's rays came through the upper windows of the small church that had not been boarded over. Daxxe's body went rigid, and Angela suddenly felt very much alone, her anger gone as quickly as it arrived.

She sat on the pew, watching him, half expecting him to grin or something, until she realized he was truly stone. Without his presence, she felt more afraid. Her mind told her it was the perfect time to leave, but her feet wouldn't respond. The feelings that slept in her for so long were now awake and demanding attention. She tried to quell the voice, but it would not be silenced. The harder she tried to convince herself she shouldn't let go of what she knew, what she could control, the more she yearned to break away.

She spent most of the day pacing the small chapel. She made it as far as the door many times, but she could not convince herself pass through it. She tried to blame her thought process on some kind of influence that Daxxe held over her, but deep down she knew her actions, and the decision, were completely hers. Her thoughts turned more to trying to figure out how to avoid some of the fallout that would surely follow if she didn't return.

She checked her watch. It was about an hour before sunset and she realized there was something she must do. She went to the small office located just inside the front doors and dug through the old rotten desk until she found what she needed. She wrote sloppily, but she was in too big a hurry to worry over penmanship.

Twenty minutes later, she slipped out of the church and headed directly for the nearest neighborhood. She had little time, but she knew she had to try or she would never be able to live with herself. She breezed in and out of a small neighborhood grocery that displayed a blue eagle on a white backing in the window.

By her watch, she reentered the church's chapel with just over ten minutes to spare. She was out of breath from sprinting whenever possible to get back in time. It took longer trying to avoid being seen, or at least absolutely noticed, by anyone. She resumed her pacing, waiting and trying to ease the renewed concerns and to warm her painfully cold hands.

Am I making the right decision? What's gotten into you Girl? Are you crazy, or are you crazy? Nope, you are totally insane! This is just some wild dream that you'll wake up from and laugh. What would Orin think? Wait, who's...

She pinched herself just to make sure it wasn't all imagination.

Okay, so I have lost my mind. I can't believe I'm doing this! Why does this feel so right, like I've finally found what I've been searching for my whole life?

She moved back and forth over the same path repeatedly for several minutes, entirely forgetting one of her internal questions. She completely lost track of time, so totally engrossed in her struggle, that she was ignoring her outward senses.

Daxxe touched her shoulder as she passed. She practically jumped straight up, out of her skin, and only stifled the back half of her scream.

"Oh my God! Don't do that!"

"I didn't mean to startle you."

Daxxe took his hand off of her shoulder.

"Per our arrangement, you are still hear. Are you ready?"

"No, but I don't think it will get any better."

"You'll be fine, and you'll need this."

He handed her Jamat's amulet. The look on her face indicated she was unsure, but she still took it. She held it in her open palm, gazing into the jewel held within a gilded lattice of thick metal. She could see her reflection in the tiny facets, and although afraid, she could see a sense of peace in her reflected expression. She closed her hand and gripped the medallion tightly, physically admitting her resolve. She nodded yes, struggling to keep her arms from trembling.

"Place the amulet around your neck. Adjust the length of the chain so the medallion hangs directly in front of your heart."

Angela did as she was told, although her attention focused solely on the amulet. She didn't realize Daxxe was speaking until she looked up at him again, but she had not processed anything he said. In that instant, he clasped his hands together and pointed at the amulet.

A burst of bright blue energy encircled his hands and shot from his fingers like a bullet of light. The blast struck the amulet, causing the gem to glow brightly. The energy arced out of the medallion and coursed all over Angela's body, captive lightning. The bolts grew brighter and more frequent rapidly, and starting to pulse.

Everything suddenly stopped, her motion, her breathing, even the beating of her heart. She panicked, unsure and scared of what was happening as the power surged through her. Her nerves felt as though they were on fire, burning out of control. Her vision blurred until she could see nothing but bright blue light, succumbing and slipping away from reality. Everything went completely dark, and she couldn't hear or feel anything either.

Am I dead?

Her body rose from the floor, face up, in a prone position. Her senses returned as another bolt of energy erupted from the floor beneath her and struck her suspended body, forcing her eyes open, and her mouth in silent scream. She closed her eyes and tried to push back the pain that was slowly building within her. Her nerve endings were on the verge of giving up under the strain, but the flow kept coming.

She opened her eyes again, shrieking aloud now, and the same blue energy shot out of her mouth and eyes like spotlight-sized lasers, scorching the places she looked upon. The energy pulsed into her suspended body faster and harder than what escaped her eyes and mouth, until she was no longer visible within the aura. As quickly as it came, the energy flashed out of existence and was gone. Her limp body slowly lowered to the floor, hanging deathly still.

Daxxe watched from a distance and waited for her to regain consciousness.

She arched her back and grabbed her chest, sucking in air as if it were her last breath. The gasp forced its way down her throat, inflating her lungs audibly. She fell back to the floor, still clutching her chest and breathing very hard and irregularly. She rolled onto her right side and drew her knees up to her chest, writhing in pain. Daxxe approached her and helped her into a sitting position. Her gulps of air slowed and became more even. She managed to speak between gasps.

"Holy shit! That f'ing hurts." She was rocking back and forth slightly, blinking her eyes, trying to see more than a blue glow.

"It will pass, and as the pain leaves you it will leave behind the things that you need."

"Why didn't you tell me what was going to happen? I so want to kick your ass right now!"

"You would have changed your mind."

Daxxe fashioned a crude bed for her out of cushion pieces from the pews.

"Rest, you'll feel better soon. Every nerve and muscle in your body is now prepared to accept the flow of magic, and those conduits have been significantly strengthened. The process can be...difficult."

He helped her to the makeshift bed and supported her weight as she dropped to her knees. She stretched out but didn't want to sleep. She needed to know what just happened, and why, and what was next. She couldn't manage to voice her questions as her thoughts slowed. She felt very sleepy and couldn't keep her eyes open.

He secured the church and left her to rest. She would be safe until he returned.

Daxxe moved rooftop to rooftop, scouting the area to avoid overexerting himself. He still needed to allow himself to heal. He felt eyes follow him as he traveled, but he didn't let his predator know of his awareness. He wanted to gain the advantage, and he sensed he wasn't in the company of one of his usual foes.

Luigi followed Daxxe at a distance with the help of newly modified night vision goggles. He waited in the cold for a few hours, patience being one of his virtues, until fate rewarded the hunter.

Daxxe swooped down past a rooftop, breaking Luigi's line of sight. Not having the chance to place radar beacons in this area beforehand, the hitman double timed to catch up. The open air beside the skyscraper held nothing but falling snow.

Damn! He barely sidestepped in time to avoid the full brunt of the attack and his instincts took over. He rolled to one knee and found his feet again, only to discover that his attacker was gone without a trace.

"What is your quarrel, human?" seemed to come from everywhere at once.

Luigi stood motionless, not answering, trying to locate the voice's source. He could not determine a direction to pursue.

"I know you can hear me, human. Why do you follow me?"

"I have a name."

"Very well, human, then you can call me Daxxe, and you are?"

"Luigi, and to answer your other question, you can lead me to what I seek."

"What you seek will lead you to an untimely end."

"I can handle myself."

"And pride will get you to that end even faster."

"Show yourself!"

"Why do you need to see me again?"

Again?

Luigi pressed one of the buttons on the goggles, switching to the computer generated three-layer perspective. The new view stacked night vision with thermographic and the sonar derived three-dimensional display. He saw Daxxe's outline just before impact, but he didn't have the time to get out of the way.

Daxxe grabbed the back of the harness Luigi wore, carrying him into the air. His sniper rifle fell to the snowy rooftop and his arms were forced into a vulnerable position by the harness itself, pulled up in a full nelson.

"I don't think you understand what you're getting yourself into," explained Daxxe as he shot through the cold air.

Luigi tried to reach the holstered pistol, but the harness didn't allow him a wide enough range of movement in his current position. Daxxe clenched his fist, tightening the straps across the back of his hand and across Luigi's chest until they broke. He fell, flailing in the blowing snow, landing hard on something solid that was very close beneath him.

"Now we can talk."

Daxxe's voice again came from a distance, and the direction of the speaker was still undetermined.

Luigi found himself atop the torch on the Statue of Liberty. Daxxe stood atop the statue's head, holding Luigi's harness and his balance of weapons.

"You will not win the fight you are so intent to start, but I respect the reasons behind your actions. You got a lucky shot the first time. That kind of luck won't last."

"How do you...?"

"Know about Tracey. I know more than you can imagine. I don't approve of your course in life, but I know you are honorable none the less, which is why I'd like to propose a truce."

"Why would I make a deal with you?"

"We fight the same enemy. Why should we waste our time and effort fighting each other? Not to mention that Tracey could die if we don't come to a resolution."

Luigi assessed his situation before responding. "I'm listening."

"All you have to do is stay out of the fight. Too many have died already. I can ensure Tracey's survival."

"That conflicts with a prior commitment."

"No, it doesn't. Trass wants Tracey alive, and he wants to know what happened to her. I can make sure she lives, and you already know what happened to her by getting this far."

"And what exactly will I tell Deacon?"

"Tell him the truth. He trusts you implicitly, and he will believe you. Agreed?"

Luigi grit his teeth, annoyed and reluctant.

"Very well, but so help me, if Tracey doesn't make it, I'll hunt you to the ends of the earth."

"I'm sure you would try. Now, the deal is sealed, as you humans would say."

Luigi suddenly felt very nauseated and dizzy as he blacked out and fell from the statue.

Luigi woke up sitting in the front seat of his SUV. The phone rang a few seconds later.

"Yes."

"Luigi, it's Deacon."

"Yes, sir."

"Tracey woke up about an hour ago. She's going to be okay."

"Perfect. I'm already headed that way."

Angela woke with a start, tightly clutching the cloak draped over her as though it were a shield. She felt very strange, like she was looking at herself in the mirror and seeing a reflection that wasn't her own. She felt different, but she didn't know exactly why.

"How do you feel?"

"I'm not sure. I mean…I don't know how to explain it. I feel…"

"Different?"

"Yes, I guess different is the best word for it. Why?"

"You feel that way because you are different, to an extent. You are aware of the parts of your being you never used before. Your power is now available to you, although I must teach you how to use it."

"How so?"

412

Daxxe picked up the sword, extending the blade towards Angela, close enough for her to touch it.

"Test the sharpness of the blade."

"What?"

"Run your finger down the blade lightly to test its sharpness."

Angela reached for the blade as she was told, pulling her hand back Daxxe twisted the edge, cutting her forearm to the bone at the wrist."

"AGGH!" she screamed. "What the f…? Oh my God, oh my God!"

"Now, fix it."

"What?!? How?!?" He set the sword down as she closed her other hand over the wound, applying pressure and reeling with pain.

"Fix the cut."

"How do I do that?" she yelled at him, dropping to her knees, watching blood drip from her arm.

"Look at the cut and concentrate on the cut not being there."

Angela released her pressure and turned her hand upwards, blood running down to her palm, over her fingers, dripping to the floor, increasing the size of the puddle. Daxxe spoke before she could voice her question.

"Don't worry about the how, you may not always have the time to ponder such things. Concentrate. Focus the power you can now feel."

Angela looked at the cut, hoping it would stop bleeding. The cut tingled a little, but the blood kept coming.

"You do not have to hope. You are in control! Close the wound!"

Angela looked at her arm, pushing the doubt and fear from her mind, dispelling the ill feelings brought on by the sight of her own blood, what he did to her and his impatience, willing the wound to close. The tingling sensation returned, but much stronger than before, and the bleeding stopped. She wiped her wrist clean, almost in disbelief of what she saw nothing. Her wrist was undamaged, just as it was before he cut her. She looked at Daxxe, shocked and amazed.

"That was your first two lessons. You cannot underestimate yourself. That wound would have been was mortal for someone without your gift."

413

"And that is my gift, healing?"

"One of them. Your line, from the beginning of this earth, possesses them. You've had the ability since you were born, you just didn't know it."

"And the second lesson?" she asked as she rose to her feet, really wanting to punch him square in the face, but unsure if it would break her hand.

"Thinking under pressure. A nick on your finger isn't serious enough to trigger a fight or flight response. You kept yourself in control and mastered the fear. You did well."

The compliment pushed her anger out of the way, clearing the way for curiosity. "What else can I do?"

"That is where you have to be careful, as that simple question is the first step into darkness. If you get too far down that path, you will never make it back."

"I didn't…" started Angela, feeling hurt again.

"I know you didn't mean to imply that, and I didn't say that to discourage you. It was only a warning. You must handle your power with responsibility or it will control you. Only use it when it is necessary to do so, with the exception of practice and training, which we need to start right away."

Angela's expression lightened slightly. During the conversation, the remnants of the pain passed. She stood up fully, suffering a slight wave of dizziness, but it passed quickly.

"What was that?"

"Your body underwent some physical changes. I don't know for sure how much you will easily notice since you kept yourself in good shape. The dizziness you felt comes from the increased blood flow in your body. Don't misinterpret that as heightened pressure; it's not a physical defect, it's an enhancement. You will discover your stamina is several times stronger than it was before, and you will be able to increase your physical strength much more than you'd expect as well. Now, you can ask your other questions while you work. Here."

Daxxe handed Angela the broadsword that Jamat once carried, holding it by the blade so she could accept it between the pommel and the hilt.

"It feels lighter than it did before."

"That's because you're stronger than you were before. How does it feel in your hand?"

"Like it fits, no, that's not quite right...like it belongs there. It has an amazing balance, and it feels normal holding it. Is that weird?" She moved the sword deftly through a type of training maneuver that she had never done before, but it felt like she had for her entire life. "Yeah, that's weird."

"Prepare to defend yourself."

"What?!"

Daxxe advanced with a long wooden staff. She didn't take the time to wonder where the staff came from, she only reacted, which included moving backwards, tripping over the edge of a pew, and landing flat on her back, dropping her weapon in the process. The end of Daxxe's staff was less than an inch from her nose. He lowered the weapon and backed to his original position.

"Again."

"Wait, what are you doing? What the hell am I supposed to do? I don't know how to use this."

Daxxe advanced again, without warning or answer. Angela brought the sword up, splitting the staff in two. Daxxe reacted, swinging the two halves inward, striking both sides of her sword hand simultaneously, just hard enough to force the sword from her hand without permanent damage, as she cried out. He returned to his starting position a second time.

"Again."

Angela looked up, tears ready to fall from the pain. She could tell by the look in his eyes that he held no sympathy for her, yet he paused from her look of distress.

"An attacker will not relent until you are dead. You do not have to be perfect, but you do have to remember to think on your feet, like you did with the gash in your arm. You have reason to trust me, so there is no flight response this time, but you still have to be able to react correctly on instinct. You already have everything you need to protect yourself. Again."

chapter Thrity-seven

"Jamison, here's the hard copy from Scotland Yard."

Joshua Stone surrendered the report.

"Good, let's get Joe and the rest of the team in the meeting room. I want everyone briefed on this and everything that's happened in the last twenty-four hours. I want someone from Dr. Palmer's office here, too.

Within fifteen minutes, key personnel gathered for the meeting. Angela's seat was the only one that remained empty. Bishop stood to call the meeting to order.

"Okay people, let's get started. We need to get through this and get back out there. I want you all to know that I appreciate all of your efforts out there and here at the HQ."

Bishop gave the helm to the Commissioner.

"I'd like to offer my thanks as well. I wanted you all here so we can try to make some headway in this case. I've checked over all the blotters and logs this morning and I'm not seeing new cases linked to our killers. This makes me nervous, considering they still have the upper hand. It doesn't make sense that they would just stop what they are doing. What's going on out there?"

The group sat in silence. No one had an answer.

"Okay. We do have some new evidence. I'll let Detective Stone give you the details."

Joshua went to the podium.

"We think we know why the group has concentrated in the warehouse district, as it appears they are looking for something. The trail led us across the Atlantic to Stockholm, Sweden. After the murders stopped there, and before they started here, we could only find one common denominator. This link is a man named Alfred Sayer. His name has turned up very close to this case and his travel across Europe followed the killer's path almost exactly.

"Just before his transatlantic trip took place, he attended an auction for high-end antiquities. He only bid on one item, and the nature of the bid is what caught the attention of the locals. He opened with an offer roughly six times that of the opening price and no one else even tried to bid. His purchase was a book that held very high value for him, which appears to be what our killers seek."

"What's so special about a book?" asked Officer Davis.

"Well, we can't confirm what this book is about, but Sayer paid $1.7 million for it. According to the auction's director, the crowd was in absolute shock over the offer, as it was much higher than the book's estimated worth. He mentioned he distinctly remembered Sayer for two other reasons as well. One, he walked out of the auction carrying the book like a schoolboy carries a textbook, without any escort and without any apparent caution for the purchase. Two, he paid cash."

A few low whistles came from the audience.

"From what we've learned, Sayer personally transported this book by land and sea only, destined for New York. He used Thornquist shipping affiliates because they apparently developed the need to avoid customs before they went belly up. We have no idea why he seemed so overly concerned about the volume at this point. Mr. Sayer met his demise somewhere in the Irish Sea, but the book was not found with his body. The charter he used had a one-night stop in Dublin before it set out for New York. That ship arrived in the states, on schedule at Pier 23, with the book onboard, but no Sayer. It, along with the other freight, was received, seized, and inventoried by authorities upon arrival in accordance with the bankruptcy proceedings. All of the crates were locked up and stored. Any guesses as to where?"

"It's got to be the warehouse that caught fire a few nights ago?"

"Exactly. No employment records of any kind can be found for Sayer, so we can only assume he was working for them, or someone, under the table. The other thing we can't figure out is exactly why he was killed or why the book wasn't taken. His body was partially dismembered, making us believe our lovely group did it, but we now believe he was a courier for the killers."

"Maybe they're just covering their tracks," came from someone in the group.

"We thought about that, too, but why would they kill him like the others? That would essentially confirm they crossed the Atlantic for anyone that knew what to look for."

"Good question," added Jamison. "That's something else we'll have to figure out."

"We're also trying to track down Alan Thornquist for questioning. We haven't been able to find him as of yet, but he had several meetings with Sayer prior to the auction. He may have answers to a lot of our questions."

"What about the bodies that were dumped on our steps a couple of days ago?" asked Temple.

"They both appear to be homeless citizens. We're planning to pull Gianelli back in for the ID since he seems to know a lot of the street people in that area. Luckily it hasn't happened again, and the number of bodies we're finding seems to be tapering off. Do you see that trend in the ME's office as well Dr. Murphy?"

"Yes, it appears to be the same on our end, but that depends on when the bodies are found. We still haven't discovered any medical explanation for this group of killers, which means we haven't figured out any weaknesses from that front."

"Thank you, Dr. Murphy. The other possibility we have to consider is that they may have found what they wanted and are moving on. If they have what they want, they may be about to disappear again. If that happens, the city may be safe, but we may never be able to stop them somewhere new."

The Commissioner leaned forward to speak again.

"I also wanted to update you all on Detective Benson. We have very little to go on, and what we have is highly classified. I can tell you she is currently hospitalized. If you have any questions, please refer them to Joe individually after the briefing. That information is on a strict need to know basis. Dismissed."

Most of the officers filed out of the room. Three remained behind to talk to Joe and he gave them all the information about her whereabouts.

Jamison approached Joe after the last officer cleared the room.

"How did it go?"

"Here's a list of what I told to whom. That was pretty hard to do. I found myself wanting to believe she's not out there somewhere. Does IT have the phone system ready?"

"Yes, I just need to… I need to get them this list. We don't know how fast this guy works."

"Yes."

"Tell Trokar I know where the girl is."

"And where would that be?"

"She's in Room 317 at the St. Barnabas Hospital, under twenty-four-hour surveillance."

"You're a bit late."

"What do you mean?"

"We followed her to St. Francis two days ago. Quite a remarkable recovery, wouldn't you say?"

The line went dead as Viktor hung up. Officer Temple was about to leave his office when a knock sounded off the door.

"Come in."

Joe walked in and closed the door.

"Hi, Joe. What's up?"

"Is there something you'd like to tell me?"

"What do you mean? I was just calling in some flowers to be sent to Angela."

Joe reached across the desk, grabbing Temple by the shirtfront. Before Temple knew what was happening, he was flat on his back in the hallway with pieces of glass from his office door windows raining down on him and tinkling along the tile floor. Joe pulled him back to his feet before he could scramble away.

"I really don't want to ask you again, you son of a bitch!"

"Are you crazy man? What are you doing? I don't know what you're talking about!"

Jamison pressed play on a digital recorder as he approached. Temple used the interruption to break away from Joe's grasp and make a break

419

down the hall, bound for the stairs. O'Toole rounded the corner, swinging his nightstick like a baseball bat. It connected just below the neck. The abrupt force of the virtual clothesline pulled his feet out in front of him and slammed him to the floor flat on his back. The air exploded from his lungs and his head bounced with a sharp thud. He writhed in pain, unable to find his voice with all the air knocked from his lungs.

Joe bent down over him and pulled him to his feet. He planted two solid punches on his left side, level with his kidneys, forcing the little air he managed to take in back out of his lungs.

O'Toole and Jamison stationed themselves at each end of the hall, closing the fire doors so Joe wouldn't be interrupted and no one else in the building would see what happened.

"I'm not playing with you. You can talk, or you can leave in a body bag. Who the hell is Trokar?"

Temple said nothing, but he wouldn't look at Joe straight on. Three more punches to the stomach doubled him over. Joe brought him back upright by grabbing his face and slamming the back of his head into the wall. A drop of blood escaped the corner of his mouth and his head started to spin. The extended lack of oxygen made him very light-headed.

"This will only get worse the longer you refuse to cooperate."

"If I say anything, he'll kill me."

"Who will kill you?"

"Trokar."

"Is that his stage name or something?"

Temple looked shocked and confused, but maintained his sarcasm. "Yeah, he's got a one-man show on Broadway, four nights a week." He tried to keep from grinning.

Joe rapid fired four more punches, two low to the stomach and two high to the face. A thick stream of blood poured from his now broken nose.

"Lying to me is a really bad decision for you right now, and you can see I'm in no mood for humor."

"I don't know…who he is. I've…never met him." Temple coughed, spitting blood. "I give him the information that we know and I get a lot of money for it. That's all there is to it."

His voice was slightly slurred. He spit a bloody, broken tooth that was affecting his speech. He looked very pale as the last of his attitude left him.

"Do you know how many officers and civilians were hurt or killed? That lunatic could have Angela right now!"

Joe lost count of how many more times he hit the turncoat. His anger wasn't being vented as the punches maintained his ire. He felt at least three ribs crack under the barrage. Temple lost consciousness before Joe was too worn to exert any more force. Joe dragged his unconscious body to the end of the hall and cuffed him to the base of the radiator that was bolted to the floor. His next stop was the rest room to wash the blood off of his hands, then the command room.

"Have we found our leak?" asked Jamison.

"One of them, but I'm not positive he was the only one. I don't think this Trokar is doing this to be in the spotlight either. I've got a hunch that he's doing this for the sole pleasure of the act."

Joe's cell beeped, alerting him to a text message. The number was one of the extensions within the department's phone network. He looked at the face and read the displayed info.

"7402? Who is that?"

"It's IT."

"I think we've lost our informant."

"Why is that?"

"He called a few minutes ago to tell us about the woman helping Daxxe. He said she's been hospitalized since she disappeared, but we know that isn't the case. Someone must have been on to him."

"It's a small matter. We've created enough confusion to keep them busy for a while. They know about us, but they can't do anything about us. Have you found Daxxe?"

"Not yet. I've sent the others to follow his trail. I don't imagine he's gotten very far. Even if the woman is helping him, it will slow him down having to worry about more than just his own head."

"Has there been any word on Sayer?"

"Not yet," returned Viktor.

"I guess it makes no difference. I have what I paid for. His loyalty and service will have no value anymore in a few days."

Trokar turned to his book, indicating that the conversation was over.

"This is Anderson, what have you got?"

"We recorded another call about a minute ago. It looks like Officer Raymond Gowan placed a call to WJNY, relaying the bogus information to some woman, but her name wasn't spoken. I can safely say this isn't a money deal, and I think there are laws against me playing what they said to each other out loud. Suffice it to say that they're using a barter system."

"Got it, thanks."

Joe hung up the phone and started down the hall.

"It looks like we found the other one. Let's get to Gowan's office before he leaves. He's leaking classified info to the press in exchange for favors."

"Who's the accessory?"

"IT didn't get her name, but it doesn't matter. This should help curb the panic the media keeps creating."

Jamison trailed Joe down the hall. They decided to take the elevator instead of climbing four flights of stairs. Joe was still tired from reeducating Officer Temple on the dynamics of Departmental operating procedures.

When the doors opened on the sixth floor, Gowan was waiting to ride to the parking garage. He boarded the elevator, saying hello to both Joe and Jamison before turning around to face the doors and press the button labeled "B".

"Going down?" asked Joe.

chapter thirty-eight

Daxxe lunged forward, swinging both halves of the staff at Angela, one low and one high. Angela jumped, flipping backwards and landing on her feet on the back of one the pews, perfectly balanced.

"Good!"

Daxxe advanced as he spoke.

She turned and used the backs of the pews as stepping stones to run across, moving at an angle across the rows. She looked over her shoulder to find no one there.

Damn! She looked around for him, trying to keep from getting surprised. The chapel was very dark, and the gray glow from the winter sky provided very little light. She dropped to the floor and rolled underneath one of the pews. The seats were high enough off the floor to allow her to shuffle quietly towards the corner of the chapel, trying to improve her defensive position.

Daxxe grabbed her around the recently healed wrist and lifted her off of the floor. She screamed, and then flushed with embarrassment for the outburst. The red in her cheeks held out of anger.

"Don't be too hard on yourself. You're improvising under pressure; that's good. You also considered my physical advantage of flight and tried to prevent me from using it, also very good." He gently lowered her to the floor and released her.

"I don't like to lose."

"That's also a very good thing, but it's a double-edged sword. Like your power, misdirected pride can destroy you as well."

Angela took the constructive criticism with grace, realizing he wasn't reprimanding her, just using exaggeration to teach.

"It is of the utmost importance that you know your enemy. That knowledge cannot be absolute, but that cannot be helped. Observing patience to watch an adversary can be the difference between victory and defeat, and as in all things, 'the best offense is a good defense'."

He motioned for her to sit, pulling a small loaf of bread, a block of cheese, and a piece of roasted beef from the knapsack. Angela started to ask where it came from, but decided she didn't really need to know.

"The opponents you will face in the future are more complex than the ones you're accustomed to facing as a police officer. Like me, they can rely on senses besides sight to see you and they can read your thoughts. With practice, you will be able to close your mind to them, but it's a vulnerability you need to be aware of in the meantime. Remember what happened in the catacombs, when you could see me in pitch-black darkness? That will help you more than you can predict or imagine."

Daxxe paused to eat his half of the simple meal.

"Will I be able to keep you out my head, too?" She grinned a little and cocked her head to the side.

"Yes," he said without looking up.

"How will I protect you against them?"

"With luck, you won't have to. I don't usually let my guard down, and they can only attack when it's dark. You'll have to deal with other mortals for the most part. Trokar likes to use what he calls familiars. They are people who are not infected with the disease, but they are convinced they want to be vampires. They act like henchmen, more like go-fors, hoping their loyalty will be repaid by being turned. They can be anyone, anywhere. You may have already met some of them and didn't know it. You have to be on watch constantly."

"Is there anything distinguishing about these familiars?"

"No, not anymore. Trokar used to put a brand on his, but he soon discovered they were much safer left anonymous. There aren't any consistent patterns or traits among them of which I'm aware, and obviously the biggest threat they pose is relaying information. You must always be cautious of what you do and say around those you don't know, and sometimes those you think you know."

Angela listened while she looked at the amulet she wore, noticing the gem set into its face turned from a deep orange to a dark, but vibrant purple.

"What's happening to it?"

"It's adapting to you. It is of the utmost importance that you always wear it. I can find you through it, and it helps magnify your power."

"So I don't have to have it for my powers to work?"

"No, it only amplifies that which you already possess. It makes the magic much stronger, but it also helps make it easier to use and control. You will need to learn how to bind it to you so it can't be taken away. By the way, we also need to get you more suitable clothing for your service."

Angela looked down at what she now considered her favorite tattered business outfit. The fabric was covered with dirt and stains, and small tears peppered the fabric. She looked up, grinning.

"You don't like it? And here I thought the dumpster-diving-executive look was in this season."

"It provides you no protection from attack, and it limits your movement."

"Can't you whip up something in that head of yours? I don't think I can run out to Bloomingdale's pick up something new if I'm supposed to be dead."

He gave her a smirk as he finished eating and put the food away. "Stand up and be still."

Daxxe backed a few feet away, chanting words Angela never heard before and could not speak, but she understood what he was saying. It was like hearing a foreign language you didn't know, but understanding what was said anyway.

"From the power held within, make this body a second skin. Light as air, hard as rock, strong attacks it must block." He moved his fingers in the arm before him, tracing patterns into the air. The path of his fingers started to manifest into something visible.

Angela resisted fidgeting and squirming because it felt like tiny bugs crawled all over here. She glanced down, seeing her clothes changing before her eyes.

"Forge the points with the strongest ore, fire from the very core. Start the shade of the deepest blues, changing as the wearer choose. Protect the feet from below and help with fleet when she decides to go. For the head, the strongest helm, to hold away wind, water, and spell. On the hands, gauntlets make, the movement not to take. Bind with cloth that will not tear to protect the skin oh so fair. Cloak the armor as a shroud, from without allow no sound."

The tingling intensified as the suit continued to metamorphosize. The sigil floating in the air before Daxxe flew into Angela, hitting the breastplate of her new clothing as it took its final shape. She felt it meld with the armor and seal tightly against her skin. It was snug, but not too tight, much like a wetsuit. A hooded robe covered her, the hem almost touching the ground.

"That was quite an experience."

Angela opened the robe, took it off, and hung it over one of the pews at a place she wiped clean, looking at the new wardrobe underneath. He body, from the groin to her shoulders was encased in a dark blue armor, shaped exactly to her body. She could wear other clothes over it and no one would be able to tell it was there. Her boots had a thick, textured sole, with armor covering the top of her foot and her legs from the knees down, and an extra piece flared up in front of her kneecap to protect the joint. Her thighs were not armored, but a black, metal-like cloth covered her skin. The backs of her hands and fingers had the same blue armor, and her forearms were covered as well with vambraces of the same hue. The same black metal mesh ran underneath everywhere. The helm covered her entire face, except for directly over her eyes and mouth, with a nose guard allowing unhindered breathing. The helmet sides dropped down on the edges to provide protection for her neck. A harness, mounted across her back, accepted the broadsword she inherited from Jamat perfectly. She sheathed it, discovering the sword and the harness seemed to interpret her thoughts, and the sword felt light as a feather. In the sheath, the broadsword's handle rested just below her shoulder, completely concealed by the cloak. When she reached back to draw the blade, she felt the blade slide up to meet her hand.

"Do you approve?" he asked.

"Yes, and I love the color. This will be the rage this spring. What did you mean about the color when you spoke the spell, uh, incantation...what's the right word?"

"Incantation. You understood my words?"

"Yes, and no. I have never heard those words, and I know I couldn't speak them, but I still understood. It was like having a universal translator from a sci-fi movie."

"That is excellent. You are adapting to your gifts faster than even I imagined you would. Go to the mirror by the entrance and look at yourself."

427

Angela did as she was told, amazed at how easily she could walk and move. It felt as if she wasn't wearing anything, the armor seeming to have no weight at all and it moved with her. She could feel the air moving over her skin, yet it didn't affect her temperature, she just felt it. She was almost startled by her reflection when she first saw it, looking strong and fierce. She thought she saw a slight blue glow in her own eyes, but it was gone after she blinked. She leaned closer to the mirror.

"Wow!"

Did I just…

"Close your eyes and imagine that you don't want to be seen."

"Okay."

"Open your eyes."

Angela gasped and reached out to touch the mirror. She could see her arm, but she had no reflection in the mirror. She could see Daxxe standing directly behind her as if she wasn't even standing there. She blinked and could see herself again in the mirror.

"What just happened?"

"The armor is enchanted. It can take on whatever appearance you choose. I want you to have every advantage possible."

"Because I'm a girl?" she asked, teasing and a little agitated at the same time.

"Because I didn't think Jamat would need it and you saw where it got him."

"I'm sorry, I didn't…" she offered as he turned away from him slightly.

"It's alright. You forget that I can sense your thoughts. I know what you meant. Now, back to the armor."

Angela could sense Daxxe's desire to change the subject. She realized she hurt him, even though she didn't intend to. She made a mental note to keep from making that mistake again.

"The armor will react the way you want it to, but you must keep it in your mind."

"I showed back up in the mirror because I lost my concentration, right?"

"Excellent. You will always be able to see yourself; it is your appearance to others that is altered. It is a good defense, but don't rely on it completely. As I said, our enemies have other means of seeing. Now, we must continue your training. You will learn much more as we go."

"Trokar has undoubtedly discovered I am still alive, which means they'll be looking for me. He needs the last book and he knows I have it."

"If he knows, why didn't he take it when he got the Book of Chaos?"

"He didn't know it then. Once four of the books are together, they can provide the location of the fifth, assuming the person possessing the Books knows the spell. Trokar knows."

"How long do we have?"

"Not very, but more than you probably realize. I am very skilled in the arts. I cannot control the flow of time, but I can expand and compress it."

"I don't understand."

"How long would you say it's been since we left St. Francis?"

"It's been about 24 hours. It was night when I woke up and it's the next night now."

"Twenty-four hours have passed for us, but not by the clock. I've been controlling the spell since last night, which takes a considerable amount of energy. That's part of the reason I'm healing so slowly."

"Wouldn't someone notice that?"

"Have you ever had nights of really good sleep, and other nights that it seems like your head never hit the pillow? Or days that drag so slowly it hurts, while others feel like they are over before they began? Mortals explain the day going by very fast or very slow as their own perception, but it happens because the flow of time is being altered."

"Everyone feels that way at one time or another, but you are saying the magic is what makes that happen? No one can tell the difference?"

"Very good, you are a quick study. Now, no more questions, prepare yourself."

"For…"

Daxxe's kick hit Angela squarely in the chest, hurling her over the pews and into the wall, leaving a dent in the sheetrock from the impact. Angela couldn't find her breath, but it wasn't because of the blow. The attack caught her completely off guard, jarring her body, but leaving her unhurt. She looked up, seeing Daxxe bear down on her. She rolled to the right, barely making it out of the way. She could tell that he wasn't pulling his punches anymore.

Daxxe turned to find the church empty.

"Ah, deception."

Daxxe looked around the church, but he didn't see her. He backed down the row at the end of the pews, keeping his back towards the wall.

"You're doing well, and you've realized we can't see each other unless we're within line of sight. Controlling the situation by keeping the defensive is good strategy."

Daxxe moved into a shadow and disappeared. Angela dared a quick glance, not even a second long, tracking her trainer as he moved around the church, keeping the altar between them.

I can't stay here much longer. The church is small, he'll find me soon.

She looked around. The stands for the choir spanned the wall behind the altar, and the passage leading to the stands stood directly behind it. When Daxxe reached the back of the church, she made her move, staying out of sight. She kept low, making it through the doorway, and entering a hallway running under the right end of the stands. She went to the right, waiting to get the jump on him when he passed. A blow to the small of her back sent her to the floor. Daxxe stood behind her.

"Always be aware of your surroundings."

Angela rolled backwards, pulling her legs up to gain momentum. At the point her feet were directly above her, she pressed against the floor will all her strength, adding speed and direction to the thrust. She landed in a fighting stance, facing Daxxe, about fifteen feet down the hall. She tried to keep from grinning with the amazement she felt at actually pulling off a move like that.

Nikola followed directly behind Mekune, rapidly losing patience.

"How long have we been in this tunnel?"

The question, his fourth thus far, irritated Mekune.

"I lose track."

They followed the tunnel with Damok, Nikola, and Tira, searching below ground for over five hours. The path they followed was not very long, but it branched off, going in two directions, leading to more tunnels and turning into a complex labyrinth of passages. The walls were solid rock, looking as if they were cut by hand, but no markings designated the tunnels from each other. The only way they could successfully traverse the maze would require a map that they didn't have.

Damok held Mekune back, letting the distance between them and the others grow.

"Where the hell are we?"

"I don't know."

"It will be dawn soon."

"I know. We'll be fine. These tunnels must lead somewhere, but the light won't reach us."

"What about the others? I can feel Nikola's need to feed."

"They'll just have to learn, and they need to know how long they can go without food anyway. I'm thinking we should split up to cover more ground. Daxxe is probably weakened to the verge of death, so it will be an easy kill when we find him."

Mekune passed instructions to the others, and the group split apart. He thought their search was pointless, but they'd have to answer to Trokar when they returned. They had to be sure Daxxe wasn't in the tunnels if they went back without his head on a pole.

Angela stood her ground, waiting for Daxxe to attack again. She was unsure how she could best him, so she focused on protecting herself.

Daxxe lunged as she expected. She rolled backward onto her back and planted her feet on his stomach and chest. He was heavier than she expected, but her legs held since she wasn't catching all of his weight. She nudged his momentum to steer it over her and she added a hard push with her legs. He hurtled down the hall, unable to right himself with his wings in the cramped confines of the small hallway.

She pulled her feet back down hard towards the floor and popped back up to a standing position. She turned around and took the offensive while he was still airborne, launching herself into the air and drawing her sword in mid-flight. She landed squarely on his chest with the tip of her sword at his throat.

"Do you yield?"

"I'm impressed. You're adapting well and you only made one mistake."

"What's that?"

Daxxe twisted his chest sharply, causing Angela to fall into the wall and land on the floor.

"You went for the kill instead of protecting yourself, and you were off balance."

Daxxe stood and helped Angela back to her feet. She sheathed the blade and rubbed the outside of her upper right arm.

"When you go for the killing stroke, you have to make sure you are ready and you must be able to do what is necessary. In that scenario, an adversary would be willing to do almost anything to survive. Anything could happen when death is so imminent."

"You're right. I should have remembered from my time in the department. I've seen people jump from a six-story window trying to keep from getting caught, and the fact that the fall will kill them never enters their minds."

"That's right. Now, we need to get the police to stop looking for you. Proof of your death will take some wind from their sails, and they will be able to focus only on Trokar's clan, likely with renewed fervor since they've lost one of their own."

"How should we do that? I mean…how am I going to die?"

"I've been thinking about that, and the collapse of St. Francis could work into it perfectly."

"Wait a minute, how do you know the church collapsed? We were just there yesterday or the day before…"

Angela trailed off, confused. She realized that she was not really aware of how much time had passed, and she was unsure of the extent of his abilities.

"I know because I'm the one that did it. It was close enough to the supply depot where you started to be a feasible destination, and since you wandered off before, Joe will be able to accept you doing it again. The collapse itself will go down in history as a freak accident because they won't be able to find an explanation for why it happened."

Angela nodded her head in approval. "That's good, but how did you know I wandered off from Joe before? Are you digging around in here again?" she asked, tapping her helm.

"You carry the guilt on your conscience. It stays fresh in your mind because you can't forgive yourself for doing it. I don't have to dig. I have to shield my eyes from it the way it stands out."

Angela didn't even realize it until Daxxe pointed it out, and it brought up all her other feelings about Joe. She knew he would blame himself for what happened, just like her dad did with his own family years before. She regretted that she would not be able to see him again to tell him the truth, but she started toying with an idea for the future.

"I do feel very badly about it. He's not had the best turn of luck in his life, and I'm afraid this will hurt him more than he can handle. I'm at odds with myself because I feel guilty and I'm afraid of what this will do, but I just know that this is what I'm supposed to do."

"In the words of Bertrand Russell, 'to conquer fear is the beginning of wisdom.' Unfortunately, the price of wisdom is almost always pain. I can promise you that your partner will be fine."

"How can you make a promise like that?"

"Because I intend to keep it. I've seen inside your mind, and I know Joe almost lost himself after he lost his family. He is a good man with a good heart, the kind of man your world needs right now. I will make sure that he makes it through his grief and continues to fight the good fight."

She could tell that he was telling the truth and not just trying to make her feel better. She was unsure how he could make such a bold claim, but she had seen more in the last few days that she never thought possible either. It calmed her nerves and allowed her a small respite from the tension wound up inside her.

"Thank you. Now, how do you intend to come up with a body? I'm pretty attached to mine."

"We have to make a trip to one of the city's graveyards."

"We're going steal a dead body?" She was shocked and revolted.

"Yes. It's the only place a dead body won't be missed."

"Won't they be able to tell it's not me?"

"No. I can alter the body by the same method that I fashioned your armor. It will be an exact physical copy of you when I'm finished."

"You won't have to revive her first, will you?"

"No. Once the soul leaves the body, there's nothing I can do. My powers do have limitations, as in Jamat's case. I can only do so much, and his injuries were too great. I could have brought him back, but he would have succumbed to his injuries and only endured more pain."

Angela felt bad again for inadvertently refreshing Jamat in Daxxe's mind.

"You must stop worrying about it. I cannot avoid every remembrance. I mourned his passing, and he is in a much better place now. In the end, we will be reunited."

Daxxe started for the door, asking Angela to follow. She retrieved her black cloak, drawing the hood over her head as she walked.

Mekune rounded a corner from one tunnel to another that crossed it. Damok stood about one hundred feet away.

"This is useless!"

"Yes, it is. I think we've made a complete circle, but I can't tell if this is where we started or not. Do you know the way back?"

434

"I think so. What should we do about the others?"

"Leave them. We don't have the time to look for them, and I think this was all part of Daxxe's design anyway. We've been down here for a long time and we haven't found him. It will take more time to find a way back out. Many things could have happened already."

"What should we do about Trokar?"

"I'll think about what to tell him it as we go. With luck, Daxxe already surfaced somewhere and was handled."

Mekune worked back down the tunnel, tracing his path backwards to the best of his memory. All the paths looked the same, so he lashed out at the wall by one of the corners, leaving deep cuts in the rock with his claws. He marked the walls in the same fashion at every intersection they went through, varying the marks slightly to make them unique.

chApter thirty-nine

The phone rang for the fifth time, forcing the voice mailbox to pick up the call. Denise hung up, frustrated. Where is Raymond? She needed to talk to him before the evening news and check the wire to see if anything else was reported.

Ray was an older man that never married, telling her on many occasions that he hadn't met the right one, but he still had urges he couldn't ignore. She used him several times, taking care of his urges in return for information for her exclusives, but she wanted to break it off. She felt guilty for leading him on less than half an hour earlier, and she wanted to tell him she wouldn't use anything he told her if he didn't want her to. A knock pulled her away from the news.

"Come in."

One of the station's secretaries walked into her office. Denise recognized Stephanie. She worked at the station for almost a year and she hated Denise from the beginning. Stephanie grew up believing the value of hard work. It infuriated her when her work was barely noticed and Denise could shake this or jiggle that to get anything she wanted.

Denise was quite shocked to see her. The whole station knew how Stephanie felt, even though she didn't make a habit of telling anyone. Denise was also taken aback by her expression. It was very soft and almost friendly, not defensive like usual.

"Hello Stephanie."

"Can we talk?"

"Yeah, sure."

"I wanted to apologize for the way I've treated you, and I appreciate what you are doing."

"Um, thank you, but why do you feel like you need to apologize? I've done plenty of things to deserve the resentment."

"My problems with you were on a different level."

"What do you mean?"

"Jack and I were…involved. He would come to me and complain about you. I was…jealous. I didn't know about the abuse, but I wasn't seeing the signs either."

Stephanie opened her jacket and lowered it to her elbows to expose her upper arms, revealing the splotches of deep, purple bruises, not covered by the sleeveless top.

"He said it was an accident. Thank you for pressing charges against him, or I would have suffered much more."

Denise sat silently for a moment, unsure of what to say. She never truly dealt with the abuse, instead burying it away and went on with her life. Her ambition would overpower her fear, but now, all those feelings were being pulled to the surface. Denise tried to resist the surge, but tears welled up in her eyes. Stephanie moved around the desk and gave her a hug and they both cried for a few moments, releasing the pain and fear they hid so well, and forming a bond that would only strengthen over time. They talked as Denise fixed her hair and freshened her makeup for the evening news.

She picked up the hard copy of the information from Raymond and looked at it for a few minutes. She was tempted to use it for her news cast, but she had several changes of heart lately. She fed the paper through shredder as they left her office.

chapter forty

The wind blew ferociously at Daxxe and Angela. She saw wisps of snow and sleet twist in the cold blasts of air. She could feel the cold, but she wasn't chilled by it. Her feet made no sound as she walked, and she couldn't hear the whistle of the wind as it passed, yet she could hear the snow crunch under Daxxe's feet and easily hear anything he said.

This cloak must be enchanted like my armor.

Thirty minutes of walking put them outside an ornate wrought iron fence that encircled approximately 400 acres of headstones. Angela could see a gothic style stone gatehouse farther down Jerome Avenue as Daxxe effortlessly jumped up and let the wind carry him over the boundary. Angela jumped up, getting much higher than she expected or was necessary. Whoa! How did I do that? She rolled head-over-heels and landed several feet inside the perimeter, standing next to one of the larger headstones. The snow was exceptionally deep and showed no signs of disturbance.

Daxxe trudged forward, cutting a path through the drifts to the shallower areas away from the fence. The area was dotted with several mausoleums and many large trees. Some of the trees were marked with signs identifying their age and species. The sounds of the city slowly faded away as they moved deeper and deeper on the hallowed ground.

"What are we looking for?"

"A recent burial, and pay attention to the markers; we want someone as close to your age as we can find."

They split apart to cover more ground. Searching was not very difficult, as the newest arrivals were set apart by large, snow-covered mounds of fresh dirt. Angela approached a grave near the center of the cemetery, brushing the snow off the marker to read its face.

Candice Michelle Davidson

October 8, 1982 – February 2, 2009

Remembered always, missed forever...

She couldn't see Daxxe directly, and she didn't know where he was. Daxxe, I found something. She knew he could read her thoughts, but wondered if she could project them. It would give her another tool she could use. Within a few seconds, Daxxe landed beside her.

"That's like having a built-in cell phone."

"Just be careful when you use it. Remember, they can sense your thoughts as well as I until you learn how to shield them, but we are somewhat protected by our isolation."

"I'll be careful. Is this what we need?"

"Yes, this is what we were looking for."

Daxxe started to dig. Angela helped, but her small hands didn't move much earth.

"Can't you use your magic to uncover her?"

"No, for this I cannot. The energy that fuels magic comes from within the earth itself. Using it in that way would draw the flow directly through her body. It could damage or outright destroy it. It would definitely hinder my incantation."

They continued to dig until Daxxe's nails scratched a smooth steel surface. He could tell by the color that it was the grave vault, holding the casket within.

"Stand back."

He slammed his claws into the top of the vault, gaining purchase. He pulled back, drawing the entire lid of the vault and the remaining dirt from the ground. He set it down next to the hole and turned back to the open grave. The casket rested in the base of the vault. The outside was a glossy, pearly white with sterling silver trim and handles. He knelt and opened one half of the lid.

Angela recognized the occupant immediately. It was the girl that was found in Central Park. She recognized her from the crime scene photos, but they hadn't identified the body when she saw the photos. She was comforted that Candice was not resigned to an unmarked, pauper's grave.

Daxxe lifted the body and placed it very gently on the frozen ground. He closed the casket and replaced the top of the vault. He muttered a few words under his breath and the ground they unearthed started to flow like possessed quicksand back into the hole, restoring the original mound. Enough snow would fall before dawn to mask the evidence of their intrusion. Daxxe lifted the body over his shoulder and they took their leave.

When they returned to the chapel, Daxxe placed Candice's body upon the altar. Angela sat down on the first pew, feeling a little sacrilegious and a lot creeped out. The sight of Candice's lifeless expression would remain with her always, as she didn't look as much like the cadavers at the morgue. It seemed like some of the girl's soul was still in her body.

Angela heard Daxxe's incantation, but the meaning of the words did not come to her as before. She could feel the magic building in the room, so it seemed to be working just as the spell that created her armor. She could see the magic as wisps of glowing energy snaked up from the floor all around the church, flowing into Candie's corpse.

As the energy enveloped the body, the changes began. The mortician's makeup faded away, allowing the full deep of the lifeless pallor to become evident. The bites and scratches that riddled her corpse peeked through the gaps opening and closing in her death gown as it morphed into the stylish outfit Angela wore when Daxxe found her. The written report didn't convey the true extent of the damage.

Seeing the spell work from a distance was very different from the way it felt. The body held a strange aura, like a picture taken out of focus. The colors mixed and mingled, flowing within an invisible bubble that encased the entire body. As the colors faded away, the image again became clear, and Angela saw herself lying on the altar. The spell was complete, and her body double looked as if she would rise up at any second, alive and well. The only indication that Death was still present was the absence of the rhythmic swelling from breathing.

"Why couldn't I understand that spell…incantation…like I did the one before?"

"You learn more as your experience increases. The magic has built in safe guards of sorts. If you can't understand the words, you don't have enough power or control to cast it."

Daxxe found a choir robe to wrap around the body, making sure it was entirely covered, and lifted the body over his shoulder. "We have to get this body into the rubble of St. Francis, and we need to drop a clue that will lead the police there."

Angela stood motionless for a moment, feeling very strange. It shook her to see herself as a corpse, even though she knew the body was someone else.

The pair crossed overland to reach the destroyed cathedral. Angela was in awe at the level of destruction before her. She couldn't fathom the magnitude of Daxxe's magical strength, but she knew it was no less than awesome. He walked over the rubble to a spot that would have been inside the chapel itself.

"This looks like a good place. Stand back."

Angela backed away, understanding as Daxxe spoke.

"Air, water, wind, and fire, hold this Earth somewhat higher."

A spot about ten feet in diameter trembled and rose straight out of the destroyed building. It looked like a column of broken concrete, rebar, and splintered wood. It rose just high enough to allow a person to crouch and jump to the exposed ground underneath it. Angela approached the gap and looked down, seeing what was the floor of the chapel at the bottom of the hole. Daxxe removed the robe and dumped the body double through the opening. The sound of the corpse hitting the frozen earth as it settled as dead weight almost made her wretch. Her guilt from them exhuming the body paled by comparison.

Daxxe placed his hand on her shoulder and drew her back away from the edge.

"I told you at the beginning that there would be difficult challenges ahead. I understand your feelings, but you must realize that we are only working with a shell. The ones responsible for her death are guilty of taking her life. Her soul is no longer of this Earth and she has no need of her body."

The words comforted her and helped her gain her composure. She felt herself turn her grief and guilt at Trokar and his clan into a glowing ember of anger on the verge of bursting into flames.

Daxxe motioned his hand as he started to cast.

"Column of rock, return to your home, not at once, but stone by stone."

The bottom of the column crumbled, dropping broken pieces one at a time into the hole, like a very quick, one-piece-at-a-time Tetris game. In just a couple of minutes, the entire column resettled on the ground, covering the body. The spot looked just as it did before they disturbed it.

"Now, we have to drop a clue for the police."

Angela felt an odd tension and realized she felt it from Daxxe as well. She followed her instincts and looked towards the south. In the distance, she saw two figures emerging from the rubble.

"Not here," whispered Daxxe. "It will destroy the ruse we are trying to create. Run, they will follow."

Daxxe and Angela sprinted away, making sure they were noticed.

Mekune and Damok immediately laid chase, following them as they made their way to the shipyards along Eastchester Bay and Long Island Sound.

Without realizing it, Angela led them back to the supply depot where her entire adventure began. The racks of parts provided them several good places to establish a defense. Angela and Daxxe broke apart just before Damok and Mekune landed in the center of the yard.

"Come out, come out, wherever you are," called Damok. "We will find you, and you won't leave alive."

The vampires separated, disappearing among the racks.

Angela tracked Damok, careful to stay out of sight. She wanted them to be a good distance apart before she made a move. She felt she could hold her own against one of them, but not both.

Damok worked around a large rack of metal panels, getting closer and closer to Angela's hiding place. She threw a rock towards the rack opposite her location. The sound got his attention, drawing him away from her and giving her the chance to attack.

A quick spin cleared Damok from harm's way and put his elbow into her back between her shoulder blades. The blunt attack didn't hurt, but it threw her forward, off-balance. She slammed into a ship's keel standing on one of the metal racks.

"Well, well, look at the little girl that thinks she's all grown up and ready to play with the adults."

Damok grabbed the back of her neck. Angela felt her feet come off the ground.

"I should keep that after I'm through with you."

He was looking at the amulet hanging around her neck. Angela issued a quick thought and the breastplate of her armor let off a burst of bright light like a camera flash.

"Aagh!" He dropped her and tried to cover his eyes. "You'll pay for that!"

Damok was temporarily unable to see. He flexed his free arm, ready to strike, but without a visible target.

Angela rolled away and regained her footing. She caught her breath as she took a defensive stance. She made a point to remember that her neck was partially exposed. His touch was deathly cold and the chill on her skin lingered unnaturally.

Damok blinked several times and looked at his opponent, reaching for a full length of chain resting on the ground beside the keel.

"I will enjoy killing you. I promise that it will be very slow and painful."

Angela drew her sword and held it readied in front of her in both hands.

Damok swung the end of the chain, letting the large hook on the end gain torque. A flex of his arm sent the hook hurling towards Angela like a blunt rocket.

She instinctively blocked with her left arm, keeping the sword in her right. Damok pulled back to regain the slack and forced the chain to wrap around her forearm several times. He pulled again before she could free her arm from the tangle. Pain shot through her shoulder as she flew forward towards the ground. She ducked her head, landing on her shoulder blades and rolling forward, using the momentum to plant her feet and push up hard. She launched herself up and over Damok gracefully. She forced her body into an aerial tumble that unwrapped her arm. Damok pulled again, but it only brought the chain to the ground as Angela landed facing him.

"You'll have to do better than that or this little girl is going to kick your ass," added Angela.

Damok's expression flared with anger as he charged, exactly as she hoped. Angela swung her sword across the space before her, forcing him to pull up and stop.

"You missed!" he exclaimed.

"Wrong again."

Angela's target wasn't Damok, but a chain to his left. Her sword severed two of the links, releasing the end of a large stack of pipes. The chain on the opposite end held long enough to let her jump clear.

The stack knocked Damok to the ground, burying him in an instant. The pipes continued to fall and roll, many of them hitting him as they passed. When the slide subsided, he pushed the pipe lying across his chest away and looked at his right leg. It was bent at the knee almost ninety degrees in the wrong direction. Fire erupted in his left shoulder as the sword passed through it, severing his arm from his body.

"That's for Jamat."

She used the momentum of the sword to carry the blade past her right side and over her head, bringing the blade down full force, like a lumberjack chopping wood, on his left knee. The razor-sharp edge had a faint blue glow. Damok shrieked in pain as the lower half of his leg fell away.

"That's for Daxxe, and this is for me."

She pulled the sword up, repositioning both hands on the hilt, thrusting the blade down with all her anger and might. Damok tried to back-pedal out of the way, but he had no leverage without all four limbs. She slammed the blade, now glowing blue down its entire length, through Damok's chest, burying it all the way to the hilt. It pierced his heart and the joint of large pipe behind him. Angela withdrew the weapon and wiped the blackened residue on his shoulder before returning it to its sheath.

Damok's body twitched and shook. Blood, almost solid black in color, ran from the hole in his chest and his severed joints. The putrid flesh fell away in rotten chunks, almost dissolving before they hit the ground. Angela went for higher ground, knowing the sound would draw the others. What was left of Damok disintegrated rapidly until there was no trace of him whatsoever.

Daxxe watched Mekune move through the depot. The two fought many times, and although Mekune was very cautious, he was also somewhat predictable. Mekune kept a sharp eye on his environment as he searched, but Daxxe knew his usual patterns.

Daxxe wanted to give Angela a chance to try her powers in the field against an opponent that would not stop if she faltered. He was close enough to give her the slack to try without hanging herself. He sensed the lack of Damok's presence, which evened up the odds, but that was not what drew his attention most. Angela's skill was honing very quickly, which was what he expected, but her control over the magic increased by leaps and bounds. It was rare for a mage to control the energy as raw force so soon, but to do so instinctively was almost unheard of.

Mekune would prove to be a stronger opponent than the fallen Damok, so Daxxe gave his new protector some distance. He wanted to see her method and strategy against an unknown first hand.

Angela moved through the yard, staying to the shadows, unaware of where she would find Daxxe or Mekune. They were apparently playing cat and mouse, and she didn't want to accidentally walk into the thick of it.

Angela approached a small building near the front of the depot that was probably the yard manager's office. A halogen light on the corner of the building lit with life, forcing her to scramble for cover. It extinguished after about forty-five seconds, allowing her to see the motion detector attached to it below the lamp assembly. She stayed behind a stack of fifty-five-gallon drums, waiting to see if the security light caught the attention of Mekune. She was very vulnerable and knew she needed to make a break for the other side of the depot where she wouldn't have to watch her back as closely. However, doing so would put her out in the open and reengage the light. She cursed under her breath at the mistake because, for all intents and purposes, she had painted herself into a corner. If the light went unnoticed the first time, it was by pure luck alone. She could not count on that luck a second time.

Mekune eyed the stack of barrels, contemplating his strategy. He saw the light come on, and he saw one of his foes duck for cover. From his point, he could approach the office and cross the roof without turning on the light, giving him the element of surprise and the advantage of higher ground. His dilemma was knowing which of them hid behind the drums.

Daxxe watched from far enough away to remain hidden, but close enough to help if Angela got herself in a tight spot.

Mekune floated to the roof, crossed the pitched surface noiselessly, and stopped at a point overlooking the barrels. No one was there. The light, mounted just below his foot, turned on. The yard was empty and he knew his presence didn't trigger the switch. He sensed a presence in the open space below. He leapt into the air as Angela broke into a run. He could not see her, but he could see the snow coming off of her heels.

He bore down on her, about to slam her down to the frozen ground, when the disturbance in the snow stopped. He swept upward, staying about fifteen feet above the ground. He was not going to take the chance of flying directly into a drawn sword. The light extinguished again after forty-five seconds.

He lowered himself to the end of the footprints as the light came back on behind him. He studied the ground, hoping the imprints would provide some clue as to the direction his prey went. He felt he was being watched as soon as he touched the ground. He looked up and took a step forward, trying to find the eyes upon him.

A sharp pain shot through his legs. He saw a pale blue swath of energy move away to his left as he fell to the ground. His feet and calves still stood before him as blood spurted from his stumps. Some of the blackish ooze spattered onto Angela's legs, making them visible.

Mekune twisted his body to avoid her advance, but her blade still punctured his arm. He rolled back and tightened his muscles, pulling the sword from her hands. The weapon became visible as soon as she lost contact with it. The flat of the blade seared his palm, but he did not let go. He slashed out with his free hand, finding purchase, although he didn't know exactly where.

Angela fell to the ground, slowly fading back into sight. She scrambled to her feet when Mekune's claws latched into her thigh. He could not use her sword against her, but she couldn't get it back either.

"Aagh!"

"Come here!"

Mekune pulled his body towards her, squeezing as hard as he could, but in his weakened condition, he couldn't do much besides prevent her escape. At full strength, the bone under her quadriceps would have snapped like a pretzel since she was not protected there by her armor.

Daxxe readied himself to intervene when Angela dropped to her side, kicking with her free foot, sweeping it back and forth and repeatedly grazing Mekune's face. Each strike was swift, and the tip of her boot held a small blade. Nice addition. On the fifth sweep, a large chunk of his face separated from his skull. He released her leg and dropped her sword, unable to bear the pain in his face or the pommel burning against his palm any longer.

She rolled beyond his reach, leaving a trail of blood spots in the snow, before popping back onto her feet. She put her hand out and the sword flew into it. Her hand tightened around the handle with the same steel-hard grip as her resolve.

Mekune didn't yet realize she'd regained the weapon. He worked his way back to the lower half of his legs, trying to reattach them when she entered his peripheral vision.

"What are you looking at?"

Angela stood, silent and ready. She didn't seem to notice the blood flowing down her leg and into her boot. She was running on pure adrenaline. Her eyes narrowed as she focused.

"Helping Daxxe will only get you killed!"

"This is personal."

Angela twisted in a full circle, gaining momentum for the blade, creating a powerful blue arc in the air, grunting from the exertion. The length of the sword burst into a dark blue flame as it found it's mark.

Mekune grinned devilishly; then his head fell forward and rolled through the snow. She carried the motion for another full circle, putting the second swing across the center of his chest, slicing him and his heart clean through. She kicked his right shoulder, knocking the top half of the torso away from the rest of the body. She watched as the remains disintegrated into nothing before her.

She turned to walk away and dropped to her knees. Her thigh seared with pain, worsened by the unrelenting throbbing. She wasn't sure how much blood she lost, but she was suddenly acutely aware of her light-headedness. Gritting her teeth and slumping forward on her knees, she drew a deep breath and focused everything she had left on her leg wound.

Daxxe landed next to Angela as she fell forward and sideways into the snow. He rolled her onto her back, checking her leg. The wounds were gone and she was breathing, slowly and steadily, but she passed out from the strain. He picked her up and headed back towards the remains of St. Francis, her condition forcing him to initiate his backup plan.

Delis walked down one of the tunnels, having no idea where she was and a hard time keeping her balance. Her thirst continued to grow, becoming unbearable. A wave of nausea ran over her, forcing her to drop to her knees as a coughing fit claimed her body. She spit up blood within a few seconds and her insides ignited with imagined fire. The severity of the fit increased, mingling pieces of flesh with the bloody vomit. She fell forward as the last of her borrowed immortality passed without any knowledge that her link to Mekune was severed.

Nikola walked in the darkness of the tunnels, not sure of the direction she traveled. Her vision was blurry and she was having trouble seeing in the dark. Something bumped her shoulder. She was startled until she felt around and realized it was the handrail of a staircase. She went up the stairs, a sense of relief comforting her as she worked her way up, smelling the blood of a mortal. She was almost free and she was overwhelmingly thirsty.

She reached for the door handle when a sharp pain shot through her stomach, doubling her over, forcing her off-balance. She rolled down the stairs to the nearest landing, curling into the fetal position in intense pain. She looked at her hands, feeling something wet on them. Her stomach continued to melt, black ooze running over her hands and forearms at a quickening pace as she died with the knowledge that her gift was anything but what Damok had promised.

Daxxe gently laid Angela on the rooftop. He went to the edge, looking down at the rubble, scanning. The area was deserted, quite normal for the wee hours of the morning. He spread his wings, gliding down to the spot where they hid the body before the encounter with Mekune and Damok. He looked at Angela's badge and then he smashed the face into one of the chucks of concrete a few times, scarring the surface. He wedged the gold shield between two pieces of fallen building, leaving just under half of it exposed before he scattered some of the rubble in the immediate area and flew back to the rooftop.

A squad car rolled by, right on schedule. He spent time studying the patterns of the police around the church when he used it as a place to hide, planning his comings and goings around their watches.

Daxxe mumbled a few words and the car rolled to a stop. The search light mounted to the driver's side roof support switched on, casting a bright beam of light in the direction it was pointed. The beam moved back and forth several times before switching off. Daxxe was about to repeat his incantation of persuasion when the driver's door opened.

The policeman walked out onto the debris field, flashlight in hand, turning the light on as he approached the spot Daxxe stood only moments before. He dislodged the badge and studied it for a few seconds, and then he started running back to his car, almost falling on the loose pieces of debris as he went.

Daxxe retrieved Angela and disappeared into the night.

Joe was asleep at his desk when he felt a hand rest on his shoulder. He awoke quickly, but he was groggy at best. Fred handed him a Styrofoam cup of hot black coffee and sat down. Joe took a sip and set the cup down, bringing his hands to his face to rub the sleep away.

"Fred, I've known you a long time, and I can tell by the look on your face that you've got some bad news for me." Joe leaned his face into his hands. "Is she alive?"

"You do know me well, and I wish you were wrong this time. No, she's not."

Jamison saw Joe's body tense when he heard the words.

"What happened?"

"A uniformed officer ran across something that didn't look right to him, so he checked it out. He caught a glint of gold in his spotlight and it turned out to be her badge. She was in the St. Francis Cathedral when it collapsed."

Joe turned to face his friend.

"Are you sure? Her badge doesn't mean that..."

"I ordered the heavy rescue team down there three hours ago, Joe. I had to be sure before I said anything to you. They found her body in the rubble. We were able to make the identification, primarily from her dental records. She didn't stand a chance against that falling stone. It was quick Joe, she didn't suffer."

Joe stood up and walked away from the desk and his friend without saying a word. Fred watched him go, knowing he would need a little time and space to sort things out. He sat for a few minutes, trying to understand how his friend and fellow officer would feel at a time like this.

He stood to go back to his office when he noticed that Joe's badge was sitting on the desk. He ran for the door, but Joe was already gone. His car was still in the lot, so he was moving on foot, and unfortunately, almost impossible to follow or find. He called the dispatcher and issued a quiet APB on Joe. He was concerned about what Joe might do in his current state of mind. He knew Joe had a soft spot for his new partner and he'd already suffered great loss. It would be enough to crack any man.

Daxxe lit on the roof across from the police station. Dawn was close, putting him at great risk, but he intended to stand by his promise.

He watched Detective Anderson walk through the front doors and head down the street. He moved as though he was in a daze without a clear destination in mind. Daxxe knew he'd gotten the news and he could sense that Angela's concern was well founded. Daxxe followed at a distance until Joe turned down a darkened alley.

Joe walked about halfway down, stopping next to several large trash bins. He moved in between two of them and sat down on the snow-dusted trash. He took his service revolver out of the holster and held it before him, letting the bulk of the weight rest on his outstretched legs.

"I can't do this again." He looked up into the sky, speaking his side of his conversation with the man upstairs out loud. "I told you when you took Michelle and Celeste that I wasn't strong enough to do this again. Why do you feel the need to test me? Angela was a good kid, a good cop, and would have been a damn good partner. She was my second chance!"

"And you did not fail her," came from the darkness.

Joe jumped up and looked around. He did not expect an answer and was startled by it.

"Who is that? I'm trying to have a private conversation here!" He didn't see anyone.

"She would be disappointed to see you like this."

"Alright you son of a... Show yourself!"

"That would be considered blasphemy by most."

This is not happening. I am not having a conversation with God.

"Why can't it be happening? It's what you intended to do before you shot yourself, was it not?"

"This is too weird. I must be having some kind of stress induced surreal daydream or something. Can't be an 'out-of-body experience' since I don't see myself."

"This is no dream. I don't have much time and you need to listen to what I have to say. Angela thought very highly of you. One of her primary goals was to simply earn your approval, which I think she accomplished. She did what she thought was right, even though the cost was her life. She would expect no less from you."

"Right or not, why did you have to take her?"

"You are forgetting that waking each day is not a given right. It was her time. She has a higher calling, as you will when your time comes."

Joe started to respond when he felt a peace wash over him, relieving his tension. He felt very light-headed and saw a bright light as he passed out and fell to the snow-laden pavement.

451

The sound of the alarm clock pulled him from his slumber. He managed to find the snooze button to allow himself to think. Rays of bright sunshine flowed into the room at a near horizontal slant, indicating the day was just beginning.

As his mind began to focus, he realized he was in one of the bunks in the Precinct. Each Precinct house had one or two such temporary quarters just in case they were needed. His badge and revolver were both sitting on top of the little table supporting the alarm.

Jamison was sitting stiffly in a chair across the room. He was pulling himself from sleep as well, although he had a much rougher night from the looks of it.

"Fred, how did I get here?"

"You can be a real pain in the ass sometimes."

"I know that, but that's not an answer to my question."

"I would have to say dumb luck. I was worried about you when you took off last night. I knew you'd take the news about Angela pretty hard."

"I was…in shock, I think. I hoped for the best but expected the worst. I didn't expect the worst to happen."

"And it wasn't your fault, Joe." Jamison stood to stretch his legs. "Are you going to be okay now? I mean really okay?"

"Yeah, I think so. I wasn't last night, but I've had some time to think about it."

"You would be a popsicle right now if it wasn't for a concerned citizen. We got a call last night about some guy passed out in the snow in an alley about a mile from here. Lucky for you, you weren't out there very long. We had a doctor come check you out and give you a mild sedative so you could get some sleep."

"I don't remember any of that."

"The doctor said he didn't expect that you would. Now, you better get some more rest. I'll take care of the task force for a few hours so you can eat a decent meal and get a little more sleep."

Jamison patted Joe on the knee and walked out the room.

Joe laid his head back against the pillow and looked up, although he wasn't looking at the ceiling.

"Thank you."

ChAPTER FORTY-ONE

Jamison took his spot behind the podium for the morning briefing after Miles took roll.

"Good morning. As you have likely realized, we have seen a sharp decline in the number of homicides related to our serial killer case. I cannot tell you why, but either this group found what they wanted and moved on, or the natural predator we learned about from Joshua has been successful. We still need to remain vigilant, but we also need to reassure the public and start working back into our normal operating procedures.

"The task force leadership has already started on a statement to be issued to the public, and we are preparing all of our dispatchers with information to be provided when the calls start pouring in."

"What can we tell the public that they will believe?" came from the seated officers.

"Our plan is to give them something they can believe in, get closure, and help restore the Department in the eyes of the public. We will keep you updated. Dismissed."

A small procession of cars followed a white hearse through the streets of New York. The drive lasted almost an hour, ending at a small graveyard just outside of the city. The graves rested inside a short, white picket fence, and the area around the small cemetery and the church that shadowed it teemed with trees, helping keep some of the wind at bay. A small headstone marked a newly created grave. It was the final resting place of Ellen Louise Clark.

Julie Romanowski, Marina Makovoz, Rick Pratt and his wife got out of the limousine that trailed the hearse. Most of the other people in attendance were friends that Ellen made while she worked at the diner.

Malcolm and Emilio parked at a distance after they escorted the procession. They were given the escorting task so they could take Julie and Marina wherever they wanted to go after the service concluded. It was no longer deemed necessary to keep them under witness protection.

The church and the graveyard were both very pretty, which was one of the reasons Ellen chose it originally. She discovered the secluded church when she first moved to New York. She never told anyone about it, but she put her desire to be buried there in her will. She left the little that she owned to her roommate and the Pratt family.

The service lasted just over twenty minutes due to the cold weather. The priest handled the service gracefully under the conditions. Once concluded, everyone left the gravesite except Julie. Marina waited in the squad car with Malcolm and Emilio, giving her some time alone. She stood by the casket, placing one hand on its shiny surface.

"I miss you so much, Ellen. I promise that I'll come visit you and let you know what's happening."

Julie wiped tears from her eyes and placed something on the casket before she turned to go to the squad car. Marina comforted her new friend as they pulled away.

"We can take you wherever you'd like to go," said Emilio to both women. "The killers have been stopped.:

Their homes were under 24-hour surveillance since the incidents began, and nothing out of the ordinary occurred. At Julie's invitation, Marina decided to go back to Julie's apartment and stay with her for a few days. Julie didn't want to be there alone. The police promised to continue their watch for a few more days as a precaution, but they genuinely felt the women were in no danger.

The gravedigger lowered the casket into the earth, noticing a small photograph tucked under the bouquet of flowers attached to the top. The picture showed two people standing in front of a roller coaster called "The Shredder." Whoever took the picture held the camera at a forty-five-degree angle, and a small piece of thumb or finger was visible along the edge. It was, without a doubt, taken at Coney Island.

One of the detectives assigned to the task force approached Joe. He was back at his desk, looking a little better than he had in days.

"What's up?"

"I've got some more bad news, Joe."

"What is it?"

"One of the uniformed units found Alan Thornquist."

"And?"

"He won't be able to answer any questions, I'm afraid."

"Why is that?"

"He's dead. They found his car in the parking garage of the Hilton downtown. A guest reported an odd smell to the manager, and hotel security made the discovery. Dr. Palmer's office already confirmed he died of a cocaine overdose, and narcotics found several pounds of cocaine and almost three hundred thousand dollars in the trunk."

Joe whistled when he heard the numbers.

"I guess he was trying to get into a new line of work. It makes sense; he needed a lot of money to get off of the hook with the court and his creditors."

"It looks like his debt's been paid, and we are out of suspects. I'll get you a copy of the report as soon as it's finalized."

"Sounds good."

Angela woke with a start, disoriented. She reached over her shoulder for the handle of her sword when she realized she wasn't still facing off with Mekune or any of his kind. She then reached for and looked at her thigh. The wounds were gone, and the legging material wasn't stained or torn.

"You did well," complimented Daxxe from the pews.

"What?"

"I said that you did very well. You took care of Damok and Mekune, and you managed to save yourself in the process."

"I don't feel like I did well."

Angela rubbed her legs and arms, her body aching everywhere.

"Your body isn't used to this lifestyle yet, even with your enhanced physical attributes. The pains will pass and you will grow stronger because of them. Your weaknesses are leaving your body."

Daxxe held out a bowl holding a very aromatic and enticing liquid.

"What's this?"

"It'll help with the aches in the meantime. It's a type of herbal tea."

Angela sipped the tepid liquid.

"It's good. What's in it?"

"If I told you, you wouldn't drink it. Ignorance is bliss."

Angela made a face and kept drinking, already feeling better.

"I particularly enjoyed the move you did in front of the depot's office, very creative and gutsy."

"Thank you. I guess I seem to work pretty well under pressure, not to mention I had to fix my screw up."

Daxxe's expression showed curiosity.

"You didn't know? I guess I should have kept my mouth shut. I didn't think about the light still being able to detect me. I bolted. The idea came to me in those few seconds. At least I was thinking enough to put some snow in my mouth so my breath wouldn't be visible, drawing sight to my head."

"Mistakes are a way of life, and they're not bad if we learn from them."

"How long have we been here?"

"Almost two hours. Your body gave out after you healed yourself."

Her tired expression took on a worried cast, remembering Mekune's claws had broken her skin. "Do I have the disease now?"

"No, you can't be infected because of your gift."

"Has anything happened with the plans we set in motion at the Cathedral?"

"The police have found the body and confirmed that it's you. I nudged an officer in the right direction. By his reaction, he knew immediately what we wanted them to think happened. A heavy rescue team was called to in to clear the area."

Angela's expression grew more somber as she finished her tea.

"He's fine. I held up my end of the bargain. It will take him a little while to mourn, but he'll move on."

"I just don't like the position it puts him in. I haven't been his partner for long, but I know he's blaming himself. I wish I could let him know."

"You know you can't do that. This was the only way. You've found your calling, or it found you. You can't walk away now."

"I know. I just feel bad."

"Why haven't you mentioned your feelings about your parents?"

She shot him a look of shock, blended with frustration over the lack of privacy for her feelings.

I have to learn how to keep everyone out of my head.

"Oh, I'm a little mixed on those emotions. My mother will be upset, but she won't voice it to my father. We haven't seen eye to eye for several years, so I don't see him getting all that upset. We don't speak to each other anyway. I know that sounds bad, but my family was pretty dysfunctional."

"What about your brother?" The shock melted away in the heat of anger.

"Methinks you need to stop digging around in my head!"

Methinks! Methinks! What is wrong with me!

She stood to walk away, but he shot right back at her.

"And you need to talk about it if you're going to get your feelings at peace. Bottling it all up will not do you any favors when your cup runneth over."

She settled quickly, seeing the wisdom in his advice and the slight grin on his face at his word choice, even though she didn't like it.

"He'll miss me when he finds out, but I don't know when that'll be. He ran away from home when he was sixteen. I get a postcard from him maybe twice a year, the last one from Sydney, Australia. He goes where he wants, when he wants, and he does what he wants. I don't have a way to get a hold of him if I tried. I just feel like he, and they, deserve to know, and I feel bad for the way things turned out."

"You're human, that's to be expected."

"What happens now?"

"Well, we've made the first move. Trokar will be coming because I stand between him and the fifth Book, not to mention the rage over Damok and Mekune. We also need to go and see a friend."

"I didn't think you let yourself have friends," she asked with a puzzled look.

"This is different, and you'll see when we get there. You need to put on your cloak and wrap it tight; the air is much colder during flight. We don't have the time to walk. I'll have to fly us there."

"You can carry me that way?"

"How do you suppose you got here?"

"Touché."

Angela wrapped the cloak around her body and pulled the hood over her head. She looked somewhat like a cloistered monk. Daxxe walked behind her and put his hand on her upper arms.

"Try not the flail about this time."

They shot skyward before she had a chance to answer. The ground moved away from them very quickly as he gained altitude and changed his direction. The view of the city and its skyline was breathtaking.

"I could get used to this."

"It's a good thing because it will be happening more and more."

Angela almost screamed when he banked a very hard right turn and slipped through one of the open sides of a bell tower. When he set her down, she was trembling a little, but not from the cold.

"You could have given me a little warning."

"There's no fun in that?"

"So, who's going to protect me from you?" She popped his shoulder with a buddy punch, affectionate, not forceful.

"It comes with the job."

"Where are we now?"

"This is the bell tower of St. Christopher's. We have some business to attend to."

"St. Christopher's? Our only witness for this entire case works here."

"That's correct. I was able to keep her from being turned after she was bitten, but she's not why we're here."

"Does Marina need more assistance?"

"No more than I have already given her. She's in good hands. Now, let's get inside."

Malcolm pulled the car to the curb in front of 2420 Webster. Emilio jumped out to open the door for Julie and Marina. Julie stopped at the bottom of the stairs, tears welling up in her eyes. Being back at the apartment she shared with Ellen for the first time since her death brought all the pain to the surface.

Marina held her hand and coaxed her up the steps. "It'll be okay. We can get you through this."

Marina was doing a good job of covering her own fears. She felt a sense of security while staying at the safe house. Now that security was somewhat gone, and she didn't want to be out in the open. They discussed how much they wanted to be free of the police, but they were having second thoughts now that the time was at hand.

Emilio carried their bags to the front door of the apartment, and Marina had to unlock the door because Julie was shaking too much to get the key into the lock. Once they were safely inside, and Emilio heard the deadbolt engage, he went back to the car.

"What do you think, Amigo?"

"I think I want to keep an eye of them for a little while to make sure they're okay. I know the Precinct needs us on regular duty again, but I'd feel a lot better if we already had an actual killer locked up or dead."

"Me, too, and I just don't trust our surveillance teams wholeheartedly."

Malcolm pulled into traffic, looking directly at the officers working the scene as he drove past them. He saw them when they first arrived, which lowered his confidence in them even more. If he could find them that quickly when he didn't already know where they were set up, or who they actually were, anyone else could too.

Joe could see Angela's face in his mind from his practical joke on her a few days before. Then he thought back to her first day. She kept quiet, but she seemed to have a purpose from the very beginning. She learned quickly and she wasn't afraid to start testing boundaries after a few days. Her previous assignment was as a regular beat cop, and she was graced with having a good uptown neighborhood where she didn't see much outside of disorderly conduct, domestic disputes, and the occasional celebrity drunk.

She worked towards the promotion to Detective because she wanted to do more, and she got more than she expected. For the first couple of weeks, each new case made her sick to her stomach. She wasn't hardened to the darker side of human nature, but she never gave up, and her determination and desire fueled Joe's respect. Each time he thought she'd break and call it quits, she picked herself up and was a little stronger than before. He regretted he hadn't told her how impressed he was, or that she was more like a daughter to him than a partner.

She also reminded him of his days as a rookie, reflecting his drive and commitment in her work ethic. The promise he made to himself was getting harder and harder to keep. In his day, he would never have even considered giving up. He could hear Angela's voice asking him why he was thinking about giving up now. He found himself sitting on the edge of her desk.

"You're absolutely right kid. You don't deserve any disrespect, and that's all my quitting the force would do for you. This one's for you partner."

"Where are the others?"

Trokar paced as he awaited an answer, which did not bode well.

"They're searching for Daxxe as you ordered."

"I think you should go back and check. They've been gone far too long."

"Yes, Master."

Viktor left the terminal, headed back to St. Francis.

Trokar entered his chamber to find Shayla sitting on the bed, perched on her knees.

"What can I do to help?"

"Nothing, it's only a matter of time now. You would think I'd be more patient. I've already waited hundreds of years."

Shayla motioned him closer and massaged his shoulders as he sat in front of her. "Take me to feed with you. I'm tired of being cooped up in here. I want to kill with you. It'll make you feel better."

Trokar thought about the request, unable to remember the last time he fed since he was capable of going several days without blood. He didn't usually take Shayla with him; he brought fresh kills back for her. He wanted her to stay cloistered as it gave him less to worry about.

"Very well, but it must be quick. Viktor will return soon, and I must find Daxxe," he said, standing and turning to face her.

"Thank you, love." She gave him a deep kiss, lightly biting his lip in the process.

"Do we just sit and wait for him to come?"

"No, we'll move around since we can't go after him directly. Trokar will find his way to us soon enough. I have to proceed with caution because I am the only thing in his way, and I expect to see him take more drastic measures to locate me. He can't sense me like I can him, but he can track the book I have with the other four in his possession. I've got to get those books from him or all will be lost."

"Where should we start? Does he have any usual habits like some of the other?"

"No, I don't think so, and that makes him more dangerous. He's not as predictable as his followers and his strength as a mage is formidable."

"Is he stronger than you?"

"It's very possible. I haven't fought him personally for many years. He didn't even do his own dirty work in the Catacombs."

"Do you think you can defeat him?"

"I don't honestly know."

"It sounds like he's afraid of you to me."

"Not wanting to waste his time on what he considers trivial is probably more like it. He's quite the narcissist."

"You seem to know him pretty well."

"Better than you know."

Trokar led Shayla through the cold night air, scanning the city below. Shayla flew carefree, taking everything in, loving to be out even more since Trokar rarely allowed it. She followed him down as he descended.

"Where are we?"

"This is Brooklyn. Look right down there," ordered Trokar, pointing.

Shayla looked, seeing a small nightclub. The sign on the window identified it as a nightclub for teens. Only people from age fourteen to nineteen were allowed inside, and no alcohol was served.

She leaned over and kissed him passionately. "You know what I like. I'll return the favor when we get back."

Shayla leapt off of the roof, gliding down behind the club. Trokar followed at a short distance, watching her walk around to enter through the front door.

The man working the front door looked to be in his mid-twenties. He was in very good shape, probably from lifting weights and working out. She walked right for the door to the club.

"Ma'am, I'm sorry, but I can't let you in. Only fourteen- to nineteen-year olds are allowed tonight."

Shayla offered a mischievous pout, but the bouncer didn't waiver.

"Tell you what, if you let me in, I'll..."

She whispered the rest into his ear.

"You're joking, right?"

She only smiled and put her left hand behind his neck and pulled his head forward, kissing him while her other hand explored his physique. He was basking in his luck when it changed abruptly.

A burning pain went from his neck, up into his head, and back into his shoulder. He tried to push the tease away, but she was much stronger than she looked. He grew weaker and weaker with each passing second until the pain started going away. She stepped back, blood trickling from her lips and chin as she licked it off of her left hand.

"You should have let me in."

She opened the door and walked into the club. The bouncer blacked out and fell to the sidewalk, the only person working the door. The blood Shayla didn't take slowly pumped out of the holes in his neck until his circulatory system lost too much pressure and his heart stopped. The cold concrete under his body was stained crimson.

The inside of the club teemed with teens dancing to the sounds of popular boy bands and Hip Hop while a disco ball and colored spotlights highlighted the dance floor. On the edges of the club, several teens sat at small tables talking, drinking, watching the crowd, or trying to make out. She found the one she wanted sitting alone. She sat down next to him, speaking so only he could hear. After a couple of minutes, they both stood up and walked towards the back of the club.

The areas along the back wall were almost completely dark, and several young couples were using the privacy to increase their carnal knowledge of each other. Shayla slipped out of the back door with the high school senior in tow.

"Why do you want to do this out here, lady? It's too cold."

"It's perfect out here."

She started unbuttoning her top. The young man stood in amazement at what she was doing as a cold hand closed around his throat, scaring him to death and making his pulse throb painfully in his skull. He was trying to break free and see who blindsided him, but he was having trouble breathing. He looked askance at Shayla as she rebuttoned her top.

"On second thought, we better not. These belong to him, and he's apparently pretty particular about his property. Now I've got to go and do something ugly to make it up to him."

Trokar held the young man as Shayla approached. The boy's eyes opened wide when he saw the fang-like teeth in her mouth. He tried to swing his arm out to knock her away, but she caught his wrist and sank her teeth into his forearm, shooting icy-hot fire up his veins. She opened her mouth over and over, moving a bit farther up his arm each time. He was going numb all over.

The same pain cut into his neck as Trokar bit into his jugular. He felt his clavicle snap from the pressure of his attacker's jaw, but it didn't hurt much in comparison to the bite itself. A second bite farther away from his neck did send sharps pains through the overall haze of anguish. He turned in time to see a large chunk of flesh and the whole of his clavicle torn away from his body. The thing attacking him spit it away as though it were no more than a piece of gristle in a cheaper cut of meat. He blacked out, feeling nothing at all.

Shayla drew back from the dead boy's leg, her front completely covered with fresh blood. She licked her lips and used her fingers to mop up as much as she could, as though she were emaciated and finally given food and water. Trokar threw the body against the building's back wall, discarded it like a rag doll.

"How do you feel now?"

"Wonderful. I love the kill, but I savor teasing them. It's easy to see why mortals are so inferior. They are so weak."

"Yes, they are. We need to return to the terminal. I assume Viktor is already there."

Viktor dared borrow no more time. He slipped out of Trokar's chamber and returned to his hammock to await Trokar and Shayla's return.

Angela slipped quietly down the stairs to get a feel for the old chapel. She eased the door open to see where it entered the church and made a mental note of where things were located before returning to Daxxe.

"Okay, I've got an idea of the layout. What are we here for?"

"To fulfill one of our most important tasks."

"And that is?"

"Confession."

Angela stood, staring, almost rudely, at her mentor.

"You just lost me. Did you say confession?"

"Yes, I did. For each dark soul we vanquish, we must make amends with God."

"But aren't we on this mission to do exactly what we're doing?"

"Yes, we are, but we are no better than those we seek to destroy if we don't ask forgiveness for our transgressions. Killing is still a mortal sin regardless of why or intentions."

Angela merely nodded in agreement.

"Did you see the confessionals?"

"Yes, and they were both empty when I looked."

"Good. I sense the priest is here. I think you will like him."

"You aren't coming?" she asked.

"Not this time. You handled both enemies this night."

They waited in the ground level landing until Angela could make it across the chapel without disturbing any other parishioners and making them aware of her. Her cloak concealed her armor and the sound of her passage, but she still looked and felt out of place. She felt a sense of relief when she entered her side of the booth and sat in silence. After a few moments, she heard the other door open and close; then the panel slid open to allow communication between each side.

"Welcome to St. Christopher's. I am Father Samuels. How may I be of service tonight?"

"I need to confess Father."

"That's why I'm here my child. What have you done?"

"I've...I...this is hard...killed two men tonight."

Angela found it much harder to accept, or even downright believe what she'd actually done, when it came down to brass tacks. It had a different feel now that she wasn't pumped full of adrenaline and could really think about it.

"Is this some kind of a joke, young lady?"

"No Father, it's not. I really killed two...I guess you could call them men, but you must give me a chance to explain why."

"The 'why' is of no consequence. You cannot simply erase the fact you've killed another human being, regardless of the reason."

She sat in silence for what felt like eternity, thinking about how to respond.

"I'm not trying to erase the fact, Father, but what I did was not wrong and nothing anyone can say will change that conviction. There is a war raging in the world that most will never be aware of, yet it will determine our fate. I have been blessed with a gift that lets me fight for our survival, and like every war, there are casualties. I am only here to ask that the two that fell fighting for the other side are forgiven."

The long silence came from Samuels' side.

"Miss, I must say that I never expected to hear a confession like this in my lifetime, and now I've heard it twice in the same week. My position is somewhat unique in the fact that I can listen to those that need an ear, or I can impart advice to them, without a breath of it leaving this booth. In all my years of service, I have only broken that vow one time."

"What happened the first time?"

"Someone told me they killed and they would kill again. Your story sounds too similar to be the truth, but I can't shake the feeling that it is. I'm realizing what is really happening now."

"And what would that be, Father?"

"I cannot begin to explain how I know, but I know you are telling me the truth. I can feel it in my soul as plain as day, and I also realize that I am being presented with this same dilemma for a reason. I didn't get it right the first time."

"The first time?"

"Yes, the first time. When this happened before, I questioned my faith and broke my vow of confidence. I went to the police and told them what I knew. I felt better at first, but I realized the severity of it after I had some time to think about it. Luckily, the confessional itself prevented me from being able to identify him, so the damage I've done is minimal. I won't make the same mistake again."

"Where do we go from here, Father?"

"Forward is the only way we can. I of all people know that God works in mysterious ways, and He would not allow this to happen without good reason. I will be here when you need to return."

"I can see why he likes you," she returned, barely above a whisper.

"And who is he?"

"The one that confessed to you the first time."

Samuels sat for a few long moments, allowing the young woman ample time to slip away after he felt the door open and close. He knew he was making the right decision this time.

chapter forty-two

Joe entered Jamison's office as he was clipping the badge to his belt. The Commissioner nodded a silent approval.

"It's good to have you back, Joe. You had me a little worried there."

"I had myself a little worried. I just needed to get my head back on straight."

"For what it's worth, I think you're doing the right thing. You're exactly where we need you to be for this case. I couldn't have asked for a better cop to tackle the job."

O'Toole called the briefing to order, but the task force was already unnaturally quiet. The news of their fallen comrade spread through the Precinct like wildfire. It would be department wide within hours, and like always, several different accounts of what happened were already going around.

"We've got a lot to cover this morning, so I'll get started. On a very sad note, for those of you that don't already know, we lost Detective Angela Benson. She was inside the Cathedral of St. Francis when it collapsed. She was a good cop, and her passing personally saddens me. We'll announce the date and time the honor guard will offer their final respects. She will be decorated for her service. Now, a moment of silence please."

Every person present bowed their heads in respect. The fact that being a cop meant putting your life on the line everyday tended to hide in the background, shrouded from view. It was quite a reality check for the department when any officer lost their life in the line of duty.

"The number of bodies ending up in the morgue has visibly reduced, which is a welcome change, but we don't know the reason why. Evidence suggests this group of killers was in our city looking for something, and this trend suggests they found it. From Stone's prior experience, once they move on, they won't be back. That's a godsend for us, but it's also unacceptable. We have to put an end to this here and now.

"Dr. Palmer's staff has worked closely with forensics on the case since this all began, but the results thus far are disappointing. We do not have a proven method to bring down these vampires and keep them there. Most of the things we associate with them are no more than old wives' tales or movie magic: like garlic, silver bullets, and holy water. The research team did discover how the disease operates, even though they have yet to develop a vaccine. I'll turn the floor over to Dr. Palmer so he can bring you up to speed."

Allen approached the podium, taking O'Toole's place.

"We haven't found much that will help, primarily due to the fact we don't have a viable specimen to examine. I think the chances of getting one are going from slim to none, but this is what we've pieced together so far. When the disease infects a host, it stays relatively quiet in terms of symptoms or outward signs, but it is far from inactive. It multiplies and spreads itself into virtually every bodily system. During this spread, the disease targets bone marrow, which affects the way red blood cells are made.

"Red cells are very fragile and they only survive about 120 days in a normal person. This is because the cell starts normally, but it fills with hemoglobin which slowly crushes the nucleus and destroys it. In a normal person, approximately two million red cells die a second and the bone marrow replenishes those cells just as fast. With our vampires, the red cells only last eight to ten days, but the renewal rate stays the same as a normal person's, thus creating a deficit in the blood. This imbalance results in the pale and sickly pallor we see in them and their body's need for red blood cells. This need is extremely strong since it is directly linked to their survival.

"Their situation is complicated by the way disease mutates at this point, becoming very active and behaving like a white blood cell. The disease begins to destroy good cells to fill the void with more diseased cells. This process progresses until the disease turns on itself, ultimately resulting in a dead host. The introduction of new red blood cells from any source holds this process at bay and provides the diseased cells with a food supply, and that's where we come in.

"Uninfected humans have the closest match for the blood they need and we average about ten pints at any given time. A vampire's digestive system is very different from ours, which allows them to receive new blood in such a crude fashion. If we ingested a large quantity of blood, it would become toxic in our stomachs, making us very sick with the potential of killing us. They do not have the normal acids in their digestive systems that we need. The Study in Vampirism text identifies a vampire's body as dead, in the terms as we understand them. If the acid remained, it would destroy the ingested blood and slowly eat through the tissue of their body from the inside.

"As I said, the disease spreads itself into virtually every system of the body. It also attacks those systems as well, but with a different purpose. The other systems mutate to evolve the body into a something more adequate for survival. Until now, we thought this rate of evolution was impossible. What all this means is that once a person is infected, they undergo dramatic physical changes. They develop fangs and claws for obvious purposes. There are huge increases in stamina and muscle mass, as well as heightened senses. It's almost as if the body mutates in reverse, devolving into a more animalistic state, but one equipped for the species to survive."

He paused to take a drink of water and take inventory of his audience. Although his presentation was long, everyone was still with him and paying attention.

"We've run some other tests as well, trying to find a weakness, and we've found a few things that should be helpful. We discovered that it is not sunlight as a whole that affects a vampire, but the ultraviolet end of the spectrum. The UV light stimulates the red blood cells, triggering them to move. In their extremely weakened state, the hyperactivity literally causes them to rupture. In the short term, this will cause the vampires intense pain until they get away from the UV. If they cannot, we think the trauma can kill them. We've already requested portable Q-Beams fitted with UV producing bulbs since normal fluorescent lights don't generate enough UV to make a difference. This will give you all a basic line of defense if you come across any more of them.

"The stake through the heart theory also works, but I don't recommend getting close enough to try it. The heart is the key to the distribution of the blood in the body. Like us, they cannot survive without a flow of blood. Damage to other parts of the circulatory system proves ineffective due to their ability to heal and regenerate damaged tissue. This regeneration process is what occurred when Miller unloaded on one of them a few nights ago. The bullets passed completely through the body, and some of the wounds probably closed before the bullets stopped flying. If the heart can be destroyed, the production and distribution center for the disease is destroyed. It causes damage that's too extensive and the ability to regenerate is lost."

Palmer looked quickly at his notes, making sure he didn't miss anything. Satisfied, he turned the meeting back to O'Toole.

"Thank you, Doctor. I'm also sorry to announce that four of the five children that survived the rave party are on a downward spiral. They are all still in comatose states with steadily decreasing brain activity over the past few days. Several doctors throughout the Greater New York Hospital Association examined them, but no one found any answers. Physically, they appear to be fine, except for the puncture wounds. Each child was bitten in a discrete location and the wounds aren't healing. There isn't any reason for them to be comatose either, but they are. Doctor, do you have any thoughts on that?"

Palmer stood at his place at the table instead of returning to the podium.

"Dr. Murphy studied some of the blood itself. He's got samples from all six children, as well as three victims from the party. He's attempting to establish some kind of pattern or similarity. He also looked at the blood sample from the vampire that was found when this all began. Strict analysis of all the samples only produced one common element, the volume of the sample itself is consistently more than the sum of its component parts. In plain English, this means there is something in the blood that we cannot detect by other means. This type of situation only exists in one other place in nature, poisonous venoms. Highly poisonous venoms, such as that of the asp or Russell's viper, are virtually undetectable, and the amount of venom needed to kill an adult male is less than one CC. An amount that small spread throughout a person's blood stream is virtually undetectable, but it will still kill you. Most varieties of venom attack the central nervous system, promoting complete neurological shutdown and death. If this is the case, a vampire can introduce a type of venom into the victim, and it works slowly at destroying the nervous system. This supports the state most of the comatose kids presented with at the area hospitals. They were all incapable of speech and without fine motor control. We had one exception, and she recovered completely. We've run several tests, and we can't find anything specific about her to explain it."

Palmer sat back down.

"Thank you. We're getting a lot of heat from the parents, except for Trass' daughter. She was in our custody, but she disappeared sometime on the second day of her hospital stay. We need to be very concerned about his reaction to this. His network is very extensive, and he can get a lot done that cannot be connected to him in any way. We all know the extent of his influence and resources. I want you all to be careful. As much as it disgusts me, his people could take one of us out and we wouldn't be able to prove that he had anything to do with it. Now, I'd like to give Jamison the floor, he has some additional information and comments."

Jamison took the podium.

"Thanks to Joshua's connections in England, we got more info about what we believe this group is, or was, looking for. A man named Alfred Sayer was found dead in England and he was apparently a courier for this group. He paid $1.7 million for a book at an antique auction in Stockholm, Sweden. His trail wove through Europe, via land and sea travel only, ending somewhere in the Irish Sea. His body was found, but the book was not recovered. We contacted the owner of the auction house, and he described the book as some type of ancient text, written in an unknown language, and said Sayer wanted it very badly. Bidding began at just over $500,000, and Sayer started by raising to the $1.7 million selling price. The other bidders never made an offer. His competition was shocked into silence, but that price was considered far more than the book was worth. This book ended up in the Thornquist warehouse off the docks, the same one that caught fire, the same one that Joe was led to by a couple of homeless victims, and the same one that's very close to the rave party crime scene. The evidence also implicates the owner, Alan Thornquist, but he was found yesterday in the Hilton parking garage in his car, dead from cocaine overdose."

"As you can see, we have very little to work with out there. We've managed to control the problems with the media and our information leak was eliminated. I want you all to use extreme caution out there, and you all need to go by the SWAT Team office on the way out. We're issuing higher-powered ammunition and special body armor. The armor is lightweight Kevlar, but it's puncture resistant. It'll keep a .44 slug from going through you from ten feet, but I wouldn't suggest testing it on your own. The force of impact will leave a very nasty bruise and it can fracture bone if it lands in just the right spot. It should be sufficient enough to protect you if you go hand to hand with one of them, although we don't want to see that happen either. If you get in a tight spot, get out as quickly as you can. Don't try to take one of these bastards on by yourself. If you have any questions, please direct them individually to Joe or myself. You're dismissed."

The group filed out silently in a somber mood laced with fear. They all realized what was happening, and what would continue to happen somewhere else if they didn't get the job done. They knew they had to protect the citizens of New York from an enemy they apparently couldn't stop.

Malcolm and Emilio reached the meeting room as the officers were leaving, and it was obvious that it wasn't good. They went inside the room to Joe and the others to get a condensed briefing. They were about two days behind on their desk work and reports from being secluded with Marina and Julie.

Angela spent the daylight hours alternating between practicing with the broadsword, increasing her agility, or looking over some of Daxxe's books. The texts proved frustrating for her since she only understood some of the incantations. Some looked like complete gibberish. From what she could understand, she gathered that the magic remaining in the Earth was practically alive and able to have a mind of its own. If the mage couldn't control the magic, the magic wouldn't even let the mage try. This foresight, instilled by whom she had no idea, was a very effective safeguard. Magic running out of control could do significant damage and hurt or kill the attempting wielder.

As she went through her routines and studies, it dawned on her that she hadn't slept, nor could she really remember the last time she had. She was even more amazed that she didn't feel like she needed it. She could feel herself improving and becoming more efficient as she practiced, and she even recovered from the exertion much faster than she expected.

During one of her breaks to look at the books, she took off the amulet to study it closer and suddenly felt exhausted and shaky. Her eyes went dry and sticky and started to burn like she'd been in a swimming pool all day. Suspicious, she slipped the amulet back around her neck.

She was nauseous for a few seconds and then she was fine again. So that's why he told me to wear it all the time. The amulet obviously held more enchantments than he felt inclined to tell her.

As Angela's strength returned she noticed a strange scent hung in the air, like a mixture of flowery potpourri and brimstone. She jumped up, startled, when something moved at the edge of her vision. She didn't see anything at first, but something didn't look right. She could see an area where her vision looked slightly distorted and out of focus. She backed away a few steps, readying her sword, as something faded into view. The ethereal form manifested out of thin air right before her eyes, taking a few seconds to take recognizable shape. It was Jamat.

He floated slowly towards Daxxe, looking him over. He didn't really have discernable legs as a thick mist took the place of them below his knees. He looked to Angela after he finished his inspection.

She stood motionless, totally amazed, never before seeing anything like it, but she had no trouble accepting it after everything else over the last few days. He floated closer to her, but kept a good distance between them. He pointed at her chest with his right index finger.

Angela looked down, realizing the amulet drew his interest. He nodded his head in acknowledgement as she put her hand around it. Jamat mimicked her stance, holding his hand before his chest, and then he raised his hand up in front of his eyes, acting as though he was looked through something and waited. Angela duplicated the motion, and as the amulet broke her line of sight, something surged over her. She dropped the amulet back to her breast to find herself standing in a thick, knee deep fog. Jamat, now flesh and blood, stood in the mist.

"Thank you."

Angela debated taking a defensive stance, considering the last time they met.

"What's happening?"

"The amulet you now possess allows you to communicate with the ethereal planes. In this place, I look as you remember me, but I can take any form."

"Why are you here?"

"My soul is not at rest. I will be here for eternity unless it is released."

"Why is your soul trapped here?"

"In life, I vowed my body and soul to Daxxe, his quest, and his well-being. His quest is not ended; therefore, my vow has not been fulfilled. I can only be released if the rites are performed."

"I never heard Daxxe mention anything about rites."

"It is not his place to know. The knowledge of the rites is passed down from protector to protector. My existence in your world was cut short before I could pass the knowledge on to you."

"I thought the protectors were only replaced if something like this happened, when the predecessor was killed."

"At times it is, but the protector usually makes the decision. Immortality is a double-edged sword and not everyone is cut out for it."

"How does that work?"

"The gift can be taken away as well as given. If a new protector must be chosen, the predecessor will perform the rites. After the transference, the predecessor's soul moves to the next plane of existence and the physical body ceases to exist."

"You mean dies?"

"Not in the sense that you understand it now. We don't truly die, but the Triskelion does not permit me to tell you any more than that."

"What is the Triskelion?"

"Not what my dear, but who. I've already said too much. You will understand, in time."

"I see. So, what were the things you didn't get to tell me that you are allowed to say?"

"You have already discovered most of your abilities on your own. You are very astute and an excellent choice on Daxxe's part."

"Thank you. I didn't feel you thought very highly of me."

"I have learned much since last we met. I was quick to judge and harsh with my opinions. Wisdom and true sight have shown me the error of my ways. The gift within you is the strongest I've ever seen. Now, we must begin. I don't have much time."

"What do I need to do?"

"I'll tell you so you can perform the rites on your own."

Jamat explained the rite in detail, emphasizing the points of highest importance.

"Once complete, my soul will be released. You will gain a full understanding of your responsibilities and abilities. As I did, you will be able to summon any of your predecessors in times of need. We are permitted to share some of our wisdom and offer advice."

"Permitted by the Triskelion?"

"Yes, they…"

Jamat stopped himself midsentence before he spoke his entire thought.

"You're a very clever girl. I can see why you're so well suited to this. Again, that's something I cannot tell you. At some point, you will be able to see what I can see, and I assure you it will be wonderful. Now, we must begin the rites or they won't be finished before sunset."

Angela drew her sword from its scabbard and pointed it directly at Jamat. She held it level with the ground, whispered a required word, and released the hilt. The sword levitated in place. She took the amulet in both hands and held it as far from her as the chain would allow. A simple, spoken prayer unlocked it, allowing the gem to come loose from the body of the amulet, the weight seeming more than the original amulet in its entirety. With the gem released, Angela could read the words engraved inside the face of the amulet itself. Angela looked towards Jamat, and he nodded silently to indicate she was doing everything correctly. She read the inscription. The sapphire started to glow from within, dimly at first, then looking like a bright blue star. It pulled out of Angela's hand and floated to the spot directly above the hilt of the levitating broadsword. The gem lowered itself, melding into the hilt and becoming a part of the weapon, illuminating the blade with the same light as the gem. As Angela spoke the last word, her right hand moved of its own volition and grasped the sword's handle. It was extremely hot, almost to the point of burning, but she couldn't let it go. The blue glow started radiating from her as well. The powers in control forced her to use the point of the blade to carve two symbols into the ground. The etching looked like two Celtic crosses, touching base to base. Each cross was enclosed within a circle and a larger, also perfect circle, enclosed them both. According to Jamat, the cross represented Daxxe.

Angela moved within one circle, standing on the intersection of one cross, and Jamat stood on the same spot in the other circle. His body illuminated a brilliant red, to the point he was lost in the light. The energy poured out of him, spilling into the grooves of the etched symbols and flowing towards Angela. It seeped up into Angela, deepening the radiance to a dark indigo. The sensation was intense and she cried out in pain. It grew stronger with each instant, finally shooting through the symbols and bursting up through Jamat with a blinding flash. When Angela's eyesight returned, she no longer glowed and Jamat was gone. She was standing in the small chapel, holding her sword, and the amulet hung around her neck with the gem attached. She almost convinced herself nothing happened when she looked at the floor. The symbols were burnt into the hardwood and some places along the grooves still glowed like embers. The fragrant smell of burnt wood hung in the air.

She felt light-headed and weak and needed to get off of her feet. She found herself sitting across from Daxxe, staring at him. He was granite, unmoving and unfeeling, and she wondered what it was like for him. She couldn't fathom existing in such irony, a unique power of purity, highly skilled and creative in darkness, but completely vulnerable and helpless in the light. She wondered if he could still see and hear, or if he spent the daytime hours in a black void. Does he still think, or is he truly a big rock? A noise caught her attention. It was so slight she almost wondered if she really heard anything at all, but instinct told her to make certain.

In an instant, she slipped her hood over her head and went to investigate the noise coming from outside. She peered through a crack in one of the boards covering the lower windows of the chapel. An old pickup was parked in front of the building. An elderly man got out, wrapping his overcoat around his body tightly, trying to keep the severity of the cold air away.

He turned to approach, walking towards the front door of the little church. She got a glimpse of his Roman collar, and she bolted for the entrance. She couldn't do anything with Daxxe, and she was supposed to be dead; she had to keep the priest outside. The chapel, being a place of worship, did not have a lock on the doors. Angela panicked until she saw a large timber standing next to the doorframe; it fit perfectly into a pair of ornate brackets mounted on both sides of the door. The locking system was hidden well, even though it was in plain sight, and it kept the lock invisible from the outside. She quietly slid the board in place as she watched the inner half of the door handle move.

He tried the door. It was locked as it should be, like the large wooden double door to the main chapel, but he always double-checked it when he came out. The side door had a normal key-operated lock and deadbolt and it was not visible from the front or the grounds. It kept any over explorative vandals and miscreants out of the church itself.

Satisfied, he walked off away from the building. Angela moved back to the window, preparing for whatever he was going to do. He walked into a small, fenced in area. She hadn't noticed the small cemetery before. He walked to a spot near the center of the small graveyard and knelt before a simple headstone, wiping snow from its face and top.

Angela was surprised she could read the engraving from so far away. The grave was the final resting place of a man named Stephen Prost. She had no idea what their connection was, but she could see the priest's lips moving as he knelt. Stephen passed almost seven years earlier.

Angela started to relax when she felt someone, or something, behind her. She reacted defensively, almost laying into Daxxe with her sword.

"Don't do that!" she barked as quietly as possible, unaware Daxxe was awake.

"My apologies. He is my connection to God."

"What? I'm confused."

"The man in the graveyard, he is my connection to God, and now yours as well. I go to him each time I kill one of them, praying their souls will not suffer eternally, as did you at St. Christopher's."

"That's Father Samuels? I didn't recognize him."

"In the flesh, and our presence puts him under a great deal of pressure. He is completely devout to God and incorruptible; that is the reason I chose him."

"So why did he come to us, I mean, the police?"

"I anticipated he would approach them because his sense of integrity is very strong, but that knowledge doesn't hinder my progress. He knows my voice, some of my actions, and some of the consequences of my actions, but I have yet to be proven to exist even though many people know about me. Your counterpart, Joshua Stone, for instance, has followed me for some time, knowing I exist, but he has no means to prove it."

"He mentioned that to us, but he only spoke of you as a theory. He classified the homicides into two different groups, the innocents killed by vampires and the vampires you've apparently destroyed."

"Stone's known of me for quite some time, and until recently, he didn't remember how long. He was orphaned when he was young, and he bounced from foster home to foster home. At one point, he ran away from one of his foster families, determined to make it on his own. He ended up in a very seedy section of London, alone, cold, and hungry, and he was attacked by one of them. His was slashed open from his shoulder to the back of his leg before I could intervene. He saw me before he blacked out, and I saw the fear and shock in his eyes. I patched him up and took him to the church I was using there. They took him in, to raise him within the walls of the church. His surrogate father, the headmaster of that church, only knows me as Samuels does. From that point on, he was a good kid, and a hard worker. He left the church when he was old enough, wanting to do something that would allow him to protect other people. As an adult, our paths crossed several times, and he follows it because he's managed to piece together what happened to him so many years ago."

"It's such a small world. It's funny how things like this happen."

"It's not coincidence, it's fate. Since the destruction of Talamhan, the powers that be keep a hand in the world, and many things happen as they do because they were ordained long ago. We can't see the outcome because we need the journey to survive – we would cower from our own destinies if we knew what was coming."

"I don't follow you."

"Would you walk through a door if you knew you would be shot and killed by doing so? No, obviously, because we have a basic instinct to survive, but by not going through the door, someone else would die in your place, causing a chain reaction. You would be alive when you shouldn't be, and someone else would be dead when she was supposed to be alive. Fate doesn't give up. The skein of life would continue, finding a way to kill you and trying to fix the damage of someone else dying too soon. You have probably seen it many times, but didn't see it for what it was."

"Yes, I have. I can't remember the number of times I've heard doctor's say that someone was alive, although by all rights they shouldn't be. I've seen innocent bystanders struck with multiple gunshot wounds pronounced dead at a crime scene, only to be resuscitated in route to the hospital."

"It happens all the time and it will continue to happen throughout time."

"If that's the way it is, why do you follow these vampires? If you can't change fate, what's the point?"

"We have the advantage of seeing the past and the future, which makes fate powerless to us, but it was not this way in the beginning. Fate lost its power over us when Trokar was born. Gargoyles and vampires will follow a path without direction until one of us is completely destroyed, and the fate of the world will be decided by the victor."

Angela sat in awe, only beginning to understand the complexity of the position she chose.

"How will we stop them?"

"It will come down to a battle between Trokar and me. One of us will end up with all of the Books of Kalanak, and the future of the Earth and Talamhan will rest there."

Angela heard the old pickup start and drive away. Samuels finished his time with Mr. Prost and returned to St. Christopher's. Daxxe prepared to venture into the night as well.

"What do you want me to do? Am I to stay here?"

"No, I will need you with me. Trokar is undoubtedly growing impatient with our game, so he will send everyone he can to look for us, and I do not know how many that may be. The book I possess will be safe as it's hidden in a place Trokar cannot truly discover for now, but we still have to get the other books from him."

Angela readied herself as well, most of the preparation being mental.

"You will have to move by the land. You do not yet have the ability to fly, and we don't have the time for you to learn the magic to do it. I will move from rooftop to rooftop so you can follow on the ground. You will have no problem keeping up, and your instincts will keep you on the right path."

Daxxe walked out of the church and flew into the storm, bound for the skyline of the city. Angela ran through the snow, amazed she was easily able to keep up with him even though the snow was three to four feet deep in places. They were headed downtown.

Angela stopped in an alley behind the building Daxxe lit on. The buildings housed only businesses, so no one was in the area at night. She heard a metallic, scraping sound from up the street. She looked for the source from her hiding place. Two metal panels, set in the sidewalk, opened. They were hinged on the ends, folding up like a drawbridge, allowing a lift that carried a single man to street level. She watched him step off and fly into the air. That's it! Daxxe must have figured out where they were hiding.

The lift started to close and Angela broke into a noiseless sprint. She dove for the lift when she was within a few feet, falling a few feet down to the surface of the lift as the metal panels sealed shut. Her eyes adjusted quickly to the darkness, but the shaft offered little to see. She didn't know where the lift went, but she knew they generally lowered just below street level. They were used by businesses as a way to receive freight if they didn't have a place designed for it somewhere else. The lift continued to lower, traveling much farther than the height of one floor, reaching the bottom almost five stories below street level. The only way she could go was through an access tunnel that ran parallel to the street, and she couldn't decipher its length.

Daxxe landed in the alley where Angela stopped, but she was nowhere in sight. He heard her thoughts, but he did not know the location of the entrance. He went to her as quickly as he could and tried to locate her, but the amulet she wore did not respond. He could no longer sense her thoughts. He searched the area where he last sensed Angela's presence, but he found nothing. Wherever she went, she was on her own.

Angela walked down the tunnel, destination unknown, noticing the air had a stale, old smell to it that got stronger the farther she went. She finally saw a rectangle of light at the end of the tunnel. It was a doorway and the door was closed. She approached it slowly, even though the cloak kept her movement silent. The air pushing around the edges of the door was pungent with decay and death. She listened carefully while she adjusted to the stench, waiting almost ten minutes before daring to open it. The unrestricted flow of air almost gagged her when she cracked it open.

The passage led into a large hallway. The floor was smooth concrete, and the walls were covered with tiles in burnt orange, pea green, and tan. It looked very old and vaguely familiar.

A quick glance let her know the hallway was empty, so she stepped into the open, carefully closing the door behind her. The side of the door that faced the hallway had words stenciled on it that read:

N.Y.T.A.

Authorized Personnel Only

Not an Exit

She was somewhere in the subway system, but from the looks of it, a very old and deserted section of it. Only about half of the lights were on, and she couldn't hear anything aside from the occasional drips of water and the scurrying of rodents and larger insects. She lowered the hood of her cloak to take advantage of her peripheral vision.

The hallway ran both directions for a long way, and she could see a wider spot in the hall to her left. She walked cautiously, trying to keep herself in the best defensive position. The wider area of the platform was at one time a boarding area for the subway that ran there. The sign on the wall identified the terminal as Washington Boulevard and 5th Avenue. She walked through one of the tiled archways and found herself on the platform. The tracks would have been just beyond the edge if they were still there and in use. A stairway to the right used to go to street level, but the first landing was bricked up. She walked to the edge of the platform, looking up and down the tunnel, gasping as she discovered the source of the smell.

The platform in most subways was at least three feet higher than the level of the tracks, but she could only see half that far to the ground. The entire area was covered with remains, ranging from bare skeletons to lightly decomposed corpses.

Oh my God, this is why we didn't have more bodies!

At first glance, the count reached into the hundreds. She almost wretched when she noticed movement among the dead, some being insects and some being maggots feasting on the dead tissues. They brought their kills home and discarded them like fast food wrappers when they were done.

She dropped to her knees, doubling over until her forehead almost touched the concrete floor. She recognized a few of the bodies. They were some of the homeless people that lived in the same alley as Todd and Freddy. She spoke to one of the fresh corpses only a few days before.

Bang!

Angela got to her feet, spinning around and looking for the source of the noise. She regained her composure quickly, considering where she was and who she suspected was approaching. Noise filtered down from the hallway leading to the access tunnel, so she crept back through the arches to look up the hall. The door to the access tunnel stood open, and she realized the noise came from the door swinging all the way open and hitting the wall behind it. She held fast, noticing movement in the shadows beyond the door. Two people walked in the hallway, moving away from her.

The hydraulic closer on the door pulled it shut with a click, and she saw the two figures follow the hall around a curve and out of sight. She followed, and as she approached another terminal area, she heard voices. She was too far away to make out any words, but she could tell that at least three people were talking. I've found their lair. This is the perfect place. There's no chance of sunlight ever touching these walls, and these terminals have been deserted for years. The voices grew louder as she walked. She stopped close enough to overhear the conversation, but far enough away to be out of sight. The two she saw just fed, and they were both talking loudly and acting obnoxious.

"You've got to stay away from the drunks. I grow tired of dealing with your stupor when you return. Get it out of your system before you come back!"

"You're always a downer, Viktor. We're just having fun. You should have seen them run. They were in tears. It was great!"

Viktor was out of his hammock, and on top of the carousers in a flash, before they knew what hit them. Angela watched the shadows play out the confrontation as she moved closer, surprised that they had shadows at all. She guessed that the lack of a shadow was probably another old wives' tale.

She could tell that one of them held the other two off of the ground by their necks. Angela moved close enough to see while they made enough noise to mask her approach.

"You will not return in this condition again. Is that understood?"

Both answered positively. Viktor dropped them and returned to his hammock. The two shadows worked farther away, slowly fading.

That terminal must have been a major junction when it was in use. It's much larger.

Angela realized she wasn't in a good position when she heard the door to the access tunnel swing open again. She was standing in the main path they used to come and go. She looked up, asking for help from above, when she saw what she needed. A catwalk, attached to the wall near the ceiling, hung in the darkness. It would have been impossible to see for someone without her newly acquired gifts. The access ladder hung on the other side of the hall, and the bottom hung ten feet from the floor. A jump got her to where she needed to be, and a short climb found her lying on the catwalk, looking down through the floor grating. She focused on being hidden.

A man walked with a blond woman. She moved happily, sometimes even skipping around the man with her, giving him light touches on his face or arms.

"Oh, that was just too fun!"

"I'm glad you enjoyed it."

"Do you have to deal with Viktor right away? Can't you come to bed first?"

"No, Shayla. I have to take care of business first. Go to my chamber. I'll be there soon."

Angela watched the woman go ahead, doing what she was told.

This was the first time she actually saw Trokar. He was very tall, and he moved with confidence rooted in wisdom and the natural ability to lead. The vampire known as Viktor approached him before he reached the main area of the terminal.

"We have a problem, Master."

"What kind of problem?"

"We have not found him and some of the others are missing. I've got a bad feeling in my gut about the tunnels under the church. I think Daxxe set a trap for us. I can't sense them, but my power is far weaker than yours."

"I see. Let me take a look."

Angela couldn't understand what he said even though she recognized the language. It was the same strange tongue that Daxxe spoke to cast his incantations.

"You're right, they're dead."

"All four of them?"

"Yes, and Daxxe will pay dearly for Damok and Mekune. They were loyal servants."

"What are our orders?"

"We've got to find Daxxe. Get the others! We leave immediately!"

Angela watched a total of nine vampires follow Trokar and Viktor back to the access tunnel. She waited for several minutes, listening. Convinced she was alone, she went down the ladder and entered the terminal. It was even larger than she first suspected.

It used to be a major intersection of the old system, and it appeared as though it also served as an administrative area for the Transit Authority at one time. A number of offices sat off of the main room. Only one of the doors stood closed, so she checked the other rooms first.

It looked like the offices served as quarters for Trokar's clan. Each room held makeshift beds and some personal belongings. One room had a hammock, and it was the largest of the rooms thus far. Finding nothing of interest, Angela approached the closed door, reaching out to open it when she remembered the blond woman. She didn't leave with the others. Angela reprimanded herself for not thinking about her, then a plan formed in her mind.

Trokar entered his chamber. Shayla lay on the bed, awake and dressed in a thin cotton gown, her body easily visible through the fabric.

"Are you coming to bed, love?"

"Not just yet. I want you to do something for me that will make things more exciting."

"Anything for you."

"I want you to go to the Empire State Building and wait for me on the observation deck."

"Why there?"

"I want the city to hear your cries of passion, and I want to see all that we'll command while I enjoy you."

Shayla's eyes flickered with excitement. She dressed quickly in a black, skintight cat suit with a black leather half jacket and matching stiletto heels. She walked up to him, leaning forward to give him a kiss, stopping just before their lips touched.

"No, not yet. If I must wait, so shall you."

She strutted through the door and left.

Worry consumed him when he felt the presence of vampires slowly approaching. He took cover quickly. Luckily, they didn't have the ability to sense him. He wasn't sure how large their number, but he could feel it was a sizable group. Daxxe kept himself at a distance to retain his advantage, using his capabilities to follow them undetected. If he got too close, their other senses would detect him.

He followed the group back to the rubble of St. Francis. Trokar was with them, meaning something of importance was going to take place. It also meant that Angela faced less immediate danger wherever she was.

Trokar cast a spell of finding as the group worked towards the shore. He could feel the remains of his clansmen in the supply depot, but he had no time to waste in a physical search.

Daxxe could do no more than watch. He was not capable of attacking such a large group at once with any chance of survival.

Viktor found a section of blackened skeleton when they reached the depot. He turned the collection of scorched bones over, inspecting the damage to the frame. He paid particular attention to the outer ends of the remains.

"Daxxe didn't do this. Mekune was killed with an enchanted blade. Someone's helping him."

Trokar bent down and picked up the carcass. He gave it a small glance and tossed it aside, then wiped away the blackish dust it left on his hands.

"He must have replaced Jamat. It means little. Whoever it is will lack the experience to benefit him. His days are numbered. All of you, find him! He has to be in the city. Viktor, come with me."

The group disbanded, searching for their prey. Daxxe chose to follow one of the younger males.

"I don't like this, Master. Daxxe has been out of sight for too long."

"I agree, and that is why we will wait."

"I don't understand."

"Daxxe isn't stupid. He would never attack us as a group, and he's probably already following one of the others. When he attacks, he'll compromise his position and we will be able to find him."

"That's very clever, Master. Are you certain he won't come for us first?"

"It's not his style. He knows he can't cover himself if any of the others remain."

Trokar and Viktor went to the Verrazano Bridge to wait atop the supports. They could easily reach the mainland or the island of Manhattan from their perch very quickly.

The young male vampire was obviously a recent turn. Daxxe could have walked behind him down the center of the street without him taking notice. He had the hardest time killing the young ones. They didn't truly understand what was happening, and they didn't have enough experience to last in a fight. Most of the time, they didn't even use a fraction of their power. Daxxe wanted it to be quick. It was the least he could do. He was about to make his move when he sensed Angela.

Daxxe, I need you.

He struck fast. His prey was dead before he realized he'd been attacked and Daxxe was gone. He followed Angela's thoughts, as fast as his wings could carry him.

Trokar and Viktor took to the air. Viktor sensed Krith's drain fade as he died. They could follow Daxxe by the remnants of Krith's life force. Some of the magic within Krith would stay with Daxxe like a residue for a short time. If they responded quickly enough, they could pick up the trail. They landed before Krith's convulsions ceased. Daxxe marked himself with the kill. They left the smoldering body and followed the trail Daxxe left behind.

Officer Michelle Reilly and her partner Mike Travis drove slowly through a more remote section of the warehouse district. They were very cautious, even though the amount of recent activity in the overall area was declining. They were discussing the best deli in town when Michelle stopped the car.

"What is it?"

"Look, down there."

A man leaned over the body of a young woman. They could see her head flopping from side to side, like she was having a seizure. He dug his teeth into her neck and her body went still. Michelle slowly opened the door and slid out of the car, hearing a wet, tearing sound.

"Cover me Mike."

"Are you crazy?"

"Just do it."

Michelle crept down the alley towards the scene. At about thirty feet, the man looked up, directly at her, blood dripping from his lips.

"Don't move!"

Sven stood up, looking straight into the barrel of the officer's assault rifle. He dropped the girl's head he was holding to the ground where it joined the rest of her body. Michelle could see the terror forever trapped in the dead eyes as the killer started walking towards her.

Michelle pulled the trigger without issuing another warning, but Sven kept coming. Michelle's fear turned, fueling the rage swelling within her as she pictured herself lying in a puddle of bloody slush. She flipped the on Q-Beam taped to the barrel of the assault rifle and fired again, discharging several rounds.

Sven howled as the beam of light touched him, becoming more guttural when the hollow point shell tore through his shoulder. The UV light caught him in the eyes, blinded him and darkening the skin on his face as the cells ruptured and released the blood they contained. After a few seconds, the affected skin started to smolder, giving off a noxious black smoke. Apparently, the retrofitted Q-Beam from Special Ops worked.

Michelle pulled the trigger again, hitting the left side of his chest. The exit wound severed his left arm and took a large chunk of his back with it. He leapt into the air and disappeared into the swirling snow, leaving a dark smoke trail in his wake.

Michelle ran to the young girl in sheer fear and desperation, knowing she was beyond help. Tears welled in her eyes and her body seized up, ready to wretch convulsively. Hopefully she was dead before he decapitated her.

Sven landed on Michelle's back, slamming her to the ground. He reared back, ready to take off the back of her skull, and started shrieking right before another shot hit him. The front of his chest exploded into hundreds of black, rotten pieces right before his eyes, some dissolving into a fine powder before disappearing on the breeze. The force of the bullet knocked him off of Michelle and dropped him onto the blacktop. His feet twitched involuntarily.

Mike ran up the alley to his partner, keeping his rifle trained on Sven.

Michelle trembled and continued to cry, but she wasn't hurt beyond a few bruises and light cuts from the impact. Her back and the back of her head were covered with bits of liquefied vampire entrails that dissolved quickly into a foul smoke, completely gone with the wind, as if it never existed.

Mike called in on the radio attached to the shoulder of his flak jacket, requested an ambulance for his partner and someone from the task force. Michelle managed to get to her feet as the first wave of shock settled itself. She immediately hugged her partner. She was glad to be alive, but she still needed support.

"That was pretty gutsy, Mic. I let HQ know the UV seems to work. You're lucky it slowed him down enough to land that shot."

Michelle continued to tremble, and she wouldn't let go. She held onto her partner as though her very existence required physical contact with another human being. In all her years of duty, and all her scuffles before joining the force, she never come face to face with the fact she wasn't indestructible. The wake-up call scared her to death.

Trokar felt Sven pass, but the trail to Daxxe pulled him in a different direction.

"We have lost Sven, but it wasn't by Daxxe's hand."

"Do you think it's his new recruit?"

"It might be. Sven wasn't very old; he could have painted himself into a corner."

"He was promising though, it's a shame."

"I know and I want you to go check it out. I'll follow Daxxe's trail."

Viktor branched off, heading in Sven's general direction, but he didn't continue that way. Instead, he turned towards the subway terminal. The perfect opportunity to get the books from Trokar's chamber presented itself, letting him initiate his plan. The fight with Daxxe would weaken Trokar if not outright kill him. Viktor and his two loyal turns could finish Traokar, allowing him to take control and reign over the clan.

Shayla sat on a bench on the observation deck, exited anticipation being pushed away by frustration. She expected Trokar much earlier. He usually found a way to make her wait, but never before this long. She wanted to go back, but she was afraid he would arrive after she left and become angered.

Viktor walked into Trokar's chamber, heading straight for the bookshelves. He was disappointed that Shayla wasn't there. He looked forward to bedding down with her again.

Trokar trusted him implicitly, so he didn't check Shayla very closely. She was turned before she entered Trokar's chamber, given the knowledge of how to act and react beforehand to keep the ruse alive.

She knew Viktor's plan before she was "given" to Trokar, and she performed loyally the entire time.

Viktor literally froze with shock when he realized the Books were gone. When he regained his senses, he tore through the room.

The Books have to be here – he always kept them here.

Finally, he stopped and calmly walked back into the terminal. The Books weren't the only things missing from Trokar's chamber. He was no longer impressed with the quality of her acting.

At street level, he called to her with a benefit shared by every vampire and their turns. She responded in his thoughts.

What are you doing? He's coming here. We cannot be seen together.

Stay there; it will be a while yet. His errand is taking longer than he expected.

Viktor jumped into flight, ending it when entered the observation deck of the Empire State Building. Shayla sat on one of the benches.

"Are you crazy? He'll find out about us if he sees us together."

"I don't think that will be a problem."

"What?"

"I think he already knows. Did you tell him about Sayer, too?"

"What are you talking about?"

"I won't fall for your little games anymore. When did this stop being an act for you?"

Shayla backed away, feeling his anger. His eyes were feral. He got this way at times, and she knew she couldn't get through to him when he was this mad.

"You must be punished for your betrayal, but I'll go easier on you if you give me the Books."

Shayla was completely confused. Has he gone crazy? She backed into the safety grill that prevented visitors from jumping off or throwing things off the building. She couldn't go any farther.

"Viktor, you're confused. I don't know what you're talking about. I didn't take the Books. Trokar keeps them in his chamber; you know that."

"Do you think I'm that stupid? How can the Books be there when you took them? Do you think I can't sense your lust for power?"

Viktor knew he was right by the look on Shayla's face. For the first time since she was turned, she actually felt fear.

"Viktor, I…"

"Lying whore!"

The back of Viktor's hand struck her cheek. He didn't pull his punch, so the attack spun her all the way around and sent her spinning to the floor. He kicked her squarely in the ribs as she tried to get up. The force of the blow hurled her across the deck. Her head struck one of the support columns, rendering her unconscious.

Viktor left the observation area and cast a spell of finding. He taught himself most of the spells in the Books of Kalanak while the others were away from the lair. Some of the incantations were particularly handy.

"New York Police Department, what is the nature of your emergency?"

The 9-1-1 dispatcher's computer screen showed the call originating from a pay phone.

"She's…oh God…I can't believe…"

The caller's voice was shaky and she was crying.

"Are you hurt, Ma'am? Are you in danger?"

"No…she…she must have jumped. Oh God…it's horrible."

"What are you trying to tell me, Ma'am? Who jumped? From where?"

"A woman…she…oh my…she jumped from the Empire State Building. Oh God…I saw her hit…sidewalk. Oh God! She's dressed in black…and there's…," the sound of explosive vomit coming across the line, "dark pool spreading out under her. "

493

"Ma'am, did I understand you that you said a woman jumped from the Empire State Building?"

"Yes! She's dead! I know it!"

"Ma'am, can I get your name please?"

"I don't…I'd rather not…oh God!"

"Okay, ma'am, I'll send a unit out right away."

The computer showed the pay phone was on West 34th, between 5th and 6th Avenue. It also noted the time and date as it recorded the call. The blotter showed three other 9-1-1 calls for the same accident originating from cell phones in the same immediate area. The system was designed to prevent multiple units from responding to the same incident unless it was necessary.

The ambulance arrived first, but they silenced their sirens and doused the lights after a couple of minutes. They found a pool of liquid that looked too dark to be blood, but there was no body.

Daxxe found Angela in the bell tower of the Cathedral of St. Christopher's. She paced back and forth, keeping to the shadows, and not getting too close to the outer walls.

"What happened?"

"I didn't know where else to go. There are things you need to know."

She continued to pace, trying to resolve some inner turmoil, but not sharing it.

"Angela, what is it? You are keeping me out of your head now."

He could tell that this startled her. After looking upon her face, and hearing her thoughts when she let him back in, he could tell that she was utterly terrified. She did not speak, but pointed to her cloak. Daxxe could tell that something was inside the folds of the fabric, but it was unidentifiable from a distance. He went to the bundle and opened it carefully. He turned to Angela when the cloak's enchantments no longer shrouded the contents.

"How did you get these?" he asked incredulously.

She stopped pacing and looked towards him, but not directly at him. "I was in the right place at the right time. I can feel the power in them, how it surges off them in waves, and it horrifies me. I wrapped them in the cloak because it seems to shield me from them."

"This is outstanding! I'm sorry for the way the magic affected you. The feeling you have isn't the magic within them; it's caused by a hex they carry. It is harmless to anyone that knows nothing of the magic, but it can actually kill an inexperienced mage. It is trying to repel you, and if you hadn't relented, it could have finished you."

Daxxe gazed back at the Books, still in shock and denial that he now possessed all five.

"My quest is almost at an end."

Angela screamed as Trokar flew through the bell tower, lashing out at Daxxe as he passed and knocked him to the floor. She sensed Trokar's approach a split second before he got there, giving her enough time to avoid the brunt of the attack he carried through, but she still took a hard hit.

"Your ends, at least," Trokar said as he swept up to go back out into the night air.

Angela drew her broadsword and took a defensive position next to Daxxe. She looked for Trokar, but she couldn't find him in the winter storm beyond the tower's walls. She was near the center of the room, which allowed attack from any one of four possible directions.

Daxxe reached up and caught Trokar by the ankle as he passed a second time, pulling him from the air. He threw him down on the trap door in the floor of the bell tower with more force than the wooden cover could withstand. The door disintegrated into splinters as Trokar disappeared through the hole. Daxxe dove through right behind him. Angela started to follow, but she hesitated, thinking about the Books. She wrapped her cloak around them and jumped from the bell tower to the church's roof.

Trokar recovered before he fell all the way to the stairs, pulling up and slipping into the shadows. Daxxe was close behind him, but he still lost sight of his prey. That instant gave Trokar enough time to catch Daxxe in the back, forcing him into the staircase railing. The momentum carried him over the rail and he rolled down the steps to the next landing. Trokar jumped back up through the hole to the bell tower. With all the Books, he had no need to waste any more time on his adversary.

Damn that woman!

Trokar realized the tower was devoid of the Books and the increasingly irritating female helping Daxxe. He chose to give chase, but he barely had the time to react to Daxxe's claws slashing towards him. He pulled away, but not enough to completely avoid the attack. The blow slashed three gashes across his face. He was able to roll with the bulk of the force, recovering quickly and coming back on the offensive. He caught Daxxe in the side with a roundhouse kick, pushing the air from his lungs, but he didn't fall.

Daxxe grabbed Trokar's leg as he brought it around again and pulled up, hard. Trokar went down, landing on the back of his neck. Not letting go, Daxxe spun him around and threw him into the one remaining bell. Trokar tried to stop his momentum, but his head still hit the cast iron sound ring along the base of the bell, resonating with a dull tone as the contact set it in motion. He managed to catch hold of the lip, giving him leverage to push against. He used his free foot to kick Daxxe squarely in the face, knocking him backwards and forcing him to let go. He grabbed the clapper inside the bell's mouth and tore it from the housing under the crown. He advanced on Daxxe with the makeshift club in hand.

"I grow tired of you and your wench's meddling Daxxe. My destiny is clear. You will not stop me!" A large fresh gash ran across his forehead, marking where he hit the crack in the bell.

"It's not destiny. It's insanity!"

Trokar swung the heavy clapper. Daxxe instinctively put his arm up to block, but Trokar let the weapon loose. It flew past his arm and struck him in the side of the head. Daxxe staggered backwards to the outer wall of the tower. He heard something from the street below. The bell clanging before dawn attracted the attention of someone. The snowfall couldn't hide them completely, but the onlooker could only make out crude movement from that distance.

Trokar charged, grabbing Daxxe about the waist and lifting him up. The goal was to throw him over the edge to buy time. Daxxe swung his right arm up and buried his claws into the casement over the window, swinging both combatants out into the air. He couldn't shake

Trokar loose, so his back swing landed them both back on the floor of the bell tower.

Angela crept into the chapel, staying in the shadows along the edge of the room. The chapel was deserted, as to be expected so early in the day. An altar boy stood near the front, attending to the altar, while another one entered from the front doors, making a bee line for the other boy. Father Samuels wanted the chapel lit by candlelight at all hours, and the windows were kept closed. This provided a pleasing, warm feeling for the parishioners, and it highlighted the stained-glass depiction of Christ set into the wall above the altar.

"Did you ring the bell?"

"No, it's not the proper time. I assumed you did it, since you are always getting in trouble."

The chamber boys wouldn't have noticed Angela if she walked down the center aisle on fire, fully engaged in their argument. They stopped yelling at one another, looking at the ceiling, confused by the sounds coming from above since they were together. They both ran to the door to reach the bell tower.

Angela slipped into one of the confessionals with the Books. She looked around for somewhere to stash them until the excitement was over. The seat cushion was a little loose, so Angela pried it open to find the hollow place underneath was large enough to hold all five volumes. She set the cushion down just before the screen between the booths slid open.

"Welcome to the House of the Lord. How may I assist you?"

Angela went rigid; Father Samuels was in the next booth. She didn't know what to say. She sat motionless, trying hard to keep from even breathing.

Was he already in there?

"I'll give you a few minutes. These things aren't always easy."

The screen slid shut, and Angela heard his side of the booth open and close.

Now what? He's probably sitting out there, waiting. What now? An idea came to her. Please work.

She prayed as she opened the door and walked out of the confessional.

Samuels was surprised to see the door open. He couldn't avoid seeing the confessor, but it wasn't his fault the confessor lost anonymity. An elderly woman walked out, closed the door, and looked at Samuels.

"Excuse me, good sir, but I'm a little confused. I thought I was going into the ladies' room."

Samuels grinned, blushing slightly. "No ma'am, that's a confessional."

"Oh my dear heavens, how did I get there?"

"It's okay, ma'am. The restrooms are in the foyer just outside the chapel. I can show you if you'd like."

"No, thank you. I'm fine, sir. I can still get around on my own."

The woman moved down the aisle slowly, headed for the doors. Samuels turned to return to the altar, but something didn't seem quite right about the older woman. It took him a minute to pinpoint that the way she moved was what he noticed. She leaned forward like her back was failing, but she didn't have a cane and she moved with an outstandingly smooth grace. He turned to check the bell, turning back to look again, finding the chapel empty and knowing absolutely that something wasn't right. She could not cover the distance to the doors in so little time.

Angela exited the front of the church and ran to a point where she could see the tower. There was now a small crowd of early rising parishioners gathered on the street, watching. She was thankful that their attention was focused away from her as she moved away, using the church itself as cover. She looked up in time to see Viktor enter the tower. Daxxe was outnumbered.

Samuels started towards the front doors to investigate his hunch when the sound of the bell diverted his attention again.

Why is the bell ringing at this hour?

He walked to the door behind the altar that led to the stairs for the bell tower, which was built directly over the main chapel. A set of motor-controlled panels, activated from the podium, allowed the bell assembly to be operated from the chapel. He glanced at the controls on the podium as he passed, making sure they were off. It was not unheard of for the altar boys to turn them on occasionally as a joke, and they both happened to be at the bottom of the stairs.

"Okay, enough joking for this morning! Back to your duties."

"But," said one, starting to point up.

"Out with you both!"

The boys did as they were told, worried about getting into any more trouble. The priest started up the stairs after they left, hearing an unusual noise from above. He didn't know what it was, but the voice in his head told him he was in a bad position. He looked up and saw the ceiling of the stairwell visibly shake, and the concrete started to crack and crumble. The wooden trap door was gone.

Daxxe felt Viktor's arrival, but he didn't shift his gaze from Trokar.

"The tables are turning against you now."

Daxxe flexed to attack when the bell's damaged crown cracked in two, letting the bell fall from its mount. The impact cracked the floor, and the added weight won the contest. Daxxe, Trokar, and the bell fell towards the bottom of the stairwell. The falling debris prevented Daxxe from spreading his wings. Trokar and the bell were falling just below him.

The bell struck bottom, bursting open the door to the stairwell, stirring up dust with a gush of air strong enough to extinguish the candles. Daxxe managed to reach out and catch the wall with his claws, sliding to a stop about one-and-a-half floors from the bottom. He couldn't see Trokar through the dust and debris rising from the bottom.

Angela ran to a side door of the church that looked like a direct path into the chapel. The door gave way and opened on her third pull, setting off the fire alarm, which would draw the Fire Department at the very least.

Can this get any worse?

Entering the church, the cleverly disguised sprinkler system automatically engaged, providing her answer. She decided it best not to ask any more questions as the cold water rained down inside the room.

Daxxe watched Viktor fly past him and into the cloud below. He heard the bell shift slightly, and then it tipped over. Viktor didn't have quite that much time. Trokar was still alive. He saw the shadow of one of them slip through the door at the bottom and enter the chapel. He saw movement again as he descended to the bottom.

"Viktor, stay here and attack him when he comes through the door! Together we can easily finish him!"

Trokar was missing most of his left arm. The bell's lip cut the rest of it off when he and it hit the bottom. He cradled the severed limb in his good hand, but he needed a few minutes to repair the damage.

"Once he's gone, we have to find the woman. She has the Books!"

"What?" asked Viktor, confused.

"Kill Daxxe and bring me the woman! She has the Books!"

Viktor turned to face his Master when Angela attacked. The sound of the water pouring from the sprinklers disguised her advance and masked her scent. Her aim failed her, as the sword thrust through his stomach after it entered his back, lower than the intended target. He spun and grabbed her by the neck, pushing her to the floor into one of the several puddles collected in the debris field, her head completely submerged. She flailed wildly for a moment, then her thrashing slowed and her body dropped, limp.

Viktor stood up in time to catch the full brunt of Daxxe's attack. He flew out of the bell tower at full speed, grabbing the handle of the sword still impaled through Victor with one hand and putting his other hand against the flat of the sword where it protruded from his back. The force knocked him to the ground and ripped the blade through sinew, muscle, and bone, until it swept clear of his side. Viktor howled in pain.

Daxxe, sword in hand, turned his attention to Trokar and saw him reconnect his severed arm. He charged and thrust, piercing the damaged arm with the blade. He twisted the weapon, severing the arm in the same spot that was already damaged. Trokar screamed in pain as the lower part of his arm separated and fell to the floor. Daxxe drew back, preparing to strike again.

Viktor kicked the back of Daxxe's leg, dropping him to both knees. The surprise gave Trokar the chance to attack. He broke forward, leaping into a flying kick that landed home. Daxxe crashed backwards through the rubble and lost his grip on the broadsword.

The angle of the attack forced Trokar off balance, and unable to break his fall effectively with only one arm, he fell into the broken concrete at the base of the bell tower. The sword clattered to the ground at Viktor's feet.

Viktor stood up, wielding the weapon. Blood oozed from the gash in his side slowly but steadily. The damage was extensive, making it harder for his body to regenerate as fast as normal. Daxxe was in easy striking distance, and Trokar was weakened enough to give him the advantage. Daxxe lay unmoving as Trokar got back on his feet.

"Give me the sword, Viktor. I'm tired of this game. It's time to finish it."

"Yes, it is."

Viktor stood at the ready, but he didn't relinquish the sword.

"I told you to give me the weapon!"

"I think not, you blind fool! Your reign is over. I've mastered your precious Books and I have no intention of serving you any longer."

Trokar, enraged with blind fury, leapt at Viktor. He avoided the sword, knowing how Viktor would defend himself, and drove his elbow into the center of Viktor's back. Bones cracked audibly and Viktor dropped to the floor.

"You dare betray me! I gave you your life, and this is how you choose to repay me!"

"You live in the past, only wanting to repeat that which didn't work to begin with. You spent so many years cowering from useless mortals! Hrmph! How did you think you could rule when you're so easily seduced by a female? I've already dispatched that wench of yours!"

The news about Shayla sent Trokar over the edge, as Viktor knew if would. He leapt at Viktor, thrusting his claws forward to rend flesh from bone. Viktor thrust backward with his legs, catapulting himself to and then off of the wall and out of harm's way. Trokar did not have the opportunity to follow as a second enemy remained.

Trokar turned to deal with Daxxe and realized his enemy was no longer lying on the floor. Trokar reached for the sword, but the blade pulled itself away from him and took to the air. It sped away and planted itself, blade first, into the floor of the chapel near the doors leading to the foyer. The handle stood easily within Daxxe's reach as he stood resolutely, holding the Books of Kalanak. The top Book was open and his lips were moving. He began casting the Spell of Binding to reforge the separate volumes into one book that would be magically bound to him. Once complete, no one else would have the power to command the Books. He was, however, vulnerable until the incantation ran its course.

"No!"

Trokar started casting a spell of his own as he ran towards his adversary. Daxxe didn't react, completely unaware of his surroundings, while the intense flow of magic swirled through him. The sword vibrated violently and slowly pulled itself from the floor. It flew into Trokar's outstretched hand once it gained freedom from the foundation.

"You idiotic fool! Did you think you would defeat me? How many times have I walked away victorious from these pointless contests? I'm growing tired of dealing with you. I'm putting this to an end!"

Daxxe remained motionless and entranced, the spell almost complete.

Trokar could not cover the distance in time, so he hurled the sword with extreme force at Daxxe. It moved swiftly across a slightly arched path, moving like a knife thrower's prized blade, spinning end-over-end as it moved and burst into flames about half way in between them.

Daxxe looked up from the Books in time to see the tip of the sword impale his chest and sink deep. The force of the blow knocked him off his feet and through the doors that led into the chapel's foyer. The doors slammed into the walls behind them before swinging back shut, shattered the glass viewing panel in each door. The Books fell to the rubble in the spot he stood, still in separate volumes.

Trokar closed the distance to reach the Books he sought for so long. He scooped them up and opened the Book of Descension to cast the Spell of Binding himself before he could be interrupted. Confusion entered his mind because the pages were devoid of writing. He checked each volume to find them all the same as they started to fall apart, dissolving into nothingness.

He turned to the double doors behind him in search of Daxxe. What he saw though the broken glass window in the door was the woman, trying to stand up. The sword was impaled into the breast plate of her armor, making it difficult for her to move or gain her balance. A small trickle of blood dripped off of the sharpened edge after it seeped from a sizable gash in the armor. She could not get the proper leverage to remove it as the handle was at arm's length.

"Trokar!"

He turned to look for the source of the summons. It sounded from behind him, so he looked over his shoulder. He saw Daxxe materialize out of thin air, by the confessionals, holding a large leather-bound book. The book looked new; it's cover a dark, rich leather and pages edged in gold. The five symbols adorned the front cover, each in a different color and each glowing with magical energy. The colors flowed around the Book, and around Daxxe, denoting its master.

Angela pulled the sword out of her armor after four tries, feeling blood running inside the breastplate on her skin. Pain shot through her as she moved, coupled with the shock that the sword pierced the armor and her chest.

Thank God it held.

She dropped the weapon to the floor and started checking herself. It appeared the blade only breached the breastplate by a few inches. She couldn't see the wound and knew it wasn't mortal, but it hurt and burned from whatever enchantment was cast on the blade. She dropped to her knees, trying to catch her breath.

The blow had knocked the air from her lungs, which slowed her recovery. A slight whistling sound, coming from under her armor, grew louder with each breath, and it was getting harder and harder to breathe. She realized the wound was worse than she thought, as the tip went deep enough to puncture her right lung. She quickly grew light-headed from the lack of air and the steadily increasing pain. She concentrated on the wound using all the strength she had left to focus her thoughts. She blacked out almost immediately, her wound throbbing painfully.

"I don't have to defeat you. Your thirst for power will do it for me. It blinds you."

"When I kill you, the Books will again divide. Do you have any last words?"

"That is not a question you are in a position to ask.".."

Trokar took to the air, using his clawed hand like a pointed blade. The attack was aimed at Daxxe's heart. His talons were almost an inch deep in Daxxe's chest when his forward motion stopped. Daxxe's clasped his hand around Trokar's forearm, squeezing hard to drive his own claws deep into the flesh. Trokar flailed, trying to release himself. Daxxe swung, adding more momentum to Trokar's arc, and slammed him head first into the floor. The sharp blow dazed him and Daxxe took full advantage of the situation. He bludgeoned Trokar's body with fierce punches and kicks to the head and chest until he fell to the floor. He was still alive, but severely weakened and unconscious.

Daxxe lifted Trokar's dead weight by his right arm and right leg. He spun a full revolution, like a hammer throw contestant, and threw him directly at the large, ornate stained-glass window built high into the wall of the chapel. His body shattered the glass, spraying multi-colored slivers and shards into the frozen air that fell like demonic rain to the pristine snow below.

Daxxe ran to Angela, grabbed her arm and hoisted her body over his shoulder, carrying her to the side door. He exited the church and went directly towards the area below the now shattered window. The jarring movement brought her back to the edge of consciousness.

She saw Trokar lying in the snow, covered with multiple cuts and gashes, surrounding by pieces of broken glass. It appeared he was trying to regain his senses, but the process was going very slowly. She drifted away in the ebb and tide of awareness as her body tried to recover. She was being carried by someone, Daxxe she assumed, as he ran to a side street and pulled a manhole cover open with ease, carefully lowering her through the steel portal until she was on the tunnel's floor.

"We have little time."

Daxxe jumped into the hole, grabbing the top rung of the access ladder to stop his descent. He pulled the steel cover back into place and jumped to the tunnel floor a few feet from his protector. He lifted her body into a half sitting, half reclining position against the side of the tunnel. The curvature of the rounded wall was gentle enough at the bottom to keep her from sliding into the foul-smelling run-off that trickled along the subterranean waterway. He sat directly opposite of her and leaned his head back against the wall with a sigh of relief.

The first rays of sunshine broke over the ridge of the skyline, spilling light over the street. Daxxe could sense the sunrise, even though the rays could not breach the steel seal of the manhole cover. Angela sensed the dawn as well, and it gave her the final push she needed to awaken, although sluggish.

"We are safe now. His developing followers that remain will not survive without their mentors, but I am unsure how many more are fully mature. The clan will likely disband and they'll venture out on their own, making them easier to destroy. I must destroy the Books, and that only leaves us to worry about cleaning up."

"I don't understand. What the hell just happened?" said Angela, angry but without the energy to fully appear so. "How do you know he was still out there when the sun rose? This entire quest was to destroy him and his reign of terror, but you didn't kill him."

Daxxe closed his eyes, and looked at the ceiling of the sewer tunnel will a sullen look. "I thought I would be able to when the time came, but...I could not."

"What do you mean you can't kill him?" Her voice was getting louder and she was sitting more upright. "Will the magic not let you? Is there some twisted sense of balance in place? How will it ever end?"

"No...it's not the balance or the magic, it only deals with me. Trokar has not always been what he is now. In the beginning, when Earth was newly created from the sundering, he was known as Kurtak. He was one of the best, intelligent, strong, and honorable, but too ambitious. Over time that ambition led him down the path of darkness, as I warned you could happen. He lost sight of the understanding that we were left behind to provide unconditional protection for this new world. He grew tired of protecting a land and a people from the shadows, knowing that they didn't appreciate his efforts or would even accept him if they knew of his existence. He saw himself as superior to humans and you've seen the end result first hand."

"That still doesn't answer the question of why." Her tone was softer, expecting the other shoe was about to fall.

"I was christened with two names at birth, as was Trokar. His true name is Kurtak Gilmesh. Mine is Daxxe…Gilmesh. We are brothers."

Angela gasped in shock.

"I cannot kill him in good conscience. He can die by his own misfortune, but I now know he will not die by my hand. I know who he was, and I refuse to believe that Kurtak is completely lost."

chapter forty-three

Officer Reilly walked into Joe Anderson office after lightly rapping on the door frame. He looked up at the sound. She was catching her breath.

"Yes, oh, good morning Michelle." He leaned back in his chair, waiting.

"Detective Anderson," she started before he put his hands behind his head, interrupting her.

"Joe is fine. You don't need to address me so formally. What have you got?"

"I think the answer we have been looking for, but I cannot explain how it happened." She offered her cell phone to Joe with a picture pulled up. "I took this less than five minutes ago in the garage."

In the photo, three dead bodies were lined up on the cement floor next to Joe's unmarked car. On the chest of the middle body, both of the hook weapons rested, with a toe tag attached to one, dated the day before Angela's death, that read:

"For Detective Joe Anderson this is over. I cannot reveal my identity for obvious reasons, and I don't care what story you come up with to restore the faith in this city. I owed a debt, and this clears it for me."

"I will be damned," said Joe, handing the phone back to Michelle. She was smiling.

"I know, right, but it's over. Maybe this is the work of the natural predator Joshua told us about, not that it matters. How do you want to work this?"

"I will get with Jamison and we will come up with something that fits. It looks like that were shot, so maybe we can tell the public we cornered them and took them down." An idea formed in his mind.

"Yes, sir!" she said, snapping a quick salute and turning to walk away.

"Wait a sec Michelle."

She stopped and turned back, looking a little worried.

"I saw the report about what happened, which led me to your case file."

She lowered his eyes a bit, becoming more uncomfortable.

"This isn't about you cold cocking that fellow officer. From what I know, he had it coming. This is about you in the alley a few nights ago."

She raised her gaze, looking truly confused.

"That took some guts, and at first I thought was you were trying to be a hero. Once I got all the way through your file, a bit long I might add, I realized that you don't back down from the right thing to do, even if it could cost you. You stand up for those that are weaker than you, and the underdogs."

"Somebody has to. It doesn't feel right otherwise."

Joe nodded and walked back to his desk. He picked up a piece of paper that was sitting in the inbox and handed it to her. Her eyes when wide as she read it.

"Is this real?"

"Absolutely. I like your spunk, but you need a mentor. I would like to fill that role if you accept. Don't answer right now. Sleep on it, and let me know in the morning. Now, I need to get to Jamison's office. Good day, Michelle."

She looked at the letter again, signed by Commission Jamison and the Mayor, promoting her to the rank of Detective, with Joe's signature accepting her as his new partner.

"Call me Mic!" she yelled just as the elevator doors closed to take Joe to the right floor.

ChAPTER FORTY-FOUR

"This is Denise Rigsby, reporting live from the Cypress Hill Cemetery," started the reporter, speaking to the camera. She was dressed very professionally under a heavy coat suitable for the cold. "You can see the size of the congregation behind me to get a feel for the scope of it all, and that scope is well deserved. They are laying a posthumously-honored Detective to rest today that was key in stopping the recent string of killers in our city, that have now been identified as a group of three serial killers. Detective Angela Benson located the killers hiding in a deserted chapel and engaged them. She was able to shoot them, but one of the perpetrators was able to throw a hand grenade. It is suspected the blast felled Detective Benson, but it did not, the collapse of the old structure did. Her body was uncovered the day the church fell, but her sidearm wasn't located until the rest of the cleanup began."

Denise stepped to the right to allow the camera to focus on the service itself.

"We are staying back as a show of respect for Detective Benson, and for those family members and fellow officers she left behind. Now, for a moment of silence."

A small picture of Angela appeared in the lower left corner of the screen, displaying her date of birth and death. Alongside her picture was three pictures of the awards presented to her for her service: the Purple Shield, the Police Star, and of the Medal of Valor. The camera operator shifted the view to a procession of honor guard walking a short distance from those in attendance.

A line of honor guard fired into the chilly morning air three times. The reports echoed for a few seconds, mingling with the clear notes of "Taps" from the bagpipe soloist standing at a distance. The Mayor and the police Commissioner delivered their comments and prayers to the large group in attendance. Another pair of honor guard folded an American flag into a tight triangle of love, honor, and pride before presenting it to an older woman sitting by herself in the front row of chairs under a tent beside the grave. She accepted it gracefully, but never moved her stoic stare from the casket.

Jamison approached next, presenting the medals in a wood display box with a glass front and a bed of dark blue fabric to support them.

A few rays of sunshine found their way through the gray blanket of winter clouds and graced the congregation. The diffused light struck the casket, forming a warm, soft aura around it.

As the minutes gave way to hours, attendees slowly dispersed and drifted back to their cars and the toil of their daily lives. The attending pastor offered consolation and thanks, retaining his post until only two people remained by the grave. He simply patted them both on the shoulder as he walked past and headed for his car.

Angela watched from a secluded area along the tree line edging the cemetery's north side. She arrived just after dawn. It felt eerie as she watched the gravediggers do their work. She saw the bottom of the vault go into the ground, and watched them assemble all of the other equipment needed to make the service run smoothly. She saw the people arrive, following the long black hearse. The cars headlights were on and all the squad cars within the procession also ran their flashing emergency lights in silent tribute. The line of cars was longer than the cemetery's interior could accommodate.

It pained her to see the two most important people in her life sitting alone, mourning an untruth. She wondered how long it would take for her conscience to ease, if at all.

The absence of her father was not surprising. She would never know that her father was too ashamed to attend, taking ill after they got the call. The feelings of regret overwhelmed her, and she knew the illness would never truly pass. Marlin Benson would pass before the end of the year, leaving Susan forever alone. She already missed them, especially the special relationship she had with her mother. She was glad, at least, that she wouldn't be stuck in the middle anymore between her and her father. He saw Joe approach her mother and exchange a few words that she could not hear.

"You must be Joe," she said when he stepped before her.

"Yes, ma'am, and you must be related to Angela?"

"That's right. I'm Susan Benson, her mother. She spoke very highly of you."

"I'm sorry that she didn't have the chance to tell me much about you."

"That would have taken a lot longer. She was always pretty tight about her feelings and slow to let people truly get to know her. She

510

turned into a fine woman and I'm proud that she was my daughter. I never expected her to be taken so soon."

Susan turned back to face the casket and the grave waiting below it, her eyes misty again. She quickly regained her composure and turned back to Joe. It appeared that she'd reached some level of inner peace.

"I'd like you to have this," she said, standing up and handing the flag to Joe.

"Ma'am, I can't...it wouldn't..."

Joe wasn't sure what to do or say, so he just stilled himself to listen.

"I want you to have it. Angie told me how you looked after her and the way you treated her more like a surrogate father. I don't have to have this flag to remember the pride I felt when they gave it to me. I think you've earned this much in my book. Do you think they can display her medals somewhere with a picture of her, something to preserve her memory and maybe give an example to others?"

Joe nodded his head in acknowledgement, but he did not speak. For once in his life, he couldn't find his voice. Susan patted him on the back, but it turned into a hug before she walked away, bound for her vehicle with a long drive ahead of her. She stopped and turned about halfway across the expanse.

"Joe, if it's not an imposition, I'd like to buy you dinner in exchange for a small favor, if you're up to it. I feel like you've been a family friend for a long time. I've also got something here that I think you should see," she added, walking back to him.

"Sorry it took me a second, but we have a special display area at the Precinct where these will be displayed and protected. Her name will also be added to the Police Officers Memorial up in Albany. I have someone in mind that I will personally make sure sees it."

"I would like that very much, and I think she would, too."

She pulled a handwritten letter from her jacket pocket. It was already well worn from repeated unfolding, reading, and refolding, even though she received it only a few days before. The envelope that it came in was postmarked with the date of her daughter's death. She had committed every word to memory:

Dear Mom,

I've got a few things that I really need to say, just in case something happens to me. I want you to know that I love you very much, and you've been more than a mother, you've been a best friend. You've always been there when I needed you with the right thing to say, even though it wasn't always what I wanted to hear. I hope I make you proud.

I hope that you'll get a chance to meet Joe sometime soon. I think we're really hitting it off pretty well, and I think you would really like him. He's not your run-of-the-mill expectation, but he treats me more like a daughter than a police Officer.

Just remember that I love you, and tell Dad the same.

Love always, Angie

Joe offered the note back to Susan, unable to speak around the lump in his throat. She spoke no words, just nodded her head slightly as her eyes wet slowly, refusing to take it back. The understanding that passed between them did not need words for validation. She turned and walked the rest of the distance to her truck, wiping her eyes, while Joe turned back to his grave side vigil.

After a few more minutes, Joe finally turned to leave the earthen sepulcher, walking slowly to his unmarked police car. His right hand gripped a gold badge with a deep scar on the face. He cradled a flag, folded into a triangle, under his right arm. He reached into the pocket of his overcoat with his free hand, touching the worn note he had just put there.

He paused, looking at the forest of leafless trees bordering the grave yard, feeling as if they weren't alone. He saw only the skeletons of the dormant oaks, not willing to trust what he saw with his own eyes. He turned back towards the car, and some of his grief lifted because he knew she was in a better place.

Susan pulled her pickup closer to Joe's car and motioned him to approach.

"That's an awfully big truck, ma'am."

"It's like they say, everything is bigger in Texas. I needed it to pull our horse trailer up here. It's back at my hotel, and that has to do with the favor I asked of you. I'll buy that dinner and we can talk about it before I start my trip back home. Do you know of a good place?"

"It would be a great honor. As a matter of fact, I know the perfect place. Do you have any interest in old trains?"

Angela's vision tracked Joe until he pulled out of the cemetery, followed closely by her mother. One of the grounds men closed the gate behind them, barring access for what was left of the winter's day. She cut back through the trees as the first shovels of dirt landed on the top of her casket, easily clearing the fence and not returning to the ground.

THE END

epilogue

Night fell on the Big Apple with spring prying open winter's icy grip on the city. Snow was slowly replaced by rain as the seasons changed, allowing the city to thaw. With the disappearance of the blanketed snow, the panic and fear created by the wide spread killing spree faded in turn, replaced by tides of anger, frustration, and sadness for the fear and lives lost during the colder months. The events lost their mystique after the story broke, letting the city release a collective sigh.

The number of homicides had dropped back to a normal level. The cases were kept open internally as long as possible, even though all traces of the vampires were gone. The public was satisfied the serial killers were eliminated and the faith in the police was restored. The police retained the heightened patrols while they quietly looked for more evidence, being extra careful to keep the truth quiet, but they found nothing more.

Joshua Stone compiled all of the information he could before returning to England, hoping the cycle would not start again elsewhere. He still didn't have the answers he personally sought, but he felt closer to them than ever before. Instinct told him he would still be able to fill the holes in his past as he looked at a sketch of a gray man as the plane went airborne.

Angela continued her training, increasing her abilities with the sword and practicing the arts of magic. She channeled the fresh pain brought on by her choice to hone her skills to a very sharp edge, lethal for those she hunted.

They encountered fewer and fewer adversaries, as Daxxe predicted. Without a leader, the clan broke down, some squabbling amongst themselves about who should be in charge, and others trying to branch out to form new clans. Even so, Daxxe did not relent from his rigorous schedule to keep them both at the top of their game.

He had yet to confirm his feeling, but Angela could tell that he knew Trokar was still alive somewhere. She also had a sinking feeling that this was far from over and the worst was yet to come.

A man in black walked out of the forest and approached a small tavern in the countryside of eastern Pennsylvania. It was just after 2:30 in the morning. The bar stood alone for miles in all directions, and the barkeep was finally alone.

If you enjoyed Scourge, please stay on the lookout for the sequel **Demons**, due out in 2022.

Appendix A

A Study in Vampirism

In opening, we would like to say that the information in the following pages is very hard, if not impossible, to believe. We were more than skeptical at first, but no other explanations fit the evidence.

History

Mankind has toyed with the idea of vampirism for several centuries. The idea originated with Vlad III Dracula, son of Vlad II Dracul, in the early 15th Century in what is now Romania. He adopted the name of Vlad III Tepes, which translates to Vlad the Impaler, because of the brutality he dealt to his enemies and his subjects. He was known to set high stakes about his castle grounds, and those who opposed him were killed, dismembered or beheaded, and forced to sit tirgoviste (atop a high pole). The practice gave Vlad quite a reputation. He was also suspected to drink the blood of his slain enemies, attempting to acquire their strengths and knowledge. It was believed that in the end the evil in his soul was too great to die, and he continued to do his horrid work as the first vampire. Thus, Vlad became known as the Count Dracula. Heightened superstition and poor education helped fuel the fire until the vampire became a legendary, mythical creature.

As the fear of vampires grew, certain processes were adopted in an attempt to counteract the superstitions. The primary reason for a wake, in the beginning, was to allow time to confirm that the newly deceased was actually dead. Rural areas were, at many times, without any type of doctor, and someone could be pronounced dead by mistake. A disorder called catalepsy is "a condition of diminished responsiveness usually characterized by a trance-like state and constantly maintained immobility." The trance could last from a few moments to a few days, and someone suffering from it could appear to be dead.

Thus, at times, people were unknowingly buried alive. This attributed to the belief that a dead person could come back to life, powered by some evil spirit or force. Unfortunately, if a person was buried alive, they usually didn't stay that way. They would either die inside the coffin or be killed trying to escape. An inappropriately buried person freeing themselves from a coffin would more than likely have a wooden stake driven through their heart, as they were seen as undead.

Another disease, known as porphyria (pour-fa-ree-ah) was commonly misunderstood and the carrier would be labeled as a vampire and treated as such. Porphyrins combine with iron to produce heme, which gives the red coloration to blood. The lack of porphyrins, obviously, will make the carrier look very pale and pasty white. This imbalance also has other symptoms that seem to fit the definition of a vampire, including neurological and psychological disorders and intolerance to sunlight or bright light (photosensitivity). Extreme cases can even burn and blister in the sunlight, forcing the victim to avoid it.

Some reports state that giving blood intravenously will ease the effects of the disease. In times past, before the invention of the IV, a sufferer might resort to drinking blood to feel better. Carriers also have to deal with nausea, stomach cramping, and anemia.

The hype and fear surrounding these disorders led to the persecution of innocents. The punishment dealt out to suspect vampires ranged from flogging to outright execution.

Present Day

Scotland Yard contacted the University of Oxford Department of Medicine, concerned with a series of unexplainable events ranging from violent attacks to unexplainable deaths to homicide that plagued the city of London. The fear of a large-scale epidemic, the likes of the Black Plague, was at hand. The Yard suspected that the victims and the perpetrators all carried a common malady, and they were contracting it from the same source.

We initially turned our attention to the diseases listed above. Porphyria was ruled out almost immediately, as it is a genetic, hereditary disease. Carriers are born with it, and it cannot be contracted by any other means.

Catalepsy was also out of consideration, as it is a very rare disease. More cases happened in the few months before the study began than in recorded history to date, and a person having it in conjunction with porphyria is even more of a rarity. A sudden outbreak of catalepsy was just not possible. We started from a blank drawing board of sorts.

The study, which began in the spring of 2003, is based on medical fact. We performed hundreds of tests on all of the blood samples the Yard could provide. The samples came from a wide range of victims, consisting of young and old, both genders, and a variety of ethnic backgrounds.

The information that follows is presented in the simplest and easiest-to-read form so everyone can understand. It is vital that everyone knows of the potential danger before us.

Dr. Jacqueline Portis

Dr. Wilson Von Brandt

The Disease

Vampirism is a disease, the true origins of which are unknown. It exists in the form of a malignant cancer that has no known cure. It targets red blood cells, destroying them and creating an imbalance in blood chemistry. It also mutates white blood cells into what we call killer cells. These cells attack the red blood cells in the carrier's blood, furthering the depletion of red cells, and other tissues, using them as a source of fuel. It replicates very rapidly, and it tends to be most highly concentrated within the heart of the victim. This would be a logical location due the benefit of increased blood flow, but that would suggest that the malady is, to some capacity, sentient. Evidence suggests the population increases actually happen because the heart represents the core of the circulatory system. For example, if the disease attacked the endocrine system, the highest concentrations would be found in the lymph nodes.

Once the concentration level within the heart reaches forty to forty-five percent, the disease will begin to spread throughout the body of the victim. It requires more physical room as it grows and searches for more and more red cells. Bone marrow produces red blood cells extremely quickly and efficiently, but the disease increases the normal destruction rate of red cells several fold. Any cell available at this stage of infection will be attacked and consumed, literally devouring the victim from within. The overall health of the carrier declines very rapidly from this point forward.

Red cells have to be introduced to the victim's system from an outside source or the disease will turn on the host body, destroying itself in an attempt to survive. This introduction is a common denominator with porphyria, but it is not the same. It was found in some cases that the advance of the disease was slowed or even stopped for a short period of time by introducing new red cells. The process of introducing blood is, in fact, an empty promise. It ultimately accelerates the growth cycle of the malignant cells, increasing the speed of the downward spiral. The body can only compensate for the imbalance to a point, after which the death of the patient appears inevitable.

Transmission

Vampirism is a blood borne disease, which is very unusual for any cancer type diseases. It's almost as if the disease is a hybrid between cancer and a virus. It can only be contracted through blood transfusion or heavy local contamination. A heavy local contamination can only occur through a deep cut or puncture in which the disease is introduced. At this time, there is no process for screening blood for contamination by the Vampire Virus, as it's been dubbed. The name is misleading because it isn't really a virus either, but it behaves like one. This makes the possibility for widespread epidemic a very recognized concern.

Oddly, the disease also exists in the saliva of the carrier. This is due to the fact that the blood vessels within the mouth are very close to the surface and there is not a substantial protective barrier like the skin. The temperature and humidity conditions within the mouth contribute as well. Although no cases have been confirmed from mouth to mouth contact, (i.e. – kissing) a bite will transmit the disease without question, as referred to above as a heavy local contamination. The puncture becomes infected and it will never heal. (Also refer to the section dealing with symptoms concerning bite wounds.) This process of transmission is harder on the disease, but it only lengthens the overall process from infection to full-blown disease. Our efforts to find a cure are focused here, when it appears that the cells are weaker, offering the possibility of prevention with early detection.

The sharing of hypodermic needles between an infected person and a non-infected person is also a confirmed method of transmission. It amounts to a smaller version of a blood transfusion, but the malady is no less potent in smaller amounts.

Symptoms

Cases tend to show the infected persons present with common symptoms that occur in roughly the same order. The pallor of the skin changes first, becoming very pale. This is due to the lack of heme from the depleted red cell count in the victim. They also begin to look very frail and weak.

During the second stage, breathing will become somewhat labored as the cancerous cells infect the heart muscle, causing it to swell. The cancer also infects the brain, promoting hallucinations and other abnormal behaviors. The exact effect of the varied destruction of brain cells on the brain wave patterns in unknown, but it almost always results in very violent behavior. The infected person will try to attack anyone within reach, with a high tendency for scratching and biting. This behavior makes the carrier much more dangerous as it promotes the spreading of the disease through heavy contamination.

The lack of red blood cells may also create a pseudo-craving within the victim. This craving for red cells supports the higher occurrence of bite attacks. It is unknown if oral ingestion will stay the disease, but it is highly unlikely. The cells would not be able to survive within the digestive tract long enough, and ingested blood becomes toxic in the digestive tract of a normal person.

As the malignant cells work through the system, varying side effects can also occur. Cellular damage to the central nervous system has been noted to create spikes of strength, as well as convulsions and violent seizures. The victim's system tries to rebuild itself, but the damage to the nervous system alters the impulses from the brain. The information received by the body's undamaged cells can result in a wide range of physical changes.

It is common to see changes that support the survivalist instincts of the carrier. Please note that this instinct will be very far off normal due to the damage to the brain. The changes, most of which are physical, happen at an exponential rate. The rate was, until now, thought to be impossible. Within a matter of weeks, dramatic physical changes reached fruition. Some victims developed claws on their hands and feet, and some developed elongated canines in their mouths.

Findings

Two sub-groups formed within the overall group of victims. The first group, and the larger of the two, consisted of people infected with the disease, but without any physical manifestations. This group also presented in the morgue with little or no blood in their veins, and we were not able to determine if they carried the Vampire Virus at all.

The second group consisted of persons suffering from the disease with minor physical alterations.

Even stranger still, one case from Scotland Yard was the epitome of irony. This single case occurred during the study, so we had the opportunity to collect very recent data. The deceased was heavily infected with malignant cells. The disease mutated approximately seventy-five percent of the victim's body, and the malignant cells were evident throughout. The rate at which this cancer spreads and does damage will kill the host within four to six months of contraction, and the highest percent of concentration achievable in that amount of time is fifty to fifty-five percent. The disease was not the cause of death in this victim.

The body was badly mutilated with the heart missing entirely. Someone, or something, killed the victim. This exactly contradicted everything we had already learned about the Vampire Virus. This one victim, for whatever reason, was surviving with the disease.

We were only able to perform a small battery of tests before we no longer had a subject from which to obtain samples. The one common denominator we did find in the set of tests was the effect the disease has on the aging process. As hard as it is to believe, the disease stops the aging process in the carrier. The cells have an internal trigger that allows or hinders the aging process within the cells. The disease flips this switch to off, bringing the aging process to a halt. Attempting to determine the time of death is how we discovered this anomaly.

Time of death can be determined by the rate of decomposition of the body. This process of decay occurs at a set rate in all humans. The time of death per police reports was infinitely less than the time of death we established. The data showed that this person carried the Vampire Virus for over fifty years. After death, the immobilization of the aging process corrected itself. The corpse, within forty-eight hours after arrival in the morgue, had almost completely decomposed. The decomposition reached a certain point, and then the rate returned to normal. The best way to describe what happened is the following: A person infected with the Vampire Virus becomes, in a sense, immortal. If the carrier dies, the phenomenon of immortality reverts back to the normal way of nature, as if nothing extraordinary happened. It is our theory that the time of death established after this phenomenon is the time that the victim actually contracted the disease – they literally are undead while they carry the disease.

To date, we have not had the opportunity to prove this theory, as we have not had another vampire in the morgue. Also, we have yet to discover what determines whether or not a person will become a vampire or if they will simply die from the disease. What we do know is that all of the other victims in the sample group were not vampires; they were killed by a vampire(s) for their blood

Certain trends within the victims became apparent after we realized what was happening. Virtually all of the victims would fit into six or seven categories. The table below shows the approximate percentages:

Victim Categorical Information

Age & Sex/Categories	Alcoholic/Heavy drinker	Diabetic	Drug user	No category
Male, under 18	0.5%	1.0%	0.3%	**8.6%**
Male, 18-30	**6.1%**	1.5%	0.8%	1.9%
Male, 30-50	1.1%	0.4%	0.4%	1.5%
Male, over 50	**2.9%**	0.7%	0.1%	1.2%
Female, under 18	0.2%	**2.3%**	**7.4%**	**13.6%**
Female, 18-30	**8.9%**	**7.8%**	**5.1%**	**7.3%**
Female, 30-50	0.9%	**7.2%**	0.2%	**4.2%**
Female, over 50	0.8%	**3.4%**	0.1%	1.6%

The information represents the entire study group, which consisted of just over 800 homicides. The bold percentages point out a few very specific combinations that have a much higher rate of incidence. Several other categories were discovered, but the three shown here occurred with the highest frequency. These statistics were compiled almost four months after the homicides stopped as many of the victims were not discovered for some time.

Considering why all of these homicides occurred, these trends show that a vampire(s) have a preference of taste. The thought is horrifying, but a vampire chooses victims just like we choose food. This also makes it clear that a group of vampires, instead of one or two as was suspected at first, committed the homicides.

Resolutions

At this time, no known cure exists for vampirism. Modern medicine has yet to have an effect on the disease in any way. The only option available at this time is self-protection. The following guidelines should help prevent the Vampire Virus from becoming an epidemic.

1. Avoid being outside after nightfall. Vampires have proven to be photosensitive.

2. Try to stay in a group if you must be out at night. Most of the victims were found alone in secluded areas.

3. Watch out for others you know who fall into one of the high-risk categories discussed in the table on the previous page.

The one vampire we did get a chance to study also offers hope – they can be killed.

Appendix B

Kalanak's Journal

Year 9,563, Day 1:

Responsibility for this journal passed to me from my mentor in Year 7,286. He kept it for the prior 7,285 years since the Great War began. An attack on the keep took his life, passing everything to me. For a thousand years, I perfected my craft in solitude, learning every nuance of wizardry. I re-entered society as the strongest magi Talamhan has ever known. I lead the Order of L'Min, but its effect on the world is a small thing.

The War continues, even though 9,562 years cannot determine a victor. Talamhan is burnt and blackened. This first day of the New Year promises no hope. Battles rage on every continent, all combatants vying for the "honor" of victory. None of them see what has happened to the spoils they await, or that no one will emerge as the winner. This has gone on far too long – too long to turn back. Talamhan has suffered too much damage. She can no longer support the survivors, or life of any kind for that matter. Death is imminent – the only decisions left to us are how we will face it and how soon it will come. I have a vision of barren wastelands devoid of all life. I must meditate this night in hope of finding an answer.

Day 2:

I fear what lies ahead. I have a design that even I find hard to think of – I must put it before the council. I do not possess enough strength to go it alone, and alone I cannot this decision make. I have seen what will come to pass – this may be our only chance.

Day 5:

My Order has grudgingly agreed with me and accepted my proposal. The end that must be is understood, but no easier to accept. They feel the Dragon-kind will use the opportunity to finish us off once and for all, and then no one will remain to end the madness. I have peered into many hearts, and sympathy to our cause exists. Our leaders are too blinded by their desire for power and control to see what is coming, and in that blindness rests our hope.

Day 7:

I have dispatched my messengers to contact our allies. I can only hope that all will have word and can complete the journey by three nights hence. We will have to proceed with whom we have as I sense an unsettling rapidity in the minds of the warring leaders.

Day 10:

Amidst great tension, everyone has arrived. Most are haggard from the journey. They all appear ready to snap at a glimpse, even though no one else knows where we are. I can see into their hearts, and the anxiety is rooted in the fear of the others that are here and the thought of their people's discovering our plan. I created this huge cavern, high in the Shilon Mountains, to insure our privacy and security. This conclave is convened in the highest secrecy – the outside world is unaware of our intentions and this location did not exist until four moons ago.

Day 11:

The duties have been assigned after much discussion and argument. I, along with the strongest of my order and the strongest magi among the Dragon-kind have taken the task of the first three books. These spells will sunder Talamhan and reconstruct her into a New World. The High Priests accepted the challenge of creating the last two volumes in which they will weave the tapestry of the New World they have decided to call Earth. Earth will be void of our magic, our laws, our memories, and our very souls. Life will flourish again in our vision, unaware of the unsettling events that led to its creation. The books themselves will be the only survivors from this world, but no one will possess the knowledge or ability to understand or use them.

Day 15:

The Dragons requested an addition to the plan. They want to create a sentinel that will inhabit the New World, bound by vows of protection to Earth and her people. I spoke against this measure, feeling no other remnants of Talamhan should remain. The council has overruled my arguments – these "protectors" shall be created and exist in our image.

Day 17:

For the last six days we have worked without pause. We are all weary. At least our focus has washed away our fears, and the work is progressing faster than I anticipated. This is for the best. Our presences in the battles raging in the outside world, by now, are surely missed. Time is of the essence. I know not why I continue to write in this journal – it will cease to be just as everything else.

Day 19:

At moonset, our time will be at hand. The books are complete and all are ready. The few hours of rest we have will have to suffice, as it will be the last we ever enjoy. At first light, we will begin the incantations. If we are not discovered, the world will be set right by this time in the morrow. I fear we have missed something, but I know not what...

Appendix C

Ten codes

10-1 Receiving poorly

10-2 Receiving well

10-3 Stop transmitting

10-4 Affirmative

10-5 Relay

10-6 Going to be busy

10-7 Out of service

10-8 In service

10-9 Repeat

10-10 Out/subject to call

10-11 Fight in progress

10-12 Visitor present

10-13 Weather condition

10-14 Escort

10-15 Prisoner in custody

10-16 Prowler report

10-17 Pick-up items at _____

10-18 Domestic disturbance

10-19 Return to station

10-20 What's your location

10-21 Call _____ by phone

10-22 Take no further action

10-23 Stand by

10-24 Suspicious person

10-25 Suspicious vehicle

10-26 Burglary

10-26A Burglary with alarm

10-27 Check for DL info

10-28 Check vehicle license

10-29 Check for wanted

10-30 Not regulation

10-31 Ask to leave area

10-32 Request breath test

10-33 EMERGENCY TRAFFIC

10-34 Dead animal

10-35 Confidential info

10-36 Correct time

10-37 Officer on duty

10-38 Keys locked in car

10-39 Loud noise/music

10-40 Assist motorist

10-41 Traffic problem

10-42 Officer is at home

10-43 Stop light/sign down

10-44 Illegal parking

10-45 Intoxicated driver

10-46 Intoxicated person

10-47 Accident with injury

10-48 Accident

10-49 Meet me at _____

10-50 Traffic check

10-51 Request NCIC check

10-52 Negative NCIC want

10-53 Positive NCIC want

10-54 Phone, tried failed

10-55 Hit and run

10-56 Livestock on road

10-57 Take a report

10-58 Robbery

10-58A Robbery with alarm

10-59 Racing on highway

10-60 Mental subject

10-61 Bomb threat

10-62 Work school zone

10-63 Radio not directed

10-64 Radio not clear

10-65 Coroner needed

10-66 Chase in progress

10-67 Fire---car/house

10-68 Unknown trouble

10-69 Deceased person

10-70 Ambulance needed

10-71 Wrecker needed

10-72 Sick/injured party

10-73 Homicide

10-74 Suicide

10-75 Stolen vehicle

10-76 Abandoned vehicle

10-77 Theft

10-78 See a party

10-79 Rape

10-80 Indecent exposure

10-81 Assist a citizen

10-82 Assault

10-83 Vandalism

10-84 Animal case dog/cat

10-85 Go to scramble

10-86 Road repair needed

10-87 Direct traffic

10-88 Public service number

10-89 Trouble at jail

10-90 Need items delivered

10-91 Need road block at__

10-92 House check

10-93 Reckless driving

10-94 Assist an officer

10-95 OFFICER NEEDS HELP

10-96 Unit in route

10-97 Arrived at scene

10-98 Finished last call

10-99 Ask to work on reports

10-100 Comfort stop

If Z is added to code, weapon involved

Appendix D

The Books of Kalanak

The Books of Kalanak represent the collective work of the magi of the Council. Each book was developed for a specific purpose in the grand scheme of sundering Talamhan and forming a New World, considered the be-all-end-all solution to end the Great War.

Five books were composed – Chaos, Descension, Death, Ascension, and Life. Each book contains spells in their own right, and the range of power of those incantations varies between the volumes. As a safeguard, the individual books could not be used to alter the world on a grand scale. To truly unlock the power within the books, the volumes have to be united with a spell of binding. Very few magi know the spell, and even fewer have the ability to cast it. The spell not only binds the books into a single, master volume, it forms an exclusive bond with the spell caster. This safeguard prevents a capable mage from being forced to cast the spell for someone else.

A brief summary of each volume is below.

Fig 1

The Book of Chaos was designed to unbind the magic of Talamhan from its physical bonds to eliminate the need to summon the energy later. The spells targeted all things on Talamhan that contained magic, living or otherwise. It was denoted Chaos due to the strange and unpredictable effects the unbound energy was capable of. Without the constraints of a controlling force (mage), the magical energy could create and/or destroy at will. The Book of Chaos is the first volume of five, and it is also the second largest of the volumes. The incantations were written very precisely to release the energy in a very ordered sequence to avoid the largest number of side effects. It is bound in red leather with gilded edges, and the symbol of Chaos (Fig 1) graces the front cover and the spine. The pages, as with all five volumes, are made of a unique parchment found only on Talamhan that did not help or hinder the flow of magical energy. The Books are the only source of this parchment on Earth.

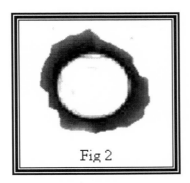

Fig 2

The Book of Descension was designed to prepare everything on Talamhan, living or otherwise, to be destroyed. The spells stripped everything down to the simplest, most basic level of existence. It forces all enchanted objects and other existing spells to discharge their magic to prevent any unseen reactions. It was believed any existing enchantments of protection or healing would cause various disruptions to the grand spell, with the possibility of preventing it from happening at all. The Book of Descension is the smallest of the volumes and the second in the set. It is bound in blue leather with silver edges, with the symbol of Descension (Fig 2) imprinted on the front cover and spine in silver.

Fig 3

The Book of Death was the actual implement of destruction for the world of Talamhan. The spells within this text are the most powerful, and ironically, the shortest and simplest to cast. This collection of incantations pulled the life-force from all living things, releasing it to combine with the magic already set loose by the Book of Chaos. The spells worked very violently. The few unfortunate enough to see what was happening saw everything explode into a blue, glowing mass of physical energy. The process was very painful, and it is said that the screams of Talamhanian creatures can still be heard on the winds of Earth. The Book of Death is bound in black leather, and the pages are gilded in gunmetal. The symbol of Death (Fig 3) is imprinted on the front cover and the spine in the same dark gray metallic color. Unique to the Book of Death, the eyes within the symbol glow a dark blue when any of the spells within are cast.

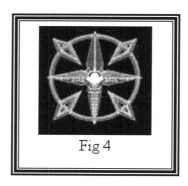

Fig 4

The Book of Ascension – was designed to re-organize all of the free-flowing energy into the shape and will of the caster, who was Kalanak himself. This text contains a single spell of great length that would forge physical shape of the New World. The incantation was supposed to make the topography of Earth, from the vast mountain ranges to the deepest oceans. It also took care of considerations like climate and atmosphere, but most importantly, it altered the way the magical energy of Talamhan reacted with the newly formed world. The energy was incorporated into the new design, but its flow and ability to be contained was highly restricted. Many, but not all things, of Earth would contain the magical energy. A highly sophisticated type of security system was intertwined, in hope the magic could not be used by the new inhabitants for the purposes of war. The Book of Ascension is bound in yellow leather, with the symbol (Fig 4) imprinted on the cover and spine in dark red. The pages of this particular text are not gilded purposefully, as the makeup of metals after the sundering would inhibit the power of the spells.

Fig 5

The Book of Life was designed to restore Earth with all living things. Every creature from the smallest single cell amoebae to the largest beasts were part of the mix. The magi of the Council attacked this large task by creating a simple building block that would be used to generate all life, and this building block was given the ability to evolve when necessary. And the close of the spell, the Earth would be thriving with living creatures in a stable, self-supporting system. The inhabitants could not be given any indication that Talamhan ever existed, so a fabricated history was incorporated into the minds of the New World. A task so vast could not occur flawlessly, and the history of Earth as we know it has discrepancies for which we cannot reconcile. The largest of these is a layer of iridium under the surface of the planet that did not exist before the sundering. Iridium was one of the new elements generated by the Book of Ascension as an inhibitor to magical energies. The layer draws and traps any energy left in the planet's core, as it was not necessary to destroy, and everything above this layer was created by the spells. The Book of Life is bound in light green leather with the symbol (Fig 5) imprinted in dark green on the face and spine. The pages are gilded with copper.

Acknowledgements

What you have read is more than a novel, it's the culmination of a dream that started over 40 years ago. The desire was fostered by reading what became my favorite books from a group of my favorite authors (Dean Koontz, Clive Cussler, Terry Brooks, Margaret Weis, and Tracy Hickman), all who provided inspiration and style influence. Many late-night sessions playing RPG games with friends let me discover just how deep my imagination could go. I think everyone has at least one good novel within them. I have too many people to thank for helping with this novel.

About the Author

Rodney McWilliams is a new author, finally taking his hobby of writing to the next level. This novel is the first of a planned series, and he has various other fiction and creative non-fiction projects in the works. He was a finalist in the Sante Fe Writer's Project annual contest for one of his short stories, which is also set to become a full-length novel.

He lives in West Texas with his wife and their herd of furry, four footed children.

With this novel, he wants to offer something a little bit different…

Connect With the Author

Learn more about Talamhanian Magic at the website.

https://www.rodneymcwilliams.com

Cover art by Mel-Cat Illustrations

https://mc-illustrations.com

Edited by Edith Rische

DEMONS

TRISKELLION
BOOK TWO

PROLOGUE

The barkeep spoke when he heard the door open as he wiped down the heavily lacquered surface of the bar.

"You'll have to come back in the morning friend. Last call was about 45 minutes ago. We closed at 2:00. You'll have to…"

His sentence trailed off when he looked up and found himself alone. Ralph Owens, proprietor of the Stalker Crossroads Pub leaned over the bar to scrutinize his roadhouse.

"Can I help you? Steve, is that you again? How many times have we had this little talk?"

The pub remained silent and still.

What is going on? I felt the cold air from outside. I know that door opened.

A sharp chill ran painfully up Ralph's spine.

"I can assure you there won't be any more little talks."

The gravelly voice came over his right shoulder as a cold hand closed around Ralph's neck, dragging him to the floor behind the bar. He flailed and gasped for breath during the short descent, and passed out as he felt his flesh rending away from his bones in violently yanked strips. Blood spattered in all directions, coating everything in a macabre Picasso-esque fashion.

Another blast of cold, early spring night air flowed into the bar as the killer silently slipped into the cover of darkness.

ChApTER ONE

"Wayne County Sheriff's Dispatch, please state your emergency."

The officer listened to the incoming call, her eyes widening to the point of popping from the sockets.

"I'll get someone out there right away, Mrs. Jones. Try to stay calm, and stay in your vehicle with the doors locked!"

The dispatcher had trouble controlling the shakes that rattled through her petite frame as she activated her two-way radio.

"Jake, this is Sierra. Get out to the Kellams-Stalker Bridge right now! Myrtle Jones spotted a dead body floating in the river."

"Come again?"

"Myrtle Jones found a dead body Jake! She said it's floating in the river under the bridge and got caught up in some driftwood!"

Sierra's voice shivered in unison with her skin riddling into gooseflesh.

"And it's...in pieces...from what I could understand. Myrtle is really shaken up."

"In pieces? Why in the hell are there body parts floating in the river?"

"I don't know, but this type of thing isn't supposed to happen out here. Jesus, it's not supposed to happen anywhere!" Her premise of peaceful country living was fading fast.

"I'm in route from Bush Road. I'm only a few miles north of her position."

"Ten...oh Christ, screw it. She's holding in the line, so I'll let her know. Please hurry Jake."

Her fingers fumbled as she disengaged from the microphone and picked up the held call with Mrs. Jones. She couldn't seem to focus on what she was doing as mental images of the crime scene swam through her mind. Nor could she recall any other time in her life that she was so disturbed.

"Mrs. Jones, I have a deputy on the way; he'll be there in a few minutes. Mrs. Jones?"

The low hum of electronic silence confirmed that she was connected to dead air. Her mind jumped into high gear, adding worse case scenarios to the already intense imagery in her mind, leaving her reeling. She felt like she was moving and sitting still all at the same time, only intensifying the dizziness and throbs pulsating in her brain. She closed her eyes as she activated the dispatcher's mike again.

"Jake, HURRY!! Something happened to Myrtle! Jake? Jake!!"

The line was silent.

Oh shit! What is going on?

She threw the hand unit to the desk, grabbing her coat from the back of her chair and her keys from the desktop. She almost fell to the floor when she jumped up, moving faster than her head was anticipating or the vertigo would allow.

A chill spread through her, making her shake more intently and forcing her thoughts to flow like cold molasses. She stood still for a few seconds to make sure she had her balance before walking outside to her Jeep. The spinning slowed to a stop when she entered the cold night, but the feeling that something was very wrong refused to be dismissed.

Thirty minutes, with good road conditions, separated the office in Honesdale from the source of the call in Stalker. She had to be in control if she hoped to complete the drive. A late cold front dropped unexpected snow on the region, making the progress even slower and more treacherous. The snowplows focused on keeping Interstate 84 clear, only getting to the rest of Wayne County when they could. She tried to call Jake on the Jeep's radio as she drove north out of town, gripping the wheel tightly with both hands when she wasn't actively using the CB handset. Her knuckles turned bone white under the pressure.

What a great time for Sheriff Hill to be gone on vacation!

The trip took the better part of an hour, and Sierra wasn't prepared for what lay ahead of her.

The bell hanging from the porch fascia chimed four or five times, alerting the people inside the house that someone was calling. The patriarch, Jason Pellam, got up from the table and went to the door.

The caller had his back to the door when it opened, looking out across the snow-covered field that covered the distance back to the highway. His tan trench coat hung around him loosely, shifting with the slight breeze rolling from the north and across the large porch.

"What can I do for you?" asked Jason.

The visitor turned, extending his hand to shake. His salt and pepper hair was mussed from a combination of wind and bed-head. His clothes were wrinkled, as if he'd slept in them. A hint of alcohol carried on his words as he spoke.

"Hello, my name is Joe Anderson. I understand you board horses here."

"That's correct Mr. Anderson. We open back up at 9:00 in the morning," offered Jason, attempting to politely prompt Joe to leave.

"I know, and I'm truly sorry. It took me a while to work up the courage to come up to the house."

Jason shifted backwards about half a step. He didn't feel threatened, but it seemed as though something wasn't quite right. His slight change of position put him in easier reach of the shotgun that leaned against the wall just inside the front door.

Joe noticed the change in Pellam's demeanor. He retreated a half step as he softened.

"Again, Mr. Pellam, I apologize for the late call. I am a detective with the New York Police Department. My partner was killed during an investigation recently. After the funeral, her mother asked if I would come out to let you know what happened, and to handle the arrangements of her daughter's horse. She couldn't bring herself to handle it personally."

Jason's posture relaxed as he took in the story.

"Who was your partner?"

"Her name was Angela Benson. Susan Benson, her mother, gave me all of your contact info and the registration paperwork for the horse. Susan said the horse's name is Ellie."

An odd look crossed Jason's face.

"What's wrong?"

"I think we need to check something. Please, come inside. I apologize for forgetting my hospitality. It's just so hard to know people's intentions these days."

"Thank you. I didn't take it personally. I'm a cop, so I get that a lot."

"Marilyn, can you set out an extra plate? We've got Joe Anderson calling."

"Sure honey," came from somewhere deeper in the house.

"You don't have to go to that much trouble, Mr. Pellam. I don't want to impose."

"It's no imposition, Joe. I think a warm house and a hot, home cooked meal may be just what you need. It'll take me a few minutes to check our paperwork. I still handle the business on paper."

Jason led Joe into the kitchen. Marilyn was just finishing the extra place setting.

"Marilyn, this is Joe Anderson. Joe, this is my wife, Marilyn."

Joe extended his hand again, but Marilyn brushed it aside and gave him a friendly hug.

"Thank you, Marilyn. I've been away from good people for so long, I don't always know how to act."

"You never mind that. Fix yourself a plate while Jason finds what he's looking for."

Joe sat and dished himself enough food to be polite. He didn't feel like eating, which was pretty regular for him these days. He'd lost about 30 pounds since Angela's death, even though his new partner tried to get him the eat all the time, pretty much only ingested things with a proof rating when he was off duty. The meal was simple, consisting of pot roast with all the fixings, soda bread, and some of the best clam chowder he'd ever experienced.

The food and the quaint, country feel to the Pellam's and their home reminded Joe of his youth and the times he got to visit his grandparents before they passed away. Although it was the first time he had ever been there, it just felt right - it felt like home.

He started his second helping when Jason came back in the room and returned to his seat at the head of the table.

"It's funny," started Jason, "I'm horrible remembering the names of our customers, but I seldom forget the names of the horses. We lease out half a dozen stalls here, and we treat the tenants as if they were our horses. We feed, groom, exercise, and work them all everyday. Our customers really appreciate that personal touch. Ellie really stood out to me because she was such a hard worker. She could go all day without breaking a sweat."

"It wouldn't surprise me for Angela to have a good horse. What was it that seemed odd to you?"

Jason handed Joe a yellow receipt copy that had the Pellam Stable's logo across the top.

"You mentioned arrangements for Ellie, but there's nothing to do. The bill was paid in full and Ellie was checked out. It was just about two months ago - February 24th to be exact."

Joe's body went rigid as he scanned the receipt. The bill was settled in cash, and the he recognized Angela's signature at the bottom. He took out his wallet and fished out a picture. He got a copy of the picture that was taken by the police department for their identification badges before her employee record was closed. He offered it to Jason.

"Is this the person that came for Ellie?"

Marilyn leaned closer when she saw no recognition on her husband's face.

"Yes, that's her. I'm not good with names, but I never forget a face."

Joe looked at them both, utterly at a loss for words.

"What is it?" asked Marilyn.

"This is…impossible. I attended Angela's funeral. She was buried on February 22nd."

Made in the USA
Columbia, SC
07 October 2024

43201470R00324